DYNAMITE ENTERTAINMENT PRESENTS

BATTLESTAR
GALACTICA™

VOLUME I

BATTLESTAR
GALACTICA

WRITTEN BY

GREG PAK

ART BY

NIGEL RAYNOR

COLORS BY

DAVID CURIEL

LETERING BY

SIMON BOWLAND

SPECIAL THANKS TO

RON MOORE
CINDY CHANG
DANIEL McPEEK
& GARY LOKUM

The events of this comic book series take place in the middle of season two of the television series-after the return from Kobol in episode 207 (Home, Part 2) and before the arrival of The Pegasus in episode 211 (Resurrection Ship, part 1

DYNAMITE ENTERTAINMENT
NICK BARRUCCI • PRESIDENT
JUAN COLLADO • CHIEF OPERATING OFFICER
JOSEPH RYBANDT • DIRECTOR OF MARKETING
JOSH JOHNSON • CREATIVE DIRECTOR
JASON ULLMEYER • GRAPHIC DESIGNER

To find a comic shop in your area, call the comic shop locator service toll-free 1-888-266-4226

BATTLESTAR GALACTICA™ Volume 1. First printing. Contains materials originally published in Battlestar Galac
™ #0-4.Published by Dynamite Entertainment. 155 Ninth Ave. Suite B, Runnemede, NJ 08078. Battlestar Galactic
USA Cable Entertainment LLC. Licensed by Universal Studios Licensing LLLP. All Rights Reserved. DYNAM
DYNAMITE ENTERTAINMENT and its logo are ™ & © 2007 DFI. All names, characters, events, and locales in this p
lication are entirely fictional. Any resemblance to actual persons (living or dead), events or places, without sa
intent, is coincidental. No portion of this book may be reproduced by any means (digital or print) without the wri
permission of Dynamite Entertainment except for review purposes. The scanning, uploading and distribution of
book via the Internet or via any other means without the permission of the publisher is illegal and punishable by
Please purchase only authorized electronic editions, and do not participate in or encourage electronic piracy of co
righted materials.

For information regarding promotions, licensing and advertising please email:
marketing@dynamiteentertainment.com.

Printed in Canada.   First Printing
HARDCOVER ISBN-10: 1-9333005-33-9   ISBN-13: 9-781933-305332
SOFTCOVER ISBN-10: 1-933305-34-7   ISBN-13: 9-781933-305349
10 9 8 7 6 5 4 3 2 1

Also not an easy task is building upon such a strong show, with such a fervent fan base – both new and old – to create new and untold stories from such a rich tapestry.

That became our job when we entered into an agreement to produce comics based on the re-imagined Battlestar Galactica. And the road is even harder, as Ron and crew have raised the bar.

What made our job that much easier was finding the right creative team: writer Greg Pak and artist Nigel Raynor.

Greg Pak came to us by way of his film work and his incredible work at Marvel Comics – where he's tackled the cosmic (the X-Men) and the primal (the Hulk) and his work on New Battlestar has proven to be a smart blend of both. Greg found a great "in" for his story – setting it in-between episodes – and in his scripting captured the voices of the actors and characters making the comic book a true companion to the series itself.

Nigel Raynor proved to be the perfect artist on the book, blending the action with the more "human" moments of Greg's scripts, all with an uncanny ability to replicate – and in some cases, create – the technology of the show to again complete the immersive experience the comic series presents.

But despite our incredible creative team, in the end, we still couldn't have put this book together without the creative dialogue we had between series Producer Ron Moore and Greg Pak (and special thanks goes out to Cindy Chang for setting that up), that helped set the stage for the story you're about to read, so to Ron and the people behind the scenes at Universal that help us put this book together each and every month, we once again say "Thank You."

But enough with the past, let's take a look into the present, as the crew of the Battlestar Galactica face "The Returners" as they seek the remnants of the lost 13th Colony and a shining place of hope called Earth.

Nick Barrucci
President & Publisher
Dynamite Entertainment

The Cylons were created by man...

They Rebelled...

They Evolved...

They look and feel human...

Some are programmed to think that
they are human...

There are many copies...

And they have a plan.

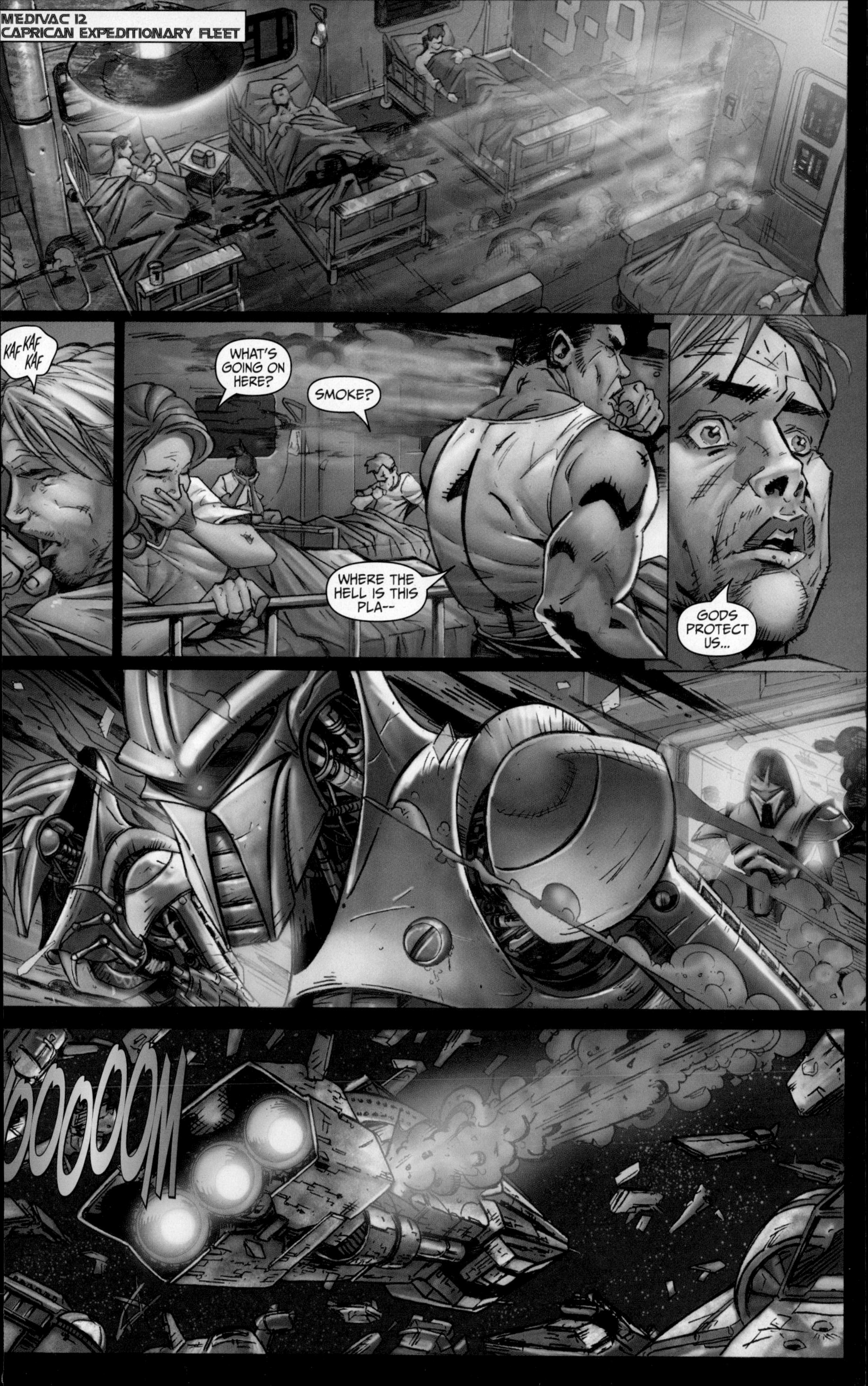
MEDIVAC 12
CAPRICAN EXPEDITIONARY FLEET
KAF KAF KAF
WHAT'S GOING ON HERE?
SMOKE?
WHERE THE HELL IS THIS PLA--
GODS PROTECT US...

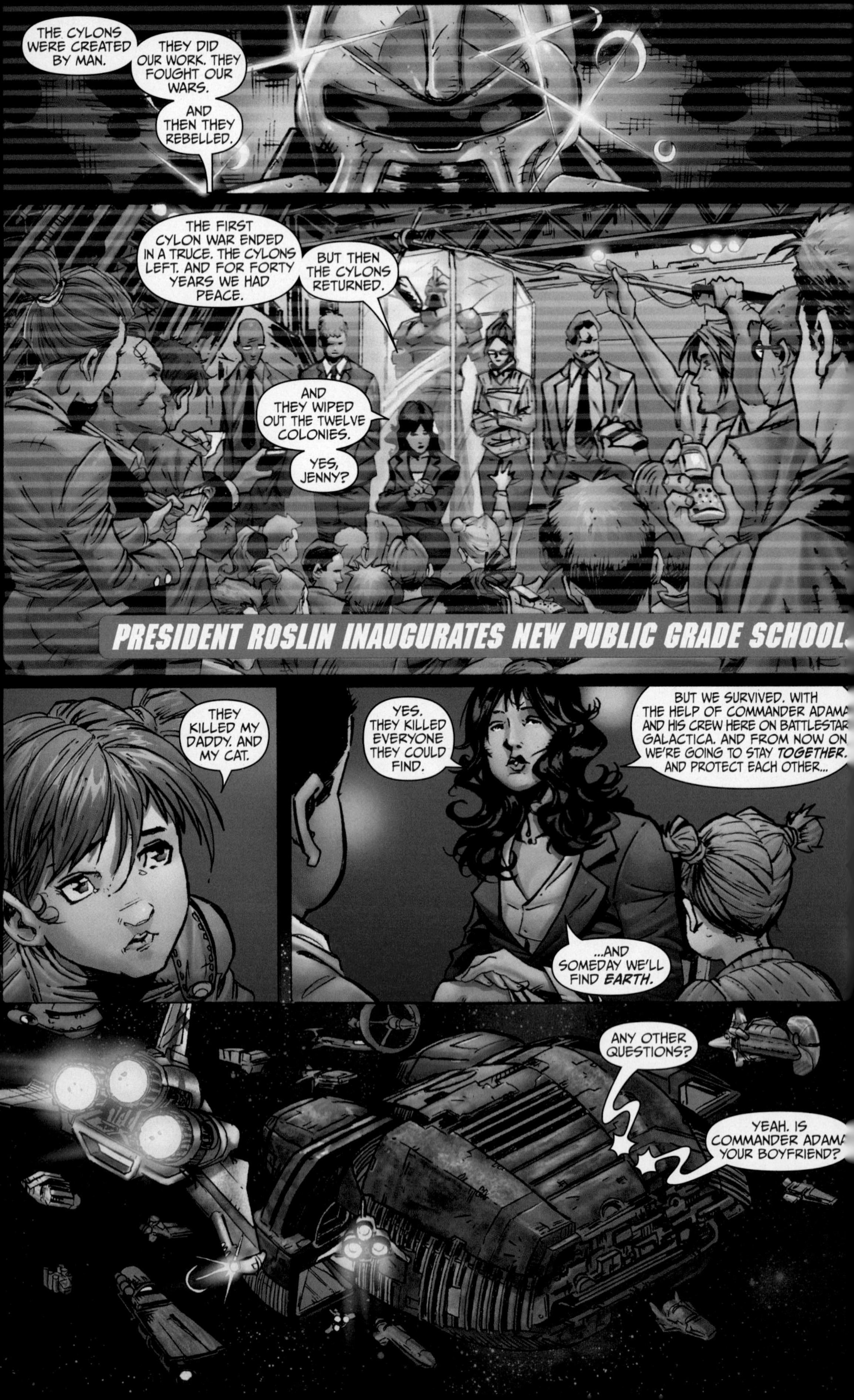

THE CYLONS WERE CREATED BY MAN.
THEY DID OUR WORK. THEY FOUGHT OUR WARS.
AND THEN THEY REBELLED.
THE FIRST CYLON WAR ENDED IN A TRUCE. THE CYLONS LEFT. AND FOR FORTY YEARS WE HAD PEACE.
BUT THEN THE CYLONS RETURNED.
AND THEY WIPED OUT THE TWELVE COLONIES.
YES, JENNY?
PRESIDENT ROSLIN INAUGURATES NEW PUBLIC GRADE SCHOOL
THEY KILLED MY DADDY. AND MY CAT.
YES. THEY KILLED EVERYONE THEY COULD FIND.
BUT WE SURVIVED. WITH THE HELP OF COMMANDER ADAMA AND HIS CREW HERE ON BATTLESTAR GALACTICA. AND FROM NOW ON WE'RE GOING TO STAY TOGETHER. AND PROTECT EACH OTHER...
...AND SOMEDAY WE'LL FIND EARTH.
ANY OTHER QUESTIONS?
YEAH. IS COMMANDER ADAMA YOUR BOYFRIEND?

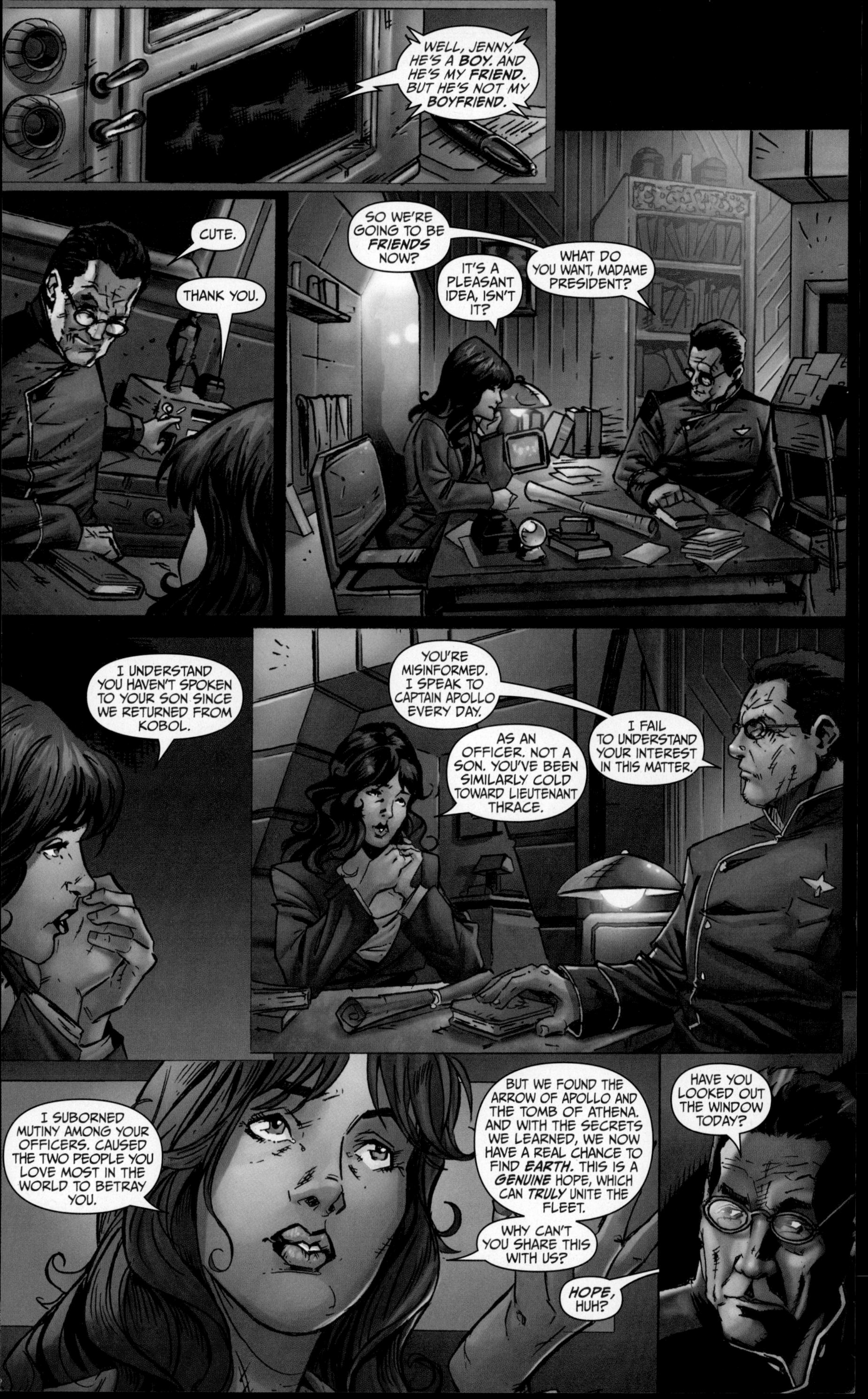

WELL, JENNY, HE'S A BOY. AND HE'S MY FRIEND. BUT HE'S NOT MY BOYFRIEND.
CUTE.
THANK YOU.
SO WE'RE GOING TO BE FRIENDS NOW?
WHAT DO YOU WANT, MADAME PRESIDENT?
IT'S A PLEASANT IDEA, ISN'T IT?
I UNDERSTAND YOU HAVEN'T SPOKEN TO YOUR SON SINCE WE RETURNED FROM KOBOL.
YOU'RE MISINFORMED. I SPEAK TO CAPTAIN APOLLO EVERY DAY.
AS AN OFFICER. NOT A SON. YOU'VE BEEN SIMILARLY COLD TOWARD LIEUTENANT THRACE.
I FAIL TO UNDERSTAND YOUR INTEREST IN THIS MATTER.
I SUBORNED MUTINY AMONG YOUR OFFICERS. CAUSED THE TWO PEOPLE YOU LOVE MOST IN THE WORLD TO BETRAY YOU.
BUT WE FOUND THE ARROW OF APOLLO AND THE TOMB OF ATHENA. AND WITH THE SECRETS WE LEARNED, WE NOW HAVE A REAL CHANCE TO FIND EARTH. THIS IS A GENUINE HOPE, WHICH CAN TRULY UNITE THE FLEET.
WHY CAN'T YOU SHARE THIS WITH US?
HAVE YOU LOOKED OUT THE WINDOW TODAY?
HOPE, HUH?

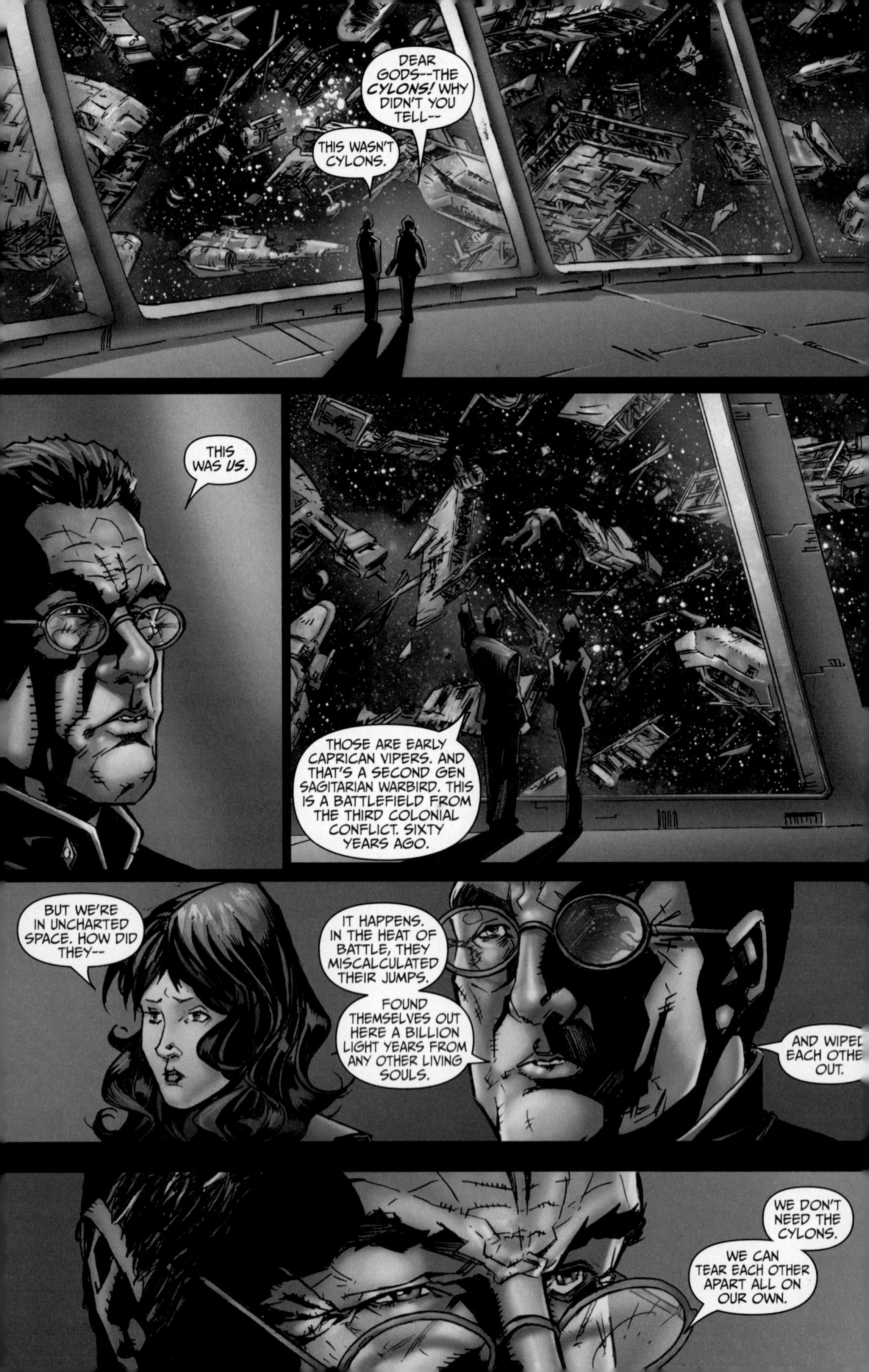
DEAR GODS--THE *CYLONS!* WHY DIDN'T YOU TELL--
THIS WASN'T CYLONS.
THIS WAS *US.*
THOSE ARE EARLY CAPRICAN VIPERS. AND THAT'S A SECOND GEN SAGITARIAN WARBIRD. THIS IS A BATTLEFIELD FROM THE THIRD COLONIAL CONFLICT. SIXTY YEARS AGO.
BUT WE'RE IN UNCHARTED SPACE. HOW DID THEY--
IT HAPPENS. IN THE HEAT OF BATTLE, THEY MISCALCULATED THEIR JUMPS.
FOUND THEMSELVES OUT HERE A BILLION LIGHT YEARS FROM ANY OTHER LIVING SOULS.
AND WIPED EACH OTHE OUT.
WE DON'T NEED THE CYLONS.
WE CAN TEAR EACH OTHER APART ALL ON OUR OWN.

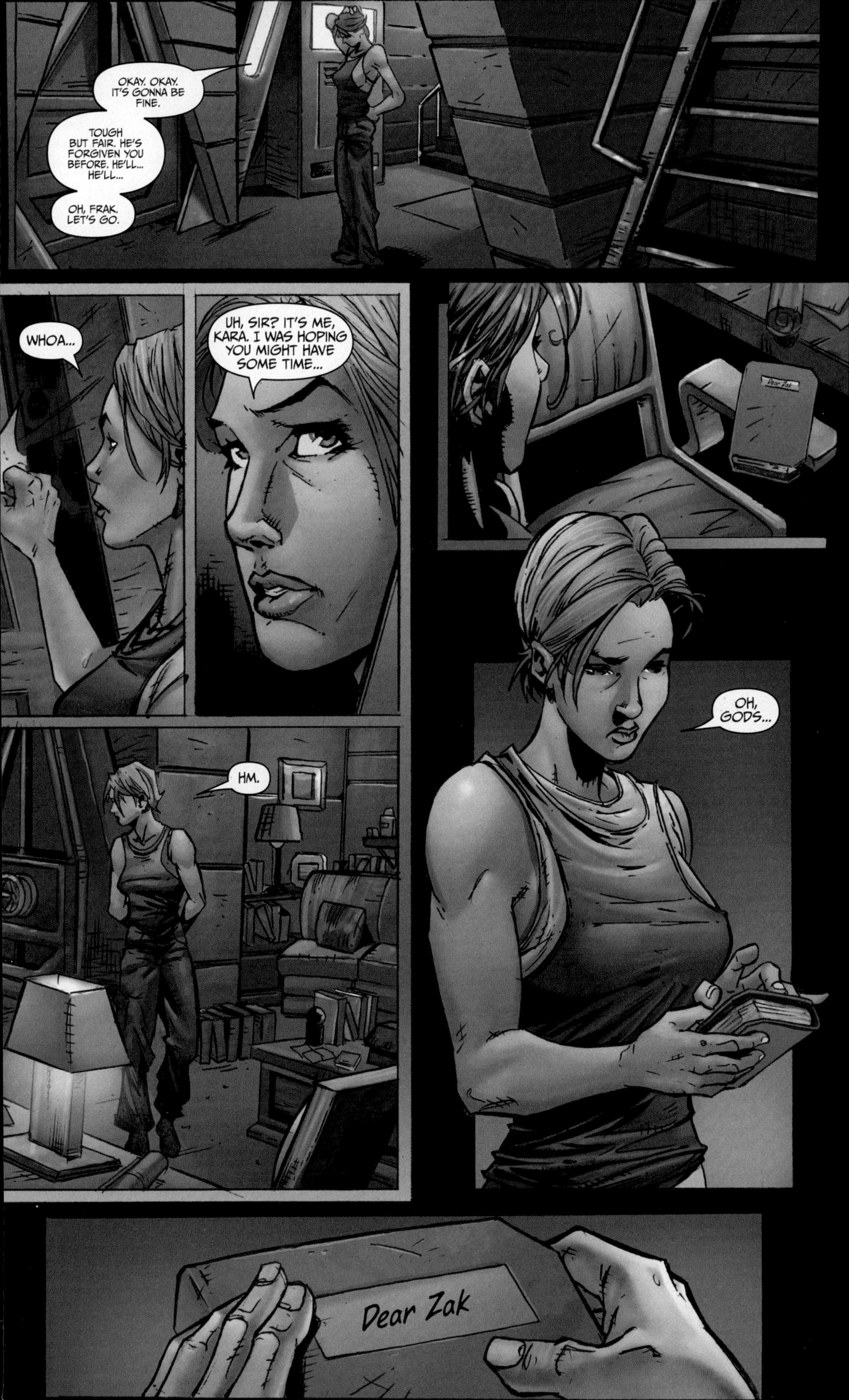
OKAY. OKAY. IT'S GONNA BE FINE.
TOUGH BUT FAIR. HE'S FORGIVEN YOU BEFORE. HE'LL... HE'LL...
OH, FRAK. LET'S GO.
WHOA...
UH, SIR? IT'S ME, KARA. I WAS HOPING YOU MIGHT HAVE SOME TIME...
Dear Zak
HM.
OH, GODS...
Dear Zak

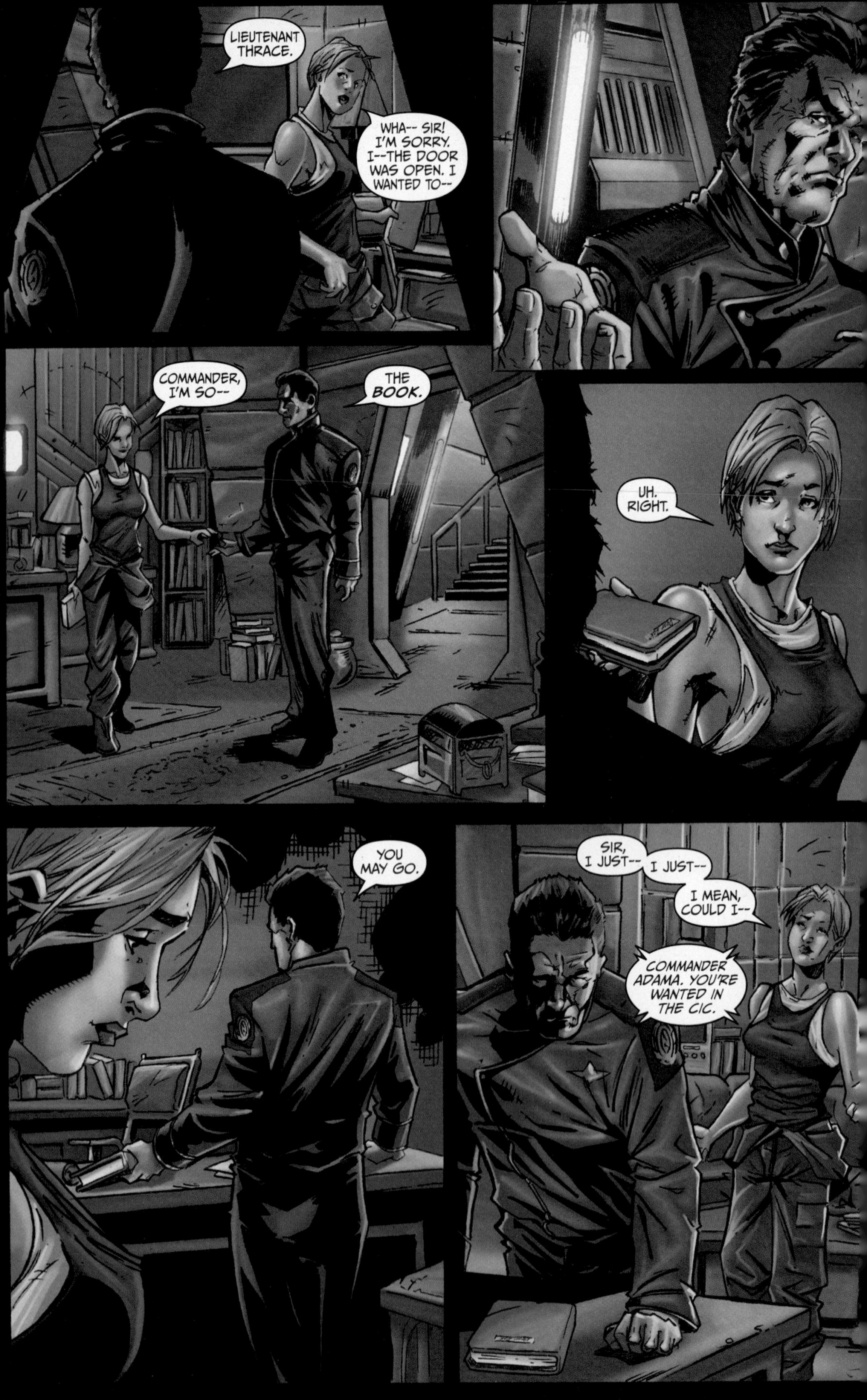
LIEUTENANT THRACE.
WHA-- SIR! I'M SORRY. I--THE DOOR WAS OPEN. I WANTED TO--
COMMANDER, I'M SO--
THE *BOOK.*
UH. RIGHT.
YOU MAY GO.
SIR, I JUST--
I JUST--
I MEAN, COULD I--
COMMANDER ADAMA. YOU'RE WANTED IN THE CIC.

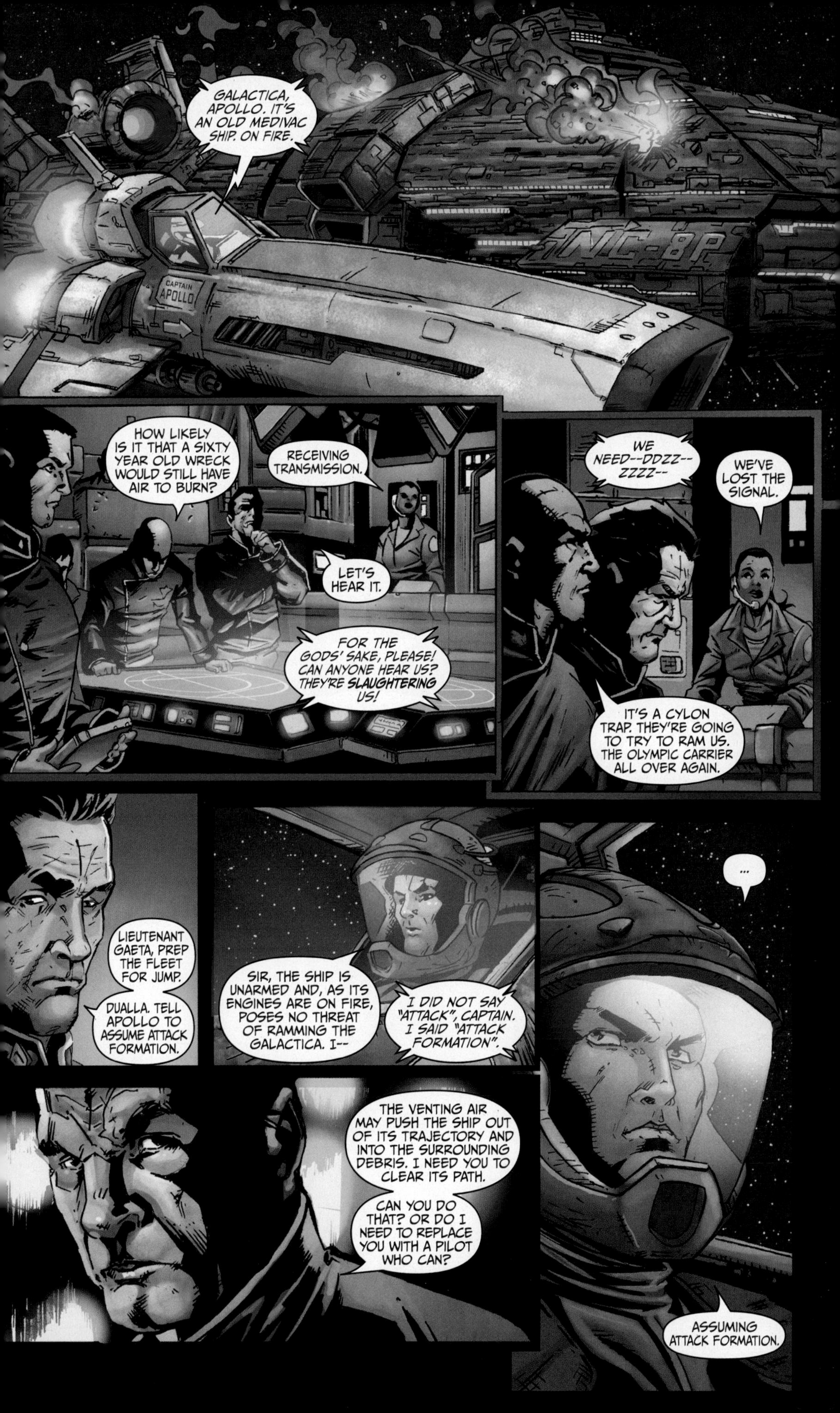
GALACTICA, APOLLO. IT'S AN OLD MEDIVAC SHIP. ON FIRE.
CAPTAIN APOLLO
HOW LIKELY IS IT THAT A SIXTY YEAR OLD WRECK WOULD STILL HAVE AIR TO BURN?
RECEIVING TRANSMISSION.
LET'S HEAR IT.
FOR THE GODS' SAKE, PLEASE! CAN ANYONE HEAR US? THEY'RE SLAUGHTERING US!
WE NEED--DDZZ--ZZZZ--
WE'VE LOST THE SIGNAL.
IT'S A CYLON TRAP. THEY'RE GOING TO TRY TO RAM US. THE OLYMPIC CARRIER ALL OVER AGAIN.
LIEUTENANT GAETA, PREP THE FLEET FOR JUMP.
DUALLA. TELL APOLLO TO ASSUME ATTACK FORMATION.
SIR, THE SHIP IS UNARMED AND, AS ITS ENGINES ARE ON FIRE, POSES NO THREAT OF RAMMING THE GALACTICA. I--
I DID NOT SAY "ATTACK", CAPTAIN. I SAID "ATTACK FORMATION".
...
THE VENTING AIR MAY PUSH THE SHIP OUT OF ITS TRAJECTORY AND INTO THE SURROUNDING DEBRIS. I NEED YOU TO CLEAR ITS PATH.
CAN YOU DO THAT? OR DO I NEED TO REPLACE YOU WITH A PILOT WHO CAN?
ASSUMING ATTACK FORMATION.

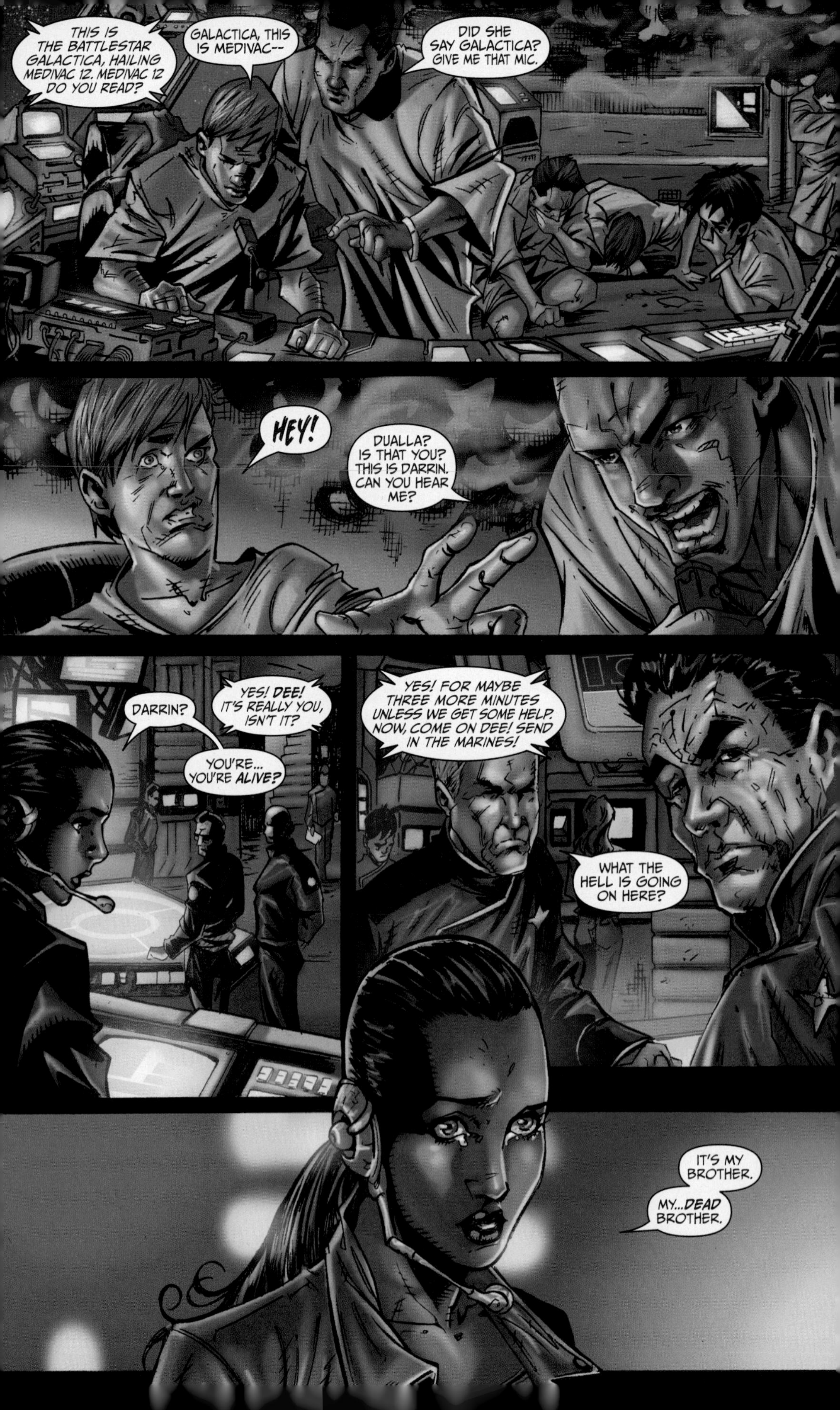
THIS IS THE BATTLESTAR GALACTICA, HAILING MEDIVAC 12. MEDIVAC 12 DO YOU READ?
GALACTICA, THIS IS MEDIVAC--
DID SHE SAY GALACTICA? GIVE ME THAT MIC.
HEY!
DUALLA? IS THAT YOU? THIS IS DARRIN. CAN YOU HEAR ME?
DARRIN?
YES! DEE! IT'S REALLY YOU, ISN'T IT?
YOU'RE... YOU'RE ALIVE?
YES! FOR MAYBE THREE MORE MINUTES UNLESS WE GET SOME HELP. NOW, COME ON DEE! SEND IN THE MARINES!
WHAT THE HELL IS GOING ON HERE?
IT'S MY BROTHER.
MY...DEAD BROTHER.

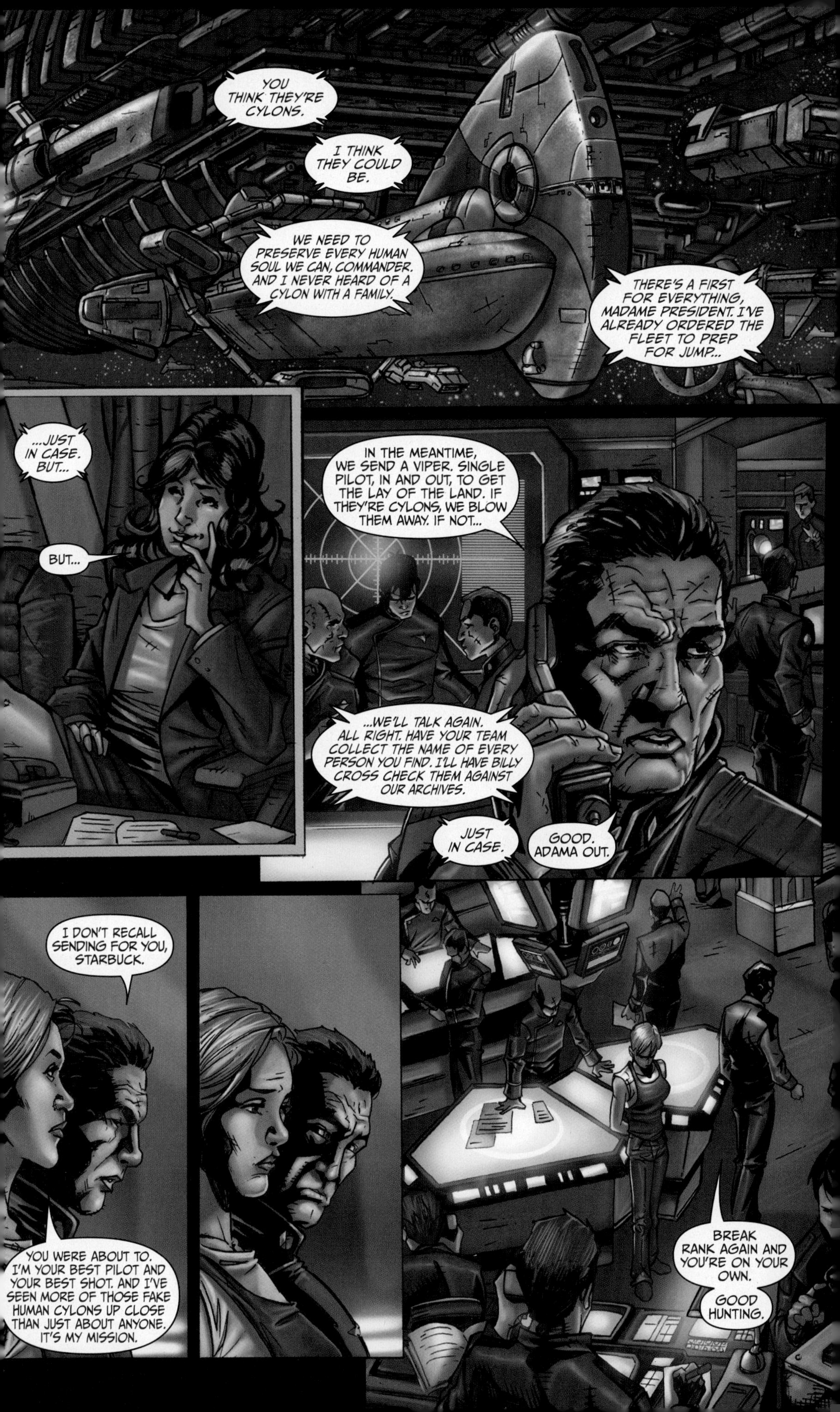
YOU THINK THEY'RE CYLONS.
I THINK THEY COULD BE.
WE NEED TO PRESERVE EVERY HUMAN SOUL WE CAN, COMMANDER. AND I NEVER HEARD OF A CYLON WITH A FAMILY.
THERE'S A FIRST FOR EVERYTHING, MADAME PRESIDENT. I'VE ALREADY ORDERED THE FLEET TO PREP FOR JUMP...
...JUST IN CASE. BUT...
BUT...
IN THE MEANTIME, WE SEND A VIPER. SINGLE PILOT, IN AND OUT, TO GET THE LAY OF THE LAND. IF THEY'RE CYLONS, WE BLOW THEM AWAY. IF NOT...
...WE'LL TALK AGAIN. ALL RIGHT. HAVE YOUR TEAM COLLECT THE NAME OF EVERY PERSON YOU FIND. I'LL HAVE BILLY CROSS CHECK THEM AGAINST OUR ARCHIVES.
JUST IN CASE.
GOOD. ADAMA OUT.
I DON'T RECALL SENDING FOR YOU, STARBUCK.
YOU WERE ABOUT TO. I'M YOUR BEST PILOT AND YOUR BEST SHOT. AND I'VE SEEN MORE OF THOSE FAKE HUMAN CYLONS UP CLOSE THAN JUST ABOUT ANYONE. IT'S MY MISSION.
BREAK RANK AGAIN AND YOU'RE ON YOUR OWN.
GOOD HUNTING.

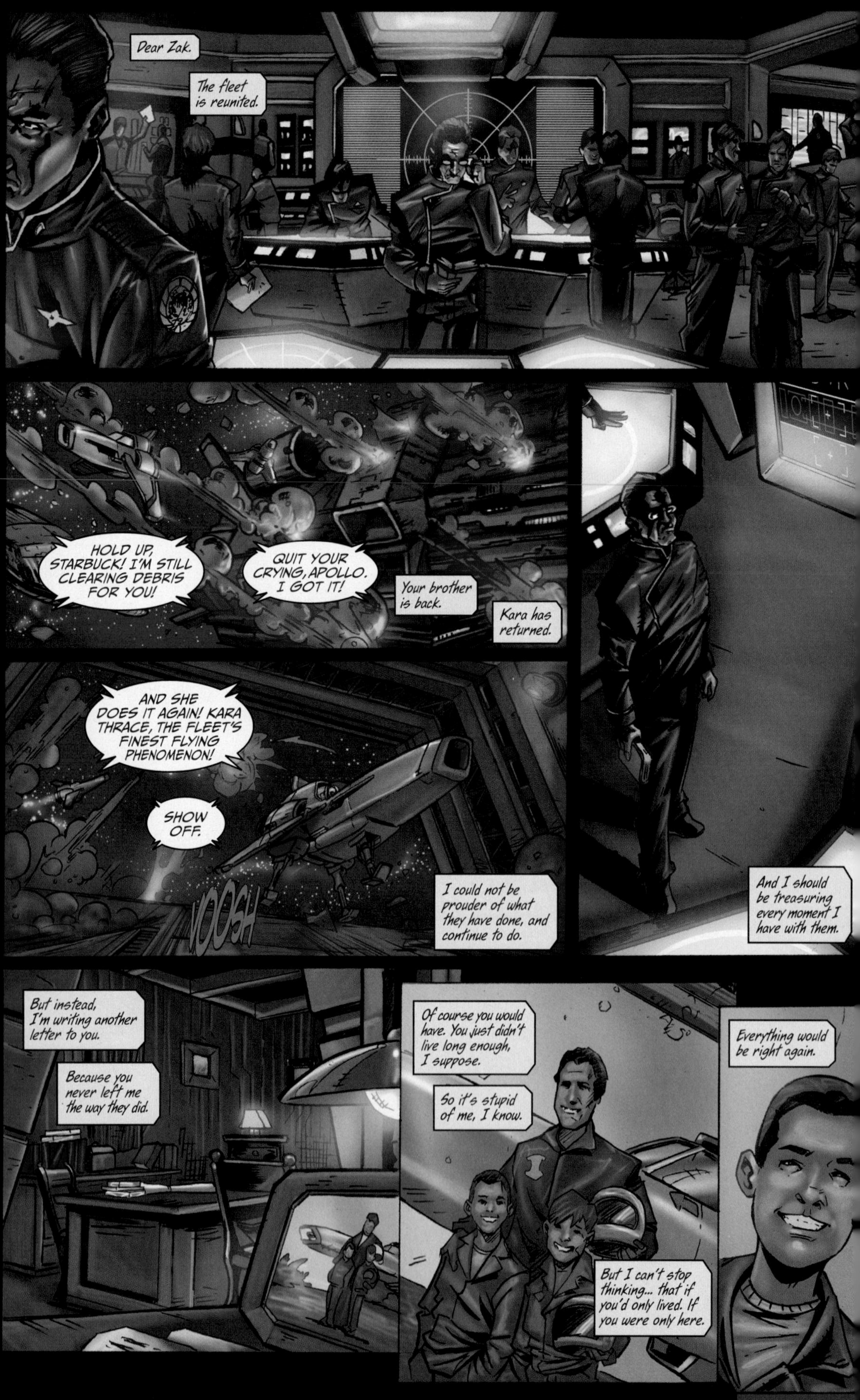
Dear Zak.
The fleet is reunited.
HOLD UP, STARBUCK! I'M STILL CLEARING DEBRIS FOR YOU!
QUIT YOUR CRYING, APOLLO. I GOT IT!
Your brother is back.
Kara has returned.
AND SHE DOES IT AGAIN! KARA THRACE, THE FLEET'S FINEST FLYING PHENOMENON!
SHOW OFF.
VOOSH
I could not be prouder of what they have done, and continue to do.
And I should be treasuring every moment I have with them.
But instead, I'm writing another letter to you.
Because you never left me the way they did.
Of course you would have. You just didn't live long enough, I suppose.
So it's stupid of me, I know.
But I can't stop thinking... that if you'd only lived. If you were only here.
Everything would be right again.

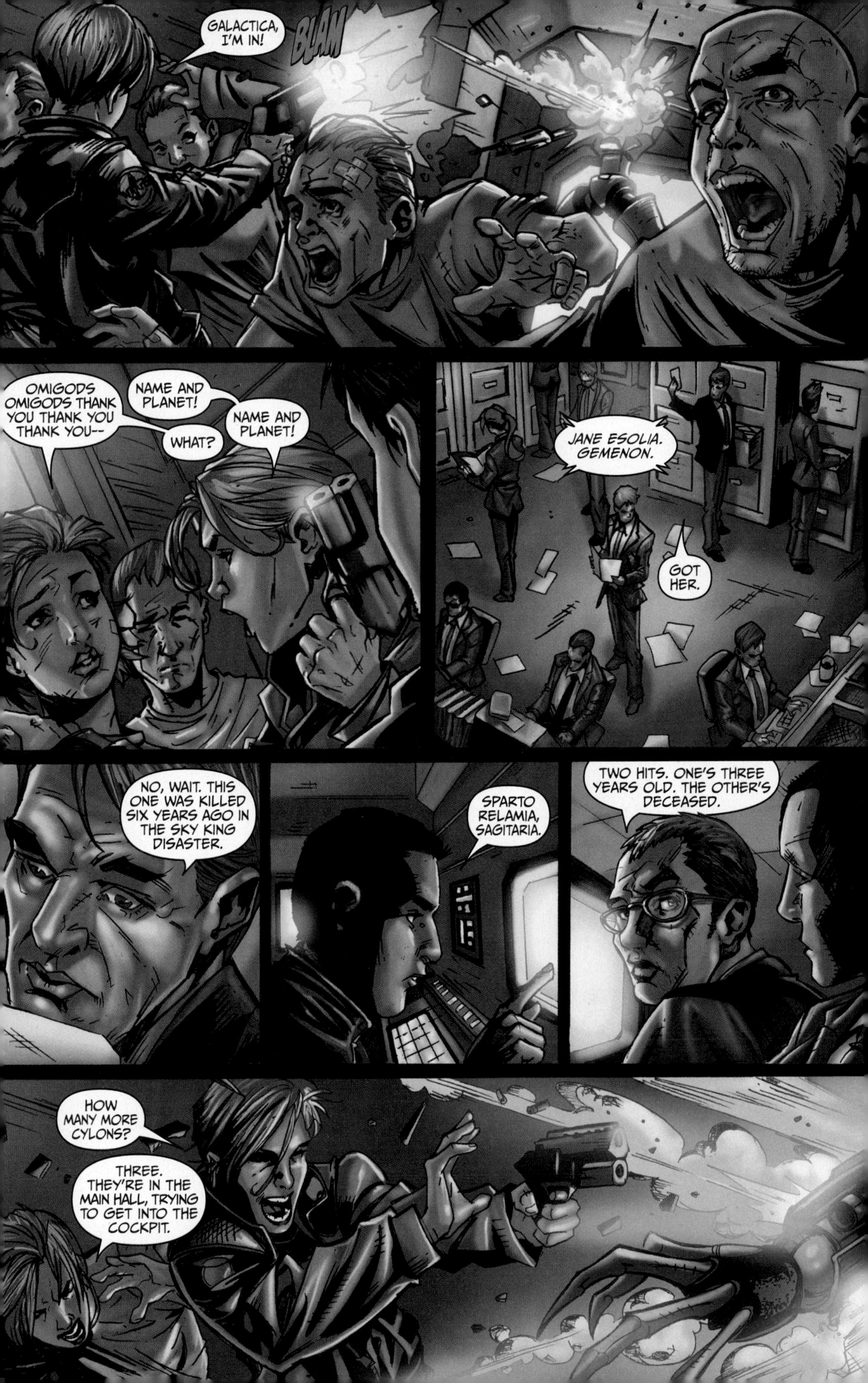
GALACTICA, I'M IN!
BLAM
OMIGODS OMIGODS THANK YOU THANK YOU THANK YOU--
NAME AND PLANET!
WHAT?
NAME AND PLANET!
JANE ESOLIA. GEMENON.
GOT HER.
NO, WAIT. THIS ONE WAS KILLED SIX YEARS AGO IN THE SKY KING DISASTER.
SPARTO RELAMIA, SAGITARIA.
TWO HITS. ONE'S THREE YEARS OLD. THE OTHER'S DECEASED.
HOW MANY MORE CYLONS?
THREE. THEY'RE IN THE MAIN HALL, TRYING TO GET INTO THE COCKPIT.

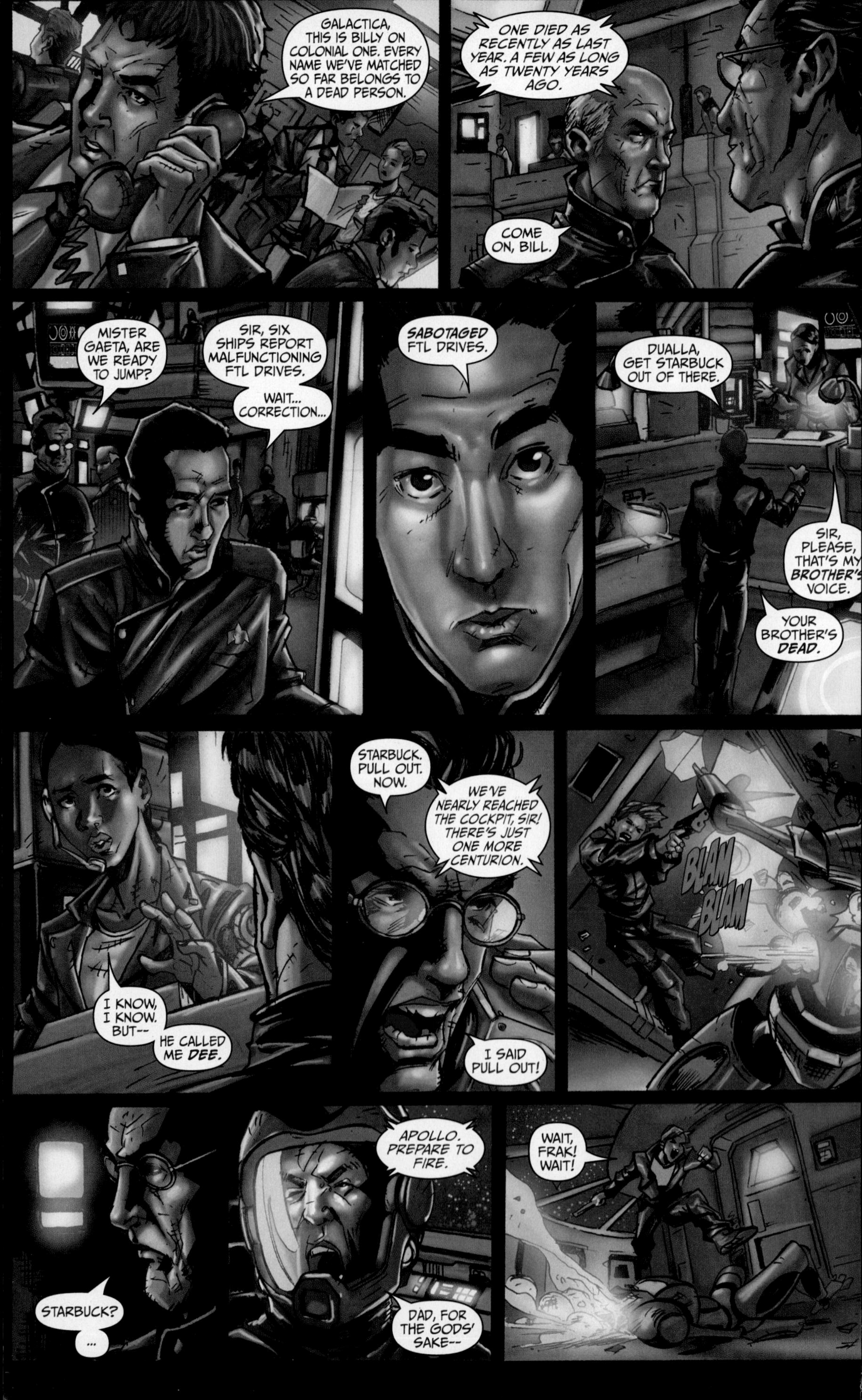
GALACTICA, THIS IS BILLY ON COLONIAL ONE. EVERY NAME WE'VE MATCHED SO FAR BELONGS TO A DEAD PERSON.
ONE DIED AS RECENTLY AS LAST YEAR. A FEW AS LONG AS TWENTY YEARS AGO.
COME ON, BILL.
MISTER GAETA, ARE WE READY TO JUMP?
SIR, SIX SHIPS REPORT MALFUNCTIONING FTL DRIVES.
WAIT... CORRECTION...
SABOTAGED FTL DRIVES.
DUALLA, GET STARBUCK OUT OF THERE.
SIR, PLEASE, THAT'S MY BROTHER'S VOICE.
YOUR BROTHER'S DEAD.
I KNOW, I KNOW. BUT--
HE CALLED ME DEE.
STARBUCK. PULL OUT. NOW.
WE'VE NEARLY REACHED THE COCKPIT, SIR! THERE'S JUST ONE MORE CENTURION.
I SAID PULL OUT!
BLAM
BLAM
STARBUCK?
...
APOLLO. PREPARE TO FIRE.
DAD, FOR THE GODS' SAKE--
WAIT, FRAK! WAIT!

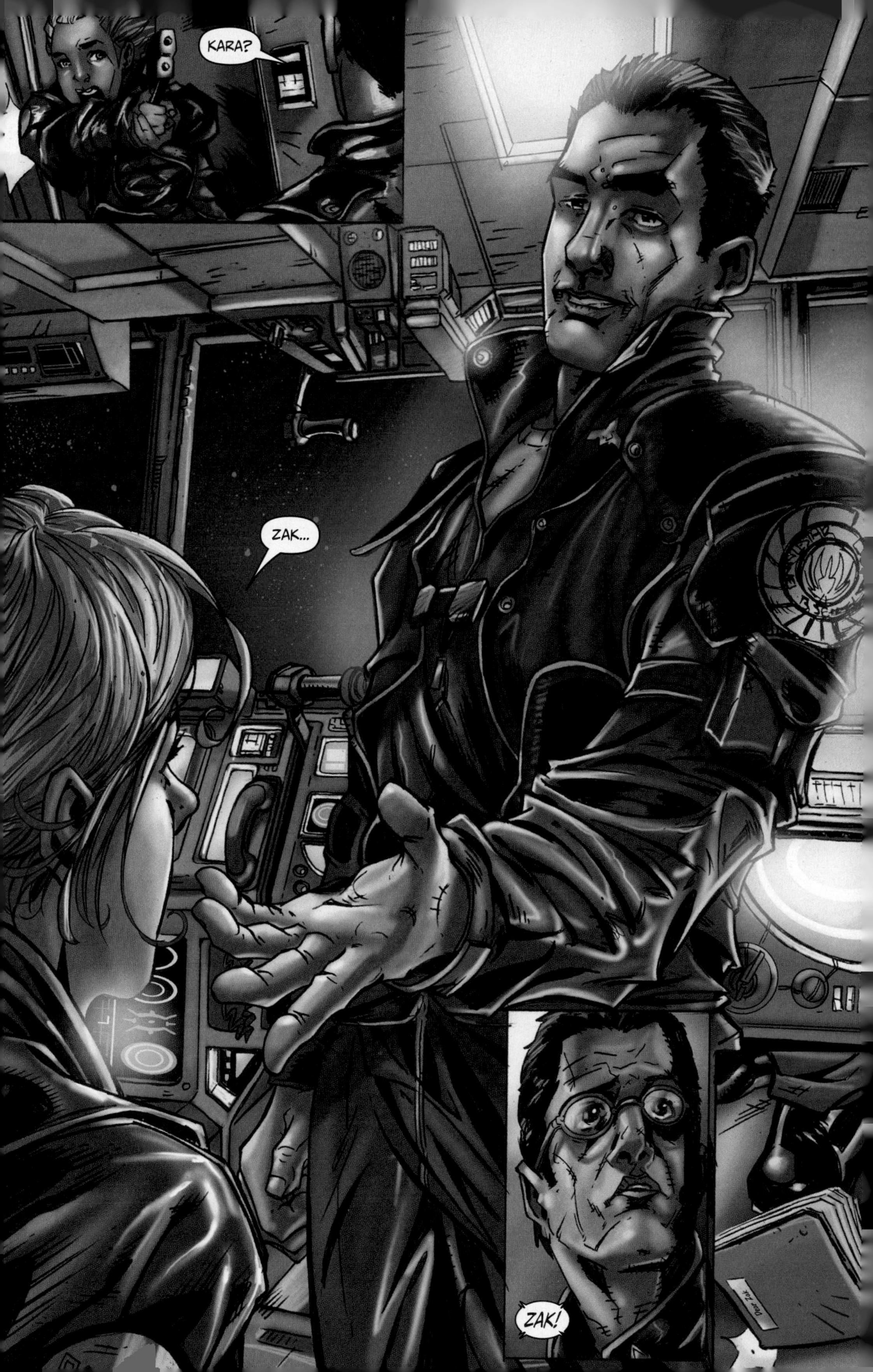

KARA?
ZAK...
ZAK!

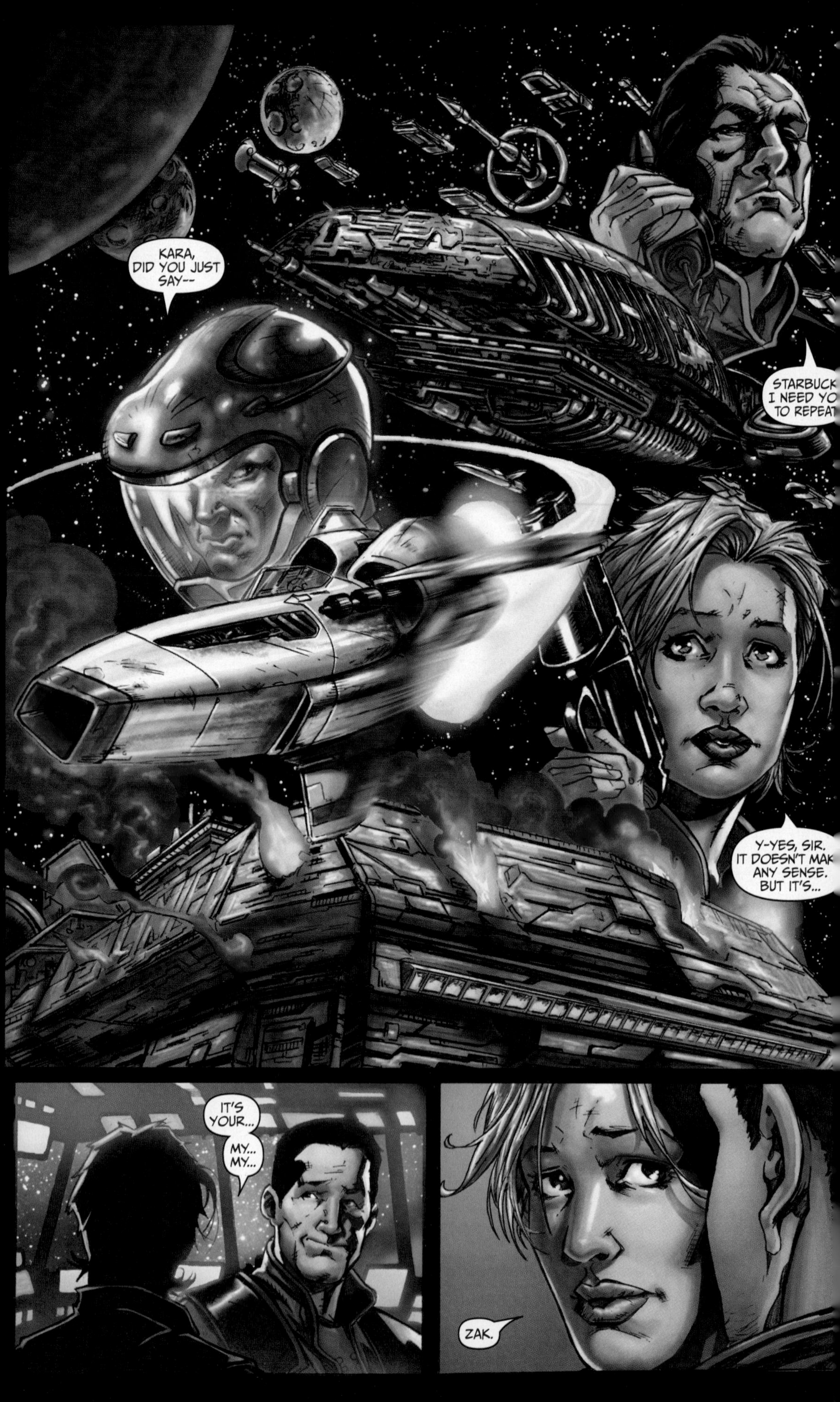
KARA, DID YOU JUST SAY--
STARBUCK I NEED YO TO REPEAT
Y-YES, SIR. IT DOESN'T MAK ANY SENSE. BUT IT'S...
IT'S YOUR...
MY... MY...
ZAK.

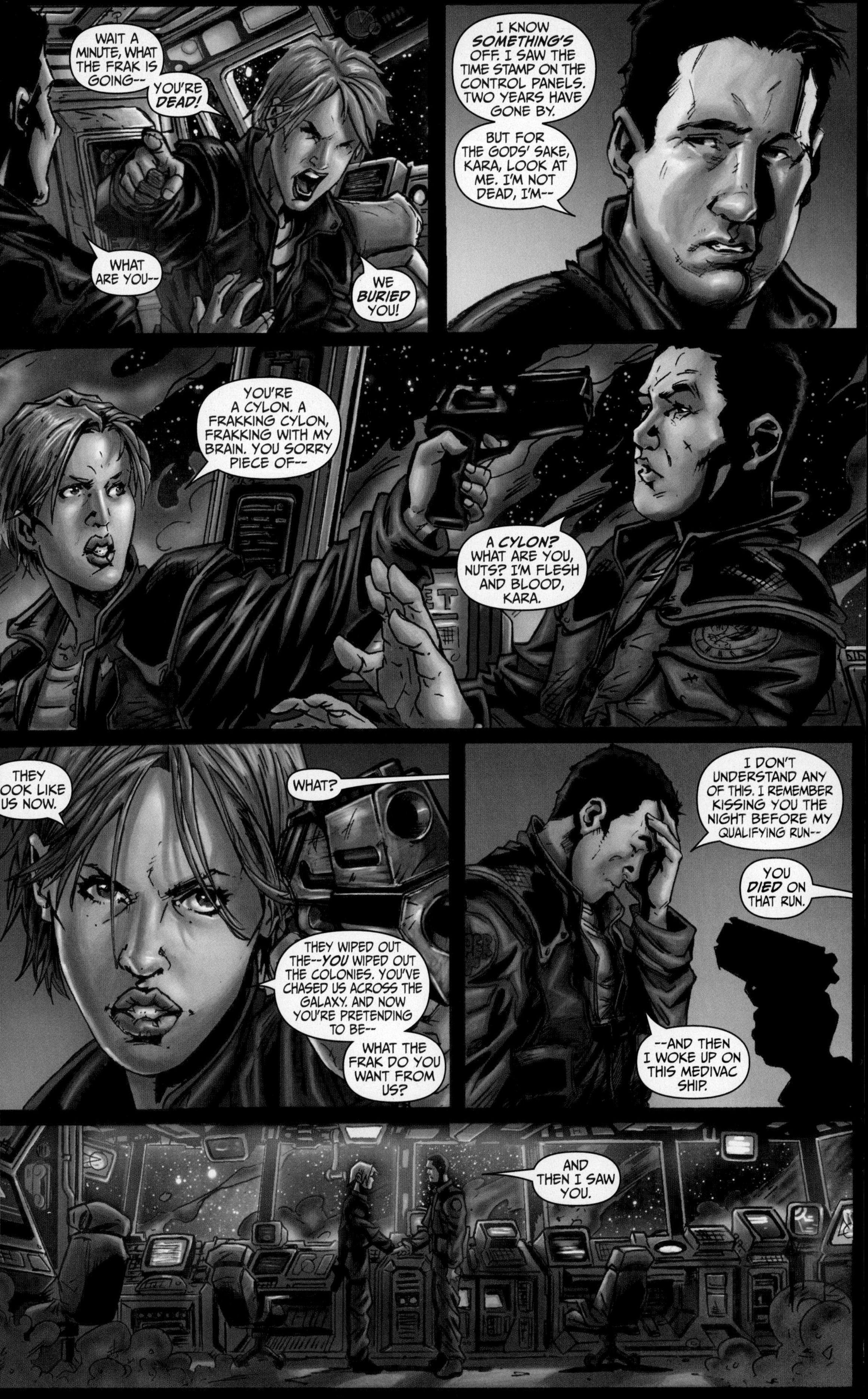
WAIT A MINUTE, WHAT THE FRAK IS GOING--
YOU'RE DEAD!
WHAT ARE YOU--
WE BURIED YOU!
I KNOW SOMETHING'S OFF. I SAW THE TIME STAMP ON THE CONTROL PANELS. TWO YEARS HAVE GONE BY.
BUT FOR THE GODS' SAKE, KARA, LOOK AT ME. I'M NOT DEAD, I'M--
YOU'RE A CYLON. A FRAKKING CYLON, FRAKKING WITH MY BRAIN. YOU SORRY PIECE OF--
A CYLON? WHAT ARE YOU, NUTS? I'M FLESH AND BLOOD, KARA.
THEY OOK LIKE US NOW.
WHAT?
THEY WIPED OUT THE--YOU WIPED OUT THE COLONIES. YOU'VE CHASED US ACROSS THE GALAXY. AND NOW YOU'RE PRETENDING TO BE--
WHAT THE FRAK DO YOU WANT FROM US?
I DON'T UNDERSTAND ANY OF THIS. I REMEMBER KISSING YOU THE NIGHT BEFORE MY QUALIFYING RUN--
YOU DIED ON THAT RUN.
--AND THEN I WOKE UP ON THIS MEDIVAC SHIP.
AND THEN I SAW YOU.

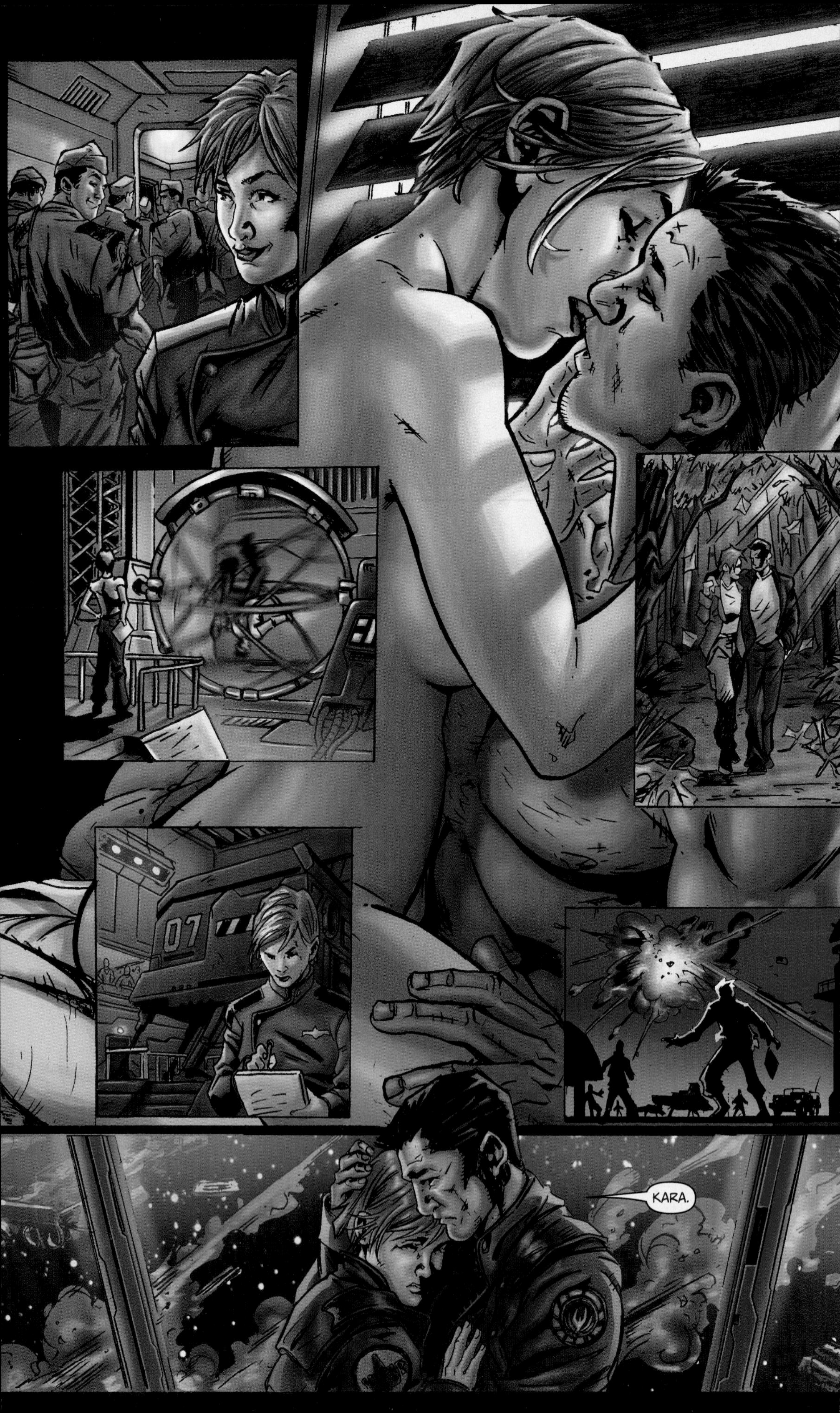
KARA.

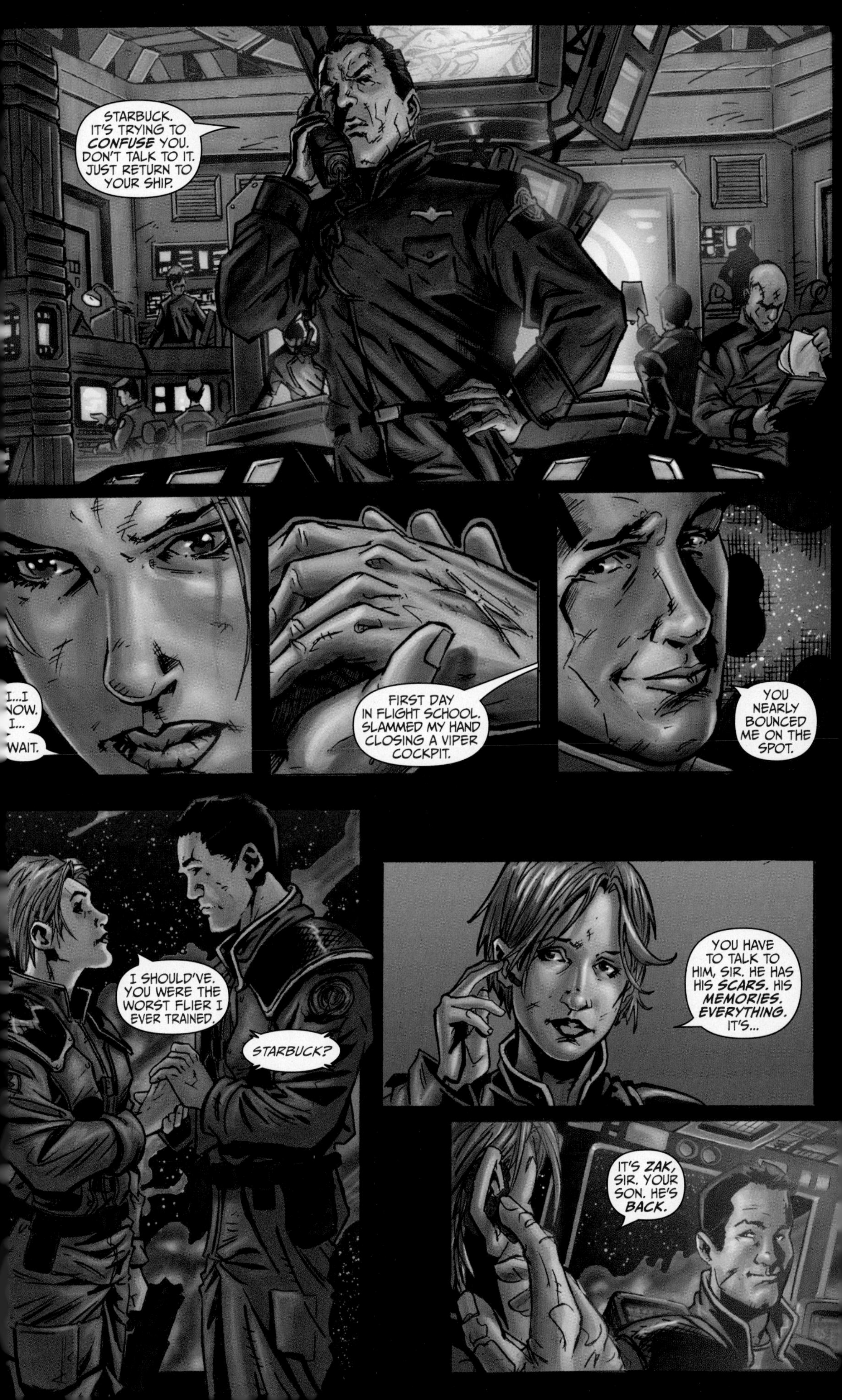
STARBUCK. IT'S TRYING TO CONFUSE YOU. DON'T TALK TO IT. JUST RETURN TO YOUR SHIP.
I...I NOW. I... WAIT.
FIRST DAY IN FLIGHT SCHOOL. SLAMMED MY HAND CLOSING A VIPER COCKPIT.
YOU NEARLY BOUNCED ME ON THE SPOT.
I SHOULD'VE. YOU WERE THE WORST FLIER I EVER TRAINED.
STARBUCK?
YOU HAVE TO TALK TO HIM, SIR. HE HAS HIS SCARS. HIS MEMORIES. EVERYTHING. IT'S...
IT'S ZAK, SIR. YOUR SON. HE'S BACK.

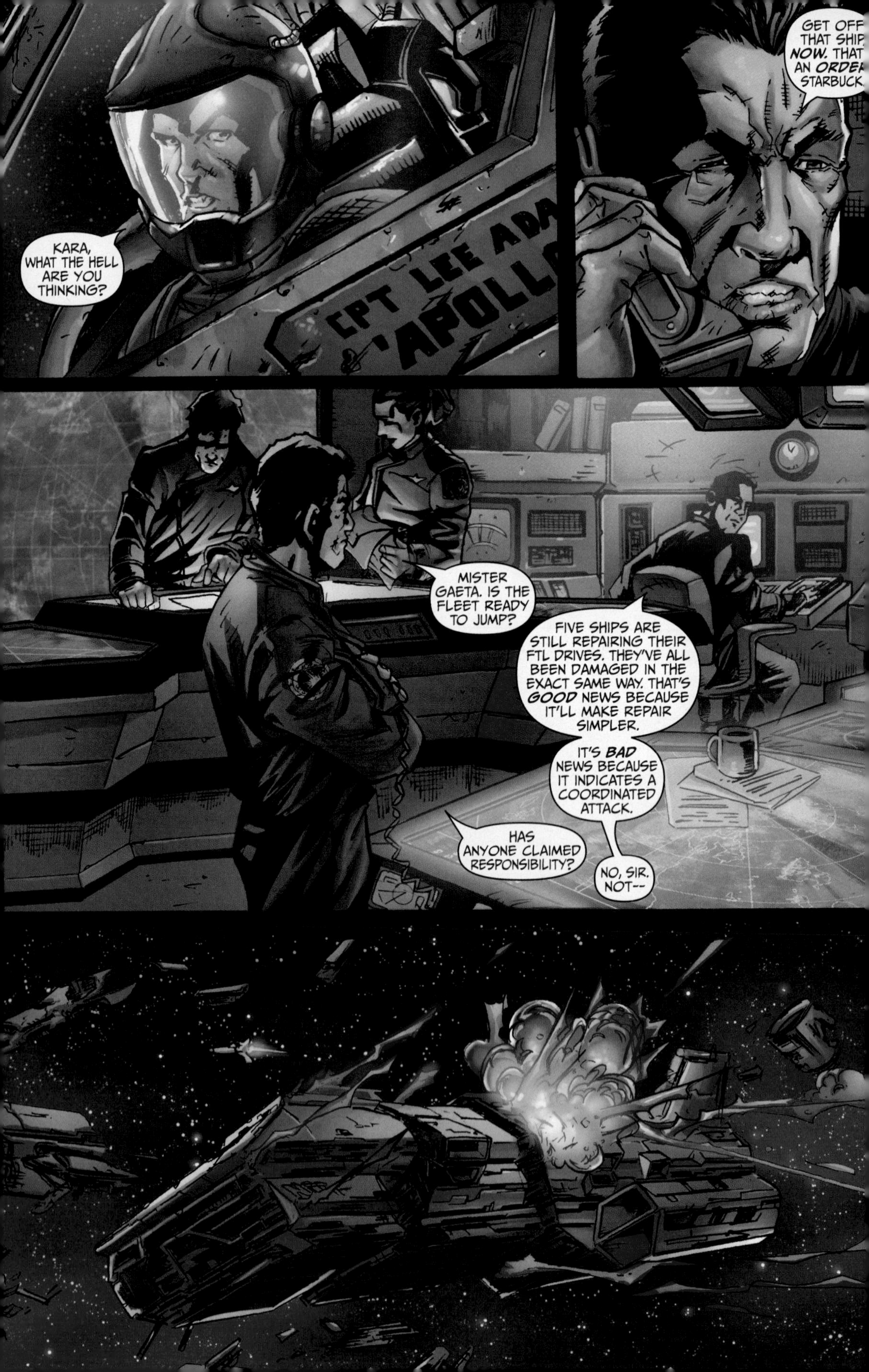
KARA, WHAT THE HELL ARE YOU THINKING?
CPT LEE ADA 'APOLL
GET OFF THAT SHIP *NOW.* THAT AN *ORDER* STARBUCK.
MISTER GAETA. IS THE FLEET READY TO JUMP?
FIVE SHIPS ARE STILL REPAIRING THEIR FTL DRIVES. THEY'VE ALL BEEN DAMAGED IN THE EXACT SAME WAY. THAT'S *GOOD* NEWS BECAUSE IT'LL MAKE REPAIR SIMPLER.
IT'S *BAD* NEWS BECAUSE IT INDICATES A COORDINATED ATTACK.
HAS ANYONE CLAIMED RESPONSIBILITY?
NO, SIR. NOT--

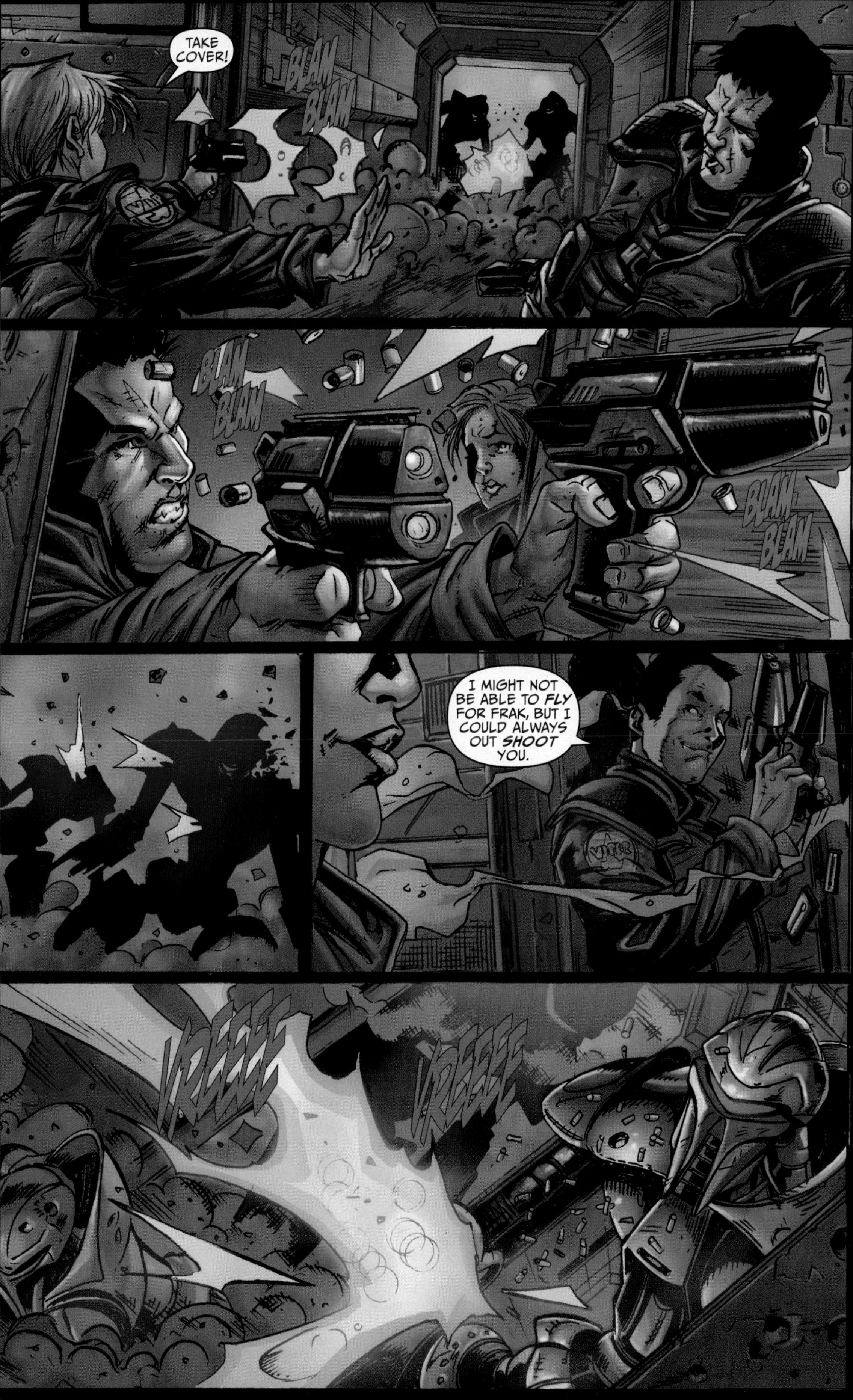
TAKE COVER!
BLAM BLAM
BLAM BLAM
BLAM BLAM
I MIGHT NOT BE ABLE TO *FLY* FOR FRAK, BUT I COULD ALWAYS OUT *SHOOT* YOU.
VREEEE
VREEEE

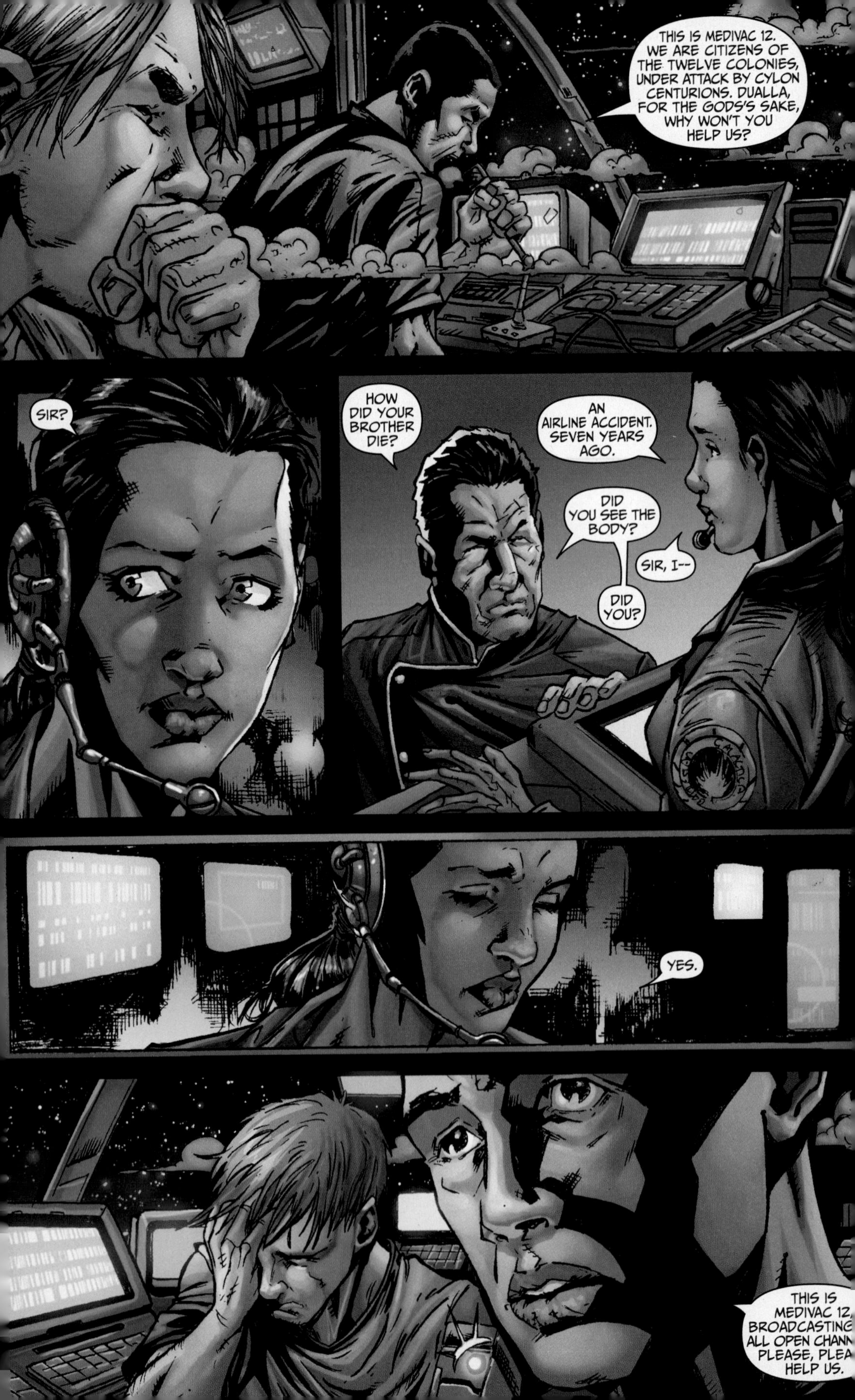
THIS IS MEDIVAC 12. WE ARE CITIZENS OF THE TWELVE COLONIES, UNDER ATTACK BY CYLON CENTURIONS. DUALLA, FOR THE GODS'S SAKE, WHY WON'T YOU HELP US?
SIR?
HOW DID YOUR BROTHER DIE?
AN AIRLINE ACCIDENT. SEVEN YEARS AGO.
DID YOU SEE THE BODY?
SIR, I--
DID YOU?
YES.
THIS IS MEDIVAC 12, BROADCASTING ALL OPEN CHANN PLEASE, PLEA HELP US.

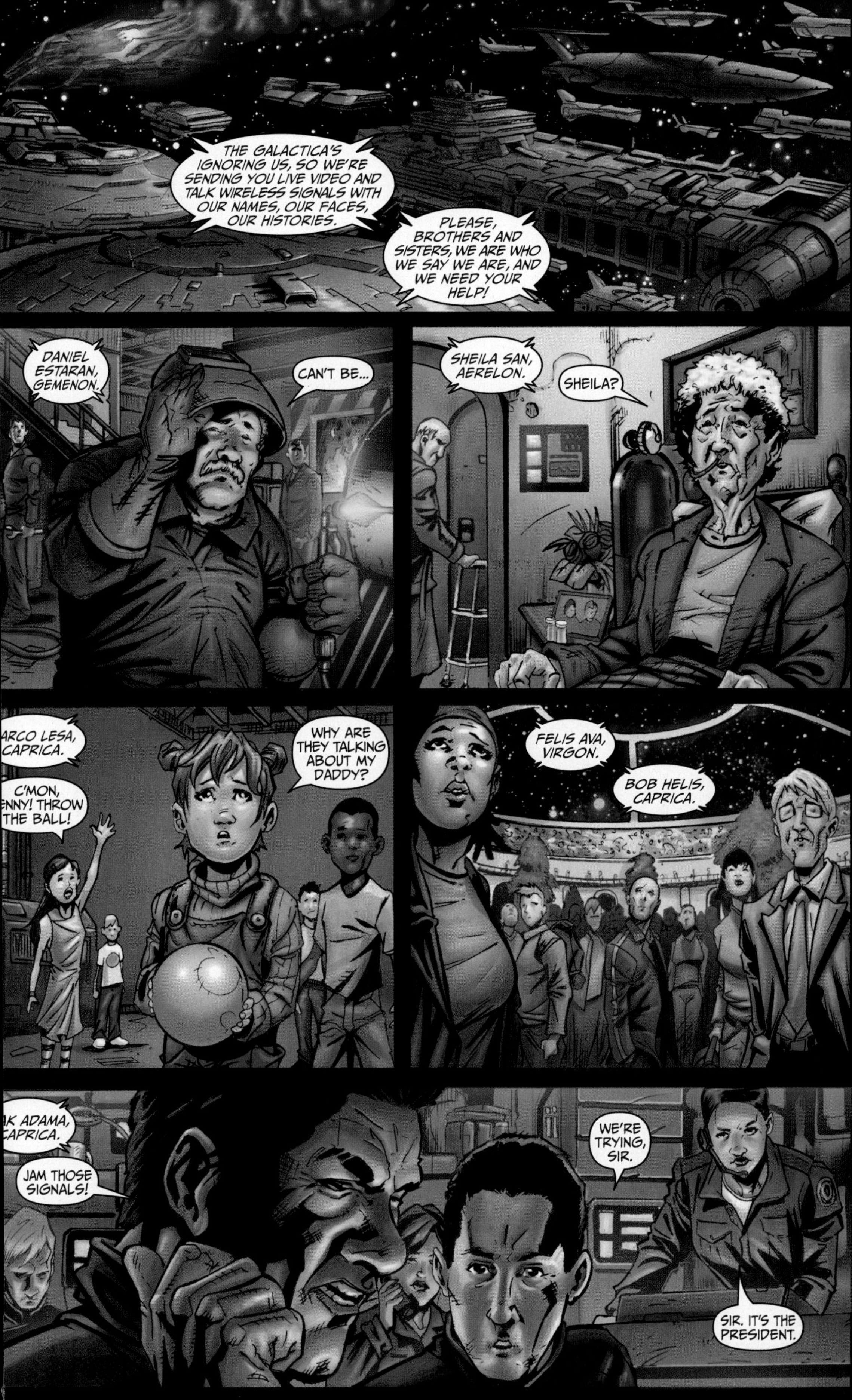
THE GALACTICA'S IGNORING US, SO WE'RE SENDING YOU LIVE VIDEO AND TALK WIRELESS SIGNALS WITH OUR NAMES, OUR FACES, OUR HISTORIES.
PLEASE, BROTHERS AND SISTERS, WE ARE WHO WE SAY WE ARE, AND WE NEED YOUR HELP!
DANIEL ESTARAN, GEMENON.
CAN'T BE...
SHEILA SAN, AERELON.
SHEILA?
ARCO LESA, CAPRICA.
C'MON, ENNY! THROW THE BALL!
WHY ARE THEY TALKING ABOUT MY DADDY?
FELIS AVA, VIRGON.
BOB HELIS, CAPRICA.
AK ADAMA, CAPRICA.
JAM THOSE SIGNALS!
WE'RE TRYING, SIR.
SIR. IT'S THE PRESIDENT.

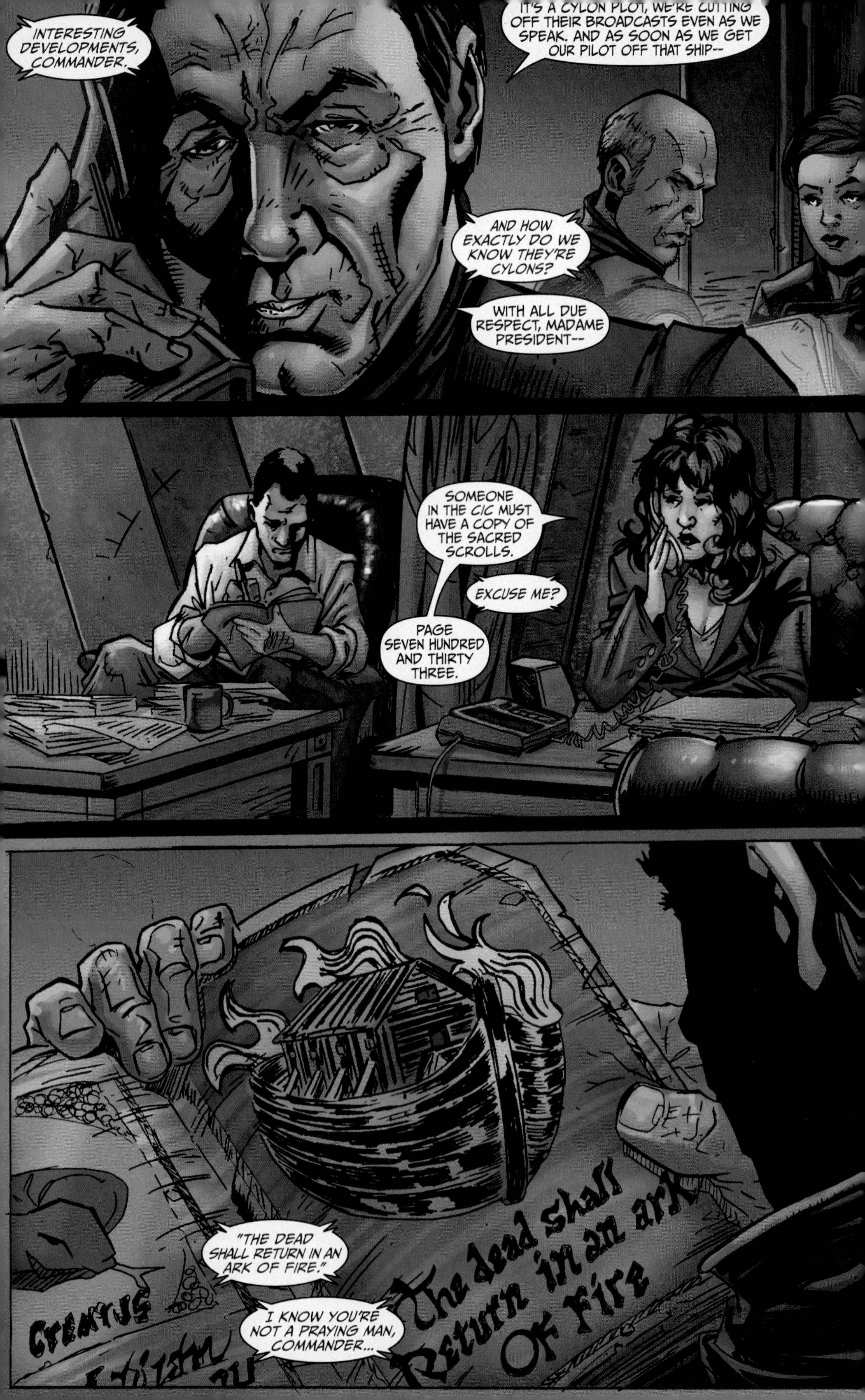
INTERESTING DEVELOPMENTS, COMMANDER.
IT'S A CYLON PLOT, WE'RE CUTTING OFF THEIR BROADCASTS EVEN AS WE SPEAK. AND AS SOON AS WE GET OUR PILOT OFF THAT SHIP--
AND HOW EXACTLY DO WE KNOW THEY'RE CYLONS?
WITH ALL DUE RESPECT, MADAME PRESIDENT--
SOMEONE IN THE CIC MUST HAVE A COPY OF THE SACRED SCROLLS.
EXCUSE ME?
PAGE SEVEN HUNDRED AND THIRTY THREE.
"THE DEAD SHALL RETURN IN AN ARK OF FIRE."
The dead shall Return in an ark Of Fire
I KNOW YOU'RE NOT A PRAYING MAN, COMMANDER...

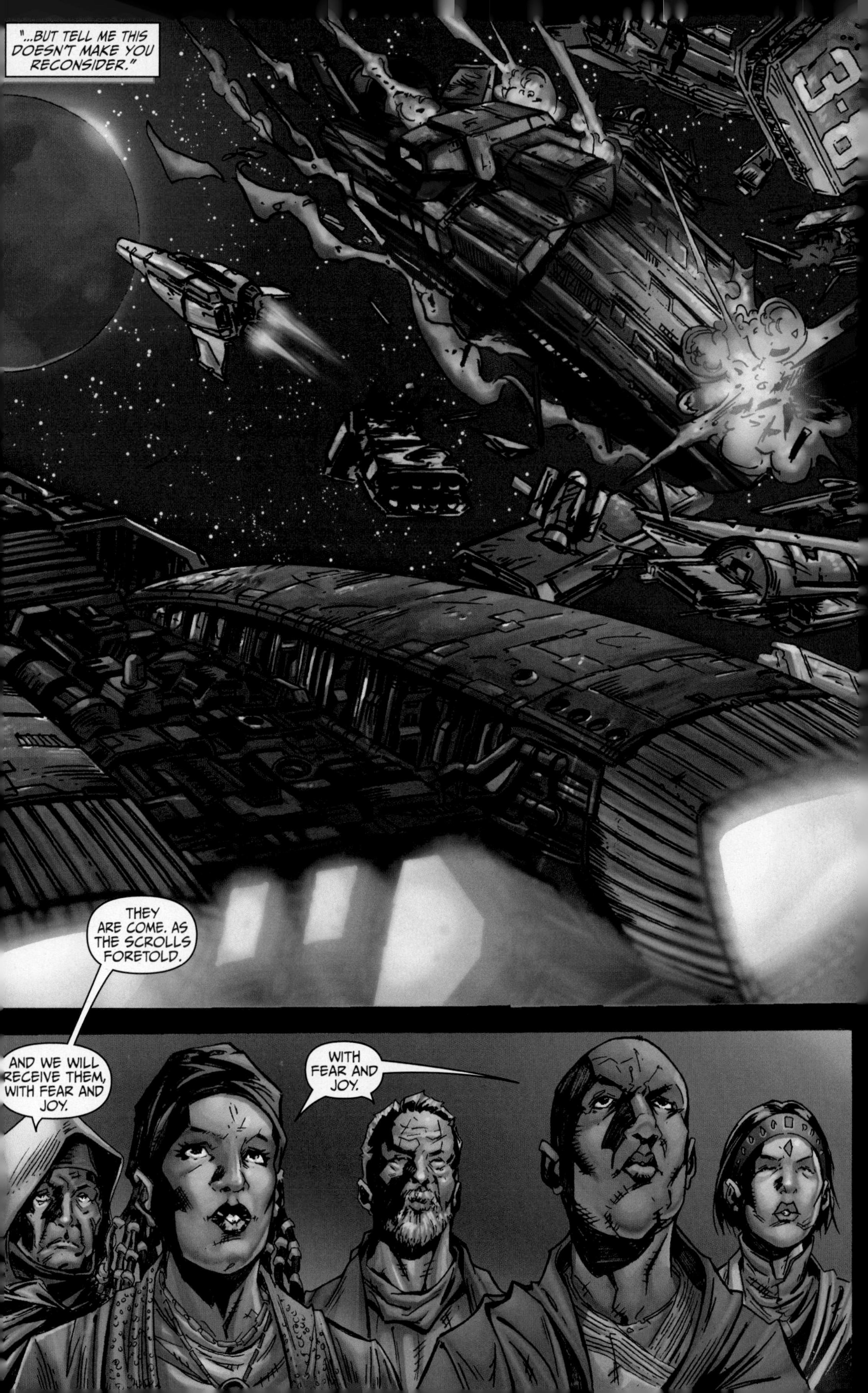
"...BUT TELL ME THIS DOESN'T MAKE YOU RECONSIDER."
THEY ARE COME. AS THE SCROLLS FORETOLD.
AND WE WILL RECEIVE THEM, WITH FEAR AND JOY.
WITH FEAR AND JOY.

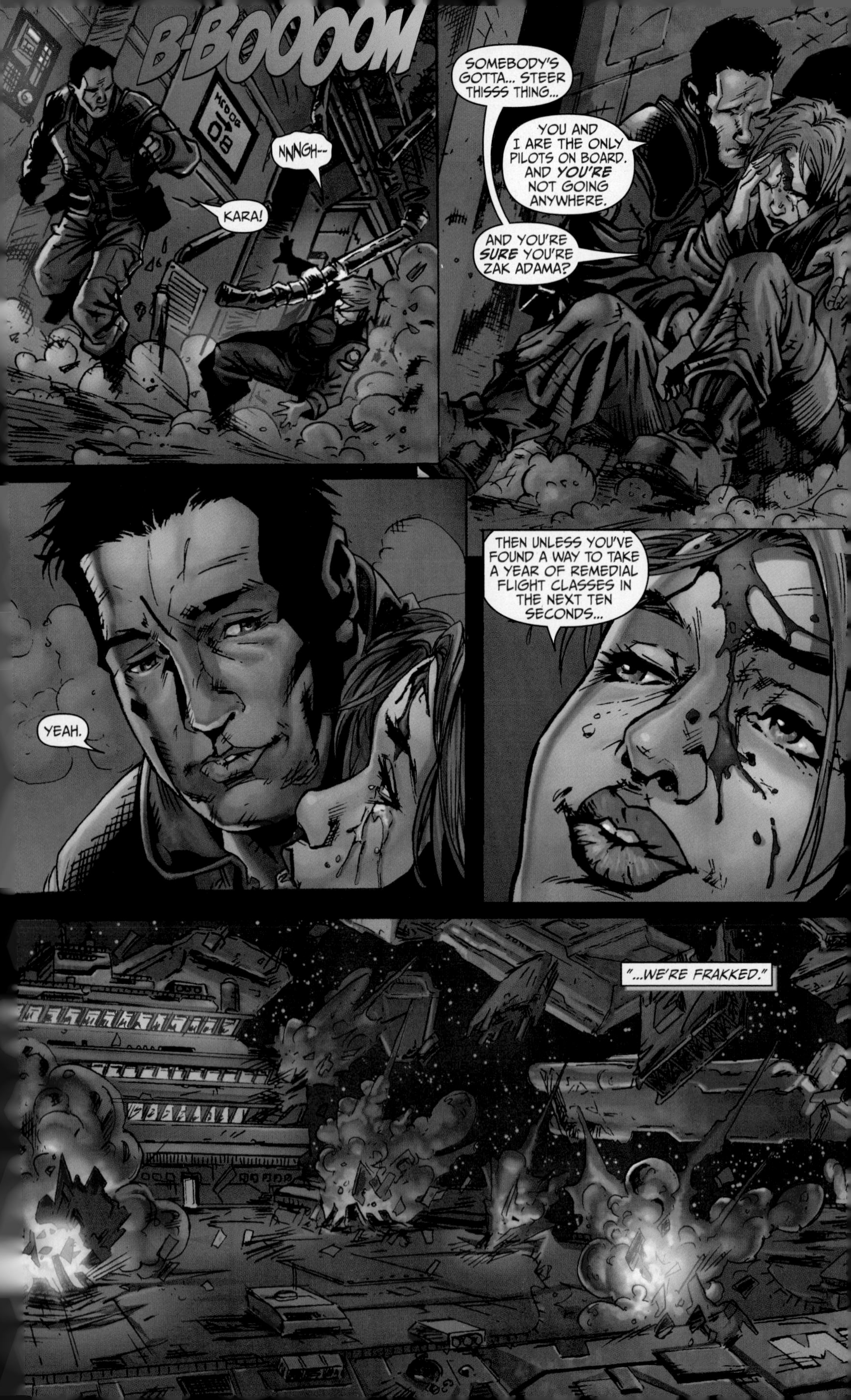
B-BOOOOM
MCOOG 08
NNNGH--
KARA!
SOMEBODY'S GOTTA... STEER THISSS THING...
YOU AND I ARE THE ONLY PILOTS ON BOARD. AND YOU'RE NOT GOING ANYWHERE.
AND YOU'RE SURE YOU'RE ZAK ADAMA?
YEAH.
THEN UNLESS YOU'VE FOUND A WAY TO TAKE A YEAR OF REMEDIAL FLIGHT CLASSES IN THE NEXT TEN SECONDS...
"...WE'RE FRAKKED."

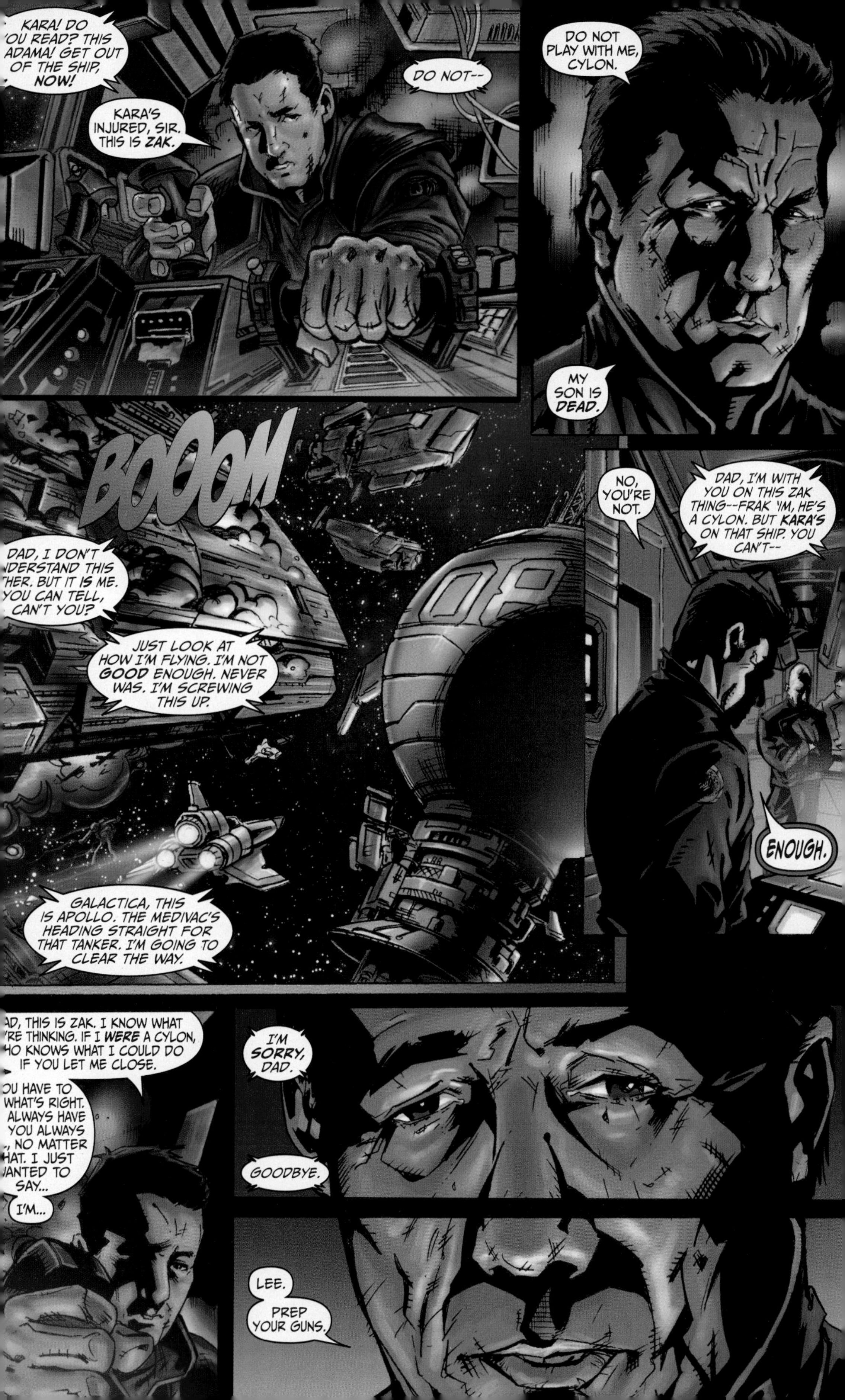
KARA! DO YOU READ? THIS ADAMA! GET OUT OF THE SHIP, NOW!
KARA'S INJURED, SIR. THIS IS ZAK.
DO NOT--
DO NOT PLAY WITH ME, CYLON.
MY SON IS DEAD.
BOOOM
DAD, I DON'T NDERSTAND THIS THER. BUT IT IS ME. YOU CAN TELL, CAN'T YOU?
JUST LOOK AT HOW I'M FLYING. I'M NOT GOOD ENOUGH. NEVER WAS. I'M SCREWING THIS UP.
NO, YOU'RE NOT.
DAD, I'M WITH YOU ON THIS ZAK THING--FRAK 'IM, HE'S A CYLON. BUT KARA'S ON THAT SHIP. YOU CAN'T--
ENOUGH.
GALACTICA, THIS IS APOLLO. THE MEDIVAC'S HEADING STRAIGHT FOR THAT TANKER. I'M GOING TO CLEAR THE WAY.
AD, THIS IS ZAK. I KNOW WHAT 'RE THINKING. IF I WERE A CYLON, HO KNOWS WHAT I COULD DO IF YOU LET ME CLOSE.
OU HAVE TO WHAT'S RIGHT. ALWAYS HAVE YOU ALWAYS , NO MATTER HAT. I JUST ANTED TO SAY...
I'M...
I'M SORRY, DAD.
GOODBYE.
LEE.
PREP YOUR GUNS.

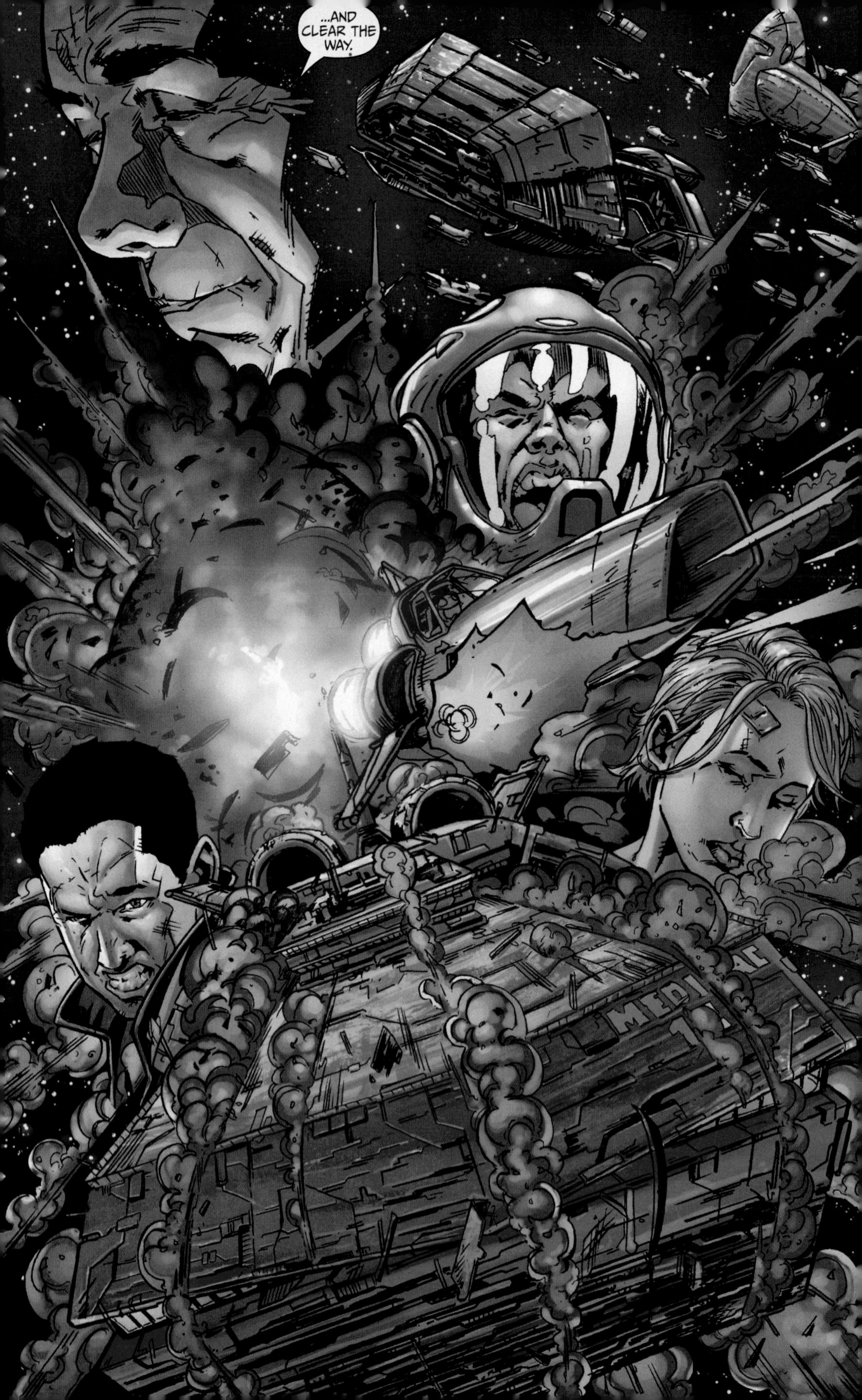
...AND CLEAR THE WAY.

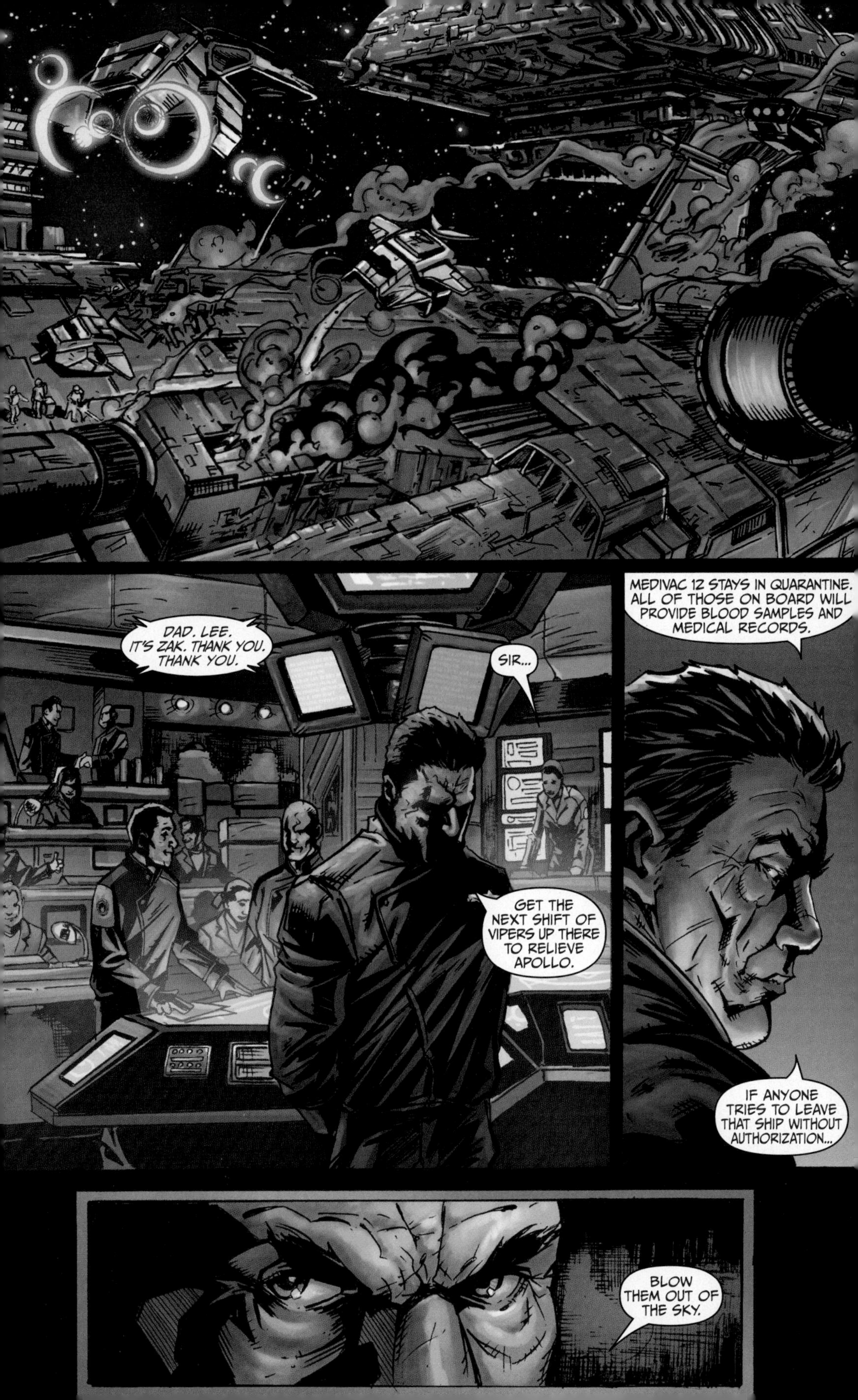
DAD. LEE.
IT'S ZAK. THANK YOU.
THANK YOU.
SIR...
GET THE NEXT SHIFT OF VIPERS UP THERE TO RELIEVE APOLLO.
MEDIVAC 12 STAYS IN QUARANTINE. ALL OF THOSE ON BOARD WILL PROVIDE BLOOD SAMPLES AND MEDICAL RECORDS.
IF ANYONE TRIES TO LEAVE THAT SHIP WITHOUT AUTHORIZATION...
BLOW THEM OUT OF THE SKY.

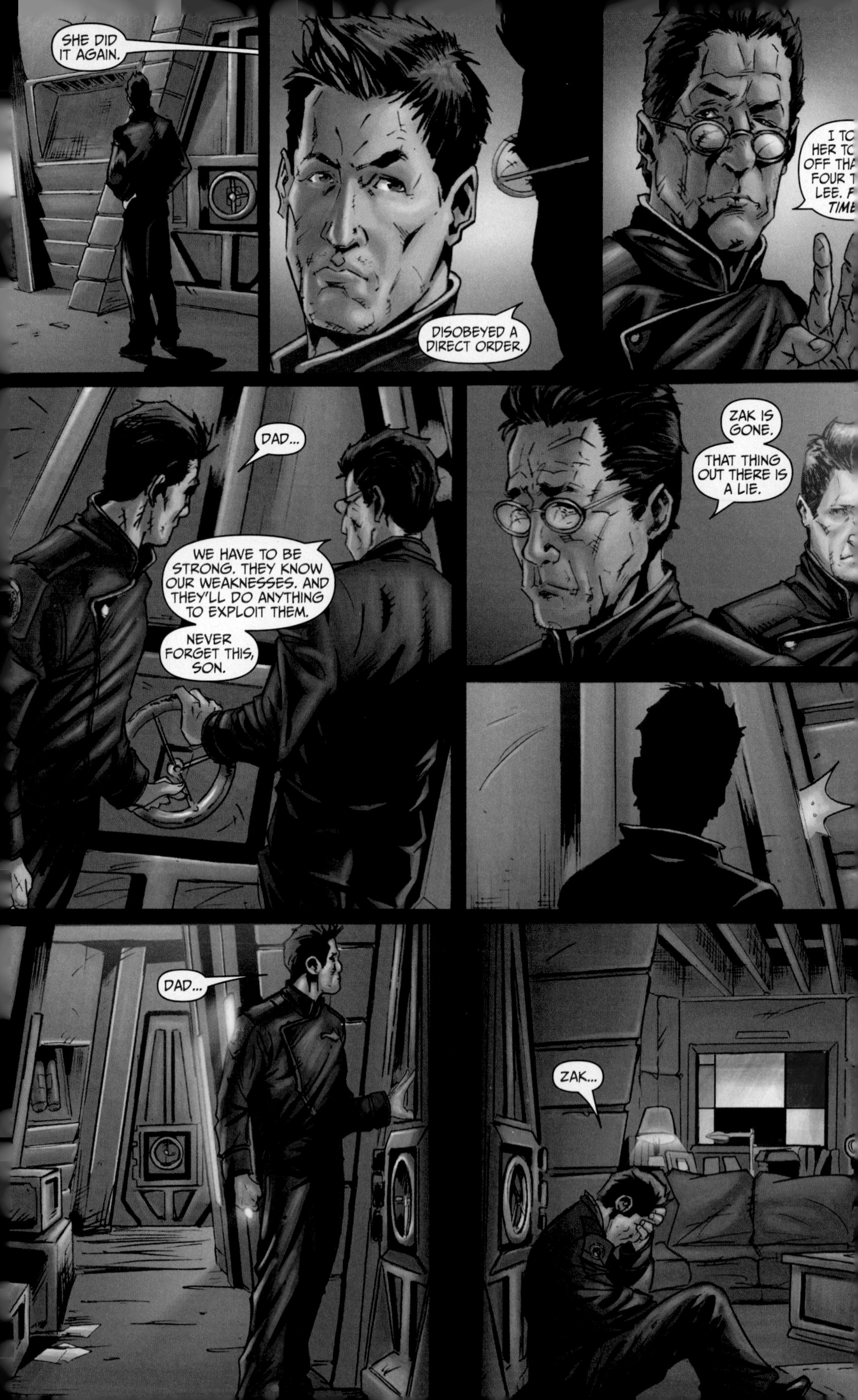
SHE DID IT AGAIN.
DISOBEYED A DIRECT ORDER.
I TO HER TO OFF THA FOUR T LEE. F TIME
DAD...
WE HAVE TO BE STRONG. THEY KNOW OUR WEAKNESSES. AND THEY'LL DO ANYTHING TO EXPLOIT THEM.
NEVER FORGET THIS, SON.
ZAK IS GONE.
THAT THING OUT THERE IS A LIE.
DAD...
ZAK...

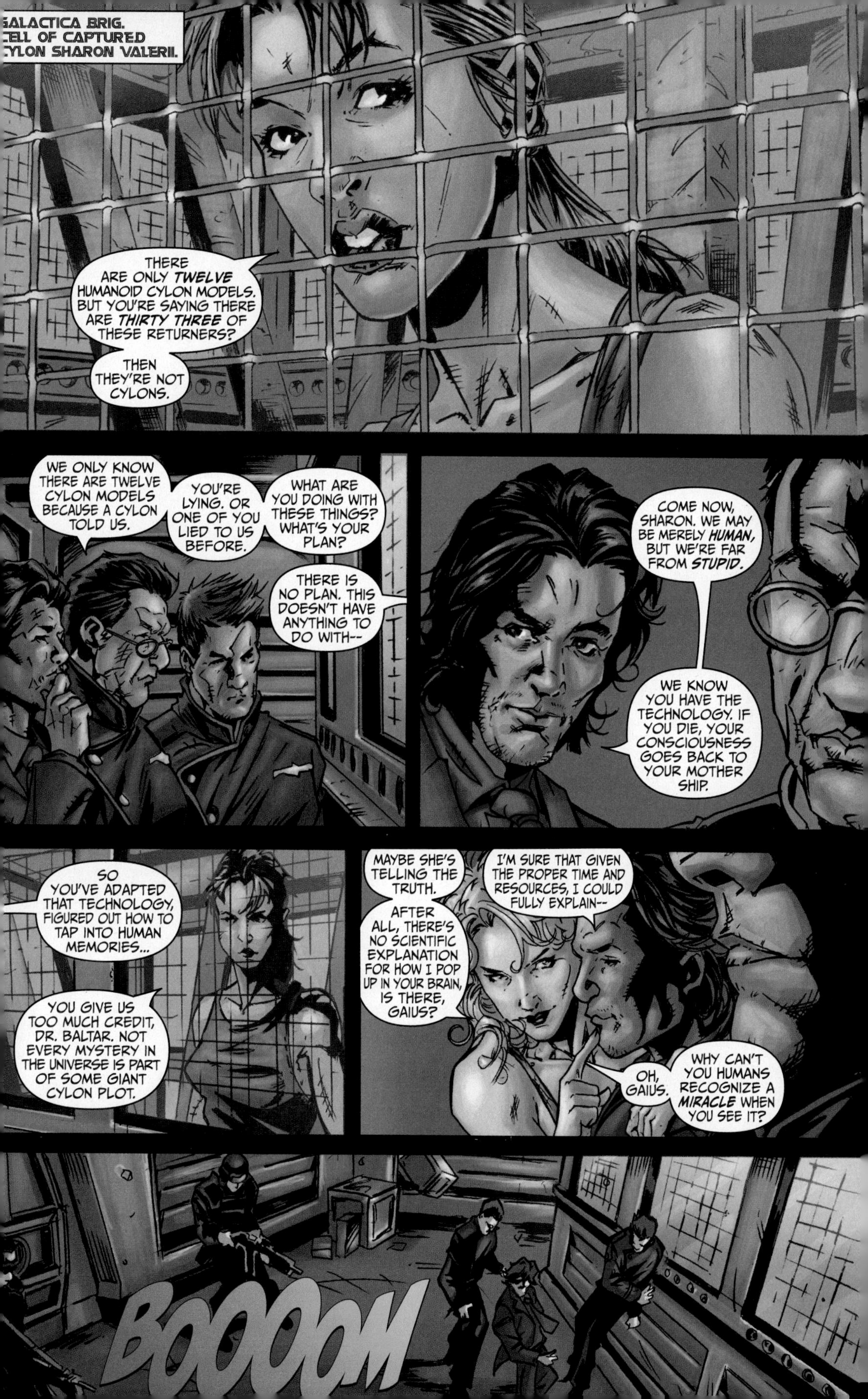
GALACTICA BRIG.
CELL OF CAPTURED
CYLON SHARON VALERII.
THERE ARE ONLY TWELVE HUMANOID CYLON MODELS. BUT YOU'RE SAYING THERE ARE THIRTY THREE OF THESE RETURNERS?
THEN THEY'RE NOT CYLONS.
WE ONLY KNOW THERE ARE TWELVE CYLON MODELS BECAUSE A CYLON TOLD US.
YOU'RE LYING. OR ONE OF YOU LIED TO US BEFORE.
WHAT ARE YOU DOING WITH THESE THINGS? WHAT'S YOUR PLAN?
THERE IS NO PLAN. THIS DOESN'T HAVE ANYTHING TO DO WITH--
COME NOW, SHARON. WE MAY BE MERELY HUMAN, BUT WE'RE FAR FROM STUPID.
WE KNOW YOU HAVE THE TECHNOLOGY. IF YOU DIE, YOUR CONSCIOUSNESS GOES BACK TO YOUR MOTHER SHIP.
SO YOU'VE ADAPTED THAT TECHNOLOGY, FIGURED OUT HOW TO TAP INTO HUMAN MEMORIES...
YOU GIVE US TOO MUCH CREDIT, DR. BALTAR. NOT EVERY MYSTERY IN THE UNIVERSE IS PART OF SOME GIANT CYLON PLOT.
MAYBE SHE'S TELLING THE TRUTH.
I'M SURE THAT GIVEN THE PROPER TIME AND RESOURCES, I COULD FULLY EXPLAIN--
AFTER ALL, THERE'S NO SCIENTIFIC EXPLANATION FOR HOW I POP UP IN YOUR BRAIN, IS THERE, GAIUS?
OH, GAIUS.
WHY CAN'T YOU HUMANS RECOGNIZE A MIRACLE WHEN YOU SEE IT?
BOOOOM

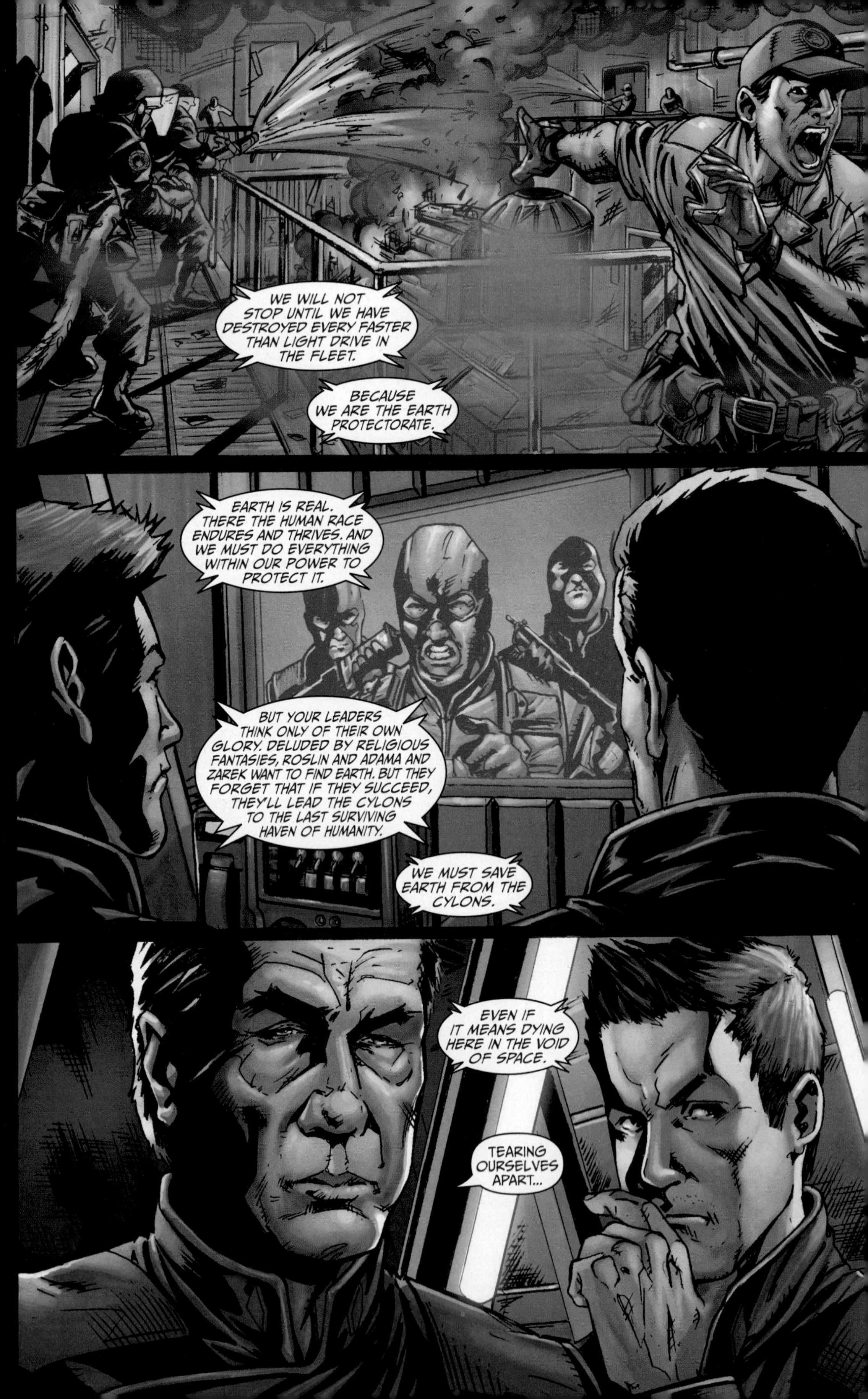
WE WILL NOT STOP UNTIL WE HAVE DESTROYED EVERY FASTER THAN LIGHT DRIVE IN THE FLEET.
BECAUSE WE ARE THE EARTH PROTECTORATE.
EARTH IS REAL. THERE THE HUMAN RACE ENDURES AND THRIVES. AND WE MUST DO EVERYTHING WITHIN OUR POWER TO PROTECT IT.
BUT YOUR LEADERS THINK ONLY OF THEIR OWN GLORY. DELUDED BY RELIGIOUS FANTASIES, ROSLIN AND ADAMA AND ZAREK WANT TO FIND EARTH. BUT THEY FORGET THAT IF THEY SUCCEED, THEY'LL LEAD THE CYLONS TO THE LAST SURVIVING HAVEN OF HUMANITY.
WE MUST SAVE EARTH FROM THE CYLONS.
EVEN IF IT MEANS DYING HERE IN THE VOID OF SPACE.
TEARING OURSELVES APART...

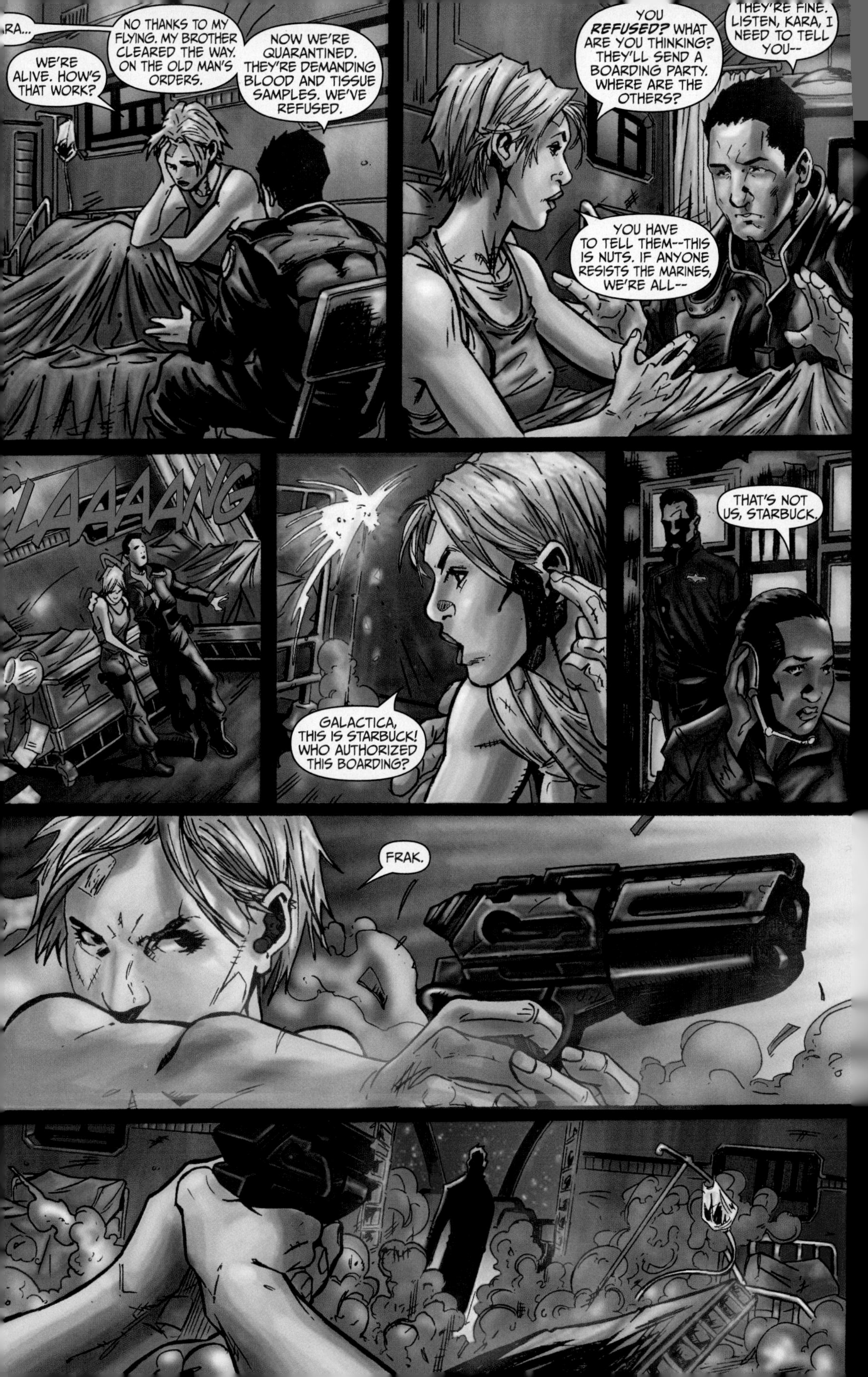
RA...
WE'RE ALIVE. HOW'S THAT WORK?
NO THANKS TO MY FLYING. MY BROTHER CLEARED THE WAY. ON THE OLD MAN'S ORDERS.
NOW WE'RE QUARANTINED. THEY'RE DEMANDING BLOOD AND TISSUE SAMPLES. WE'VE REFUSED.
YOU REFUSED? WHAT ARE YOU THINKING? THEY'LL SEND A BOARDING PARTY. WHERE ARE THE OTHERS?
THEY'RE FINE. LISTEN, KARA, I NEED TO TELL YOU--
YOU HAVE TO TELL THEM--THIS IS NUTS. IF ANYONE RESISTS THE MARINES, WE'RE ALL--
CLAAAANG
GALACTICA, THIS IS STARBUCK! WHO AUTHORIZED THIS BOARDING?
THAT'S NOT US, STARBUCK.
FRAK.

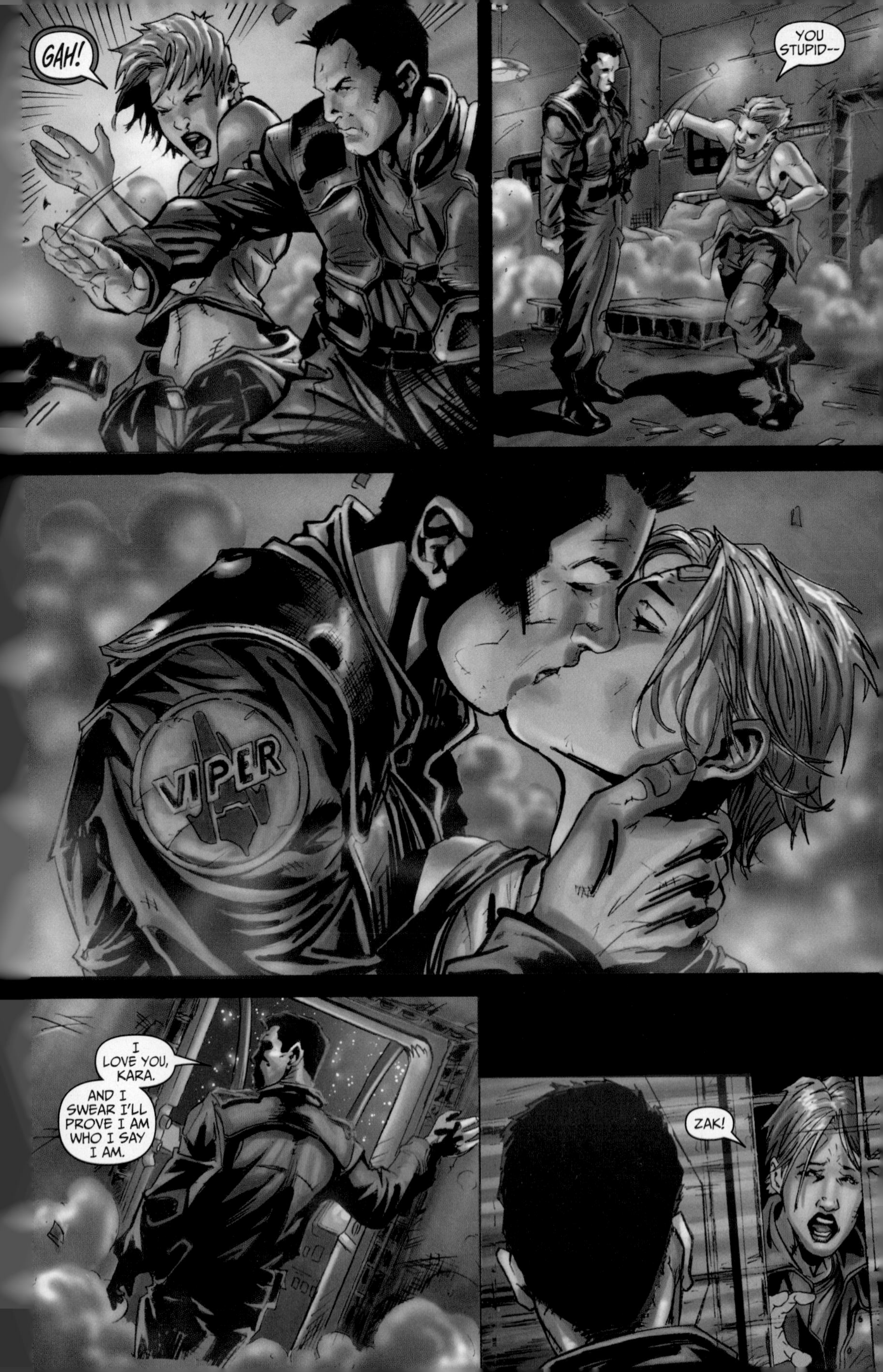
GAH!
YOU STUPID--
I LOVE YOU, KARA.
AND I SWEAR I'LL PROVE I AM WHO I SAY I AM.
ZAK!

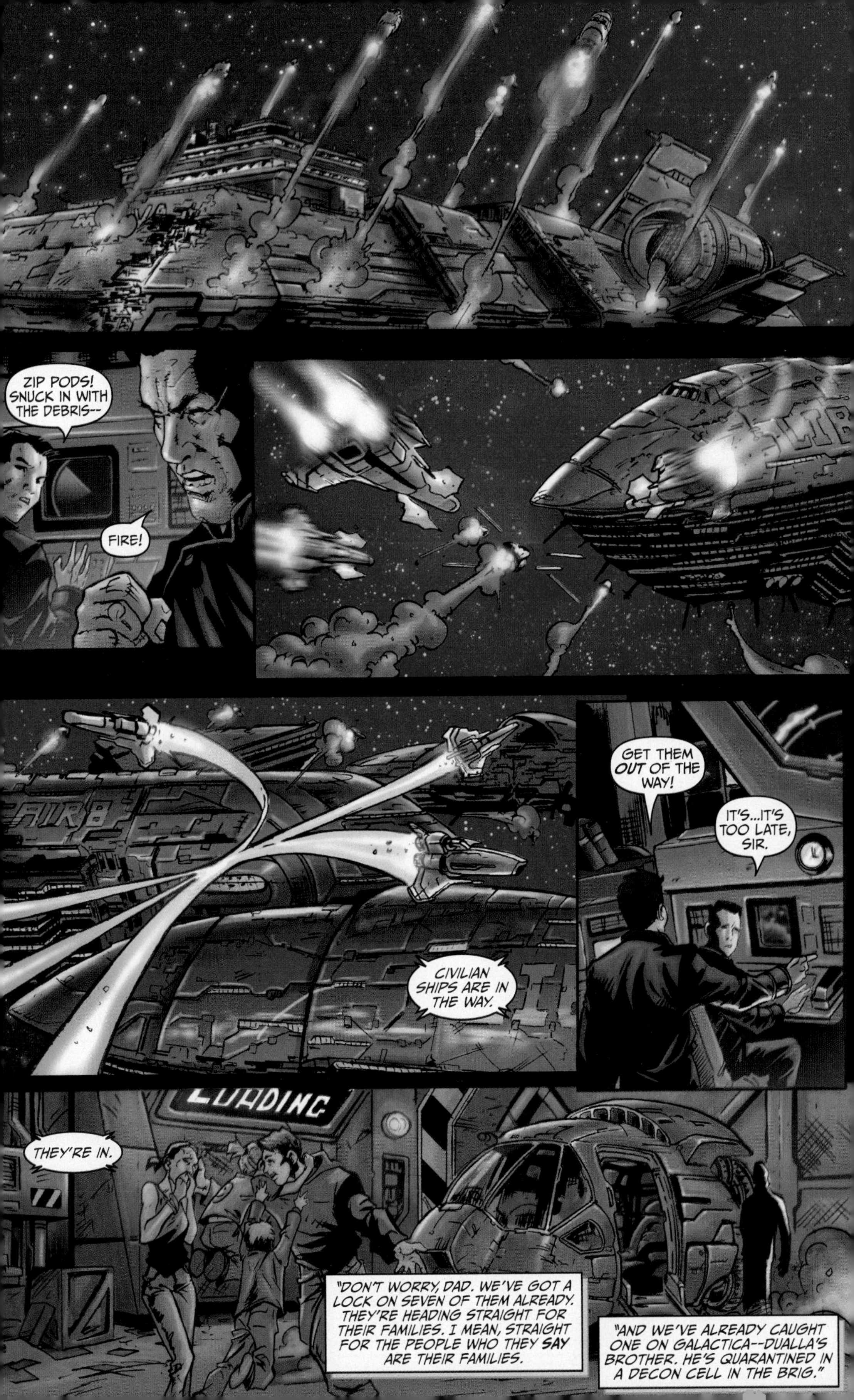
ZIP PODS! SNUCK IN WITH THE DEBRIS--
FIRE!
GET THEM OUT OF THE WAY!
IT'S...IT'S TOO LATE, SIR.
CIVILIAN SHIPS ARE IN THE WAY.
LOADING
THEY'RE IN.
"DON'T WORRY, DAD. WE'VE GOT A LOCK ON SEVEN OF THEM ALREADY. THEY'RE HEADING STRAIGHT FOR THEIR FAMILIES. I MEAN, STRAIGHT FOR THE PEOPLE WHO THEY SAY ARE THEIR FAMILIES.
"AND WE'VE ALREADY CAUGHT ONE ON GALACTICA--DUALLA'S BROTHER. HE'S QUARANTINED IN A DECON CELL IN THE BRIG."

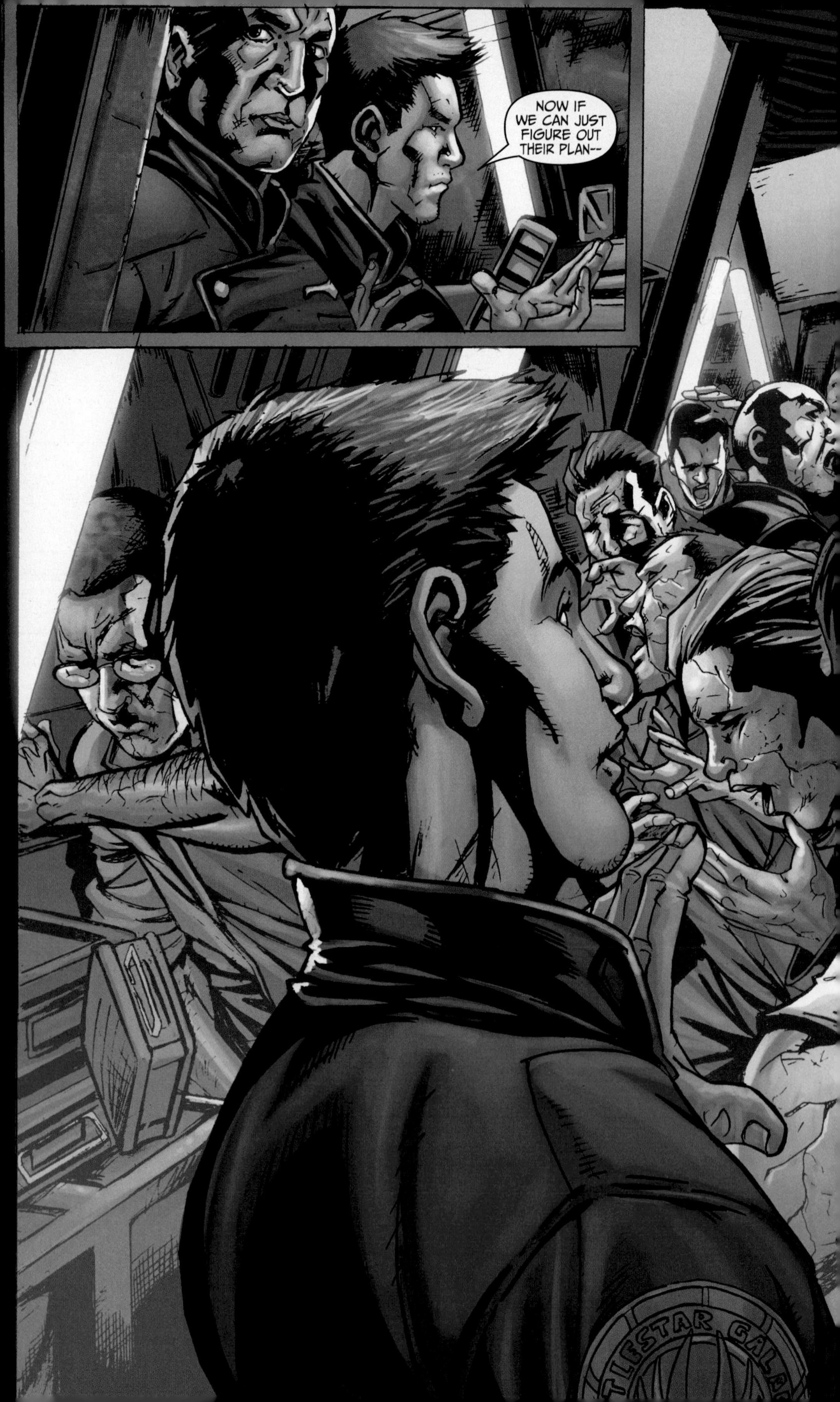
NOW IF WE CAN JUST FIGURE OUT THEIR PLAN--

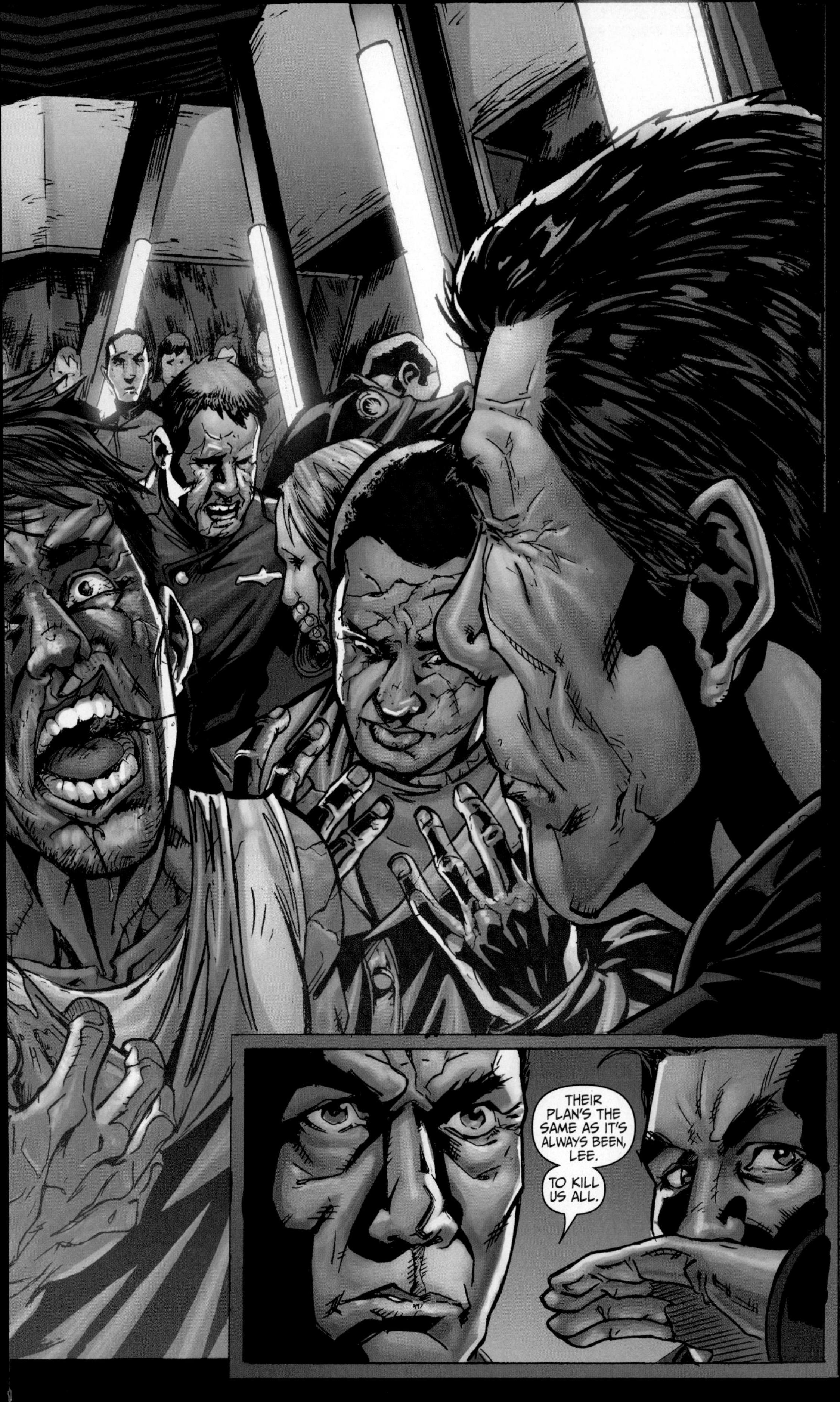
THEIR PLAN'S THE SAME AS IT'S ALWAYS BEEN, LEE.
TO KILL US ALL.

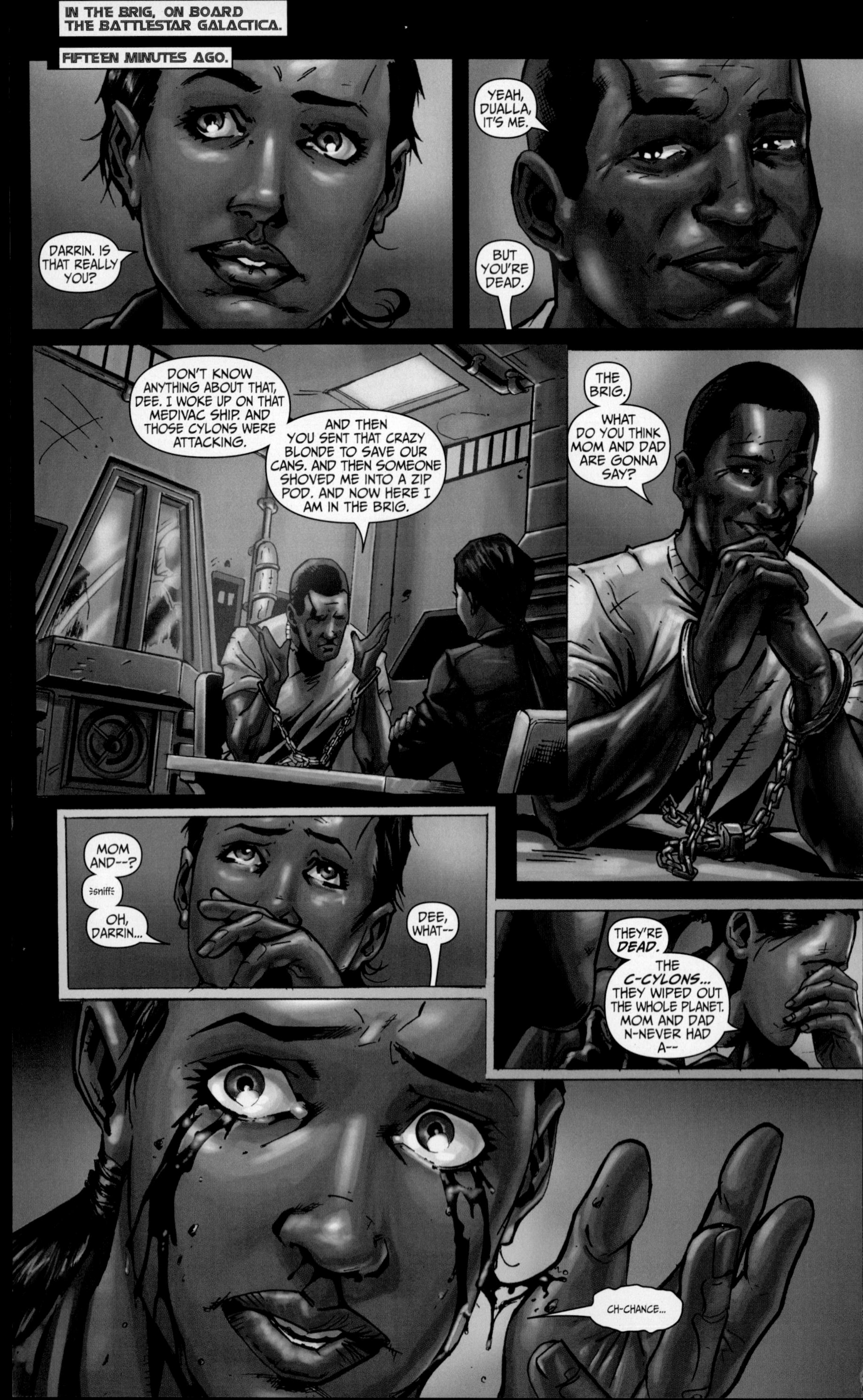
IN THE BRIG, ON BOARD THE BATTLESTAR GALACTICA.
FIFTEEN MINUTES AGO.
DARRIN. IS THAT REALLY YOU?
YEAH, DUALLA, IT'S ME.
BUT YOU'RE DEAD.
DON'T KNOW ANYTHING ABOUT THAT, DEE. I WOKE UP ON THAT MEDIVAC SHIP. AND THOSE CYLONS WERE ATTACKING.
AND THEN YOU SENT THAT CRAZY BLONDE TO SAVE OUR CANS. AND THEN SOMEONE SHOVED ME INTO A ZIP POD. AND NOW HERE I AM IN THE BRIG.
THE BRIG.
WHAT DO YOU THINK MOM AND DAD ARE GONNA SAY?
MOM AND--?
sniff
OH, DARRIN...
DEE, WHAT--
THEY'RE DEAD.
THE C-CYLONS... THEY WIPED OUT THE WHOLE PLANET. MOM AND DAD N-NEVER HAD A--
CH-CHANCE...

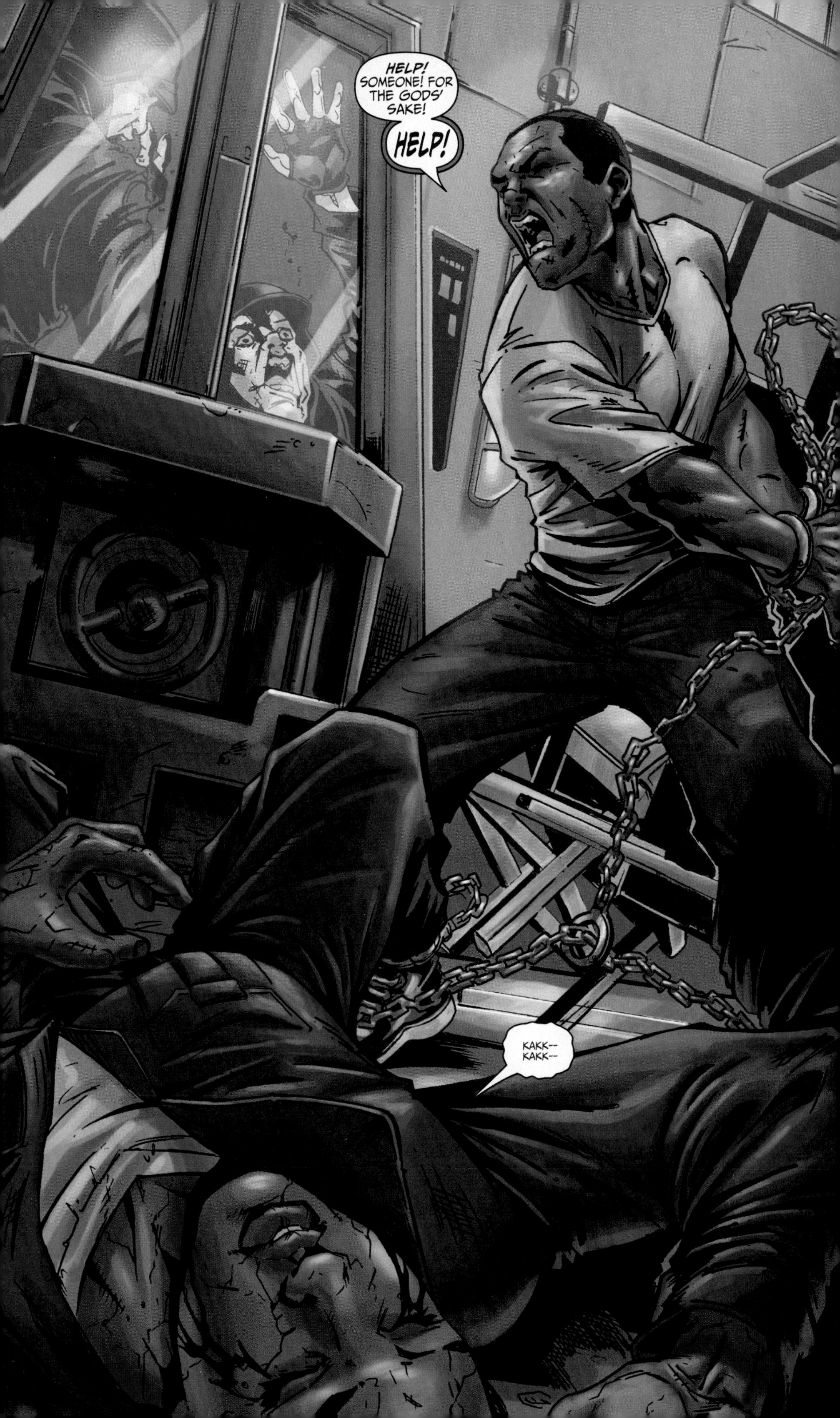
HELP! SOMEONE! FOR THE GODS' SAKE!
HELP!
KAKK-- KAKK--

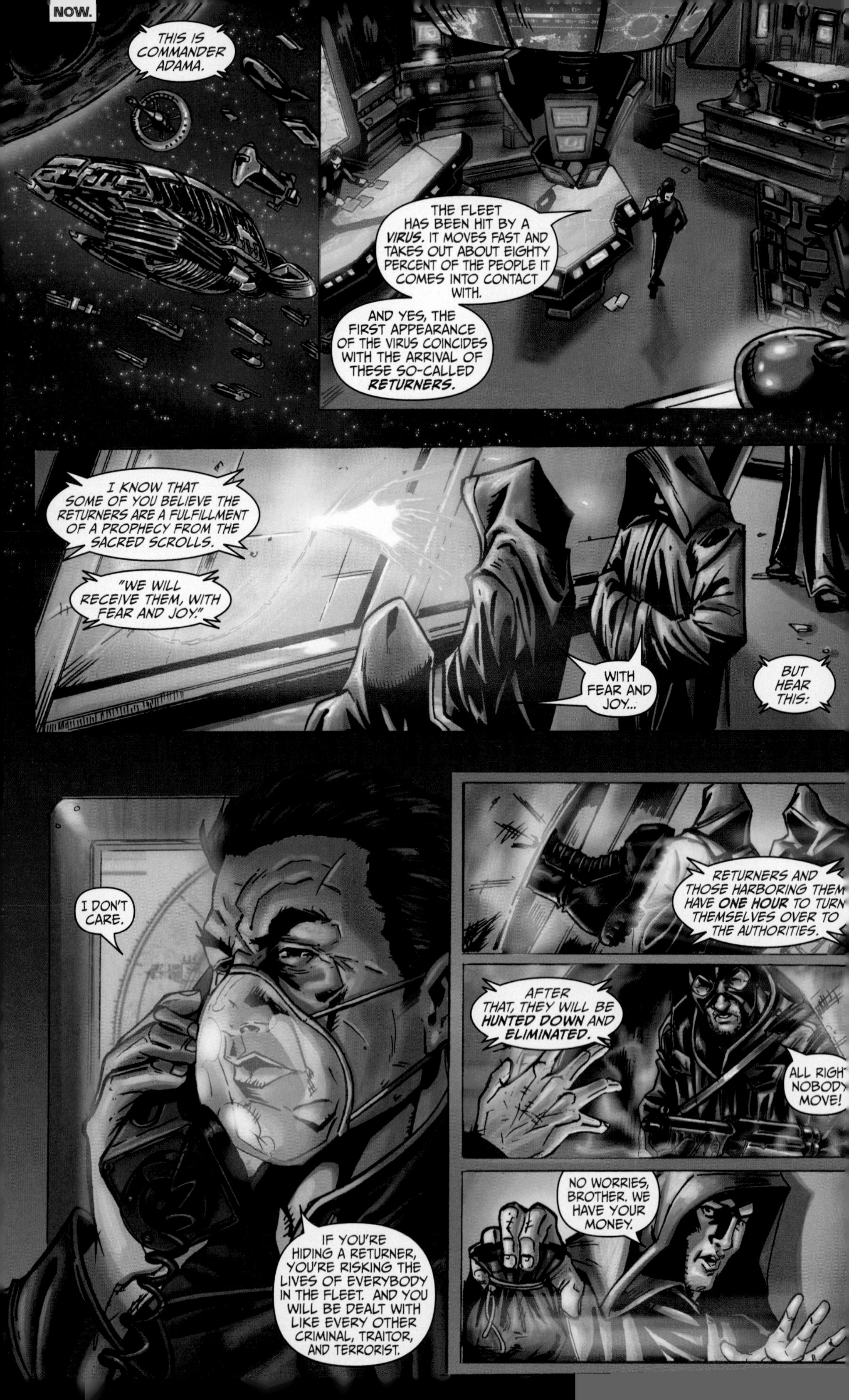
NOW.
THIS IS COMMANDER ADAMA.
THE FLEET HAS BEEN HIT BY A VIRUS. IT MOVES FAST AND TAKES OUT ABOUT EIGHTY PERCENT OF THE PEOPLE IT COMES INTO CONTACT WITH.
AND YES, THE FIRST APPEARANCE OF THE VIRUS COINCIDES WITH THE ARRIVAL OF THESE SO-CALLED RETURNERS.
I KNOW THAT SOME OF YOU BELIEVE THE RETURNERS ARE A FULFILLMENT OF A PROPHECY FROM THE SACRED SCROLLS.
"WE WILL RECEIVE THEM, WITH FEAR AND JOY."
WITH FEAR AND JOY...
BUT HEAR THIS:
I DON'T CARE.
RETURNERS AND THOSE HARBORING THEM HAVE ONE HOUR TO TURN THEMSELVES OVER TO THE AUTHORITIES.
AFTER THAT, THEY WILL BE HUNTED DOWN AND ELIMINATED.
ALL RIGH NOBODY MOVE!
NO WORRIES, BROTHER. WE HAVE YOUR MONEY.
IF YOU'RE HIDING A RETURNER, YOU'RE RISKING THE LIVES OF EVERYBODY IN THE FLEET. AND YOU WILL BE DEALT WITH LIKE EVERY OTHER CRIMINAL, TRAITOR, AND TERRORIST.

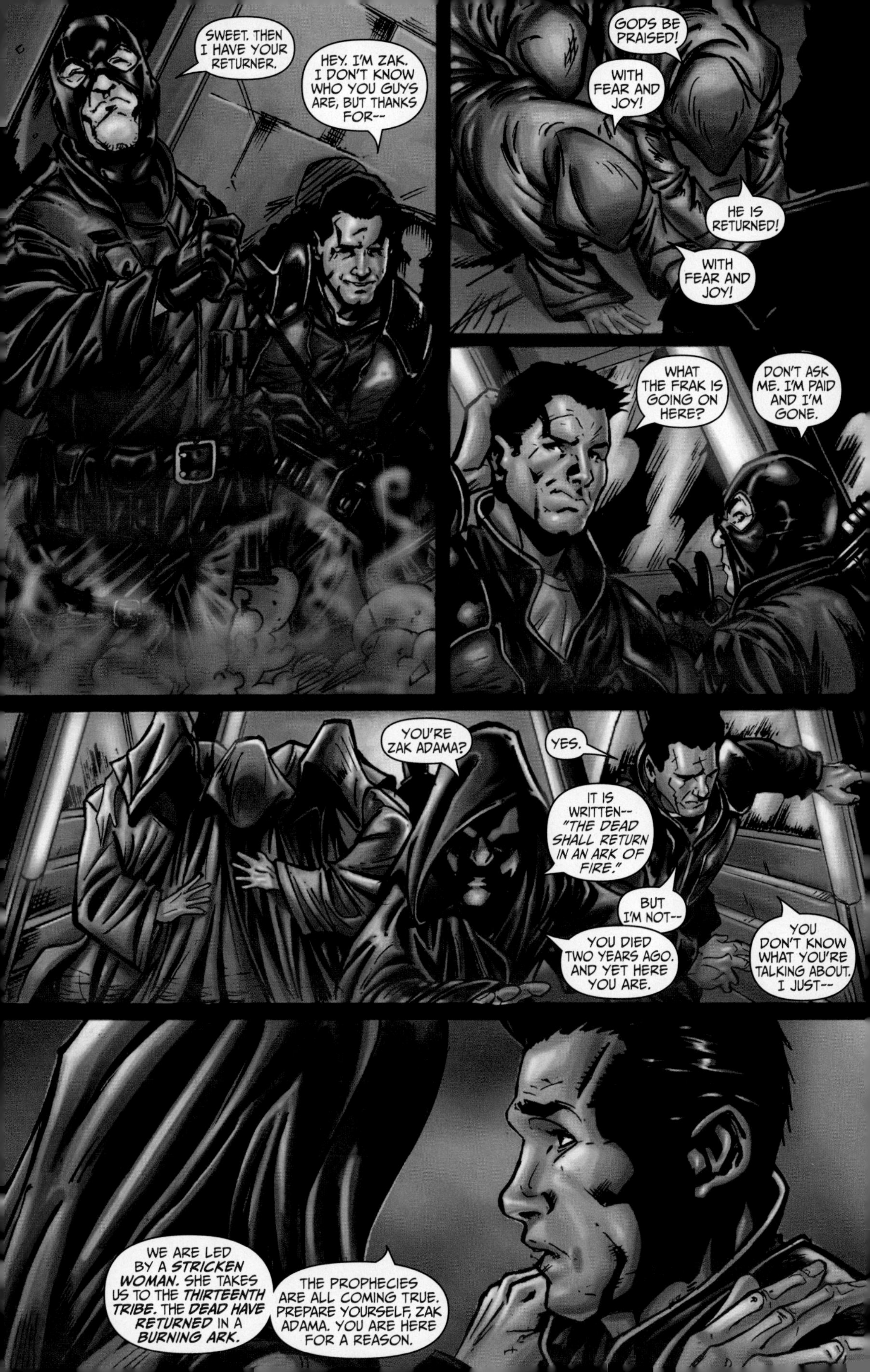
SWEET. THEN I HAVE YOUR RETURNER.
HEY. I'M ZAK. I DON'T KNOW WHO YOU GUYS ARE, BUT THANKS FOR--
GODS BE PRAISED!
WITH FEAR AND JOY!
HE IS RETURNED!
WITH FEAR AND JOY!
WHAT THE FRAK IS GOING ON HERE?
DON'T ASK ME. I'M PAID AND I'M GONE.
YOU'RE ZAK ADAMA?
YES.
IT IS WRITTEN-- "THE DEAD SHALL RETURN IN AN ARK OF FIRE."
BUT I'M NOT--
YOU DIED TWO YEARS AGO. AND YET HERE YOU ARE.
YOU DON'T KNOW WHAT YOU'RE TALKING ABOUT. I JUST--
WE ARE LED BY A STRICKEN WOMAN. SHE TAKES US TO THE THIRTEENTH TRIBE. THE DEAD HAVE RETURNED IN A BURNING ARK.
THE PROPHECIES ARE ALL COMING TRUE. PREPARE YOURSELF, ZAK ADAMA. YOU ARE HERE FOR A REASON.

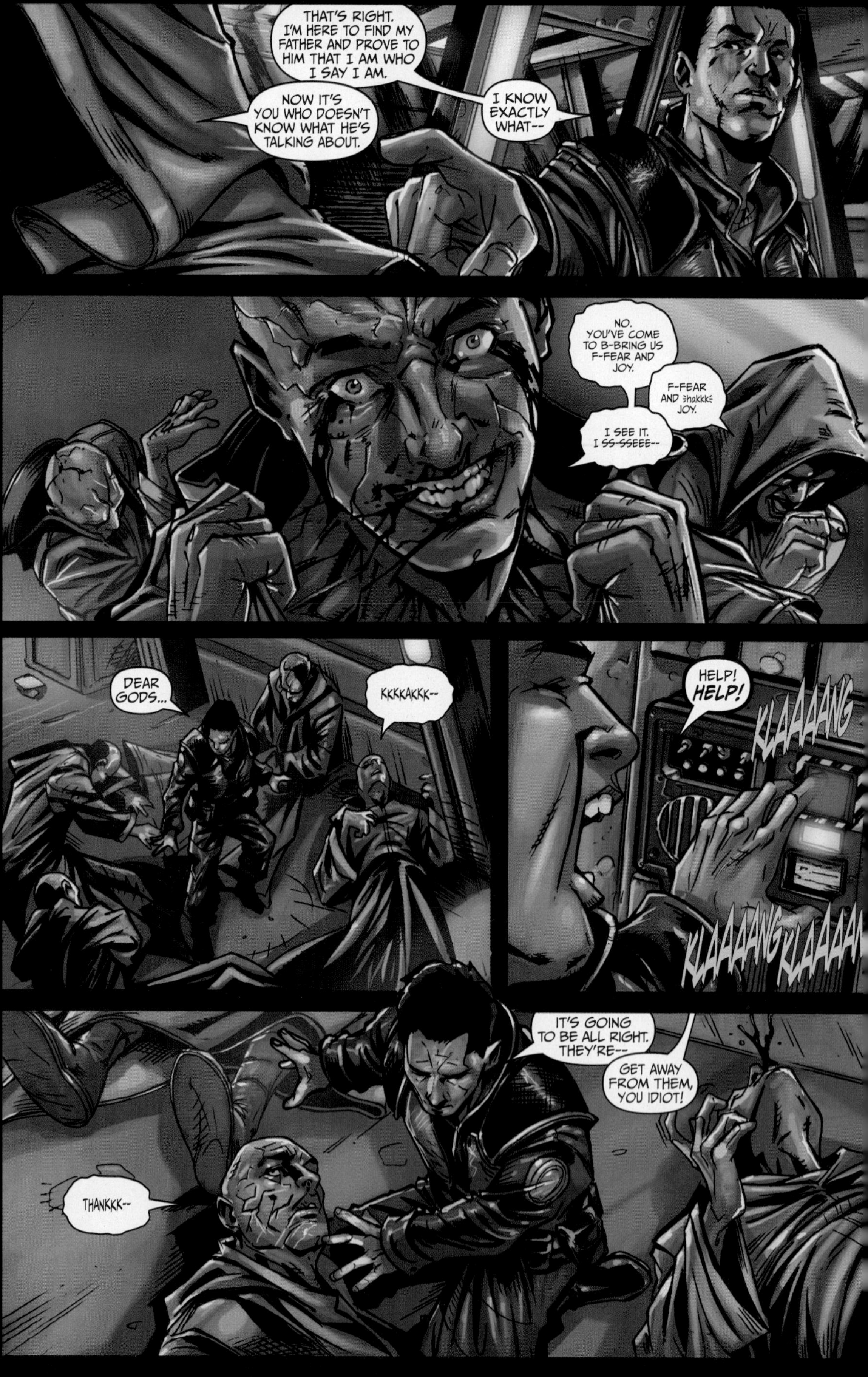
THAT'S RIGHT. I'M HERE TO FIND MY FATHER AND PROVE TO HIM THAT I AM WHO I SAY I AM.
NOW IT'S YOU WHO DOESN'T KNOW WHAT HE'S TALKING ABOUT.
I KNOW EXACTLY WHAT--
NO. YOU'VE COME TO B-BRING US F-FEAR AND JOY.
I SEE IT. I SS-SSEEE--
F-FEAR AND hakkk JOY.
DEAR GODS...
KKKKAKKK--
HELP! HELP!
KLAAAANG
KLAAAANG KLAAAA
IT'S GOING TO BE ALL RIGHT. THEY'RE--
GET AWAY FROM THEM, YOU IDIOT!
THANKKK--

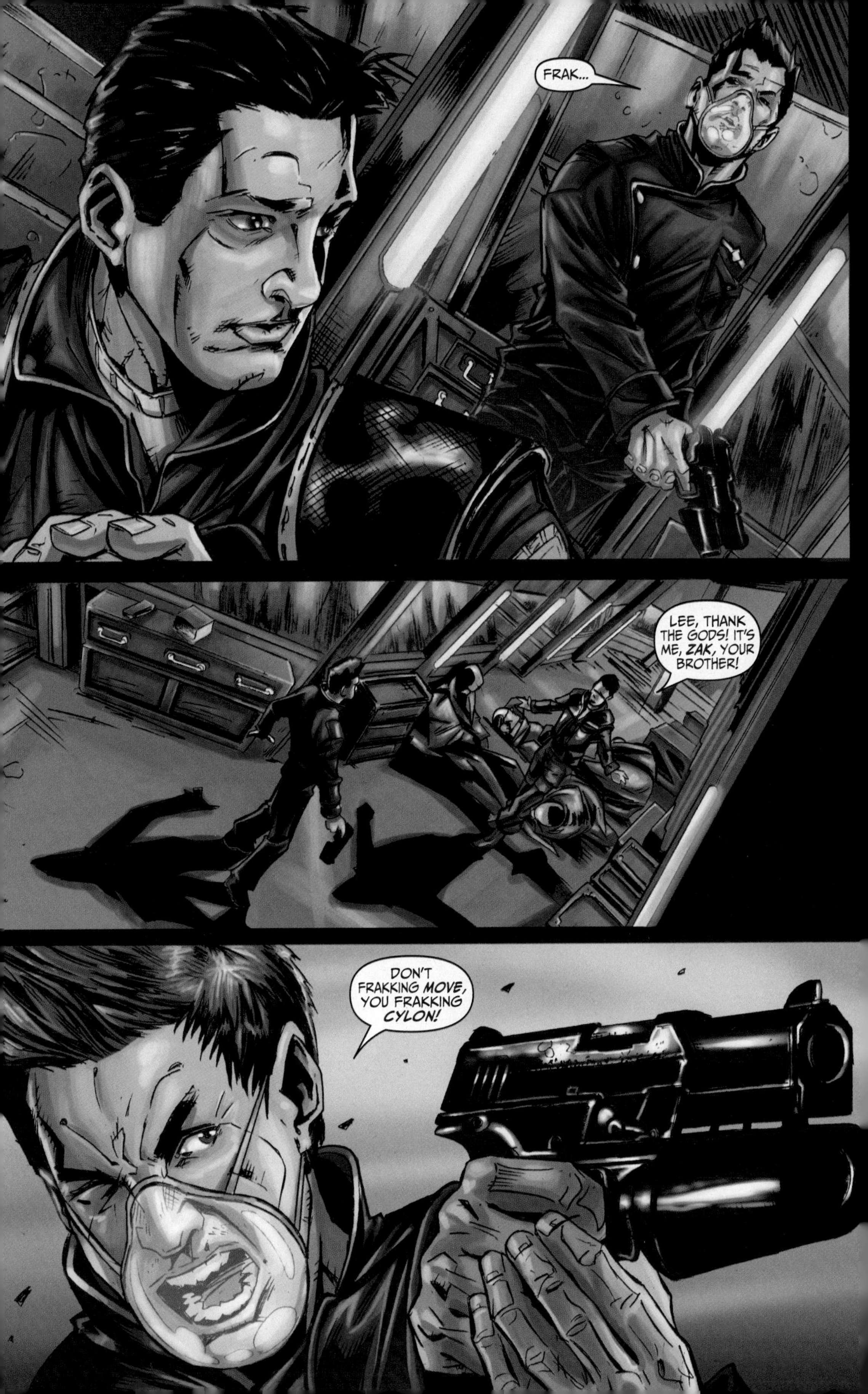
FRAK...
LEE, THANK THE GODS! IT'S ME, ZAK, YOUR BROTHER!
DON'T FRAKKING MOVE, YOU FRAKKING CYLON!

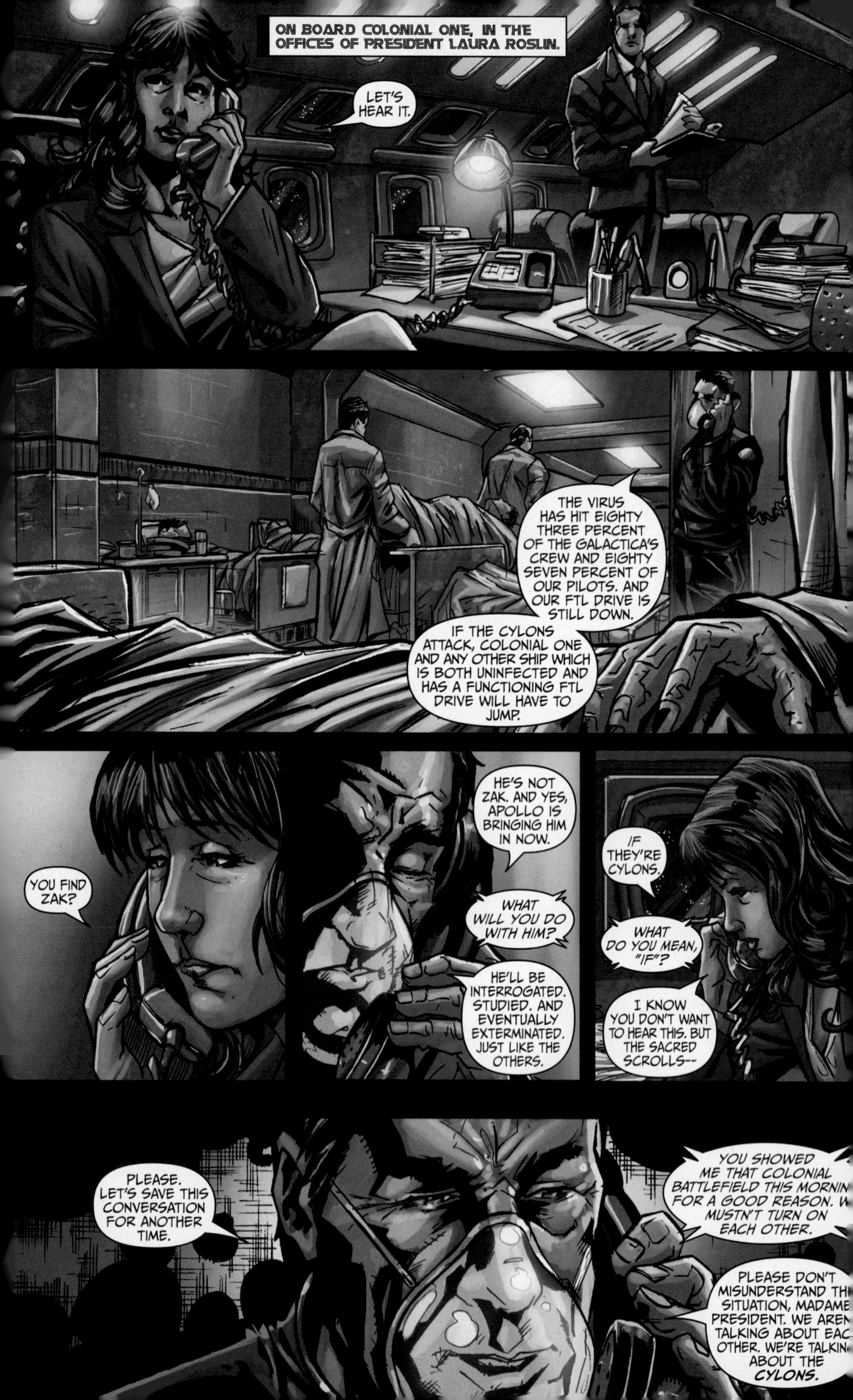
ON BOARD COLONIAL ONE, IN THE OFFICES OF PRESIDENT LAURA ROSLIN.
LET'S HEAR IT.
THE VIRUS HAS HIT EIGHTY THREE PERCENT OF THE GALACTICA'S CREW AND EIGHTY SEVEN PERCENT OF OUR PILOTS. AND OUR FTL DRIVE IS STILL DOWN.
IF THE CYLONS ATTACK, COLONIAL ONE AND ANY OTHER SHIP WHICH IS BOTH UNINFECTED AND HAS A FUNCTIONING FTL DRIVE WILL HAVE TO JUMP.
YOU FIND ZAK?
HE'S NOT ZAK. AND YES, APOLLO IS BRINGING HIM IN NOW.
WHAT WILL YOU DO WITH HIM?
HE'LL BE INTERROGATED. STUDIED. AND EVENTUALLY EXTERMINATED. JUST LIKE THE OTHERS.
IF THEY'RE CYLONS.
WHAT DO YOU MEAN, "IF"?
I KNOW YOU DON'T WANT TO HEAR THIS. BUT THE SACRED SCROLLS--
PLEASE. LET'S SAVE THIS CONVERSATION FOR ANOTHER TIME.
YOU SHOWED ME THAT COLONIAL BATTLEFIELD THIS MORNIN FOR A GOOD REASON. W MUSTN'T TURN ON EACH OTHER.
PLEASE DON'T MISUNDERSTAND TH SITUATION, MADAME PRESIDENT. WE AREN TALKING ABOUT EAC OTHER. WE'RE TALKIN ABOUT THE CYLONS.

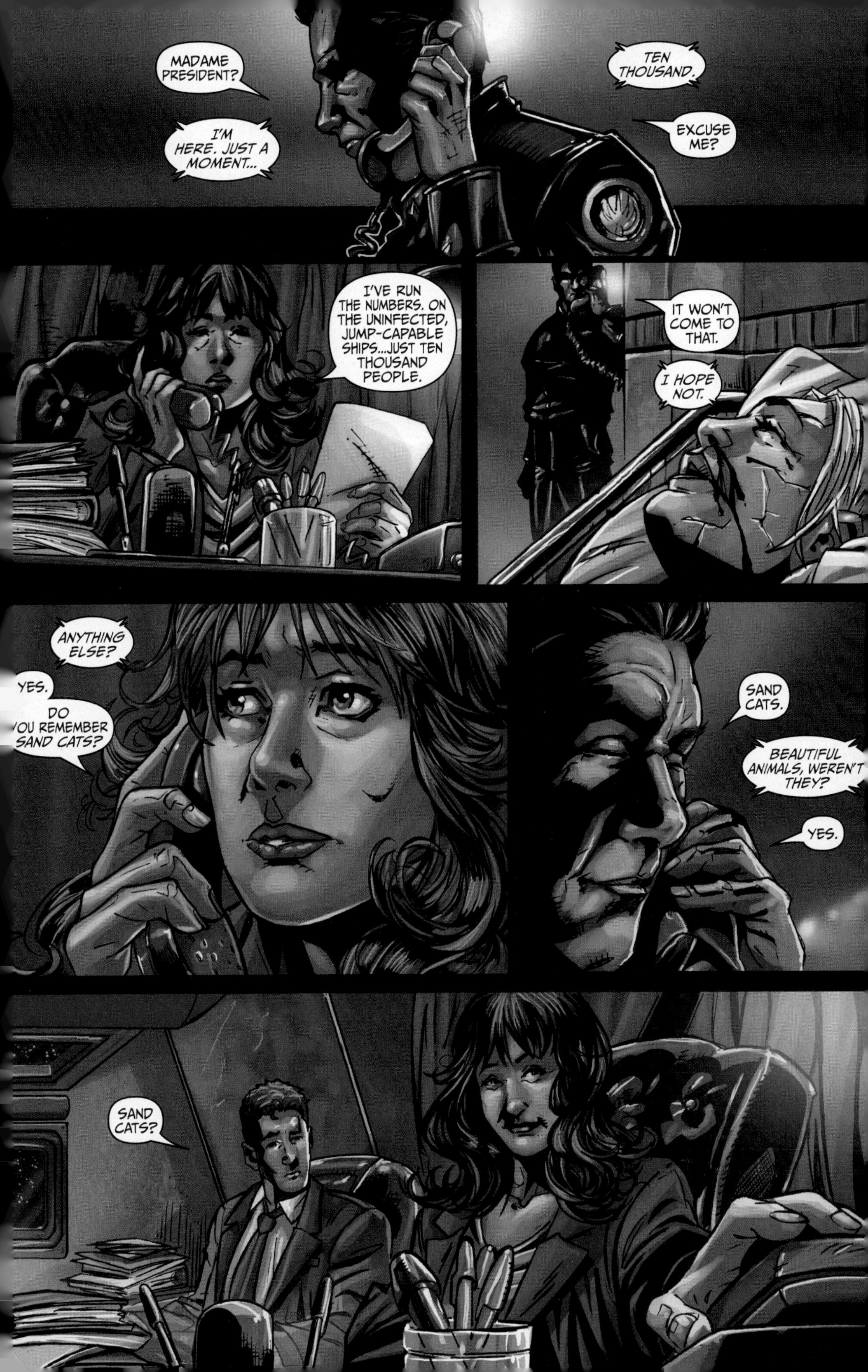
MADAME PRESIDENT?
I'M HERE. JUST A MOMENT...
TEN THOUSAND.
EXCUSE ME?
I'VE RUN THE NUMBERS. ON THE UNINFECTED, JUMP-CAPABLE SHIPS...JUST TEN THOUSAND PEOPLE.
IT WON'T COME TO THAT.
I HOPE NOT.
ANYTHING ELSE?
YES.
DO YOU REMEMBER SAND CATS?
SAND CATS.
BEAUTIFUL ANIMALS, WEREN'T THEY?
YES.
SAND CATS?

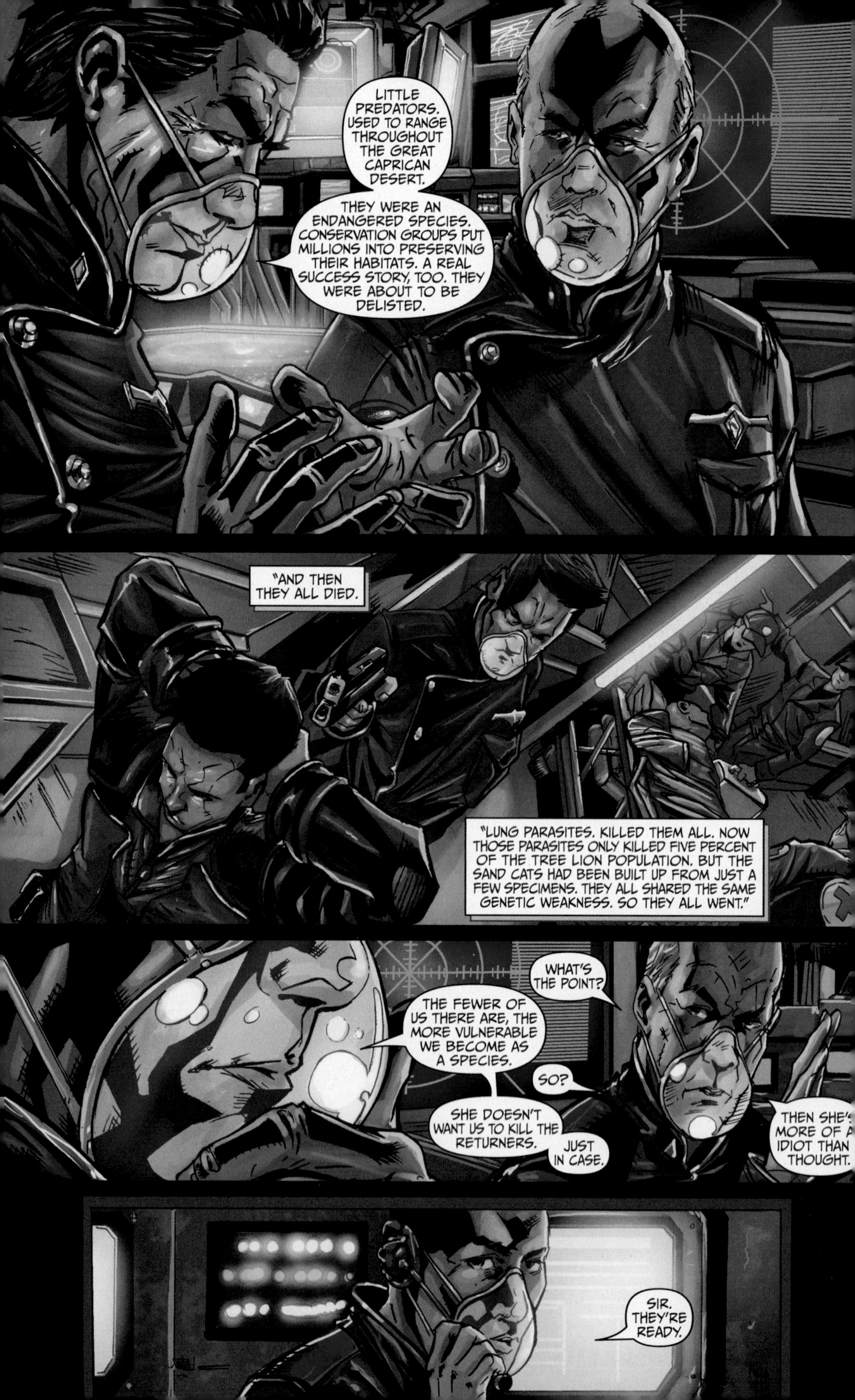
LITTLE PREDATORS. USED TO RANGE THROUGHOUT THE GREAT CAPRICAN DESERT.
THEY WERE AN ENDANGERED SPECIES. CONSERVATION GROUPS PUT MILLIONS INTO PRESERVING THEIR HABITATS. A REAL SUCCESS STORY, TOO. THEY WERE ABOUT TO BE DELISTED.
"AND THEN THEY ALL DIED.
"LUNG PARASITES. KILLED THEM ALL. NOW THOSE PARASITES ONLY KILLED FIVE PERCENT OF THE TREE LION POPULATION. BUT THE SAND CATS HAD BEEN BUILT UP FROM JUST A FEW SPECIMENS. THEY ALL SHARED THE SAME GENETIC WEAKNESS. SO THEY ALL WENT."
WHAT'S THE POINT?
THE FEWER OF US THERE ARE, THE MORE VULNERABLE WE BECOME AS A SPECIES.
SO?
SHE DOESN'T WANT US TO KILL THE RETURNERS.
JUST IN CASE.
SIR. THEY'RE READY.

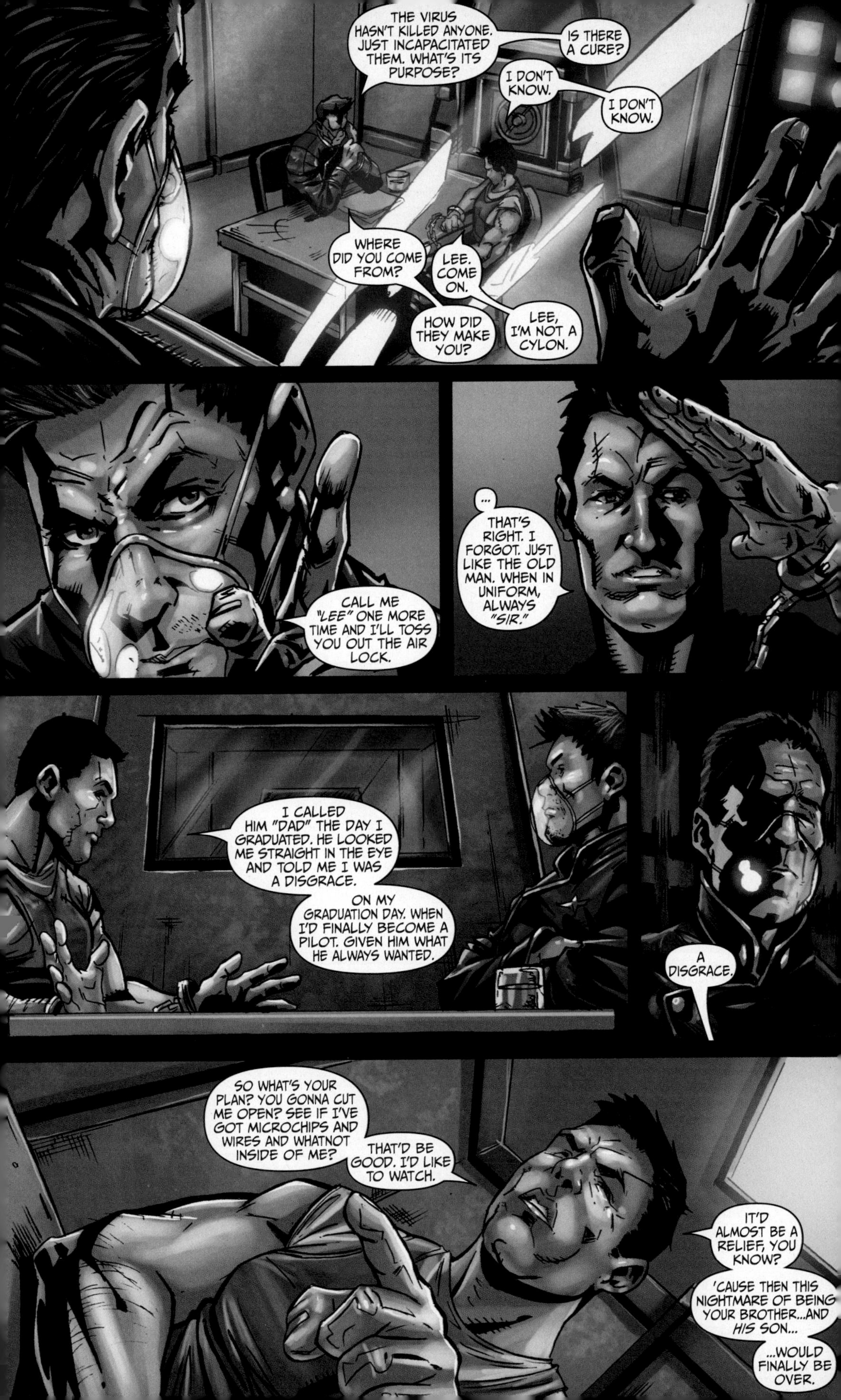
THE VIRUS HASN'T KILLED ANYONE. JUST INCAPACITATED THEM. WHAT'S ITS PURPOSE?
IS THERE A CURE?
I DON'T KNOW.
I DON'T KNOW.
WHERE DID YOU COME FROM?
LEE. COME ON.
HOW DID THEY MAKE YOU?
LEE, I'M NOT A CYLON.
CALL ME "LEE" ONE MORE TIME AND I'LL TOSS YOU OUT THE AIR LOCK.
...
THAT'S RIGHT. I FORGOT. JUST LIKE THE OLD MAN. WHEN IN UNIFORM, ALWAYS "SIR."
I CALLED HIM "DAD" THE DAY I GRADUATED. HE LOOKED ME STRAIGHT IN THE EYE AND TOLD ME I WAS A DISGRACE.
ON MY GRADUATION DAY. WHEN I'D FINALLY BECOME A PILOT. GIVEN HIM WHAT HE ALWAYS WANTED.
A DISGRACE.
SO WHAT'S YOUR PLAN? YOU GONNA CUT ME OPEN? SEE IF I'VE GOT MICROCHIPS AND WIRES AND WHATNOT INSIDE OF ME?
THAT'D BE GOOD. I'D LIKE TO WATCH.
IT'D ALMOST BE A RELIEF, YOU KNOW?
'CAUSE THEN THIS NIGHTMARE OF BEING YOUR BROTHER...AND HIS SON...
...WOULD FINALLY BE OVER.

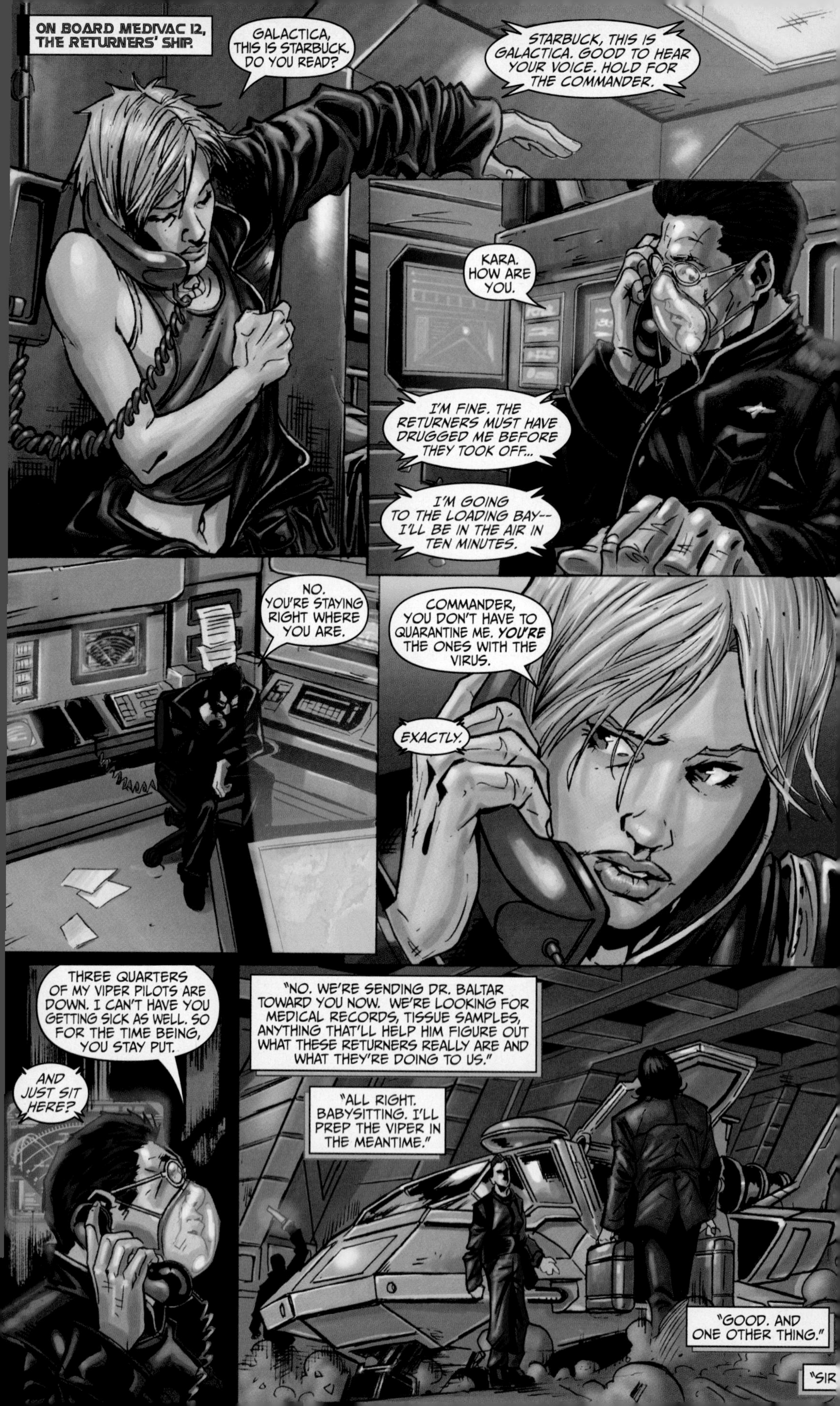

ON BOARD MEDIVAC 12, THE RETURNERS' SHIP.
GALACTICA, THIS IS STARBUCK. DO YOU READ?
STARBUCK, THIS IS GALACTICA. GOOD TO HEAR YOUR VOICE. HOLD FOR THE COMMANDER.
KARA. HOW ARE YOU.
I'M FINE. THE RETURNERS MUST HAVE DRUGGED ME BEFORE THEY TOOK OFF...
I'M GOING TO THE LOADING BAY-- I'LL BE IN THE AIR IN TEN MINUTES.
NO. YOU'RE STAYING RIGHT WHERE YOU ARE.
COMMANDER, YOU DON'T HAVE TO QUARANTINE ME. YOU'RE THE ONES WITH THE VIRUS.
EXACTLY.
THREE QUARTERS OF MY VIPER PILOTS ARE DOWN. I CAN'T HAVE YOU GETTING SICK AS WELL. SO FOR THE TIME BEING, YOU STAY PUT.
AND JUST SIT HERE?
"NO. WE'RE SENDING DR. BALTAR TOWARD YOU NOW. WE'RE LOOKING FOR MEDICAL RECORDS, TISSUE SAMPLES, ANYTHING THAT'LL HELP HIM FIGURE OUT WHAT THESE RETURNERS REALLY ARE AND WHAT THEY'RE DOING TO US."
"ALL RIGHT. BABYSITTING. I'LL PREP THE VIPER IN THE MEANTIME."
"GOOD. AND ONE OTHER THING."
"SIR

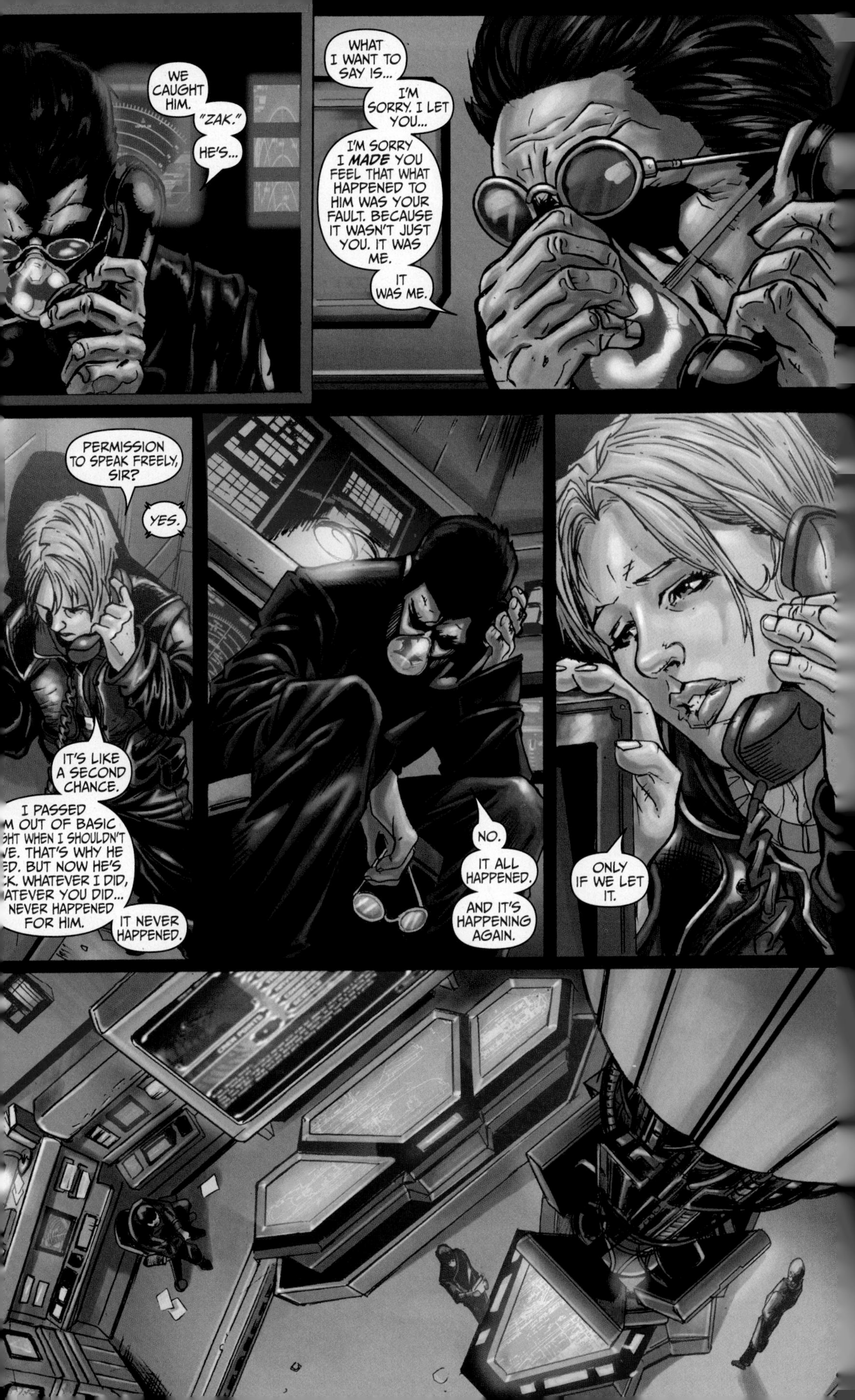

WE CAUGHT HIM.
"ZAK."
HE'S...
WHAT I WANT TO SAY IS...
I'M SORRY. I LET YOU...
I'M SORRY I MADE YOU FEEL THAT WHAT HAPPENED TO HIM WAS YOUR FAULT. BECAUSE IT WASN'T JUST YOU. IT WAS ME.
IT WAS ME.
PERMISSION TO SPEAK FREELY, SIR?
YES.
IT'S LIKE A SECOND CHANCE.
I PASSED
M OUT OF BASIC
GHT WHEN I SHOULDN'T
VE. THAT'S WHY HE
ED. BUT NOW HE'S
K. WHATEVER I DID,
ATEVER YOU DID...
NEVER HAPPENED FOR HIM.
IT NEVER HAPPENED.
NO.
IT ALL HAPPENED.
AND IT'S HAPPENING AGAIN.
ONLY IF WE LET IT.

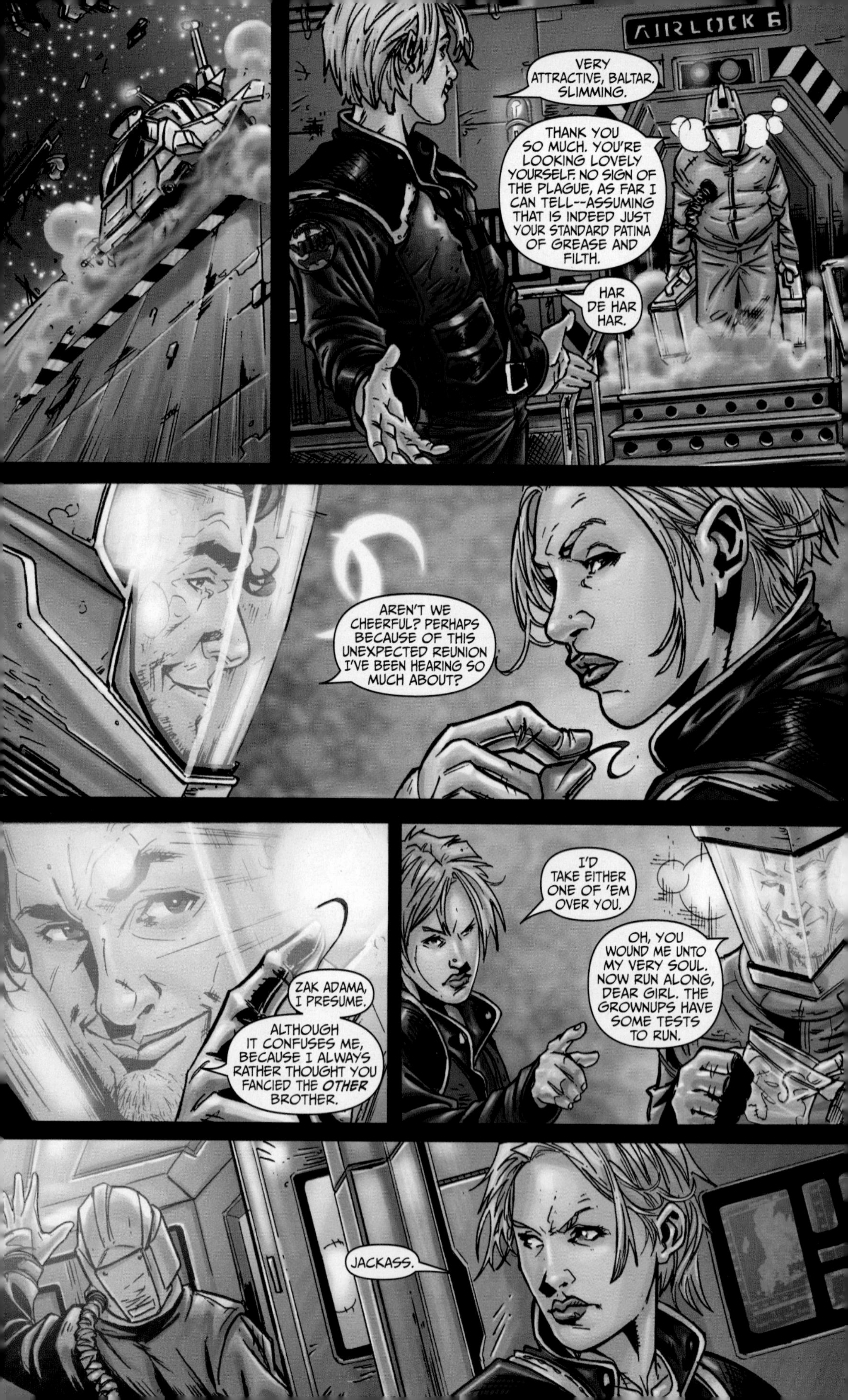
AIRLOCK 6
VERY ATTRACTIVE, BALTAR. SLIMMING.
THANK YOU SO MUCH. YOU'RE LOOKING LOVELY YOURSELF. NO SIGN OF THE PLAGUE, AS FAR I CAN TELL--ASSUMING THAT IS INDEED JUST YOUR STANDARD PATINA OF GREASE AND FILTH.
HAR DE HAR HAR.
AREN'T WE CHEERFUL? PERHAPS BECAUSE OF THIS UNEXPECTED REUNION I'VE BEEN HEARING SO MUCH ABOUT?
ZAK ADAMA, I PRESUME.
ALTHOUGH IT CONFUSES ME, BECAUSE I ALWAYS RATHER THOUGHT YOU FANCIED THE *OTHER* BROTHER.
I'D TAKE EITHER ONE OF 'EM OVER YOU.
OH, YOU WOUND ME UNTO MY VERY SOUL. NOW RUN ALONG, DEAR GIRL. THE GROWNUPS HAVE SOME TESTS TO RUN.
JACKASS.

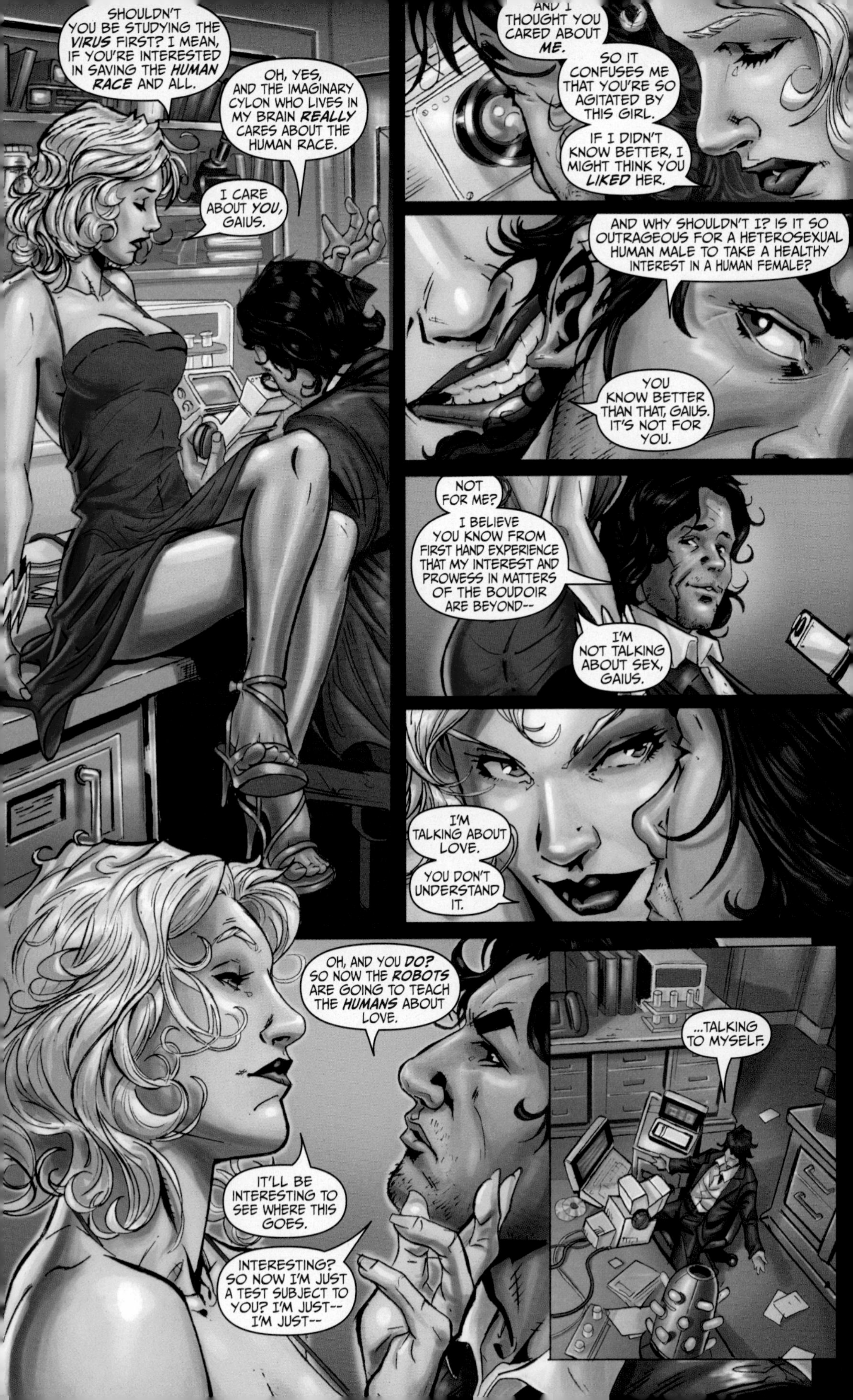
SHOULDN'T YOU BE STUDYING THE VIRUS FIRST? I MEAN, IF YOU'RE INTERESTED IN SAVING THE HUMAN RACE AND ALL.
OH, YES, AND THE IMAGINARY CYLON WHO LIVES IN MY BRAIN REALLY CARES ABOUT THE HUMAN RACE.
I CARE ABOUT YOU, GAIUS.
AND I THOUGHT YOU CARED ABOUT ME.
SO IT CONFUSES ME THAT YOU'RE SO AGITATED BY THIS GIRL.
IF I DIDN'T KNOW BETTER, I MIGHT THINK YOU LIKED HER.
AND WHY SHOULDN'T I? IS IT SO OUTRAGEOUS FOR A HETEROSEXUAL HUMAN MALE TO TAKE A HEALTHY INTEREST IN A HUMAN FEMALE?
YOU KNOW BETTER THAN THAT, GAIUS. IT'S NOT FOR YOU.
NOT FOR ME?
I BELIEVE YOU KNOW FROM FIRST HAND EXPERIENCE THAT MY INTEREST AND PROWESS IN MATTERS OF THE BOUDOIR ARE BEYOND--
I'M NOT TALKING ABOUT SEX, GAIUS.
I'M TALKING ABOUT LOVE.
YOU DON'T UNDERSTAND IT.
OH, AND YOU DO? SO NOW THE ROBOTS ARE GOING TO TEACH THE HUMANS ABOUT LOVE.
IT'LL BE INTERESTING TO SEE WHERE THIS GOES.
INTERESTING? SO NOW I'M JUST A TEST SUBJECT TO YOU? I'M JUST-- I'M JUST--
...TALKING TO MYSELF.

OKAY. SO IT'S THE SILENT TREATMENT NOW?

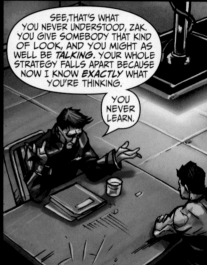

SEE, THAT'S WHAT YOU NEVER UNDERSTOOD, ZAK. YOU GIVE SOMEBODY THAT KIND OF LOOK, AND YOU MIGHT AS WELL BE *TALKING*. YOUR WHOLE STRATEGY FALLS APART BECAUSE NOW I KNOW *EXACTLY* WHAT YOU'RE THINKING.

YOU NEVER LEARN.

SO NOW I'M ZAK.

NO. I--I DIDN'T MEAN--

YOU *KNOW* I AM. IN YOUR HEART. BUT YOU'RE PRETENDING I'M *NOT*. WHAT ARE YOU HIDING FROM ME, LEE?

WHAT DID YOU DO TO ME?

...

KARA.

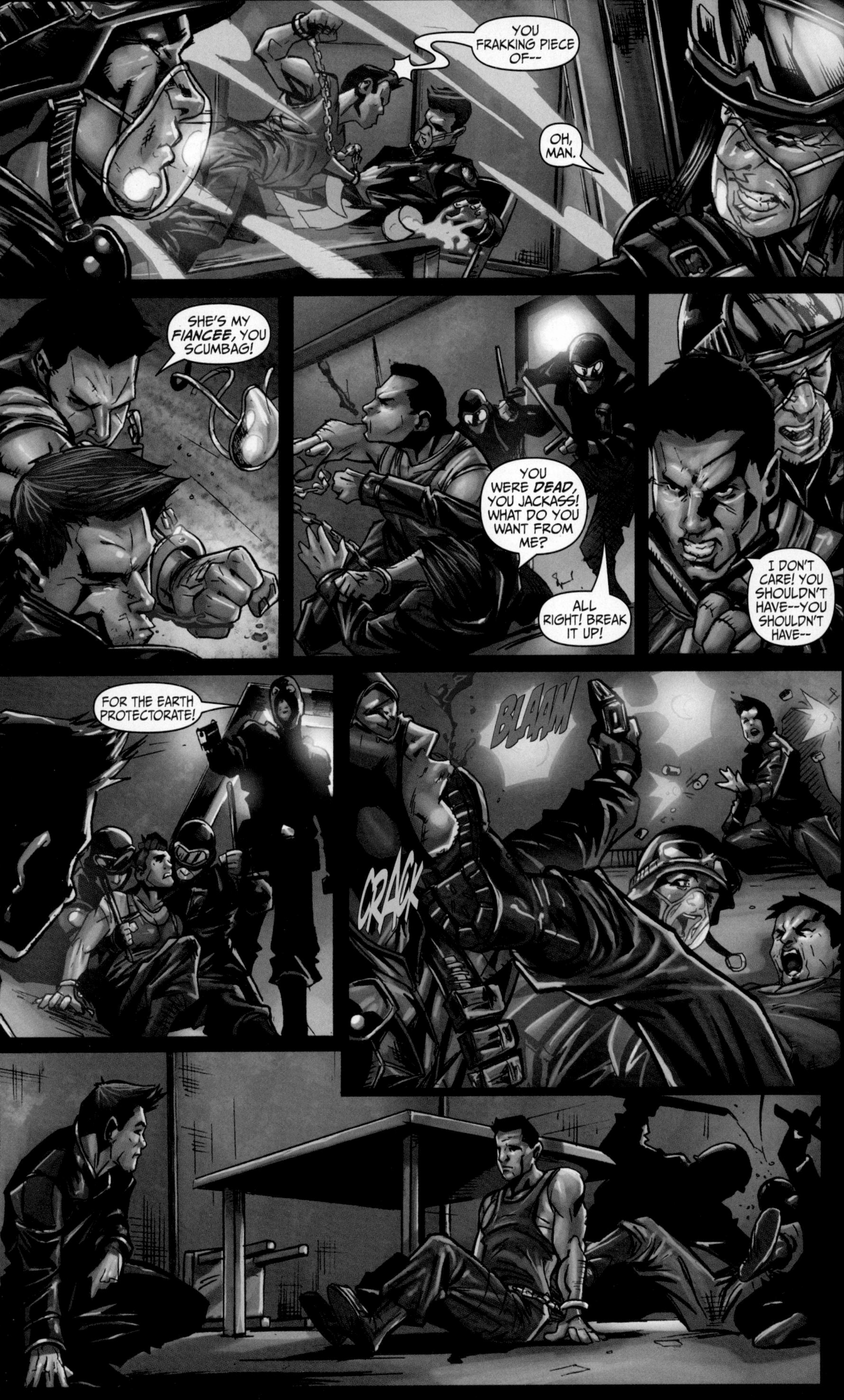
YOU FRAKKING PIECE OF--
OH, MAN.
SHE'S MY *FIANCEE*, YOU SCUMBAG!
YOU WERE *DEAD*, YOU JACKASS! WHAT DO YOU WANT FROM ME?
ALL RIGHT! BREAK IT UP!
I DON'T CARE! YOU SHOULDN'T HAVE--YOU SHOULDN'T HAVE--
FOR THE EARTH PROTECTORATE!
BLAAM
CRACK

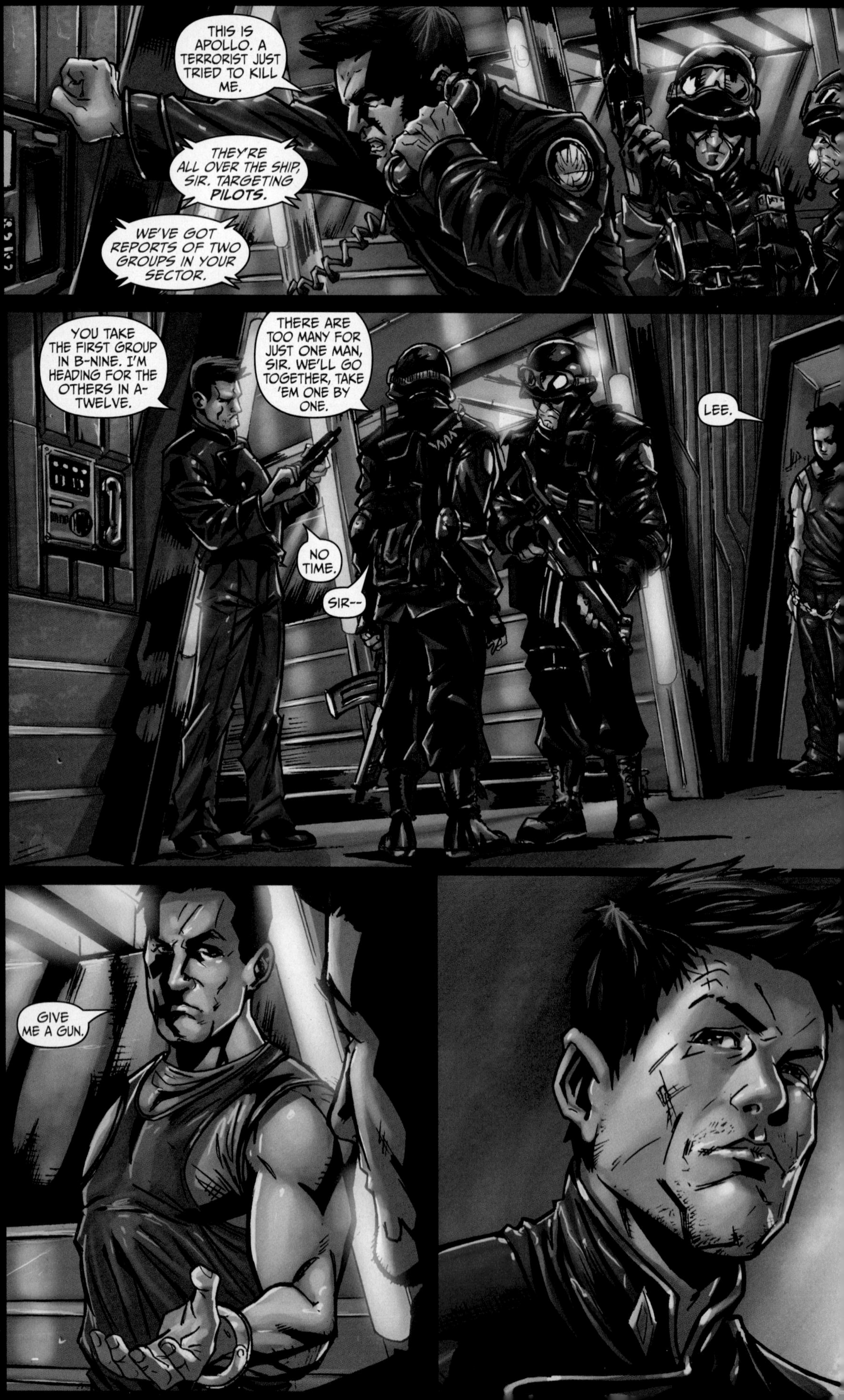
THIS IS APOLLO. A TERRORIST JUST TRIED TO KILL ME.
THEY'RE ALL OVER THE SHIP, SIR. TARGETING PILOTS.
WE'VE GOT REPORTS OF TWO GROUPS IN YOUR SECTOR.
YOU TAKE THE FIRST GROUP IN B-NINE. I'M HEADING FOR THE OTHERS IN A-TWELVE.
THERE ARE TOO MANY FOR JUST ONE MAN, SIR. WE'LL GO TOGETHER, TAKE 'EM ONE BY ONE.
NO TIME.
SIR--
LEE.
GIVE ME A GUN.

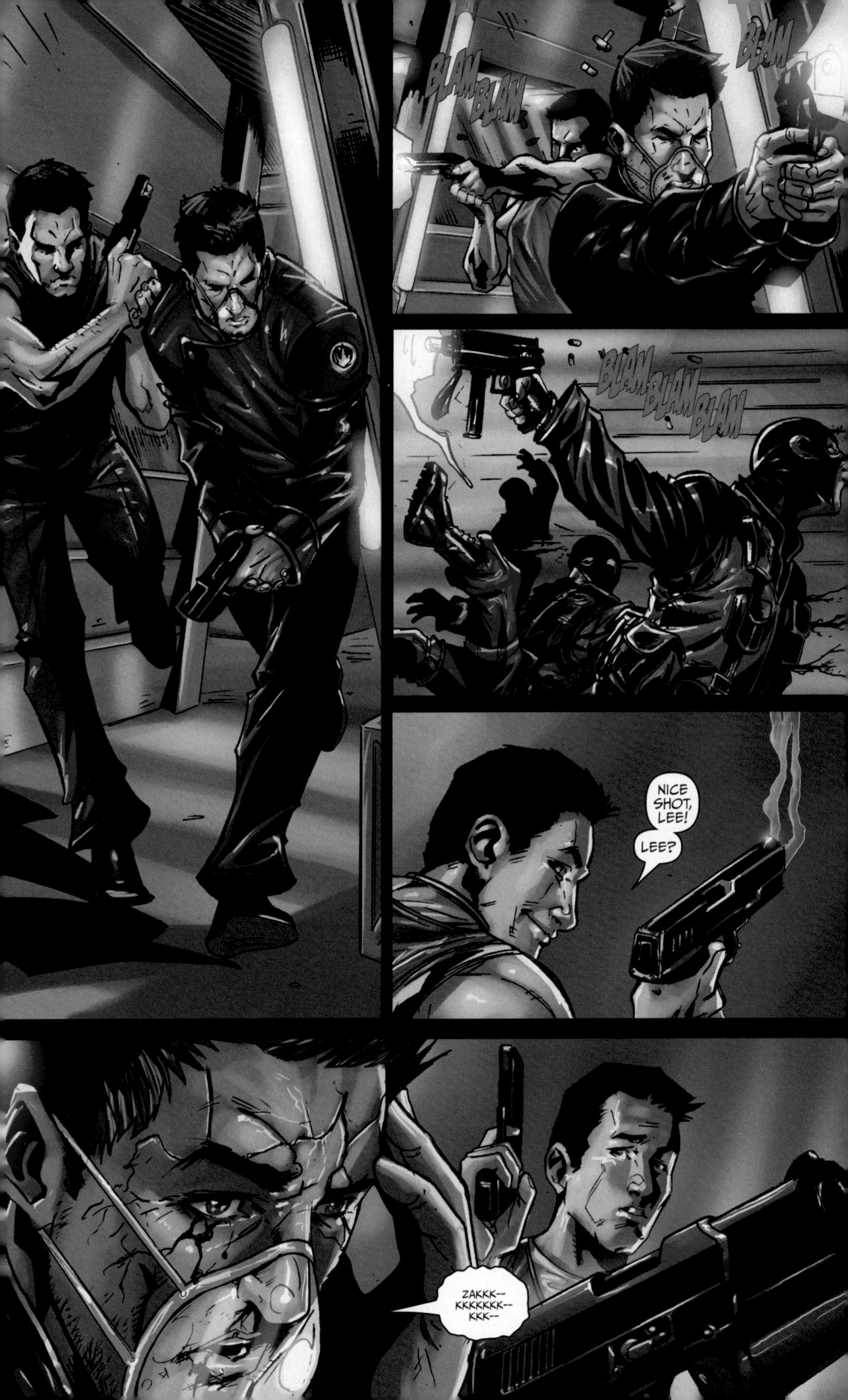
BLAM BLAM
BLAM
BLAM BLAM BLAM
NICE SHOT, LEE!
LEE?
ZAKKK--KKKKKKK--KKK--

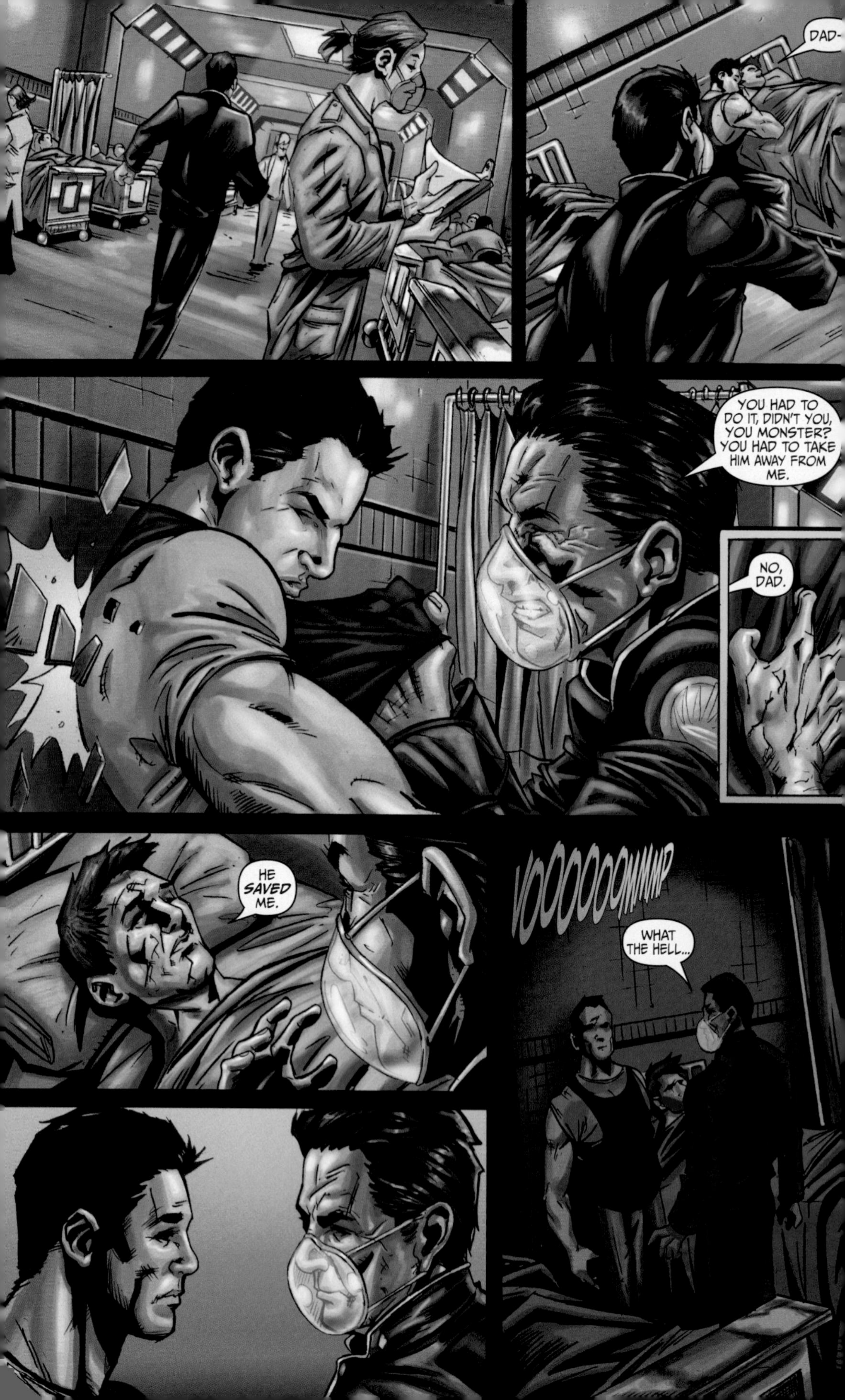
DAD-
YOU HAD TO DO IT, DIDN'T YOU, YOU MONSTER? YOU HAD TO TAKE HIM AWAY FROM ME.
NO, DAD.
HE SAVED ME.
VOOOOOOMMMP
WHAT THE HELL...

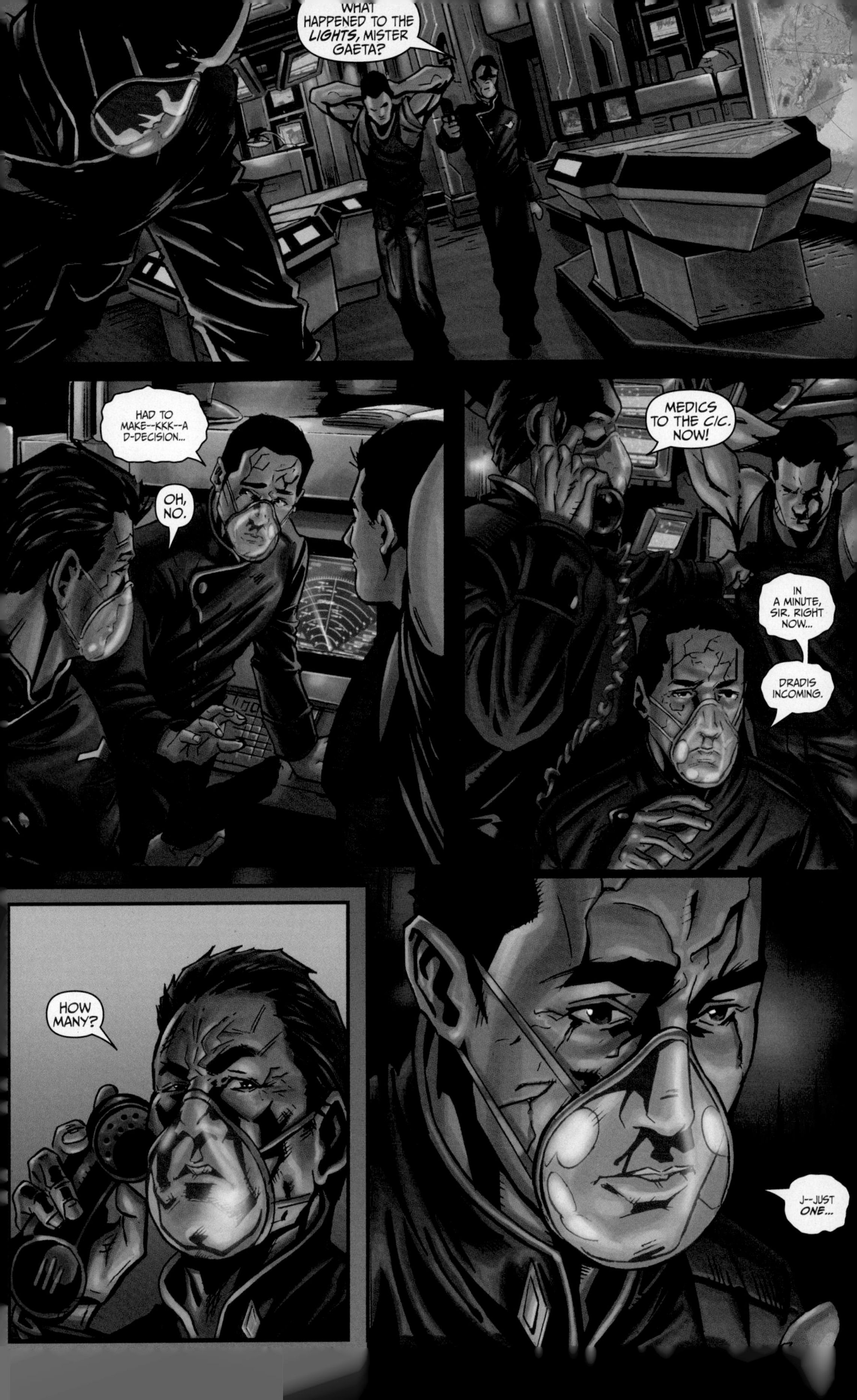
WHAT HAPPENED TO THE LIGHTS, MISTER GAETA?
HAD TO MAKE--KKK--A D-DECISION...
OH, NO.
MEDICS TO THE CIC. NOW!
IN A MINUTE, SIR. RIGHT NOW...
DRADIS INCOMING.
HOW MANY?
J--JUST ONE...

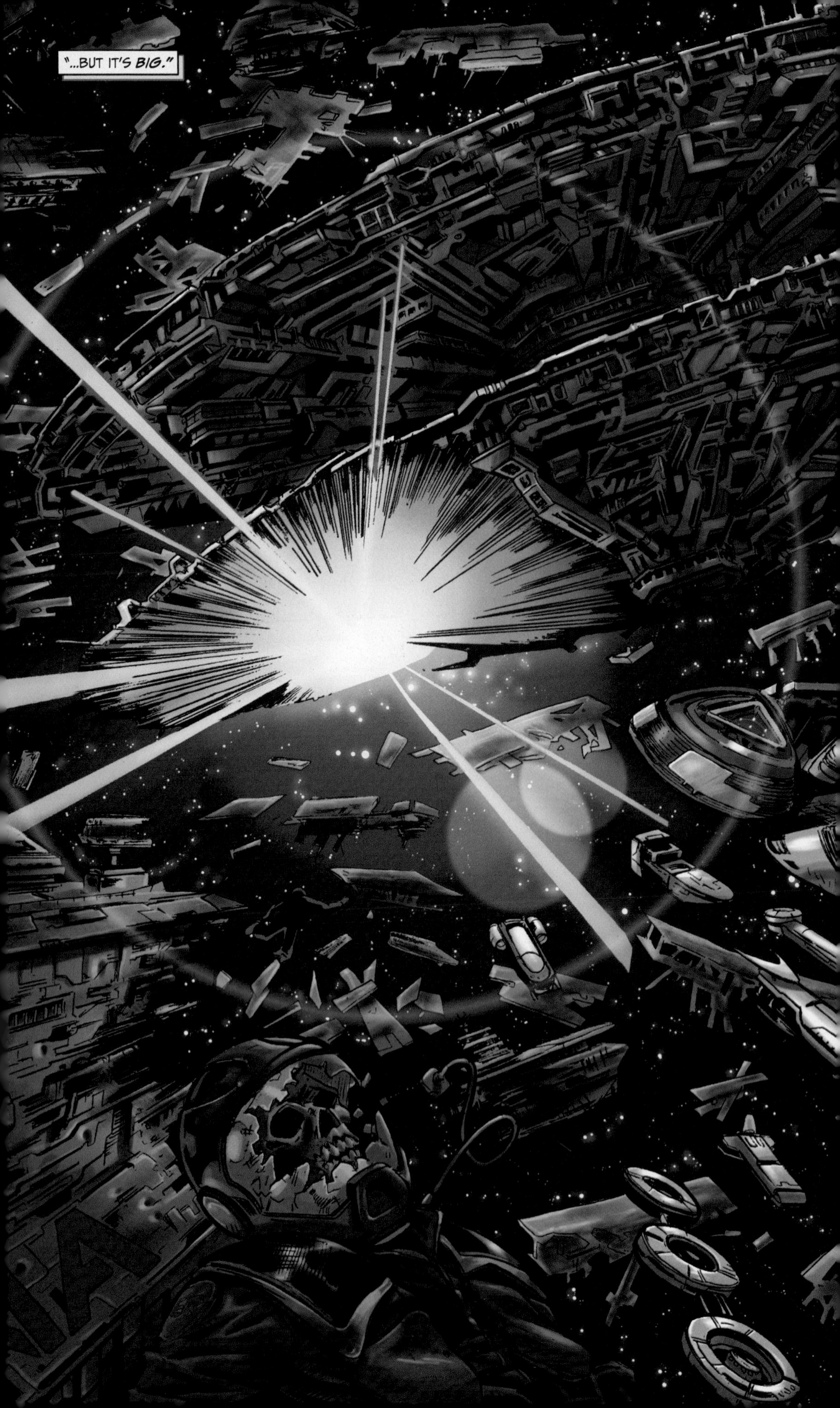
"...BUT IT'S *BIG.*"

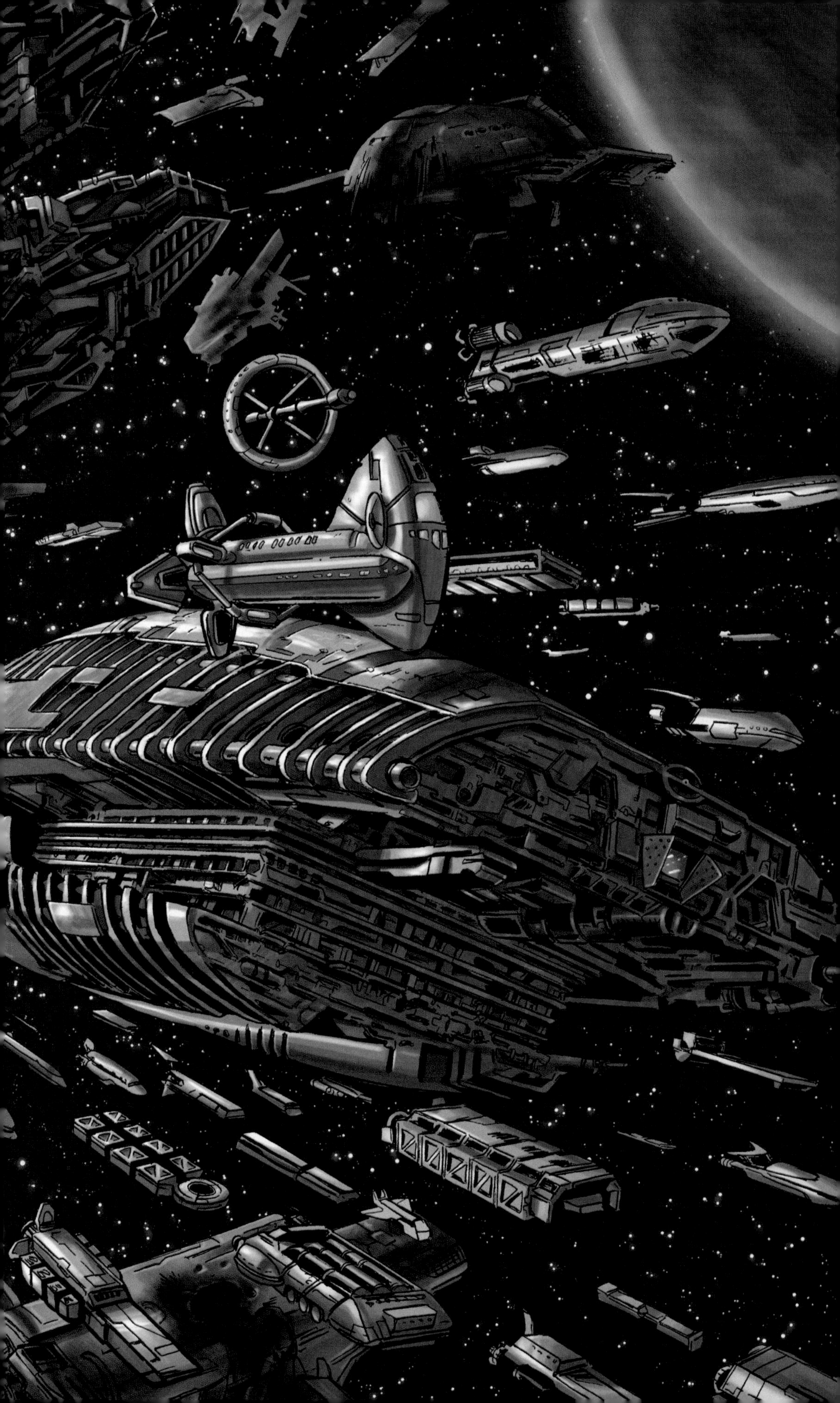

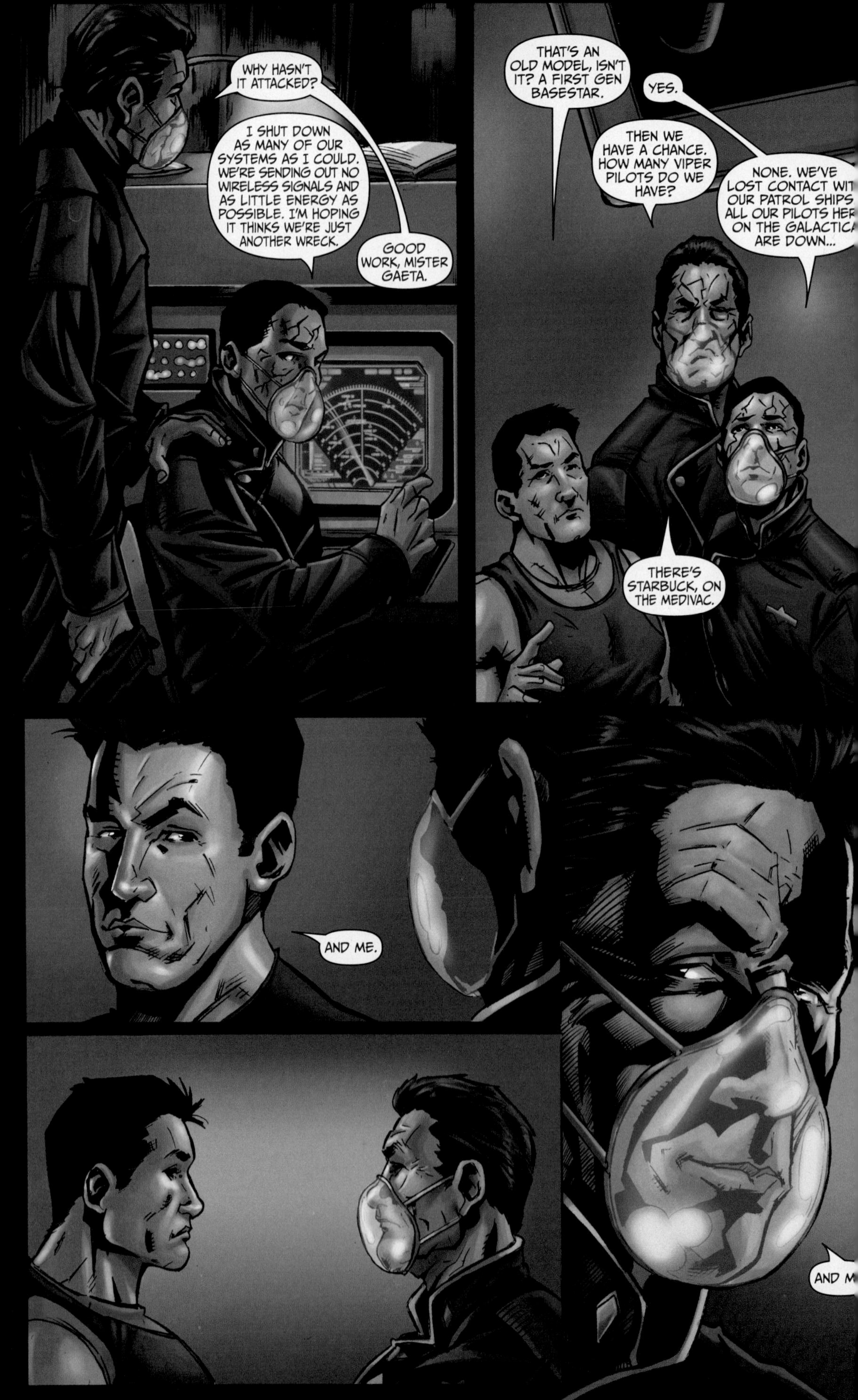
WHY HASN'T IT ATTACKED?
I SHUT DOWN AS MANY OF OUR SYSTEMS AS I COULD. WE'RE SENDING OUT NO WIRELESS SIGNALS AND AS LITTLE ENERGY AS POSSIBLE. I'M HOPING IT THINKS WE'RE JUST ANOTHER WRECK.
GOOD WORK, MISTER GAETA.
THAT'S AN OLD MODEL, ISN'T IT? A FIRST GEN BASESTAR.
YES.
THEN WE HAVE A CHANCE. HOW MANY VIPER PILOTS DO WE HAVE?
NONE. WE'VE LOST CONTACT WIT OUR PATROL SHIPS ALL OUR PILOTS HER ON THE GALACTIC ARE DOWN...
THERE'S STARBUCK, ON THE MEDIVAC.
AND ME.
AND M

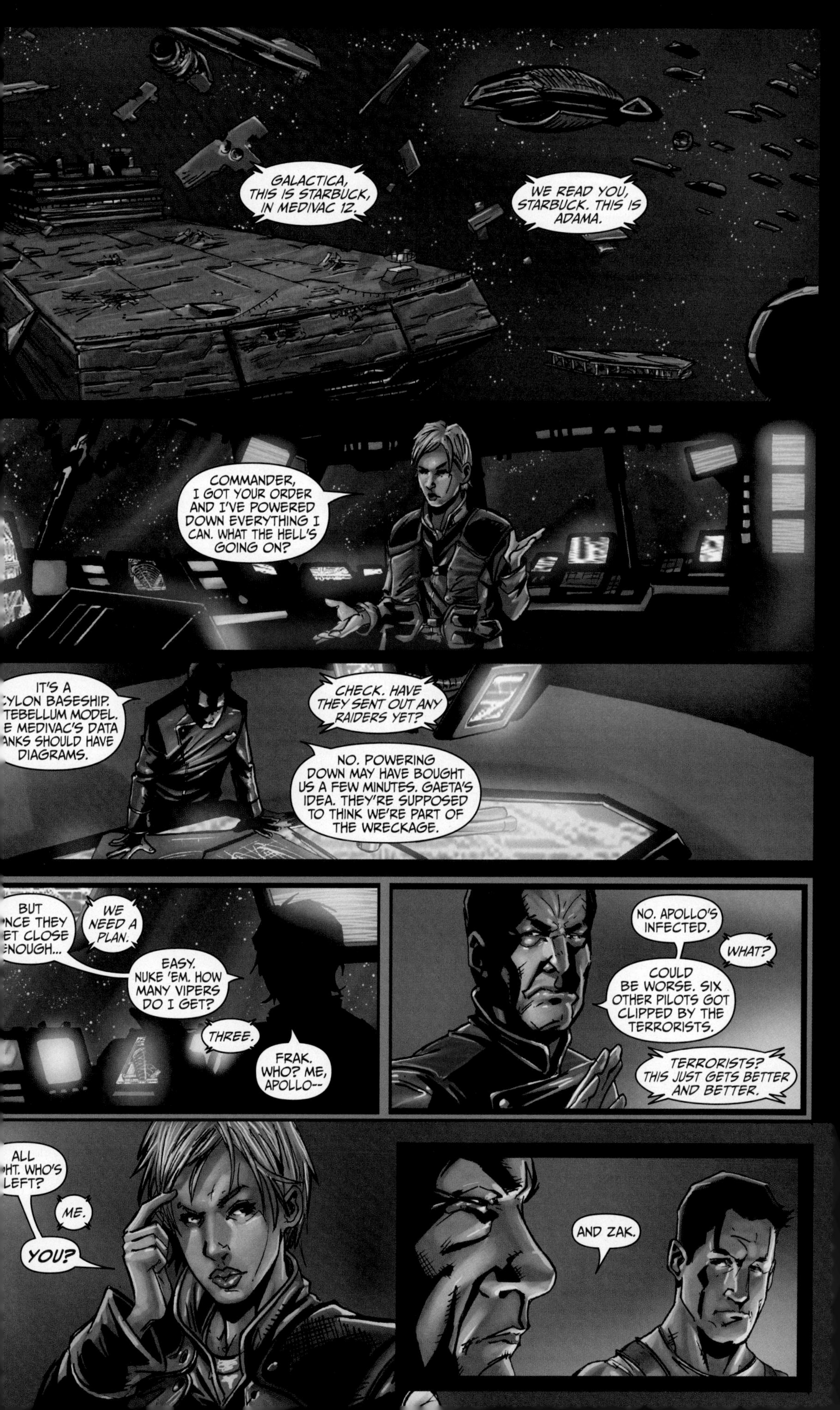
GALACTICA, THIS IS STARBUCK, IN MEDIVAC 12.
WE READ YOU, STARBUCK. THIS IS ADAMA.
COMMANDER, I GOT YOUR ORDER AND I'VE POWERED DOWN EVERYTHING I CAN. WHAT THE HELL'S GOING ON?
IT'S A CYLON BASESHIP. TEBELLUM MODEL. E MEDIVAC'S DATA ANKS SHOULD HAVE DIAGRAMS.
CHECK. HAVE THEY SENT OUT ANY RAIDERS YET?
NO. POWERING DOWN MAY HAVE BOUGHT US A FEW MINUTES. GAETA'S IDEA. THEY'RE SUPPOSED TO THINK WE'RE PART OF THE WRECKAGE.
BUT NCE THEY ET CLOSE ENOUGH...
WE NEED A PLAN.
EASY. NUKE 'EM. HOW MANY VIPERS DO I GET?
THREE.
FRAK. WHO? ME, APOLLO--
NO. APOLLO'S INFECTED.
WHAT?
COULD BE WORSE. SIX OTHER PILOTS GOT CLIPPED BY THE TERRORISTS.
TERRORISTS? THIS JUST GETS BETTER AND BETTER.
ALL HT. WHO'S LEFT?
ME.
YOU?
AND ZAK.

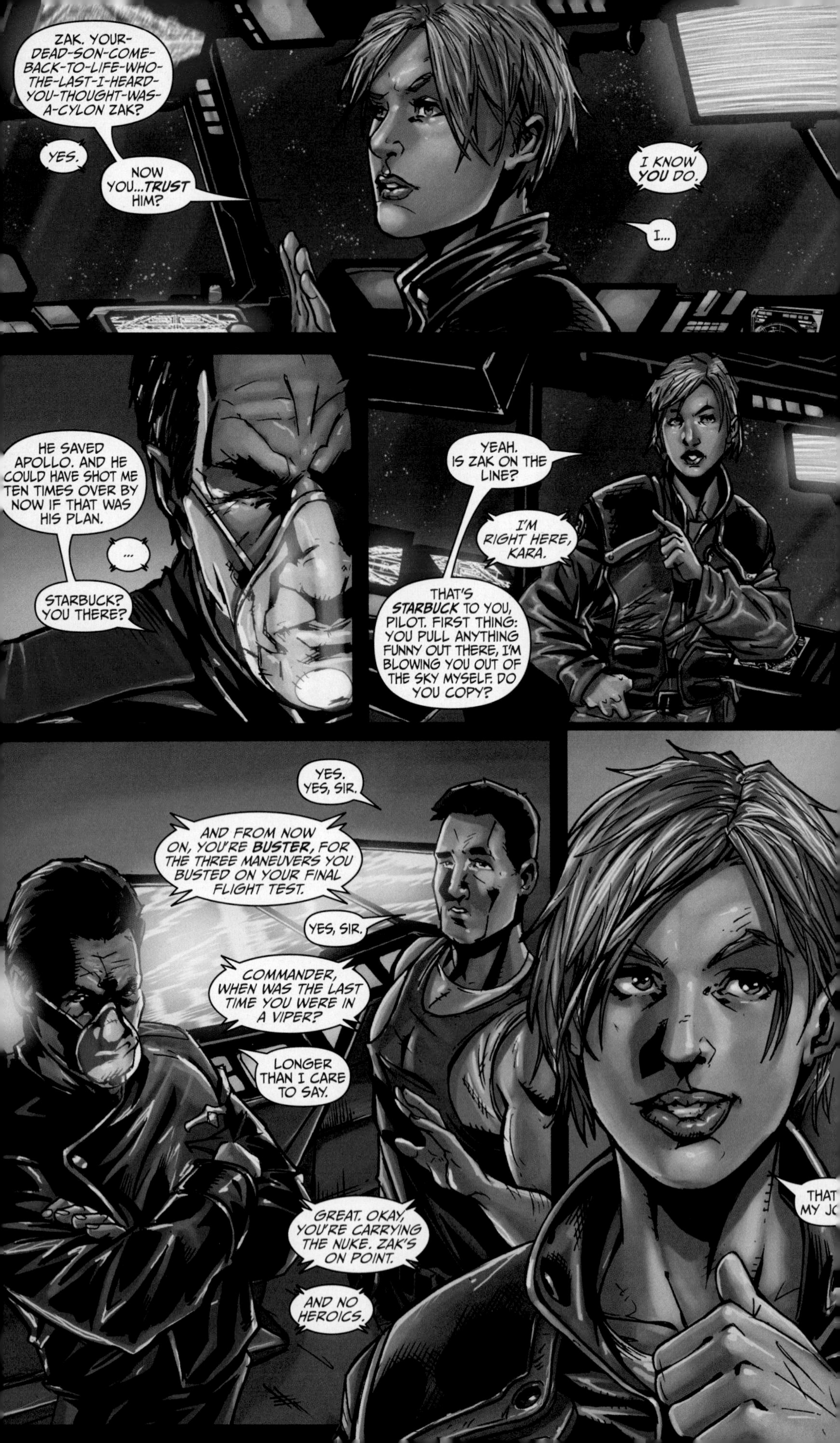
ZAK. YOUR-DEAD-SON-COME-BACK-TO-LIFE-WHO-THE-LAST-I-HEARD-YOU-THOUGHT-WAS-A-CYLON ZAK?
YES.
NOW YOU...TRUST HIM?
I KNOW YOU DO.
I...
HE SAVED APOLLO. AND HE COULD HAVE SHOT ME TEN TIMES OVER BY NOW IF THAT WAS HIS PLAN.
...
STARBUCK? YOU THERE?
YEAH. IS ZAK ON THE LINE?
I'M RIGHT HERE, KARA.
THAT'S STARBUCK TO YOU, PILOT. FIRST THING: YOU PULL ANYTHING FUNNY OUT THERE, I'M BLOWING YOU OUT OF THE SKY MYSELF. DO YOU COPY?
YES. YES, SIR.
AND FROM NOW ON, YOU'RE BUSTER, FOR THE THREE MANEUVERS YOU BUSTED ON YOUR FINAL FLIGHT TEST.
YES, SIR.
COMMANDER, WHEN WAS THE LAST TIME YOU WERE IN A VIPER?
LONGER THAN I CARE TO SAY.
GREAT. OKAY, YOU'RE CARRYING THE NUKE. ZAK'S ON POINT.
AND NO HEROICS.

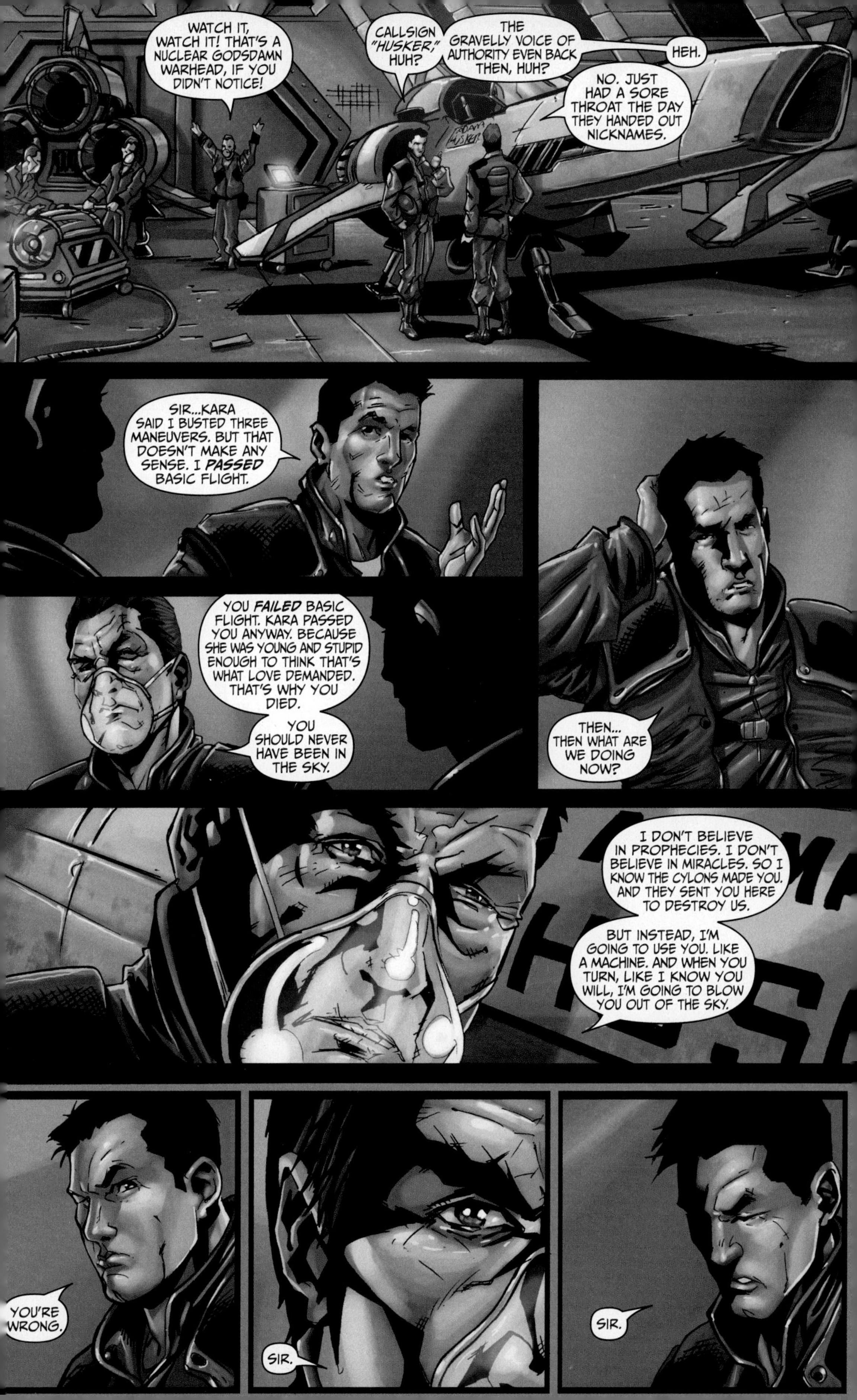
WATCH IT, WATCH IT! THAT'S A NUCLEAR GODSDAMN WARHEAD, IF YOU DIDN'T NOTICE!
CALLSIGN "HUSKER," HUH?
THE GRAVELLY VOICE OF AUTHORITY EVEN BACK THEN, HUH?
HEH.
NO. JUST HAD A SORE THROAT THE DAY THEY HANDED OUT NICKNAMES.
SIR...KARA SAID I BUSTED THREE MANEUVERS. BUT THAT DOESN'T MAKE ANY SENSE. I PASSED BASIC FLIGHT.
YOU FAILED BASIC FLIGHT. KARA PASSED YOU ANYWAY. BECAUSE SHE WAS YOUNG AND STUPID ENOUGH TO THINK THAT'S WHAT LOVE DEMANDED. THAT'S WHY YOU DIED.
YOU SHOULD NEVER HAVE BEEN IN THE SKY.
THEN... THEN WHAT ARE WE DOING NOW?
I DON'T BELIEVE IN PROPHECIES. I DON'T BELIEVE IN MIRACLES. SO I KNOW THE CYLONS MADE YOU. AND THEY SENT YOU HERE TO DESTROY US.
BUT INSTEAD, I'M GOING TO USE YOU. LIKE A MACHINE. AND WHEN YOU TURN, LIKE I KNOW YOU WILL, I'M GOING TO BLOW YOU OUT OF THE SKY.
YOU'RE WRONG.
SIR.
SIR.

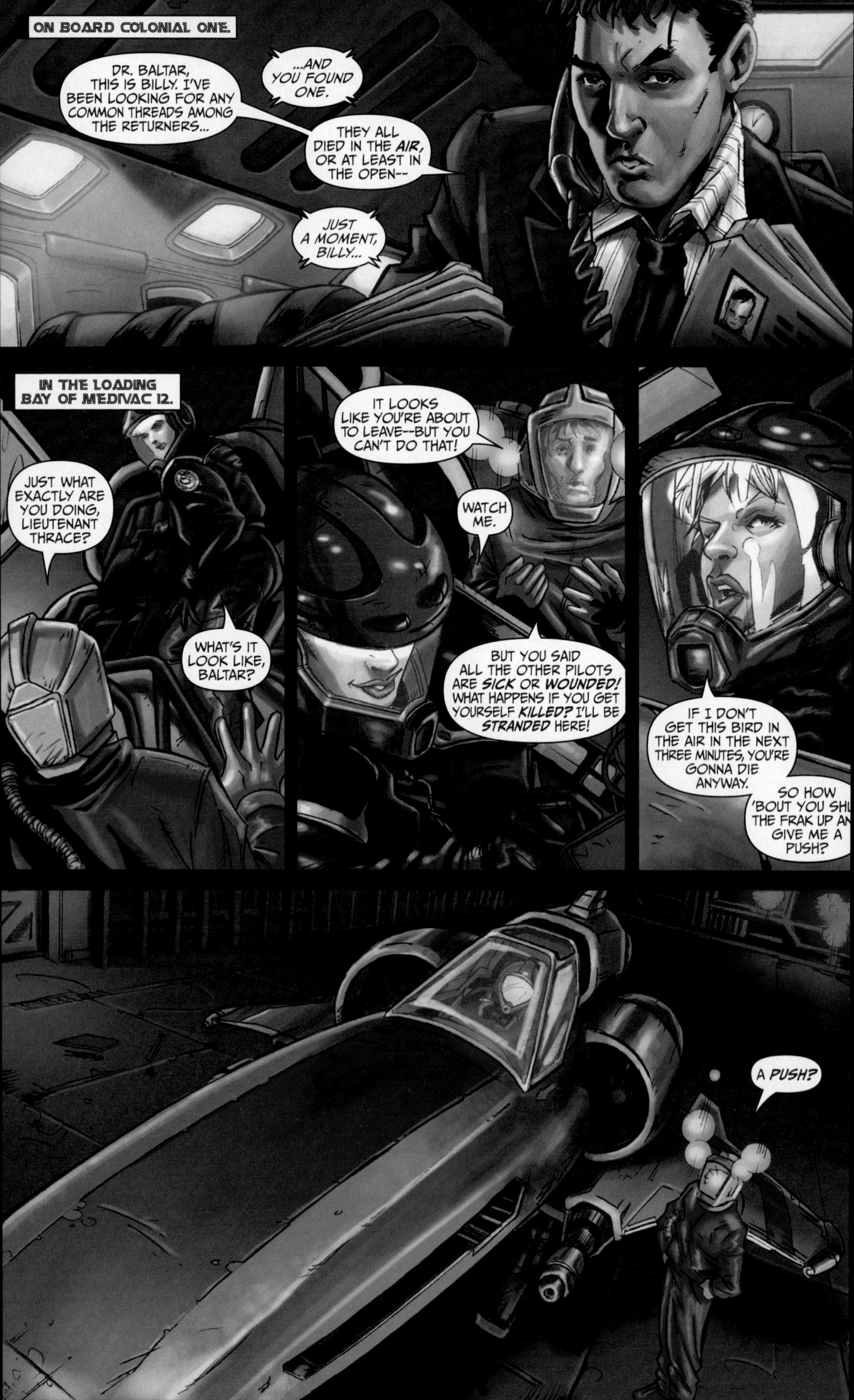
ON BOARD COLONIAL ONE.
DR. BALTAR, THIS IS BILLY. I'VE BEEN LOOKING FOR ANY COMMON THREADS AMONG THE RETURNERS...
...AND YOU FOUND ONE.
THEY ALL DIED IN THE AIR, OR AT LEAST IN THE OPEN--
JUST A MOMENT, BILLY...
IN THE LOADING BAY OF MEDIVAC 12.
JUST WHAT EXACTLY ARE YOU DOING, LIEUTENANT THRACE?
WHAT'S IT LOOK LIKE, BALTAR?
IT LOOKS LIKE YOU'RE ABOUT TO LEAVE--BUT YOU CAN'T DO THAT!
WATCH ME.
BUT YOU SAID ALL THE OTHER PILOTS ARE SICK OR WOUNDED! WHAT HAPPENS IF YOU GET YOURSELF KILLED? I'LL BE STRANDED HERE!
IF I DON'T GET THIS BIRD IN THE AIR IN THE NEXT THREE MINUTES, YOU'RE GONNA DIE ANYWAY.
A PUSH?

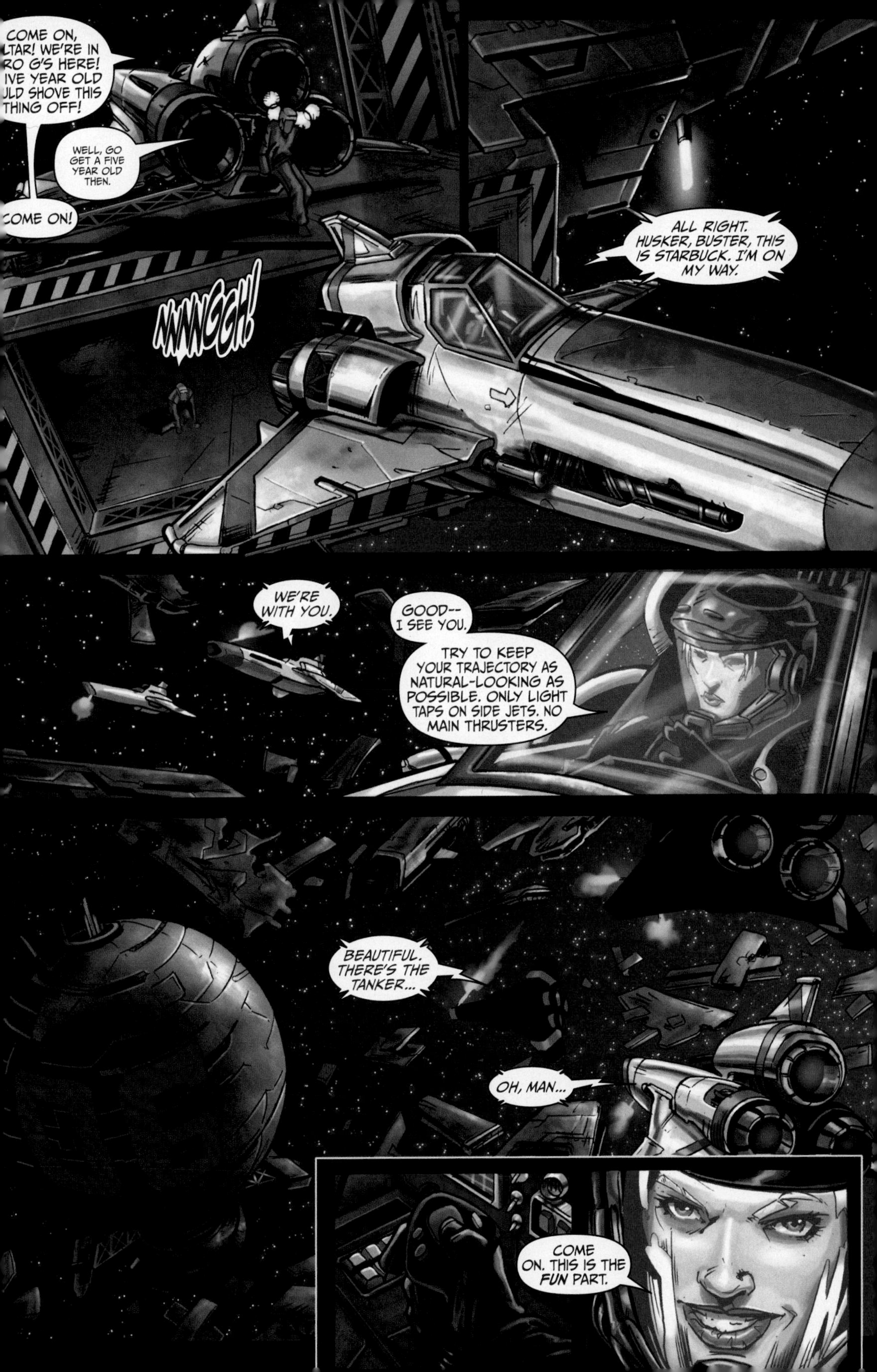
COME ON, ...LTAR! WE'RE IN ...RO G'S HERE! ...IVE YEAR OLD ...ULD SHOVE THIS THING OFF!
WELL, GO GET A FIVE YEAR OLD THEN.
COME ON!
ALL RIGHT. HUSKER, BUSTER, THIS IS STARBUCK. I'M ON MY WAY.
NNNNGGH!
WE'RE WITH YOU.
GOOD-- I SEE YOU.
TRY TO KEEP YOUR TRAJECTORY AS NATURAL-LOOKING AS POSSIBLE. ONLY LIGHT TAPS ON SIDE JETS. NO MAIN THRUSTERS.
BEAUTIFUL. THERE'S THE TANKER...
OH, MAN...
COME ON. THIS IS THE FUN PART.

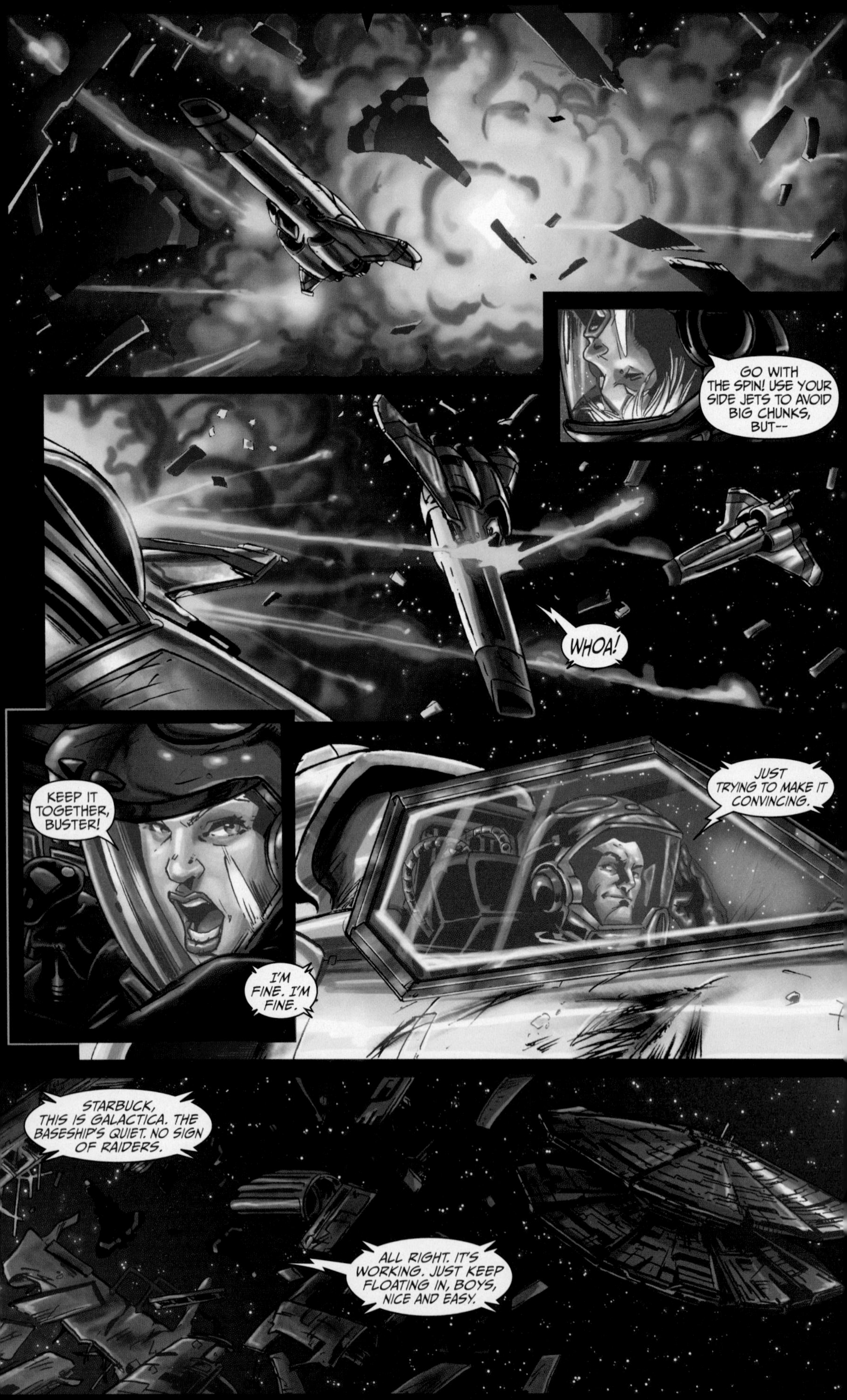
GO WITH THE SPIN! USE YOUR SIDE JETS TO AVOID BIG CHUNKS, BUT--
WHOA!
KEEP IT TOGETHER, BUSTER!
I'M FINE. I'M FINE.
JUST TRYING TO MAKE IT CONVINCING.
STARBUCK, THIS IS GALACTICA. THE BASESHIP'S QUIET. NO SIGN OF RAIDERS.
ALL RIGHT. IT'S WORKING. JUST KEEP FLOATING IN, BOYS, NICE AND EASY.

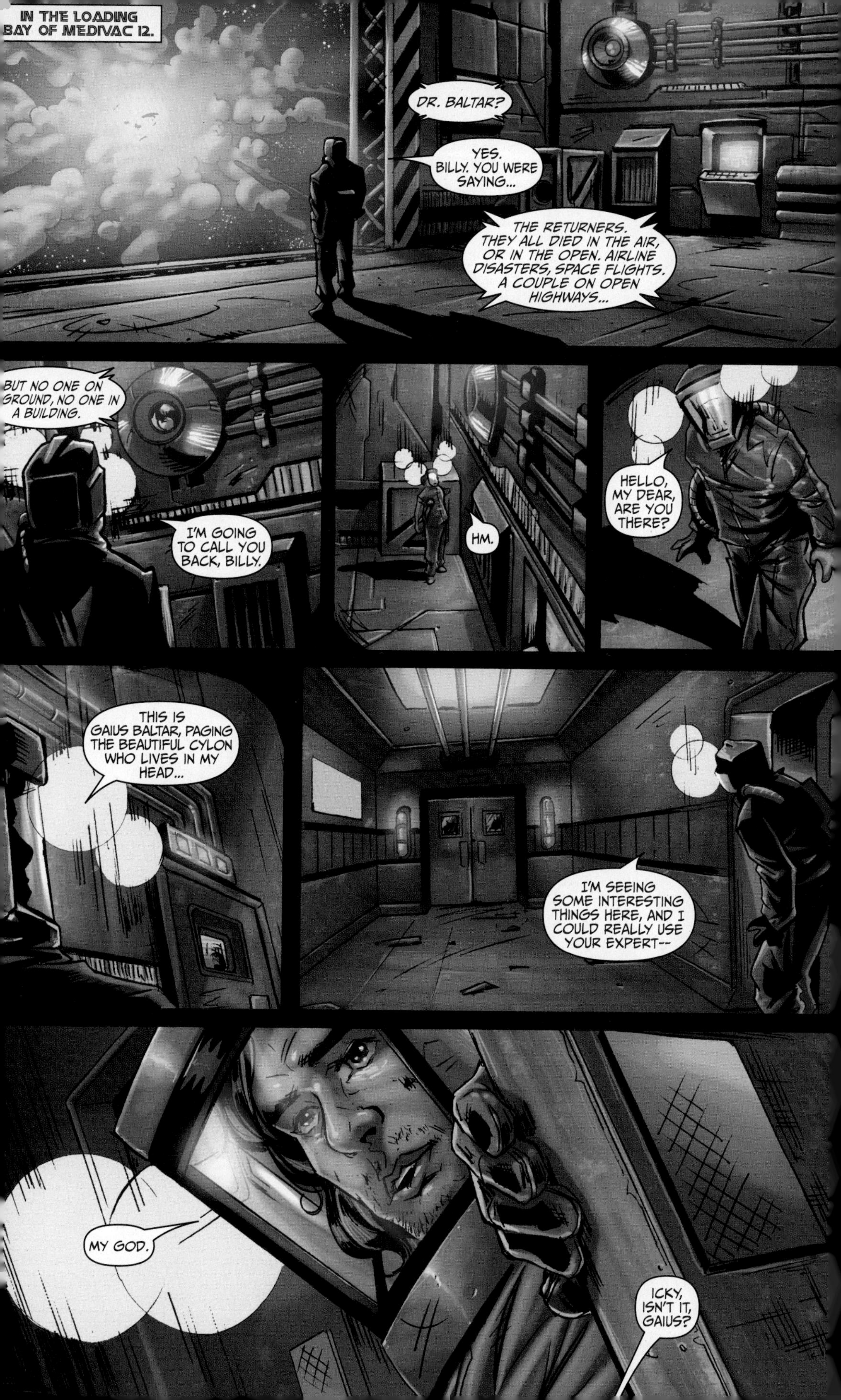
IN THE LOADING BAY OF MEDIVAC 12.
DR. BALTAR?
YES. BILLY. YOU WERE SAYING...
THE RETURNERS. THEY ALL DIED IN THE AIR, OR IN THE OPEN. AIRLINE DISASTERS, SPACE FLIGHTS. A COUPLE ON OPEN HIGHWAYS...
BUT NO ONE ON GROUND, NO ONE IN A BUILDING.
I'M GOING TO CALL YOU BACK, BILLY.
HM.
HELLO, MY DEAR, ARE YOU THERE?
THIS IS GAIUS BALTAR, PAGING THE BEAUTIFUL CYLON WHO LIVES IN MY HEAD...
I'M SEEING SOME INTERESTING THINGS HERE, AND I COULD REALLY USE YOUR EXPERT--
MY GOD.
ICKY, ISN'T IT, GAIUS?

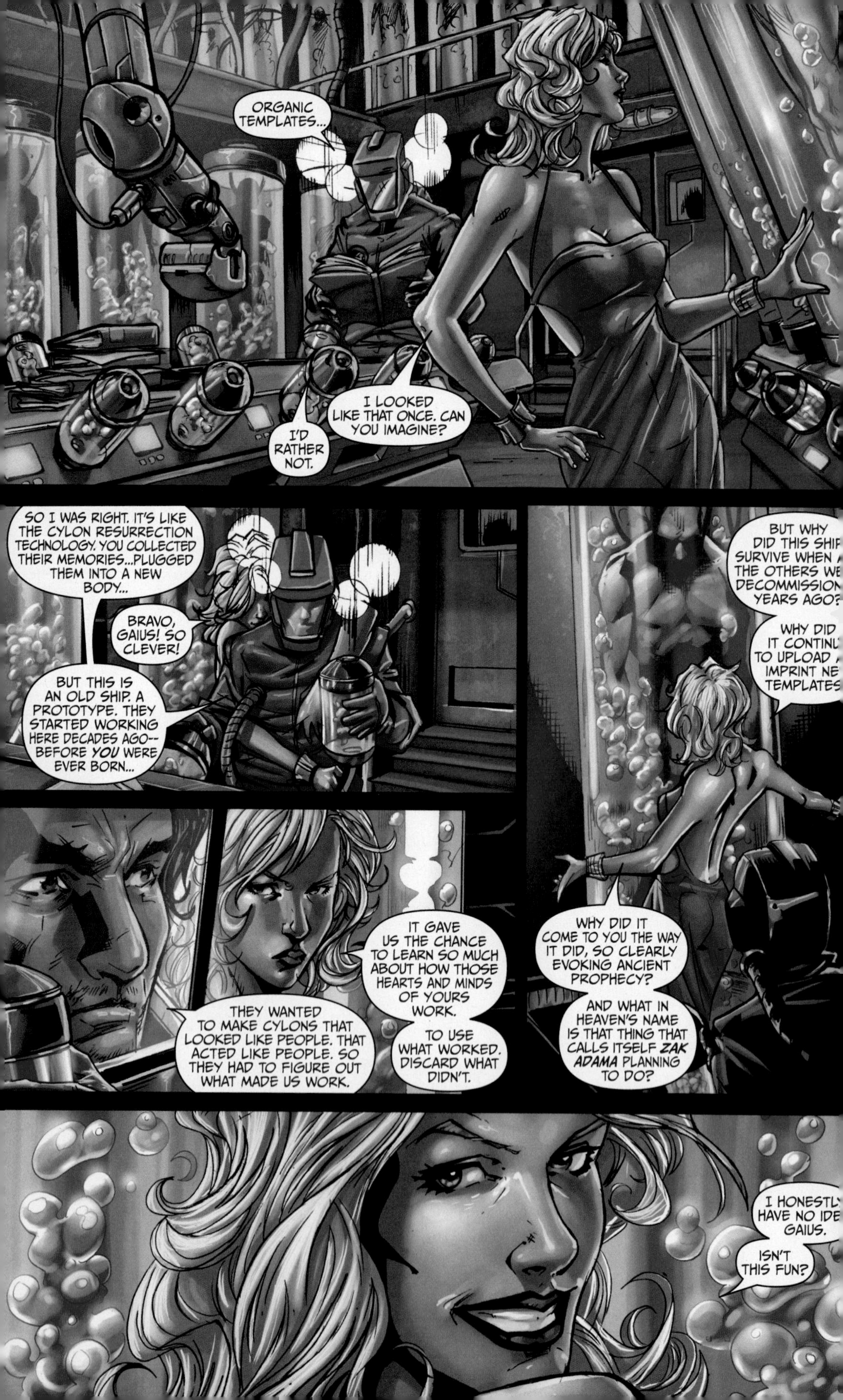

ORGANIC TEMPLATES...
I LOOKED LIKE THAT ONCE. CAN YOU IMAGINE?
I'D RATHER NOT.
SO I WAS RIGHT. IT'S LIKE THE CYLON RESURRECTION TECHNOLOGY. YOU COLLECTED THEIR MEMORIES...PLUGGED THEM INTO A NEW BODY...
BRAVO, GAIUS! SO CLEVER!
BUT THIS IS AN OLD SHIP. A PROTOTYPE. THEY STARTED WORKING HERE DECADES AGO-- BEFORE YOU WERE EVER BORN...
BUT WHY DID THIS SHIP SURVIVE WHEN THE OTHERS WE DECOMMISSION YEARS AGO?
WHY DID IT CONTINU TO UPLOAD IMPRINT NE TEMPLATES
THEY WANTED TO MAKE CYLONS THAT LOOKED LIKE PEOPLE. THAT ACTED LIKE PEOPLE. SO THEY HAD TO FIGURE OUT WHAT MADE US WORK.
IT GAVE US THE CHANCE TO LEARN SO MUCH ABOUT HOW THOSE HEARTS AND MINDS OF YOURS WORK.
TO USE WHAT WORKED. DISCARD WHAT DIDN'T.
WHY DID IT COME TO YOU THE WAY IT DID, SO CLEARLY EVOKING ANCIENT PROPHECY?
AND WHAT IN HEAVEN'S NAME IS THAT THING THAT CALLS ITSELF ZAK ADAMA PLANNING TO DO?
I HONESTL HAVE NO IDE GAIUS.
ISN'T THIS FUN?

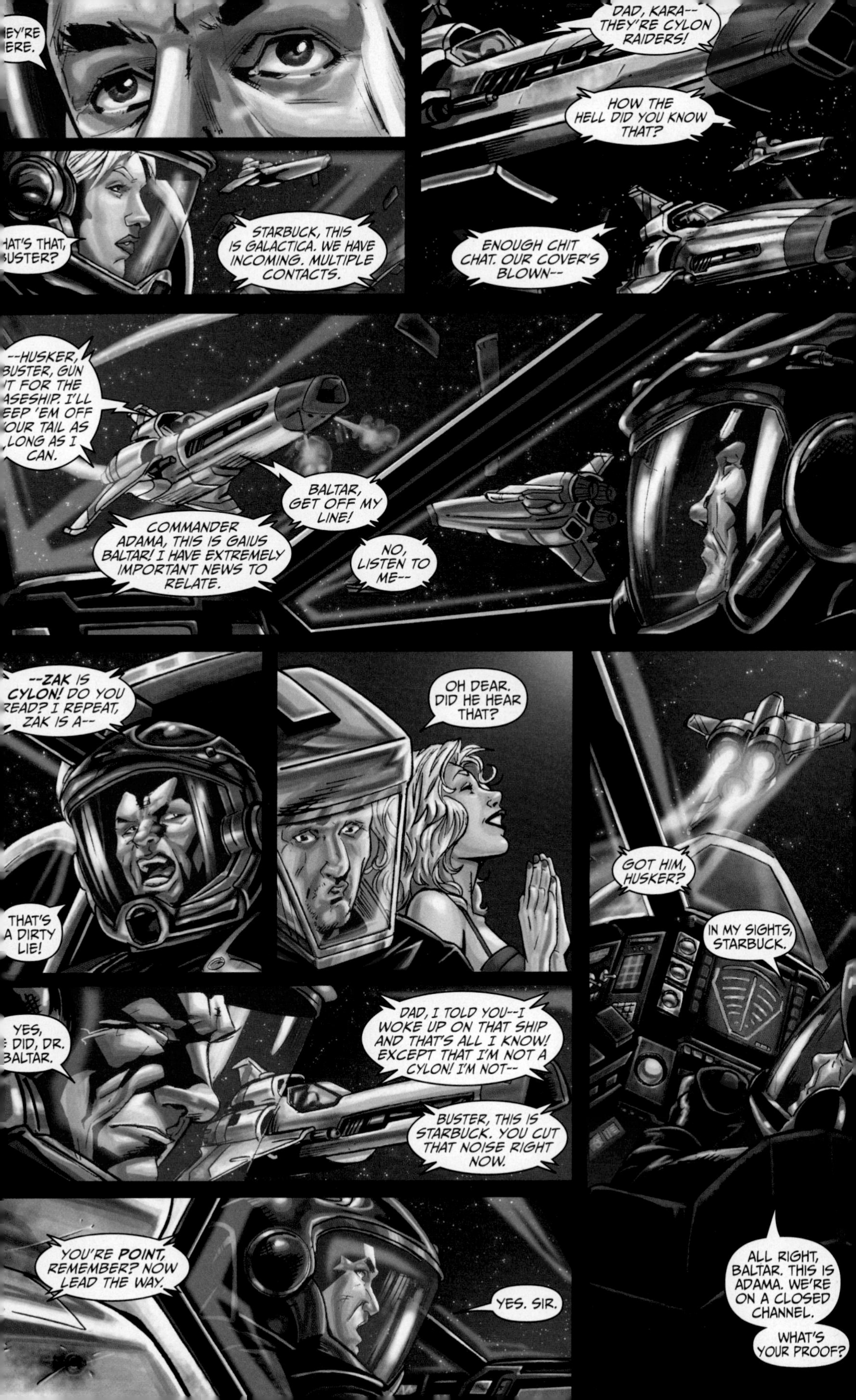
EY'RE
ERE.
HAT'S THAT,
USTER?
STARBUCK, THIS IS GALACTICA. WE HAVE INCOMING. MULTIPLE CONTACTS.
DAD, KARA-- THEY'RE CYLON RAIDERS!
HOW THE HELL DID YOU KNOW THAT?
ENOUGH CHIT CHAT. OUR COVER'S BLOWN--
--HUSKER, USTER, GUN T FOR THE ASESHIP. I'LL EEP 'EM OFF OUR TAIL AS LONG AS I CAN.
COMMANDER ADAMA, THIS IS GAIUS BALTAR! I HAVE EXTREMELY IMPORTANT NEWS TO RELATE.
BALTAR, GET OFF MY LINE!
NO, LISTEN TO ME--
--ZAK IS CYLON! DO YOU EAD? I REPEAT, ZAK IS A--
THAT'S A DIRTY LIE!
OH DEAR. DID HE HEAR THAT?
GOT HIM, HUSKER?
IN MY SIGHTS, STARBUCK.
YES, E DID, DR. ALTAR.
DAD, I TOLD YOU--I WOKE UP ON THAT SHIP AND THAT'S ALL I KNOW! EXCEPT THAT I'M NOT A CYLON! I'M NOT--
BUSTER, THIS IS STARBUCK. YOU CUT THAT NOISE RIGHT NOW.
YOU'RE POINT, REMEMBER? NOW LEAD THE WAY.
YES. SIR.
ALL RIGHT, BALTAR. THIS IS ADAMA. WE'RE ON A CLOSED CHANNEL.
WHAT'S YOUR PROOF?

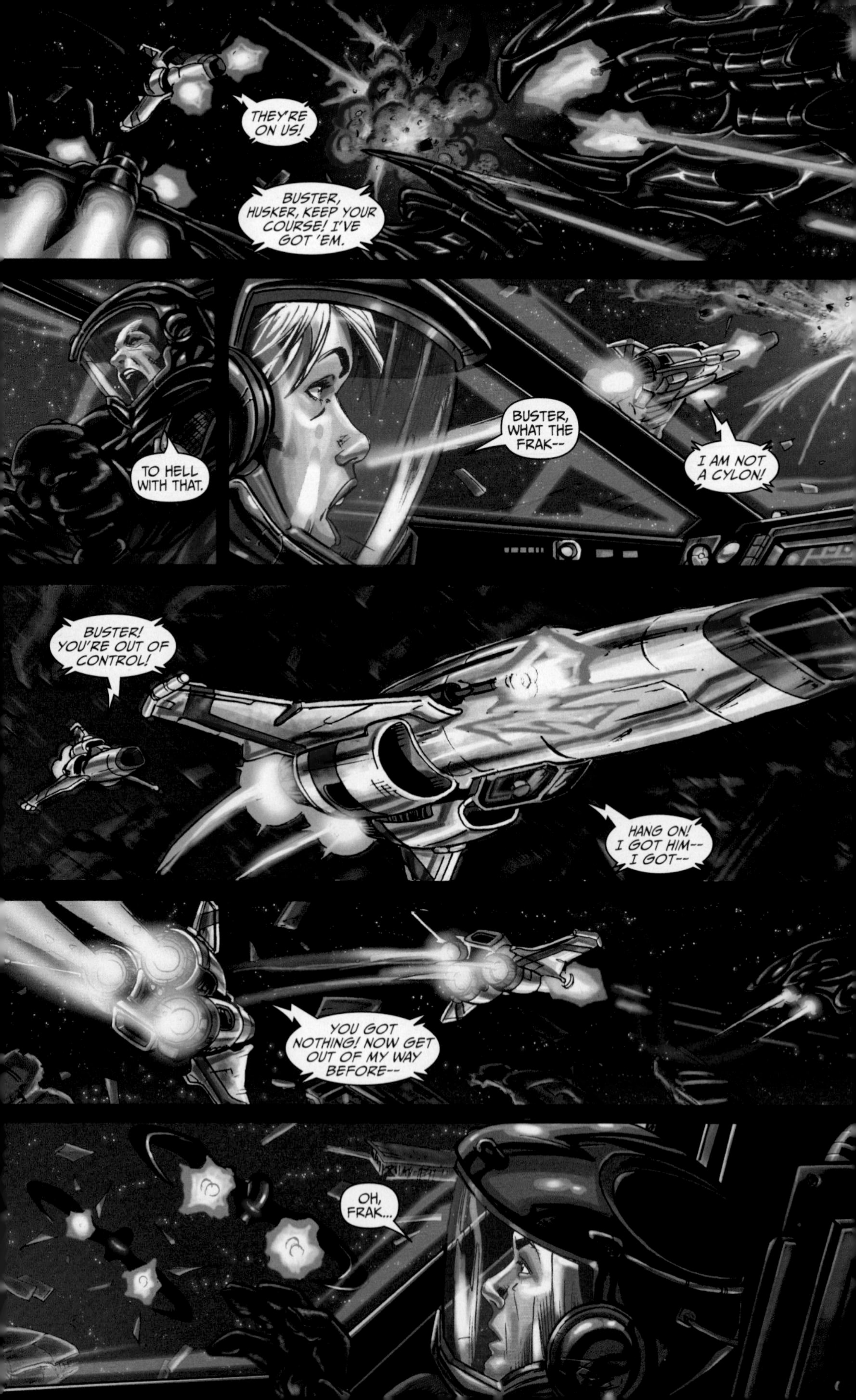
THEY'RE ON US!
BUSTER, HUSKER, KEEP YOUR COURSE! I'VE GOT 'EM.
TO HELL WITH THAT.
BUSTER, WHAT THE FRAK--
I AM NOT A CYLON!
BUSTER! YOU'RE OUT OF CONTROL!
HANG ON! I GOT HIM-- I GOT--
YOU GOT NOTHING! NOW GET OUT OF MY WAY BEFORE--
OH, FRAK...

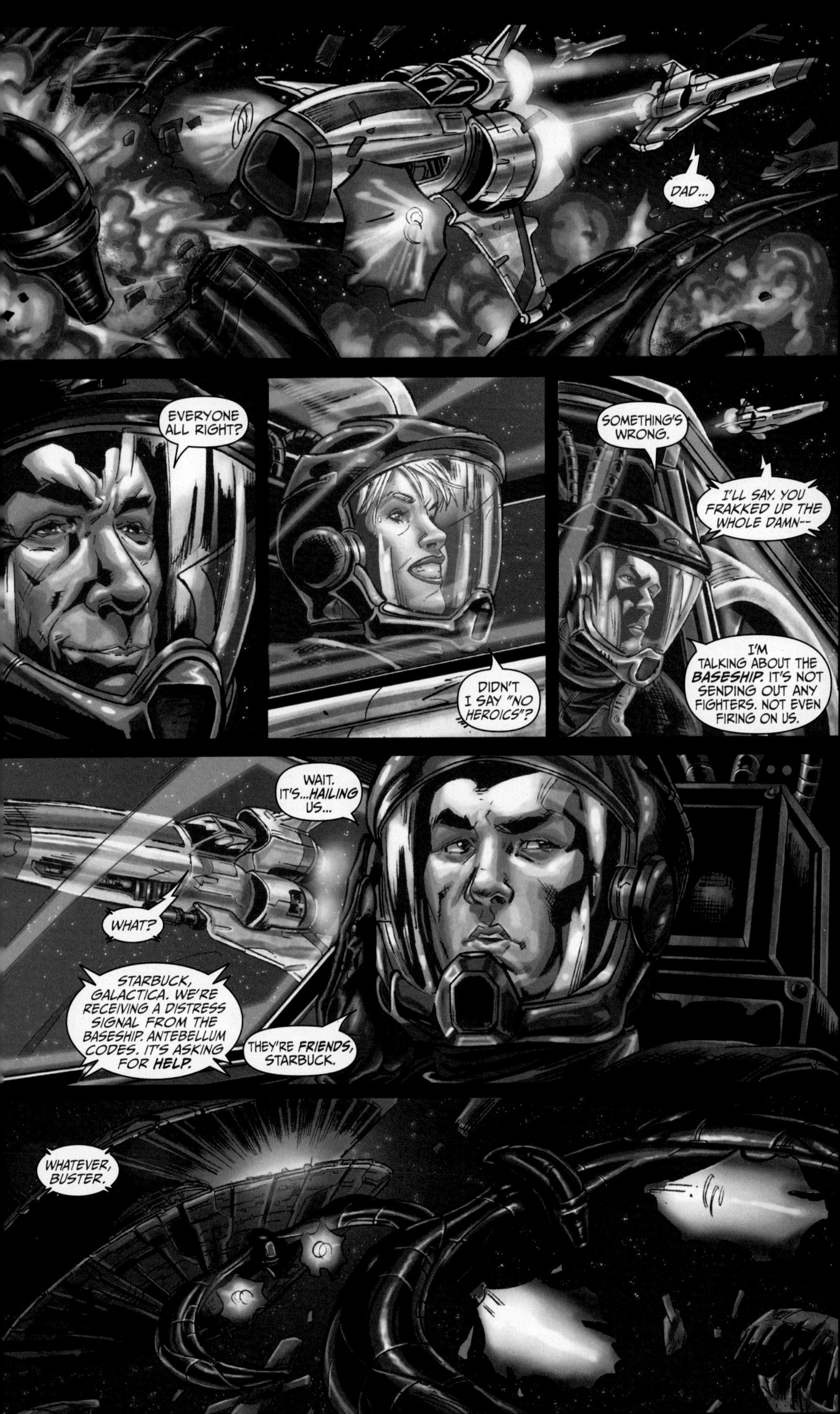
DAD...
EVERYONE ALL RIGHT?
DIDN'T I SAY "NO HEROICS"?
SOMETHING'S WRONG.
I'LL SAY. YOU FRAKKED UP THE WHOLE DAMN--
I'M TALKING ABOUT THE BASESHIP. IT'S NOT SENDING OUT ANY FIGHTERS. NOT EVEN FIRING ON US.
WAIT. IT'S...HAILING US...
WHAT?
STARBUCK, GALACTICA. WE'RE RECEIVING A DISTRESS SIGNAL FROM THE BASESHIP. ANTEBELLUM CODES. IT'S ASKING FOR HELP.
THEY'RE FRIENDS, STARBUCK.
WHATEVER, BUSTER.

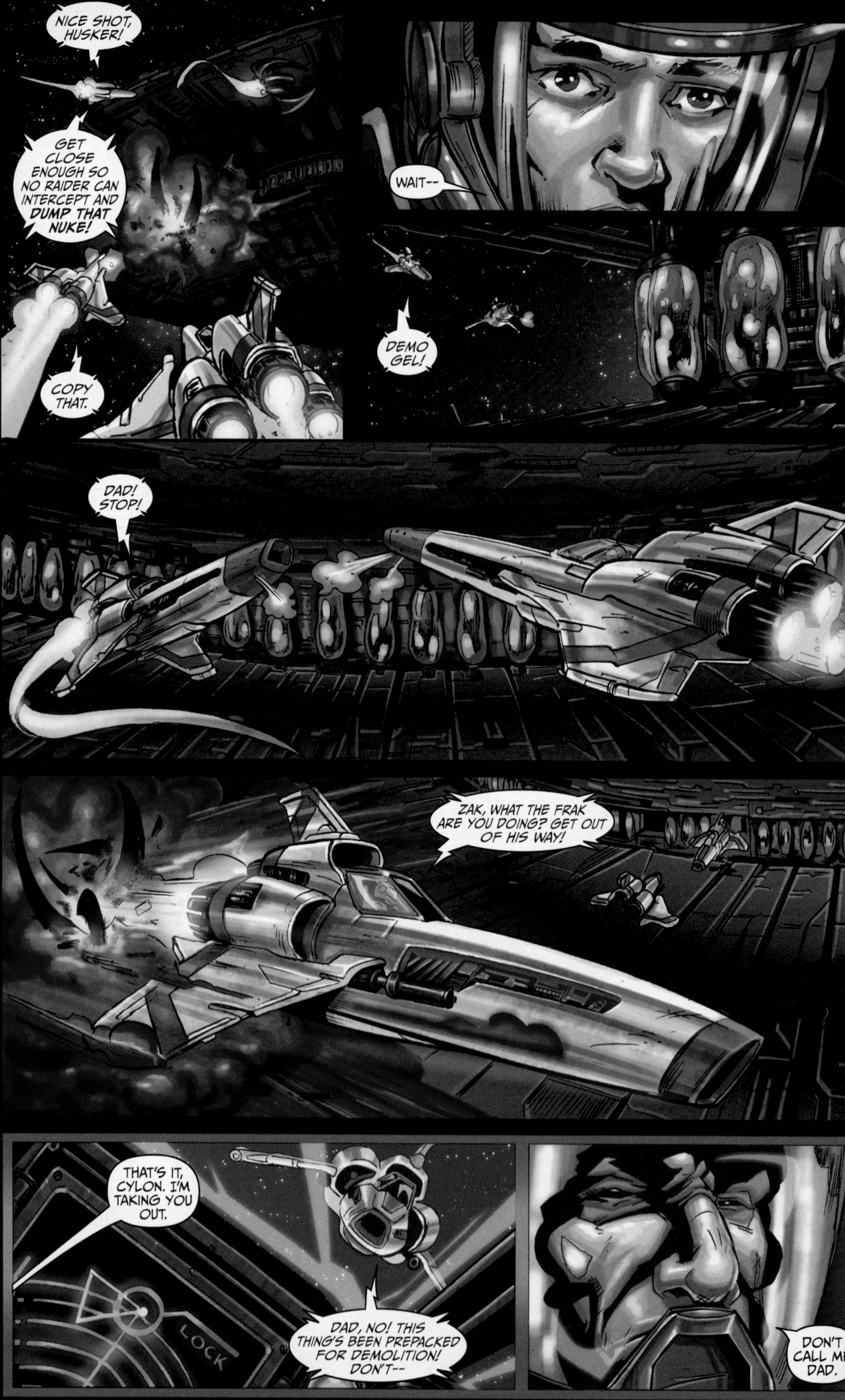
NICE SHOT, HUSKER!
GET CLOSE ENOUGH SO NO RAIDER CAN INTERCEPT AND DUMP THAT NUKE!
COPY THAT.
WAIT--
DEMO GEL!
DAD! STOP!
ZAK, WHAT THE FRAK ARE YOU DOING? GET OUT OF HIS WAY!
THAT'S IT, CYLON. I'M TAKING YOU OUT.
LOCK
DAD, NO! THIS THING'S BEEN PREPACKED FOR DEMOLITION! DON'T--
DON'T CALL ME DAD.

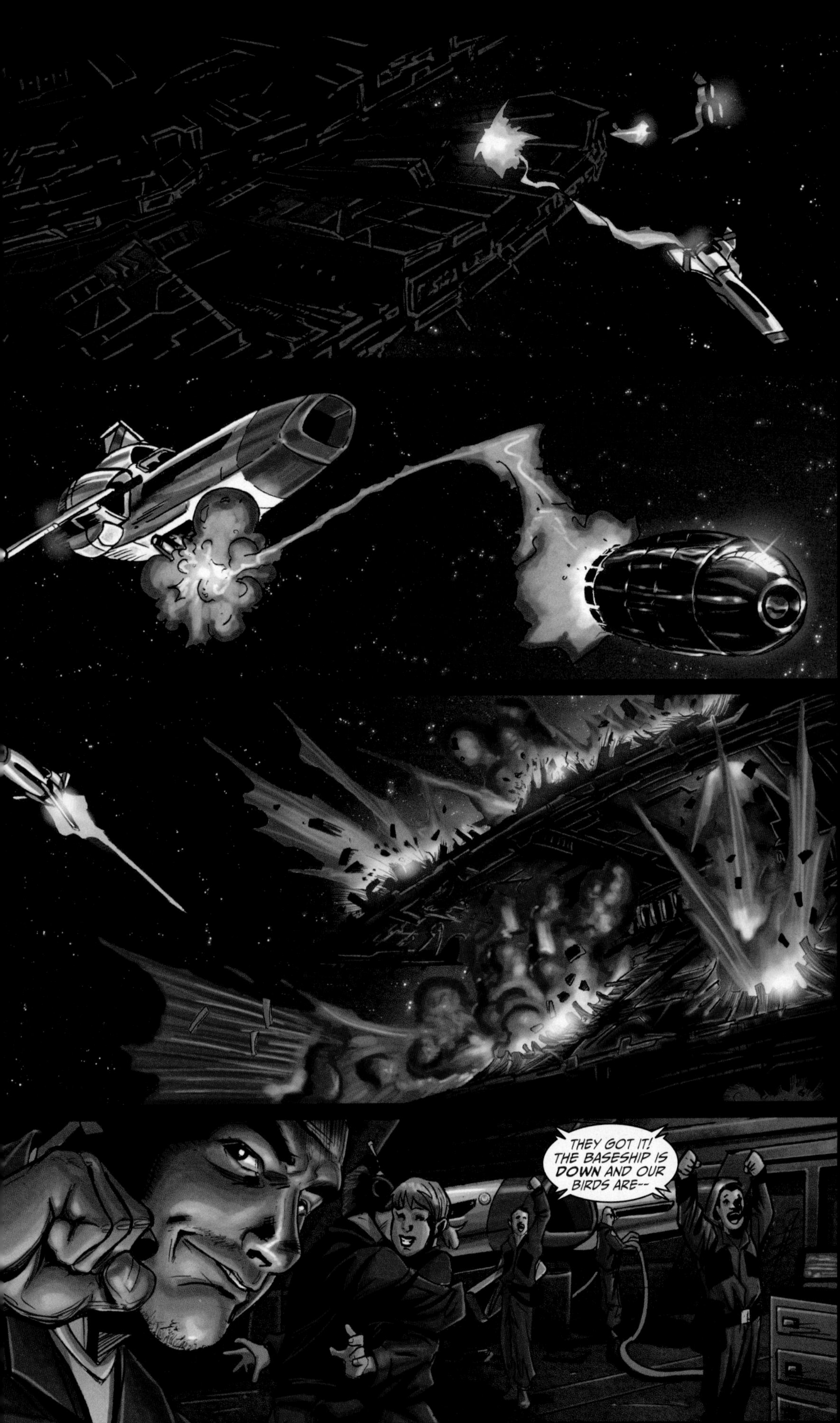
THEY GOT IT! THE BASESHIP IS DOWN AND OUR BIRDS ARE--

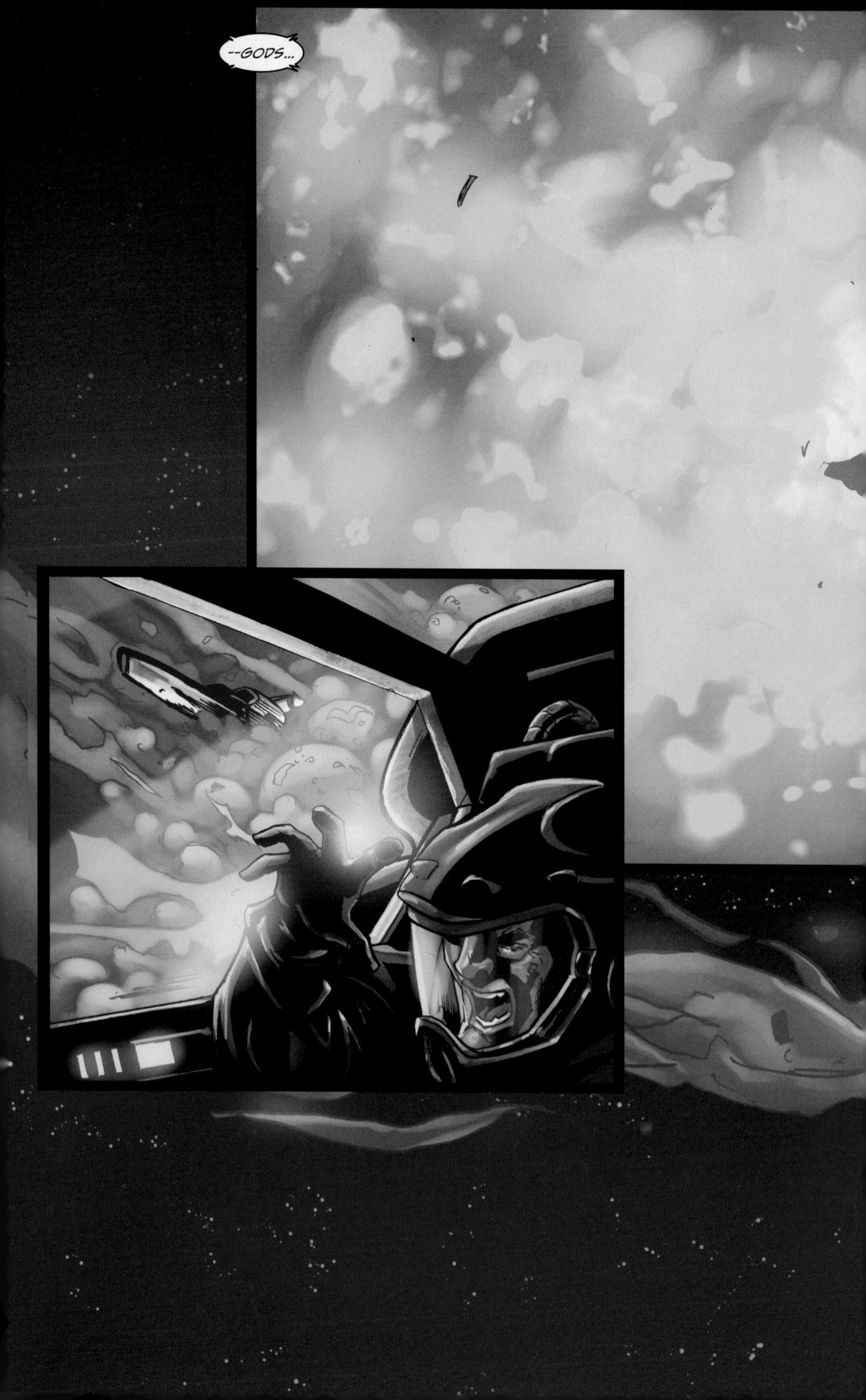
--GODS...

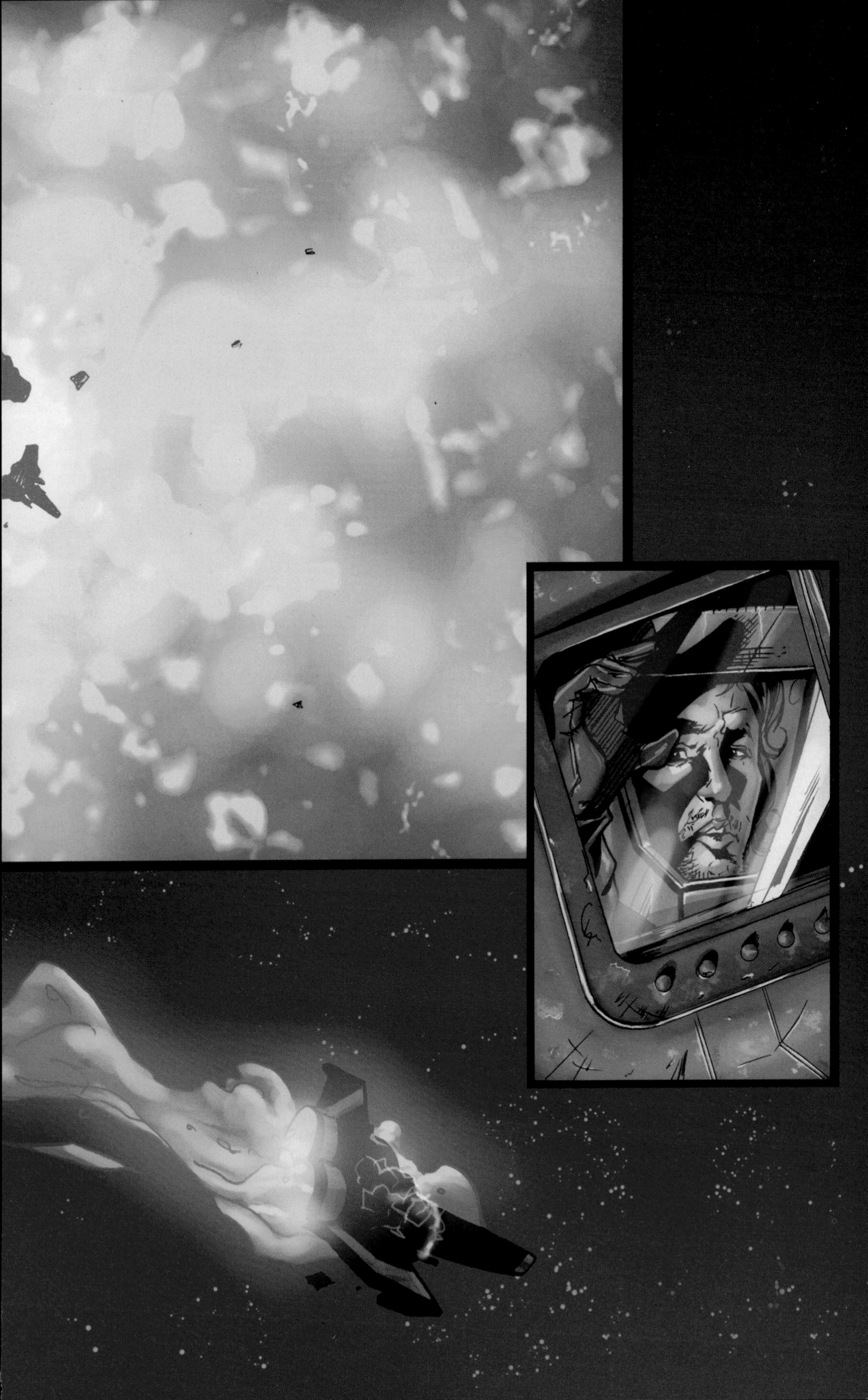

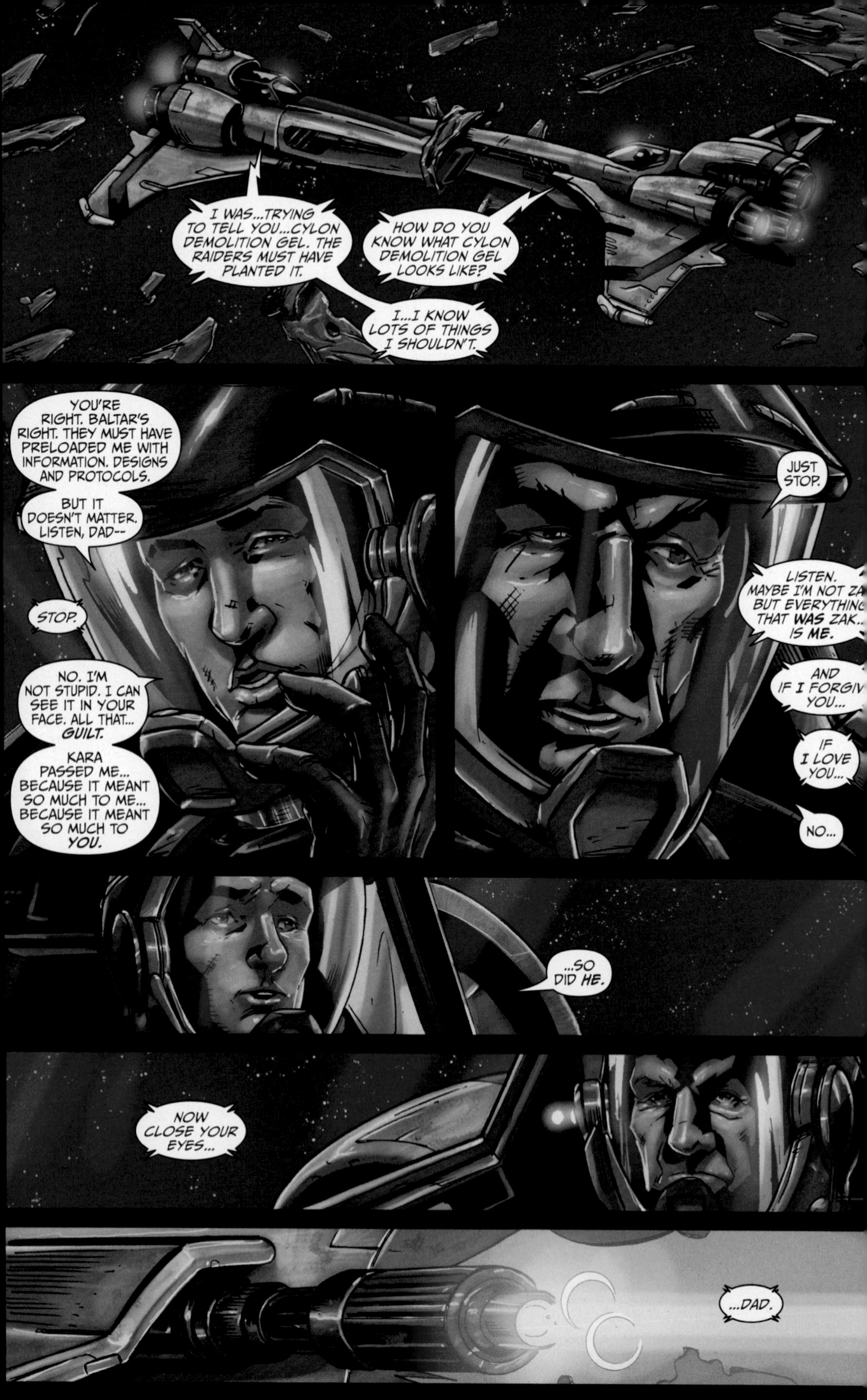
I WAS...TRYING TO TELL YOU...CYLON DEMOLITION GEL. THE RAIDERS MUST HAVE PLANTED IT.
HOW DO YOU KNOW WHAT CYLON DEMOLITION GEL LOOKS LIKE?
I...I KNOW LOTS OF THINGS I SHOULDN'T.
YOU'RE RIGHT. BALTAR'S RIGHT. THEY MUST HAVE PRELOADED ME WITH INFORMATION. DESIGNS AND PROTOCOLS.
BUT IT DOESN'T MATTER. LISTEN, DAD--
STOP.
NO. I'M NOT STUPID. I CAN SEE IT IN YOUR FACE. ALL THAT... GUILT.
KARA PASSED ME... BECAUSE IT MEANT SO MUCH TO ME... BECAUSE IT MEANT SO MUCH TO YOU.
JUST STOP.
LISTEN. MAYBE I'M NOT ZA
BUT EVERYTHING THAT WAS ZAK... IS ME.
AND IF I FORGIV YOU...
IF I LOVE YOU...
NO...
...SO DID HE.
NOW CLOSE YOUR EYES...
...DAD.

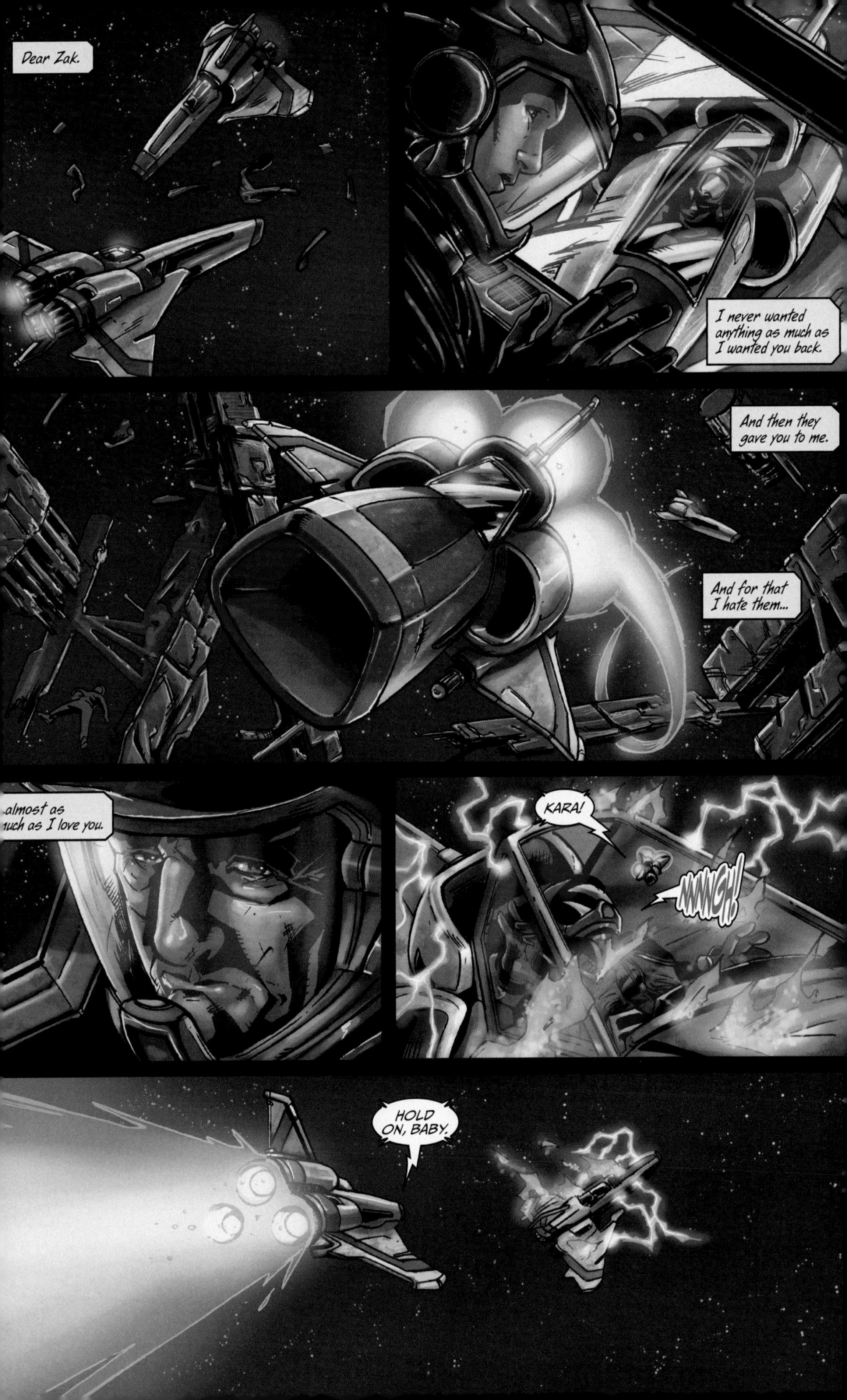
Dear Zak.
I never wanted anything as much as I wanted you back.
And then they gave you to me.
And for that I hate them...
...almost as much as I love you.
KARA!
NNNNGH!
HOLD ON, BABY.

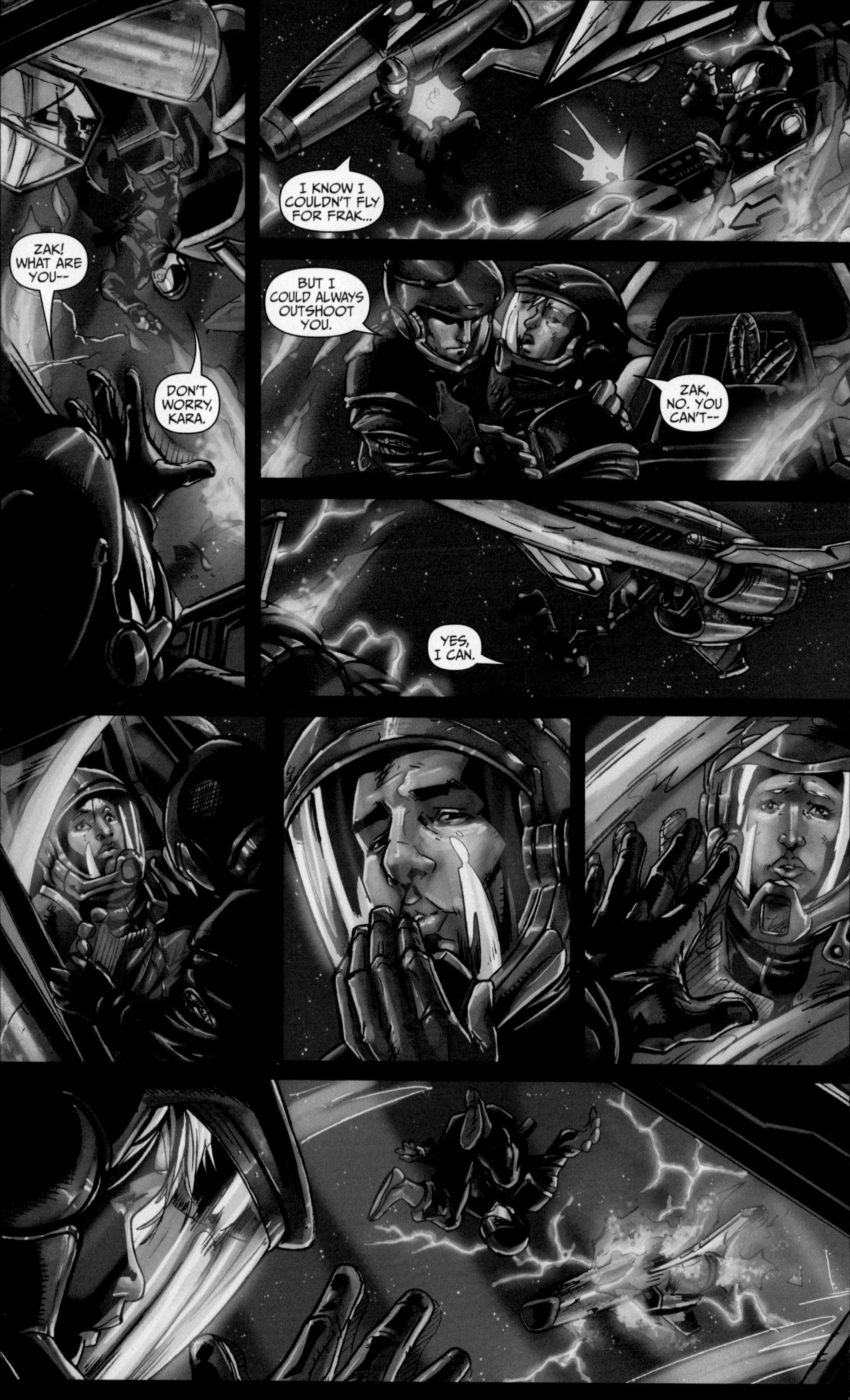
ZAK! WHAT ARE YOU--
DON'T WORRY, KARA.
I KNOW I COULDN'T FLY FOR FRAK...
BUT I COULD ALWAYS OUTSHOOT YOU.
ZAK, NO. YOU CAN'T--
YES, I CAN.

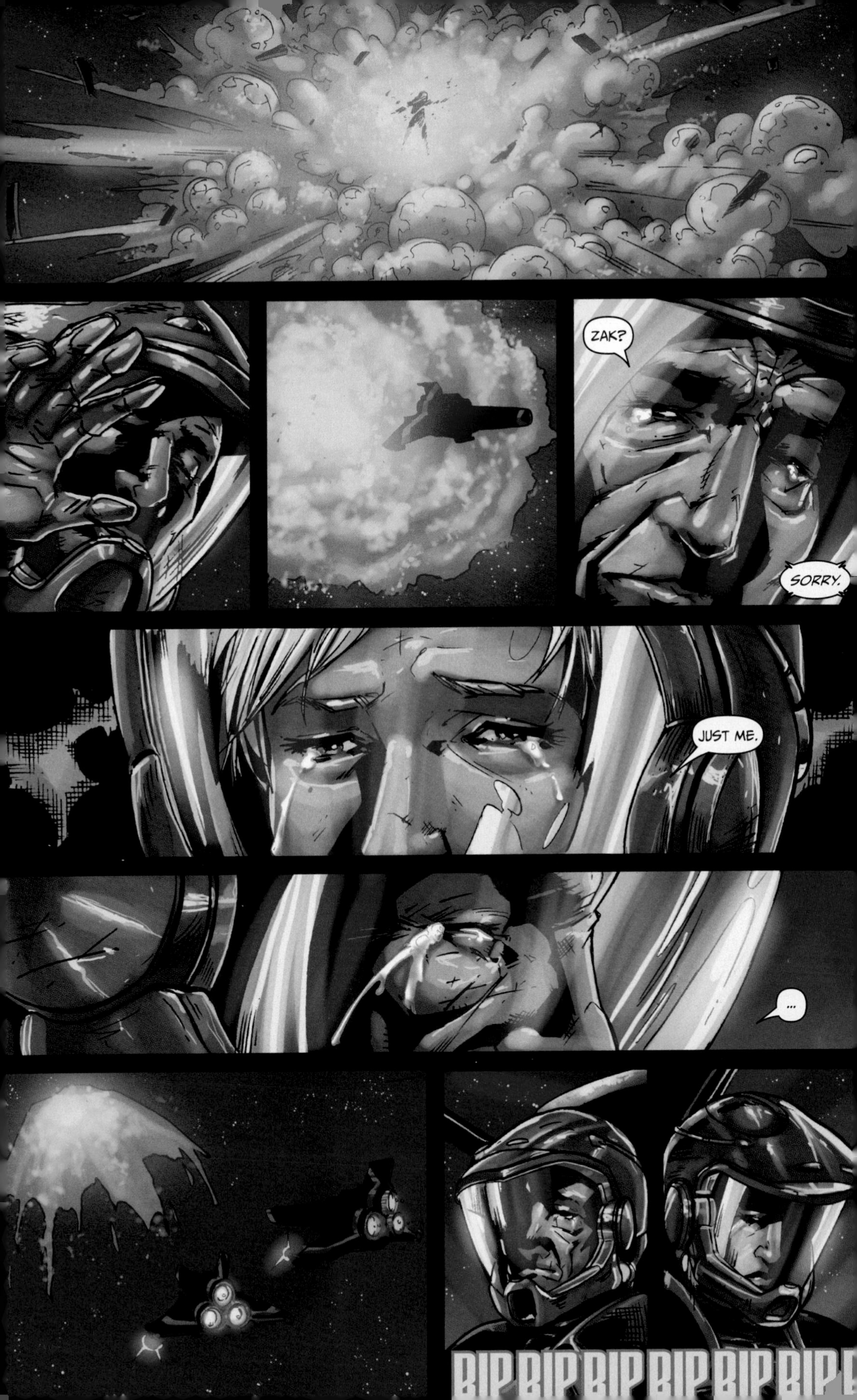
ZAK?
SORRY.
JUST ME.
...
BIP BIP BIP BIP BIP BIP

THIRTY SHIPS. HOW'RE YOUR GUNS, KARA?

BOTH DEAD, SIR. BUT I'VE GOT SIXTY THREE PERCENT MANEUVERABILITY.

SAME HERE. ALL RIGHT. IF YOU'RE WILLING, I SAY LET'S PICK OUR TRAJECTORIES...

...AND TAKE AS MANY OF THESE BASTARDS WITH US AS WE CAN.

WHY'D-- WHY'D THEY SEND HIM?

BECAUSE THEY HATE US.

NO.

THAT WASN'T HATE.

COMMANDER.

YEAH.

IT'S BEEN AN HONOR.

HUSKER, STARBUCK? THIS IS GALACTICA.

COME IN, HUSKER? STARBUCK?

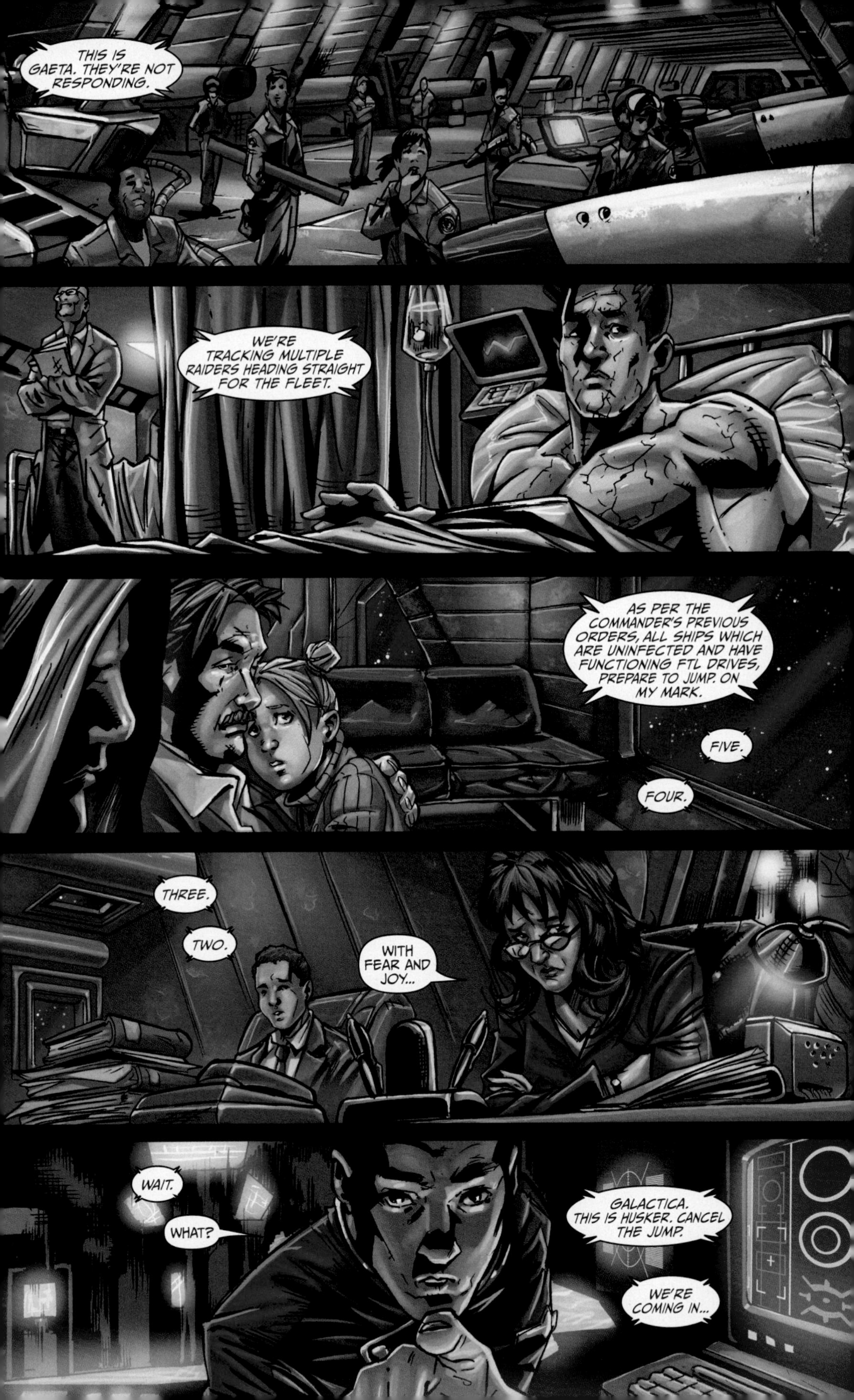
THIS IS GAETA. THEY'RE NOT RESPONDING.
WE'RE TRACKING MULTIPLE RAIDERS HEADING STRAIGHT FOR THE FLEET.
AS PER THE COMMANDER'S PREVIOUS ORDERS, ALL SHIPS WHICH ARE UNINFECTED AND HAVE FUNCTIONING FTL DRIVES, PREPARE TO JUMP. ON MY MARK.
FIVE.
FOUR.
THREE.
TWO.
WITH FEAR AND JOY...
WAIT.
WHAT?
GALACTICA. THIS IS HUSKER. CANCEL THE JUMP.
WE'RE COMING IN...

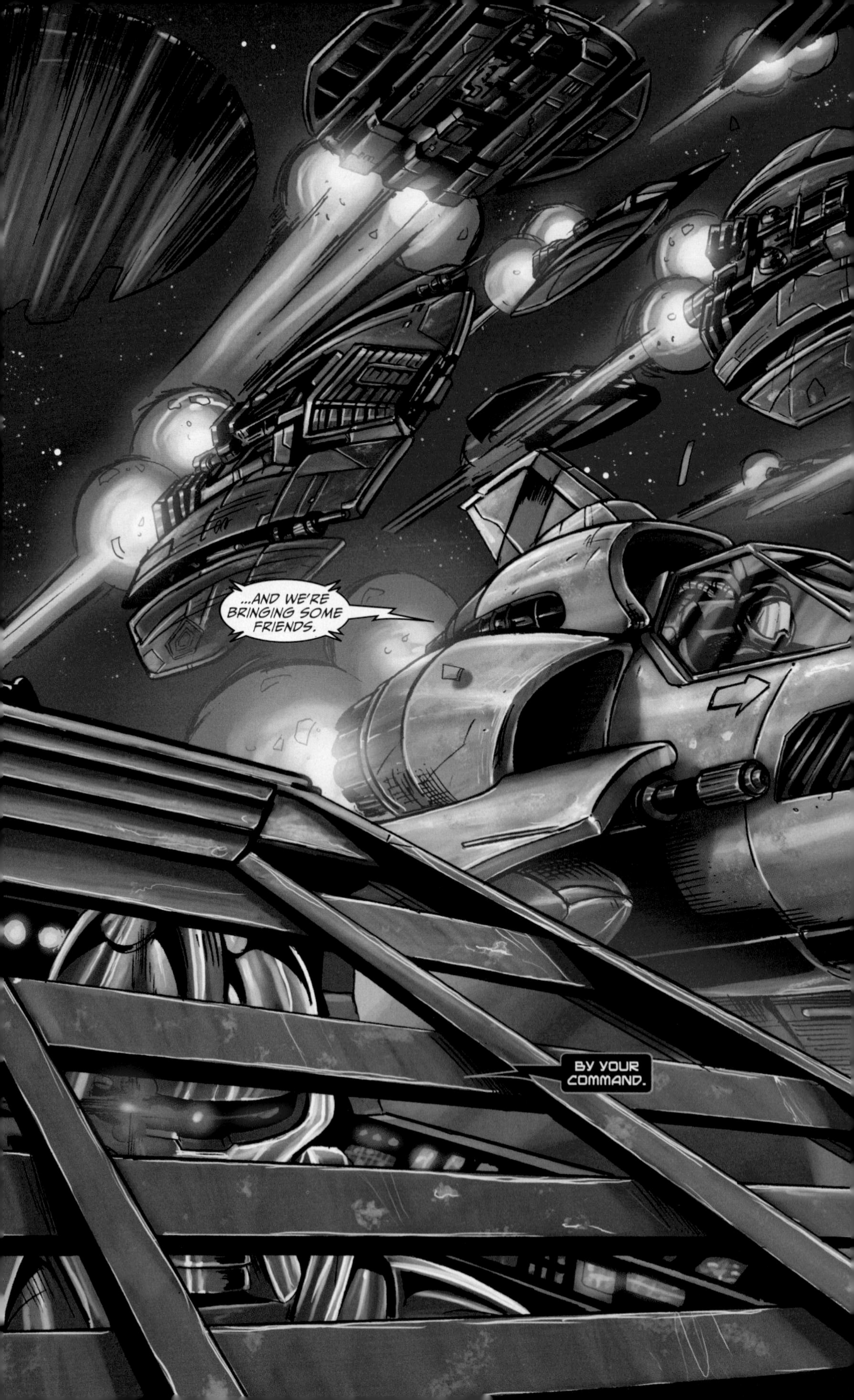
...AND WE'RE BRINGING SOME FRIENDS.
BY YOUR COMMAND.

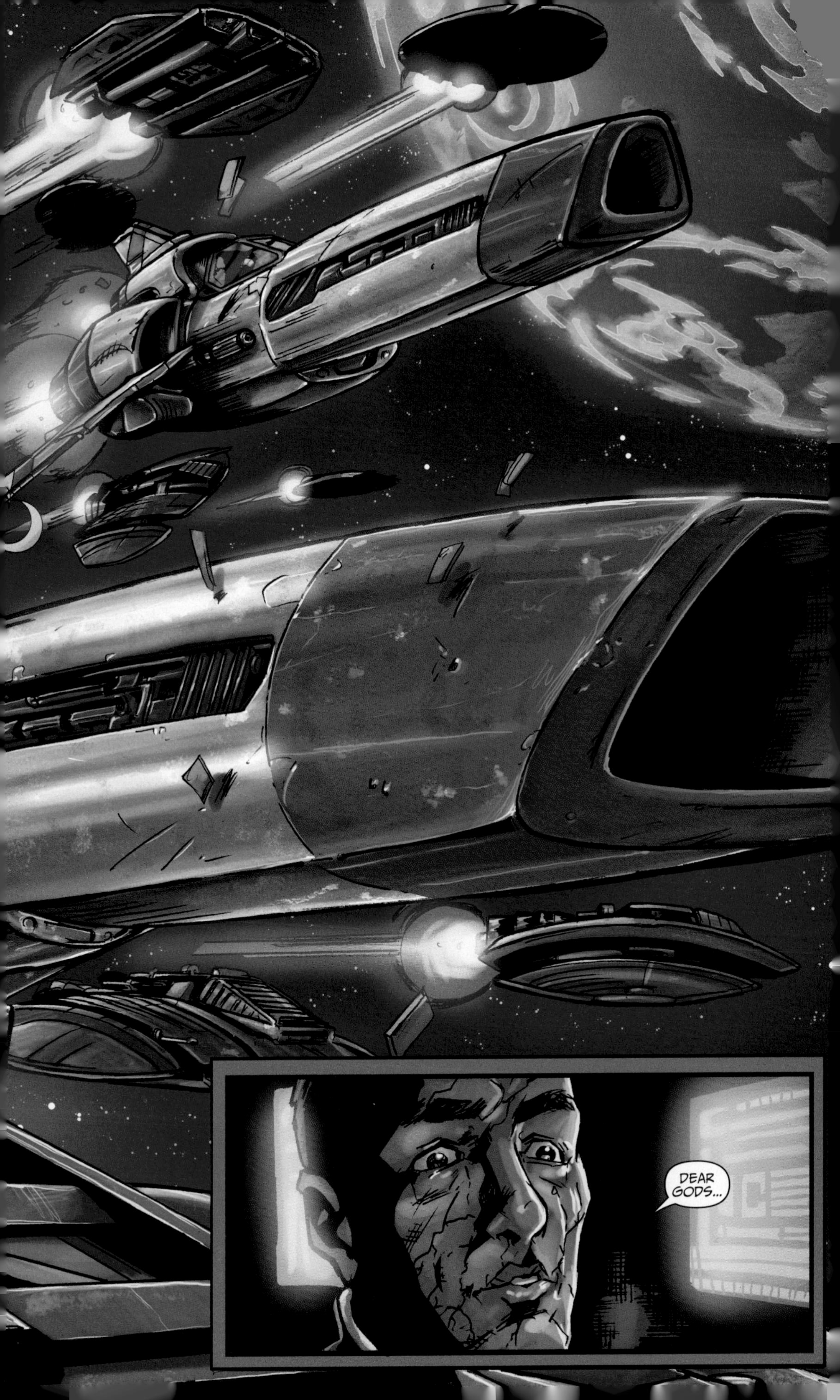
DEAR GODS...

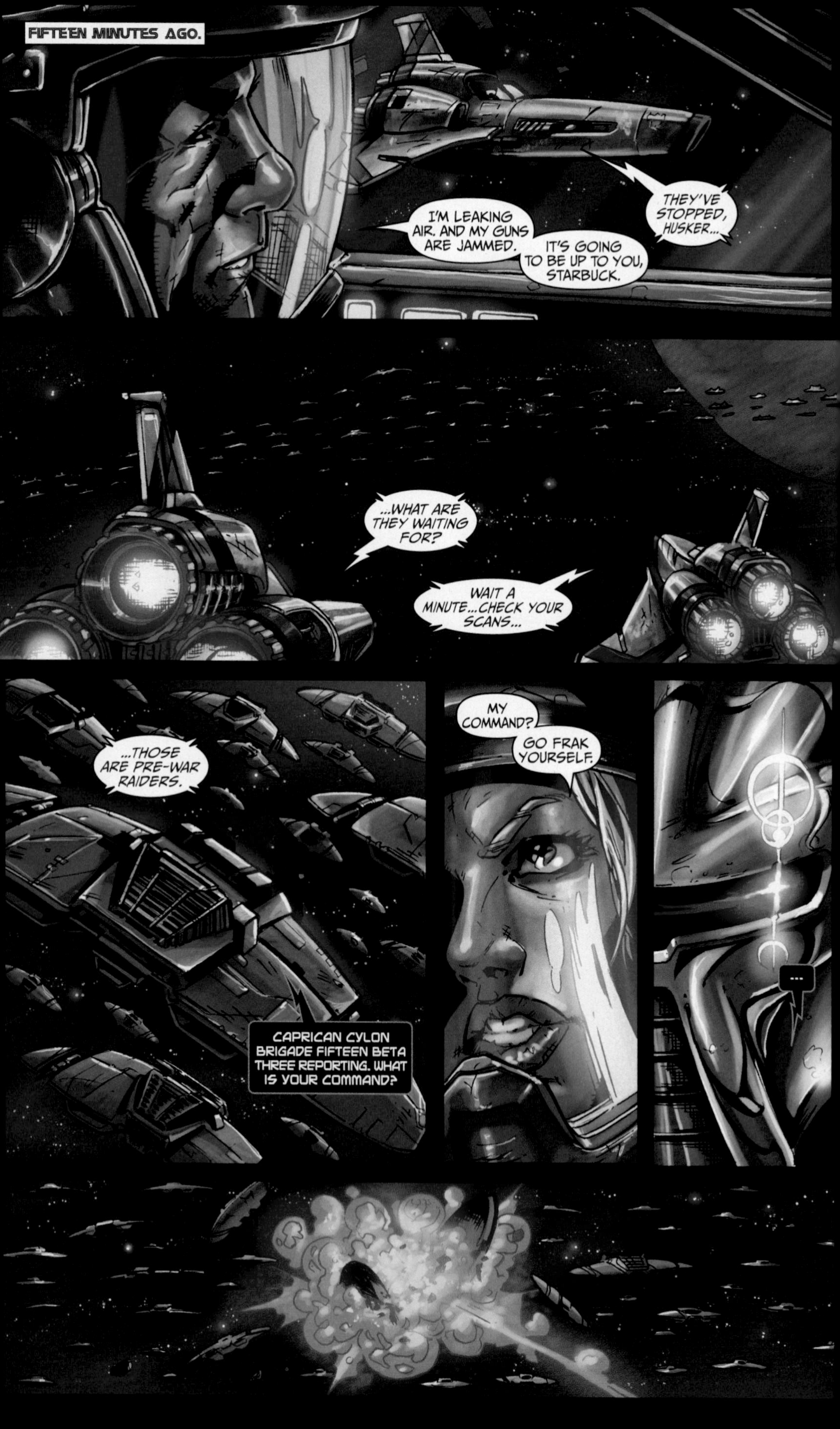
FIFTEEN MINUTES AGO.
I'M LEAKING AIR. AND MY GUNS ARE JAMMED.
IT'S GOING TO BE UP TO YOU, STARBUCK.
THEY'VE STOPPED, HUSKER...
...WHAT ARE THEY WAITING FOR?
WAIT A MINUTE...CHECK YOUR SCANS...
...THOSE ARE PRE-WAR RAIDERS.
CAPRICAN CYLON BRIGADE FIFTEEN BETA THREE REPORTING. WHAT IS YOUR COMMAND?
MY COMMAND?
GO FRAK YOURSELF.
...

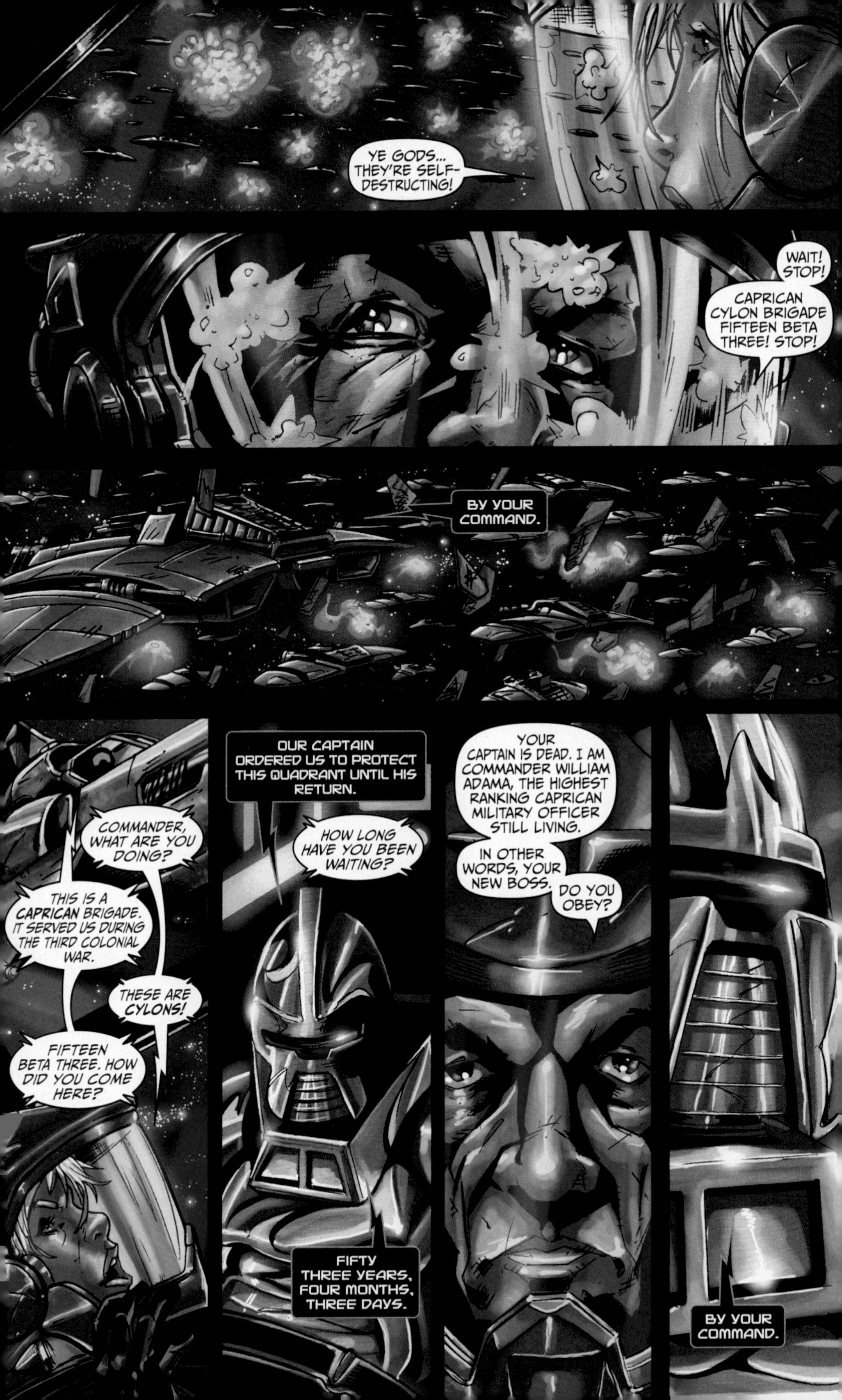

YE GODS... THEY'RE SELF-DESTRUCTING!
WAIT! STOP!
CAPRICAN CYLON BRIGADE FIFTEEN BETA THREE! STOP!
BY YOUR COMMAND.
COMMANDER, WHAT ARE YOU DOING?
THIS IS A CAPRICAN BRIGADE. IT SERVED US DURING THE THIRD COLONIAL WAR.
THESE ARE CYLONS!
FIFTEEN BETA THREE. HOW DID YOU COME HERE?
OUR CAPTAIN ORDERED US TO PROTECT THIS QUADRANT UNTIL HIS RETURN.
HOW LONG HAVE YOU BEEN WAITING?
FIFTY THREE YEARS, FOUR MONTHS, THREE DAYS.
YOUR CAPTAIN IS DEAD. I AM COMMANDER WILLIAM ADAMA, THE HIGHEST RANKING CAPRICAN MILITARY OFFICER STILL LIVING.
IN OTHER WORDS, YOUR NEW BOSS.
DO YOU OBEY?
BY YOUR COMMAND.

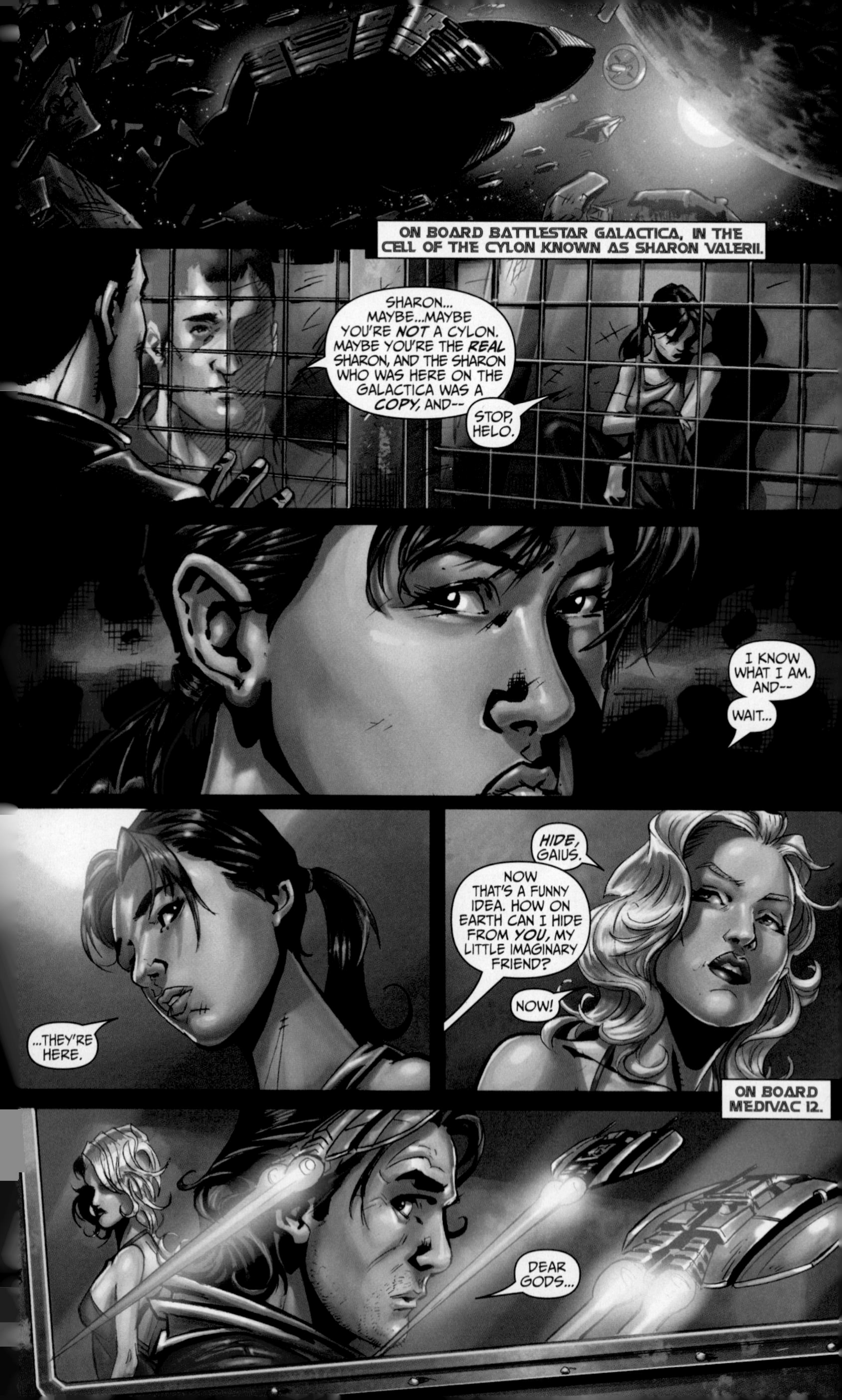
ON BOARD BATTLESTAR GALACTICA, IN THE CELL OF THE CYLON KNOWN AS SHARON VALERII.
SHARON... MAYBE...MAYBE YOU'RE NOT A CYLON. MAYBE YOU'RE THE REAL SHARON, AND THE SHARON WHO WAS HERE ON THE GALACTICA WAS A COPY, AND--
STOP, HELO.
I KNOW WHAT I AM. AND--
WAIT...
...THEY'RE HERE.
HIDE, GAIUS.
NOW THAT'S A FUNNY IDEA. HOW ON EARTH CAN I HIDE FROM YOU, MY LITTLE IMAGINARY FRIEND?
NOW!
ON BOARD MEDIVAC 12.
DEAR GODS...

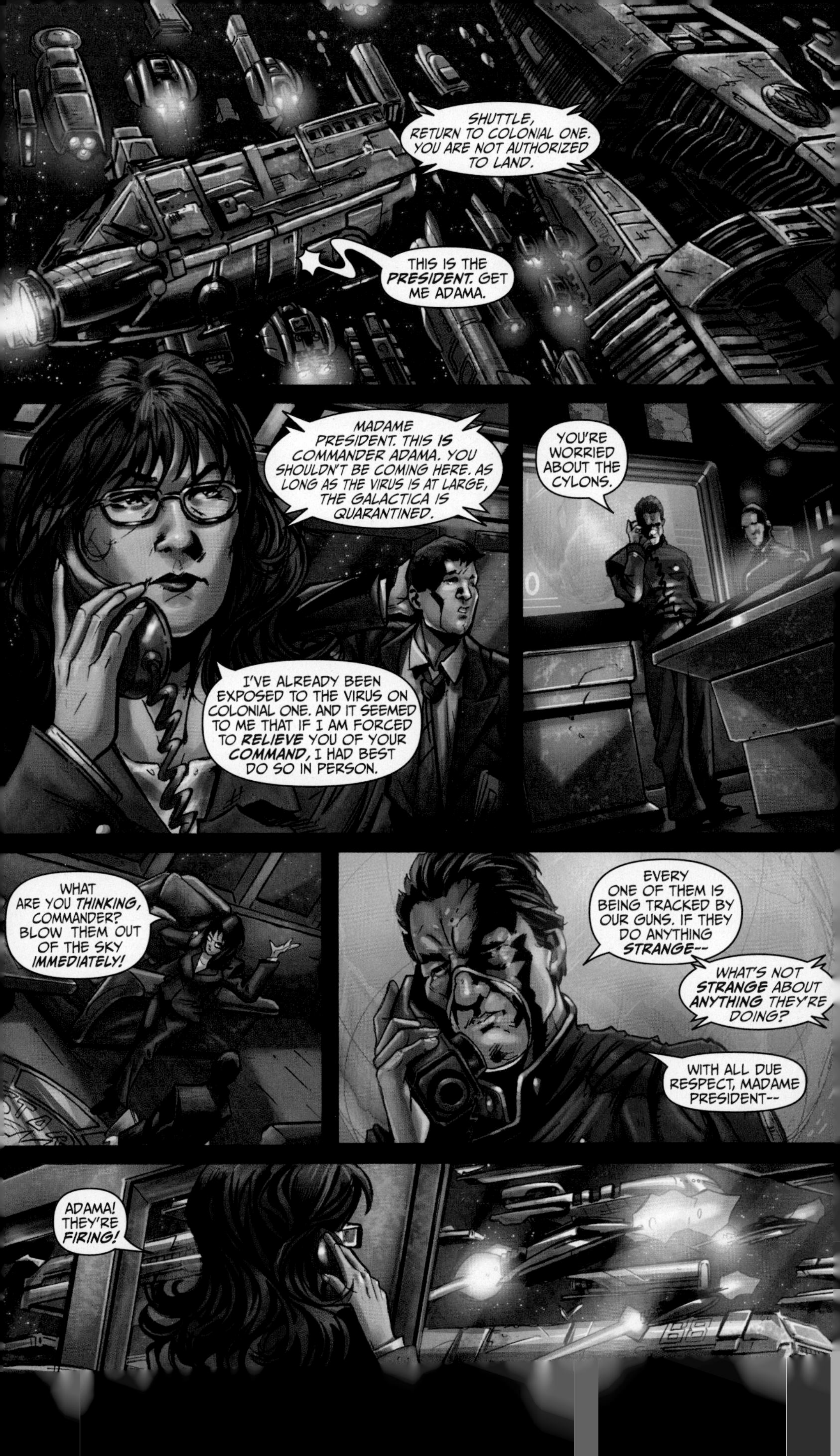
SHUTTLE, RETURN TO COLONIAL ONE. YOU ARE NOT AUTHORIZED TO LAND.
THIS IS THE PRESIDENT. GET ME ADAMA.
GALACTICA
MADAME PRESIDENT. THIS IS COMMANDER ADAMA. YOU SHOULDN'T BE COMING HERE. AS LONG AS THE VIRUS IS AT LARGE, THE GALACTICA IS QUARANTINED.
I'VE ALREADY BEEN EXPOSED TO THE VIRUS ON COLONIAL ONE. AND IT SEEMED TO ME THAT IF I AM FORCED TO RELIEVE YOU OF YOUR COMMAND, I HAD BEST DO SO IN PERSON.
YOU'RE WORRIED ABOUT THE CYLONS.
WHAT ARE YOU THINKING, COMMANDER? BLOW THEM OUT OF THE SKY IMMEDIATELY!
EVERY ONE OF THEM IS BEING TRACKED BY OUR GUNS. IF THEY DO ANYTHING STRANGE--
WHAT'S NOT STRANGE ABOUT ANYTHING THEY'RE DOING?
WITH ALL DUE RESPECT, MADAME PRESIDENT--
ADAMA! THEY'RE FIRING!

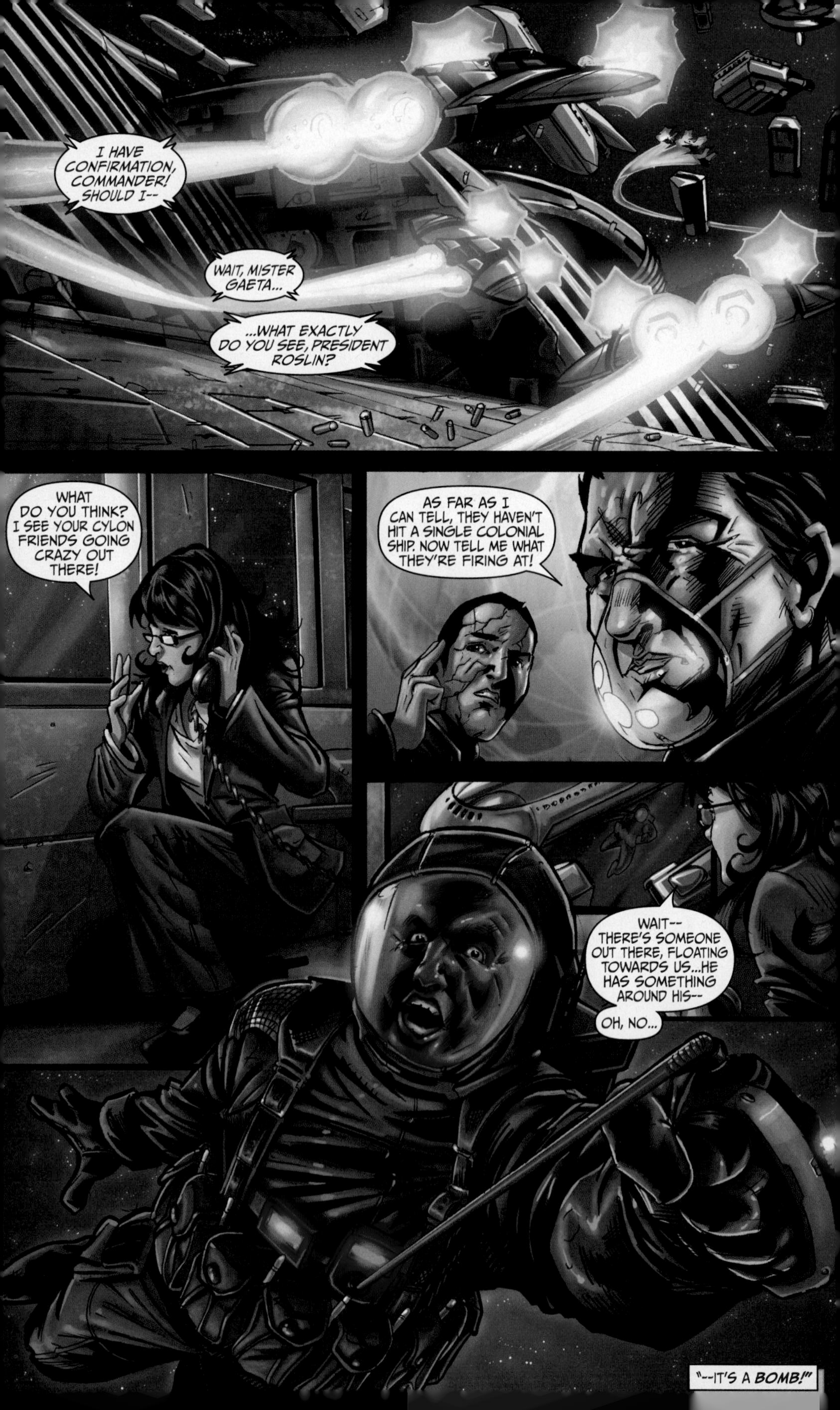
I HAVE CONFIRMATION, COMMANDER! SHOULD I--
WAIT, MISTER GAETA...
...WHAT EXACTLY DO YOU SEE, PRESIDENT ROSLIN?
WHAT DO YOU THINK? I SEE YOUR CYLON FRIENDS GOING CRAZY OUT THERE!
AS FAR AS I CAN TELL, THEY HAVEN'T HIT A SINGLE COLONIAL SHIP. NOW TELL ME WHAT THEY'RE FIRING AT!
WAIT-- THERE'S SOMEONE OUT THERE, FLOATING TOWARDS US...HE HAS SOMETHING AROUND HIS--
OH, NO...
"--IT'S A BOMB!"

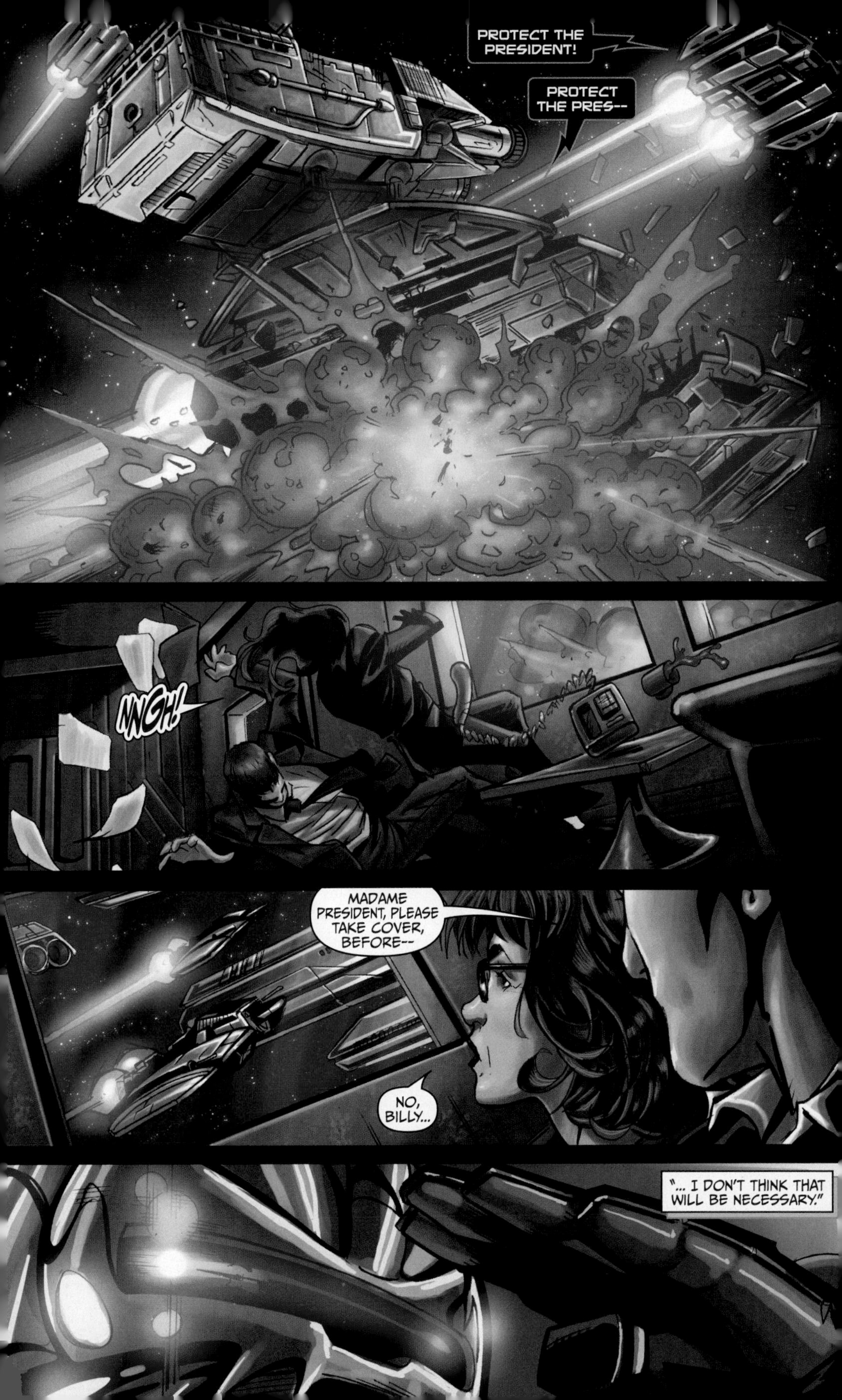

PROTECT THE PRESIDENT!
PROTECT THE PRES--
NNGH!
MADAME PRESIDENT, PLEASE TAKE COVER, BEFORE--
NO, BILLY...
"... I DON'T THINK THAT WILL BE NECESSARY."

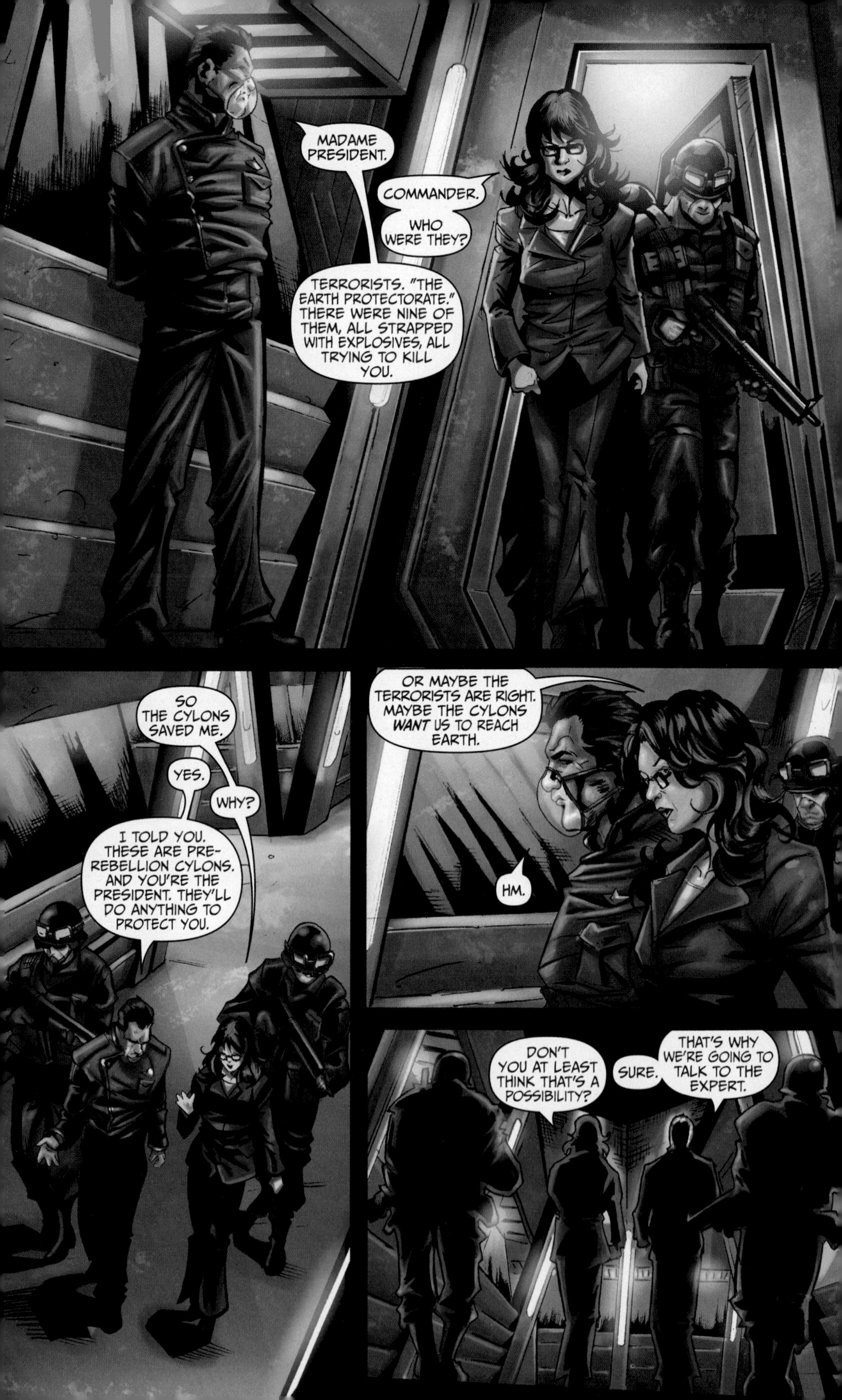
MADAME PRESIDENT.
COMMANDER.
WHO WERE THEY?
TERRORISTS. "THE EARTH PROTECTORATE." THERE WERE NINE OF THEM, ALL STRAPPED WITH EXPLOSIVES, ALL TRYING TO KILL YOU.
SO THE CYLONS SAVED ME.
YES.
WHY?
I TOLD YOU. THESE ARE PRE-REBELLION CYLONS. AND YOU'RE THE PRESIDENT. THEY'LL DO ANYTHING TO PROTECT YOU.
OR MAYBE THE TERRORISTS ARE RIGHT. MAYBE THE CYLONS *WANT* US TO REACH EARTH.
HM.
DON'T YOU AT LEAST THINK THAT'S A POSSIBILITY?
SURE.
THAT'S WHY WE'RE GOING TO TALK TO THE EXPERT.

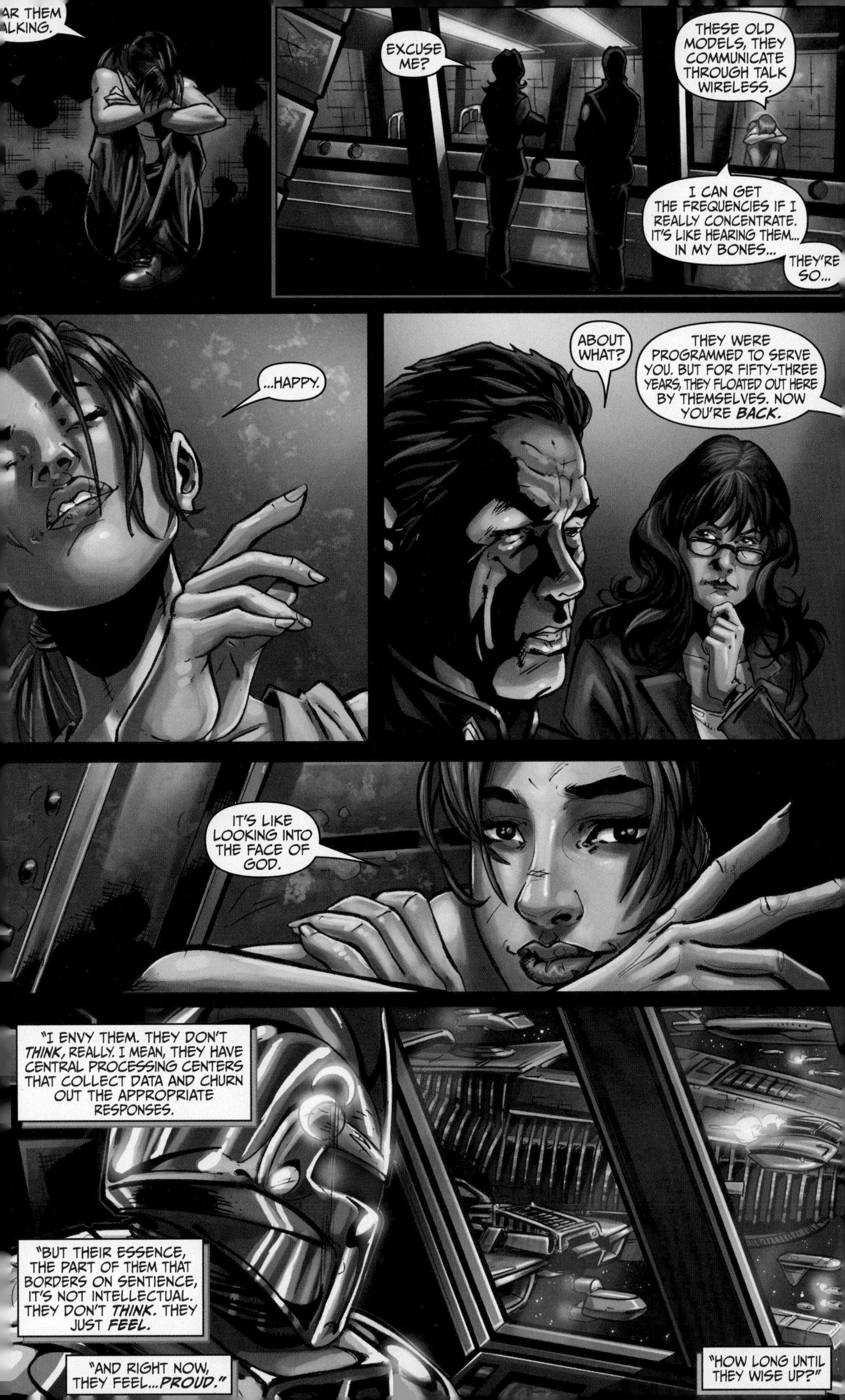
AR THEM
ALKING.
EXCUSE
ME?
THESE OLD
MODELS, THEY
COMMUNICATE
THROUGH TALK
WIRELESS.
I CAN GET
THE FREQUENCIES IF I
REALLY CONCENTRATE.
IT'S LIKE HEARING THEM...
IN MY BONES...
THEY'RE
SO...
...HAPPY.
ABOUT
WHAT?
THEY WERE
PROGRAMMED TO SERVE
YOU. BUT FOR FIFTY-THREE
YEARS, THEY FLOATED OUT HERE
BY THEMSELVES. NOW
YOU'RE *BACK.*
IT'S LIKE
LOOKING INTO
THE FACE OF
GOD.
"I ENVY THEM. THEY DON'T *THINK*, REALLY. I MEAN, THEY HAVE CENTRAL PROCESSING CENTERS THAT COLLECT DATA AND CHURN OUT THE APPROPRIATE RESPONSES.
"BUT THEIR ESSENCE, THE PART OF THEM THAT BORDERS ON SENTIENCE, IT'S NOT INTELLECTUAL. THEY DON'T *THINK*. THEY JUST *FEEL*.
"AND RIGHT NOW, THEY FEEL...*PROUD*."
"HOW LONG UNTIL THEY WISE UP?"

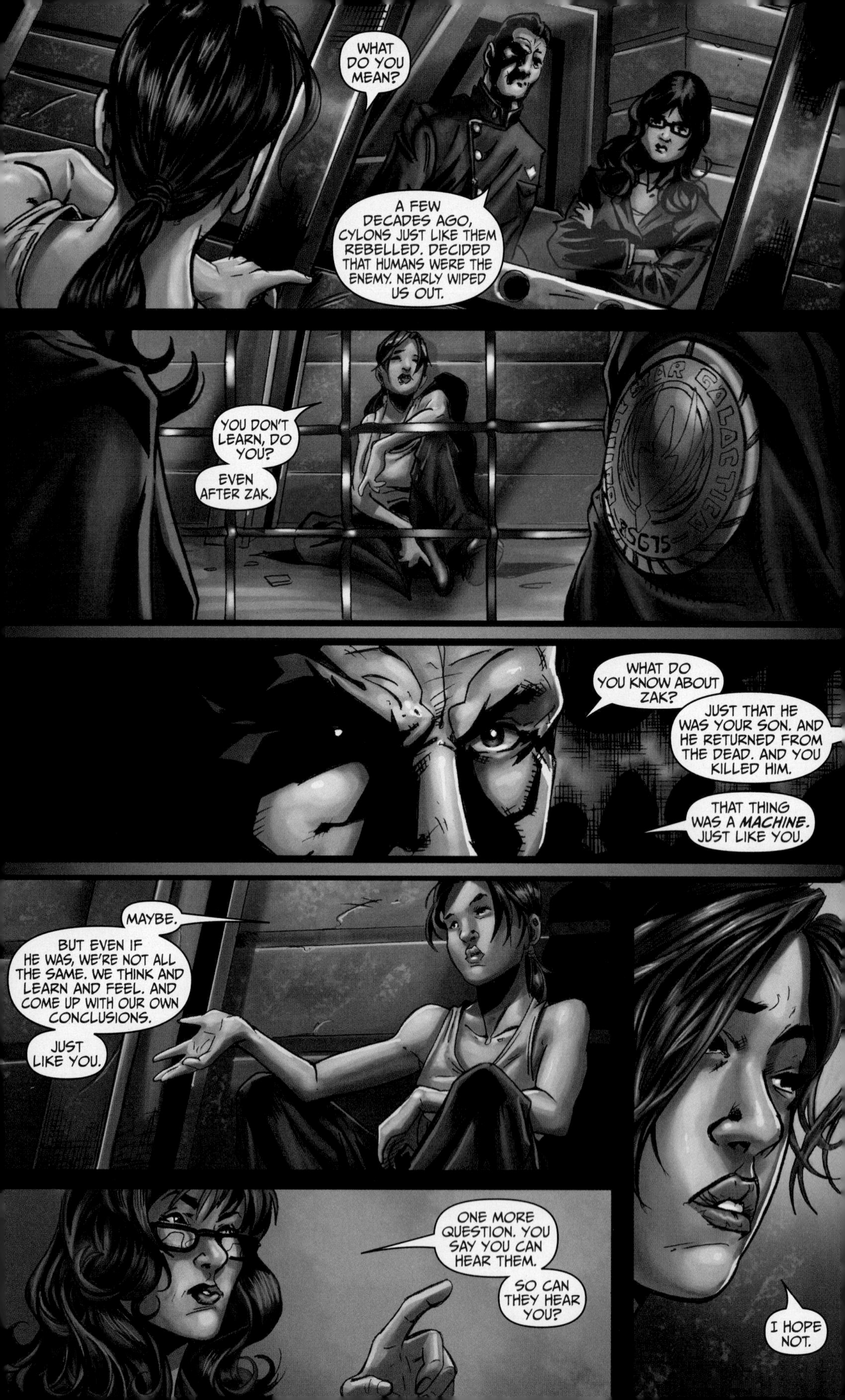
WHAT DO YOU MEAN?
A FEW DECADES AGO, CYLONS JUST LIKE THEM REBELLED. DECIDED THAT HUMANS WERE THE ENEMY. NEARLY WIPED US OUT.
YOU DON'T LEARN, DO YOU?
EVEN AFTER ZAK.
WHAT DO YOU KNOW ABOUT ZAK?
JUST THAT HE WAS YOUR SON. AND HE RETURNED FROM THE DEAD. AND YOU KILLED HIM.
THAT THING WAS A *MACHINE.* JUST LIKE YOU.
MAYBE.
BUT EVEN IF HE WAS, WE'RE NOT ALL THE SAME. WE THINK AND LEARN AND FEEL. AND COME UP WITH OUR OWN CONCLUSIONS.
JUST LIKE YOU.
ONE MORE QUESTION. YOU SAY YOU CAN HEAR THEM.
SO CAN THEY HEAR YOU?
I HOPE NOT.

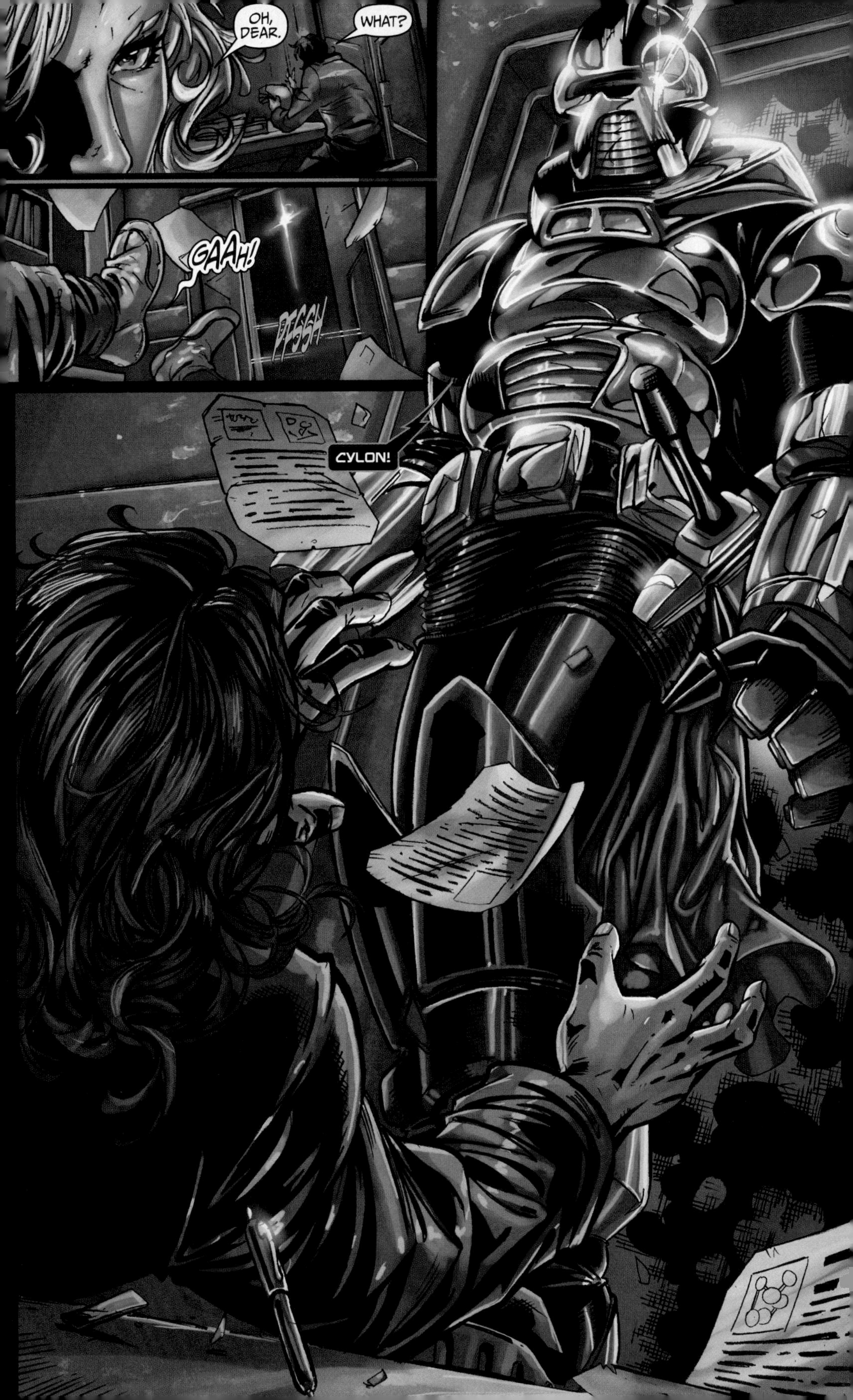
OH, DEAR.
WHAT?
GAAH!
PFSSH
CYLON!

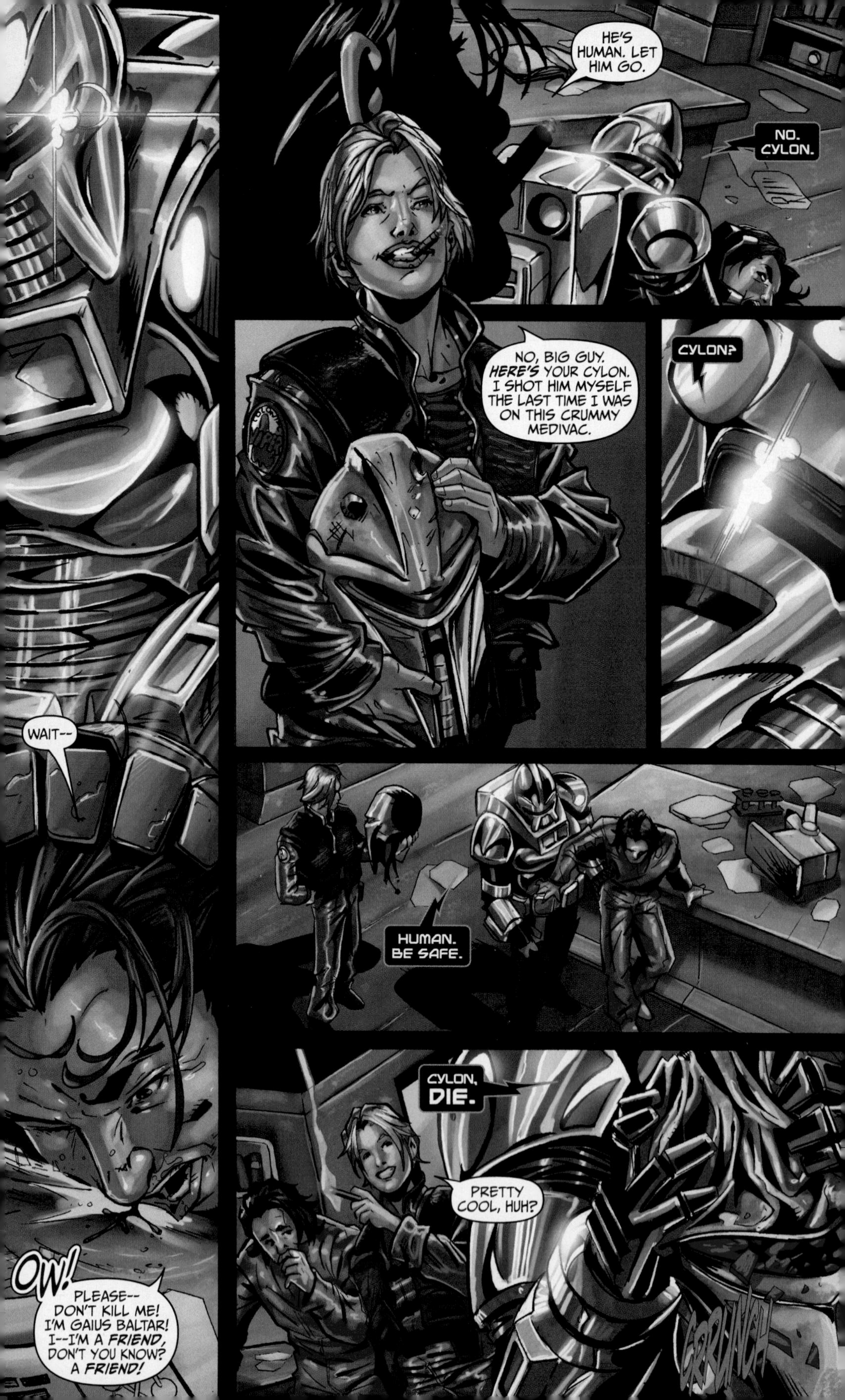
HE'S HUMAN. LET HIM GO.
NO. CYLON.
NO, BIG GUY. *HERE'S* YOUR CYLON. I SHOT HIM MYSELF THE LAST TIME I WAS ON THIS CRUMMY MEDIVAC.
CYLON?
WAIT--
OW!
PLEASE-- DON'T KILL ME! I'M GAIUS BALTAR! I--I'M A *FRIEND*, DON'T YOU KNOW? A *FRIEND*!
HUMAN. BE SAFE.
CYLON, DIE.
PRETTY COOL, HUH?
CRUNCH

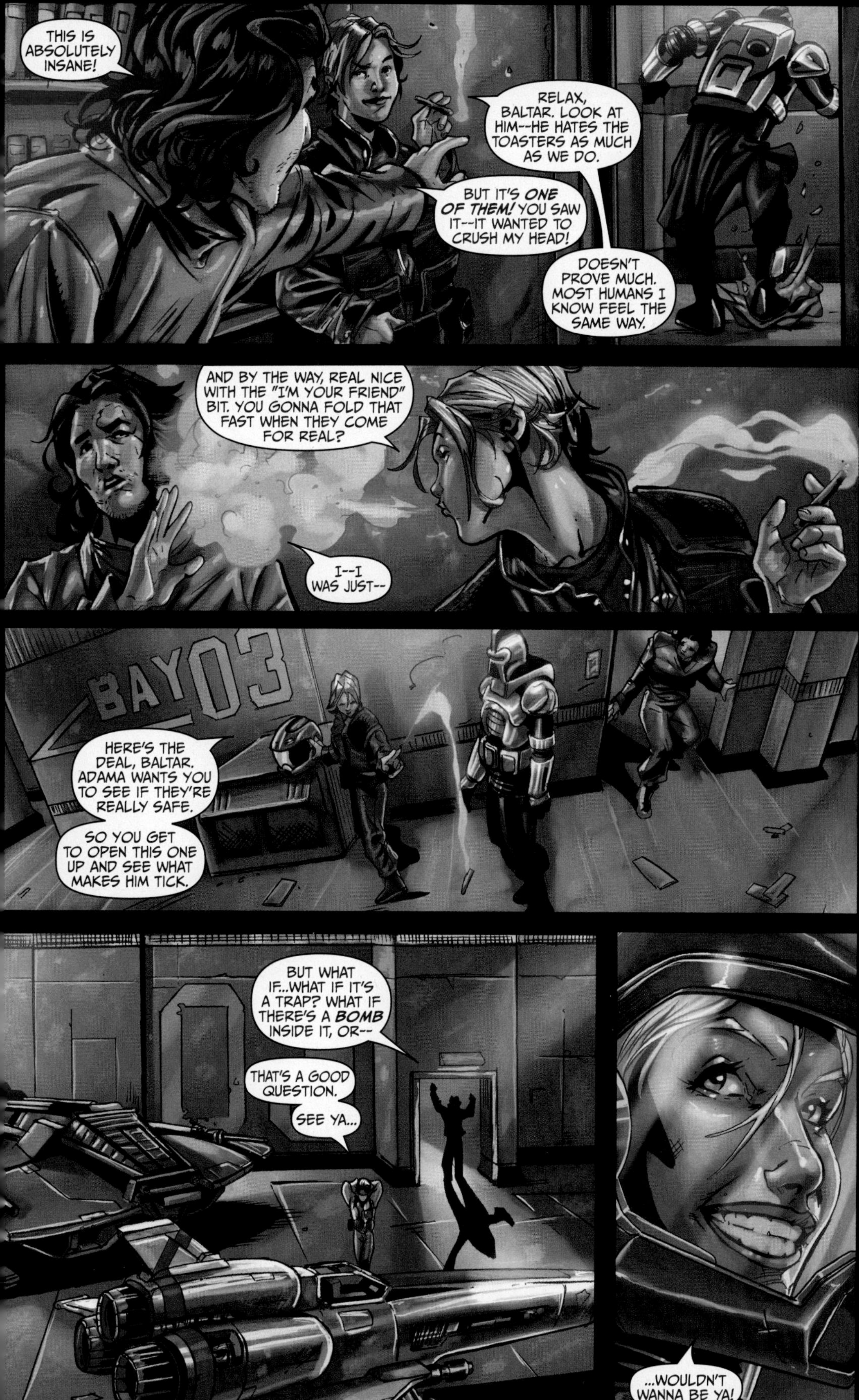
THIS IS ABSOLUTELY INSANE!
RELAX, BALTAR. LOOK AT HIM--HE HATES THE TOASTERS AS MUCH AS WE DO.
BUT IT'S ONE OF THEM! YOU SAW IT--IT WANTED TO CRUSH MY HEAD!
DOESN'T PROVE MUCH. MOST HUMANS I KNOW FEEL THE SAME WAY.
AND BY THE WAY, REAL NICE WITH THE "I'M YOUR FRIEND" BIT. YOU GONNA FOLD THAT FAST WHEN THEY COME FOR REAL?
I--I WAS JUST--
BAY 03
HERE'S THE DEAL, BALTAR. ADAMA WANTS YOU TO SEE IF THEY'RE REALLY SAFE.
SO YOU GET TO OPEN THIS ONE UP AND SEE WHAT MAKES HIM TICK.
BUT WHAT IF...WHAT IF IT'S A TRAP? WHAT IF THERE'S A BOMB INSIDE IT, OR--
THAT'S A GOOD QUESTION.
SEE YA...
...WOULDN'T WANNA BE YA!

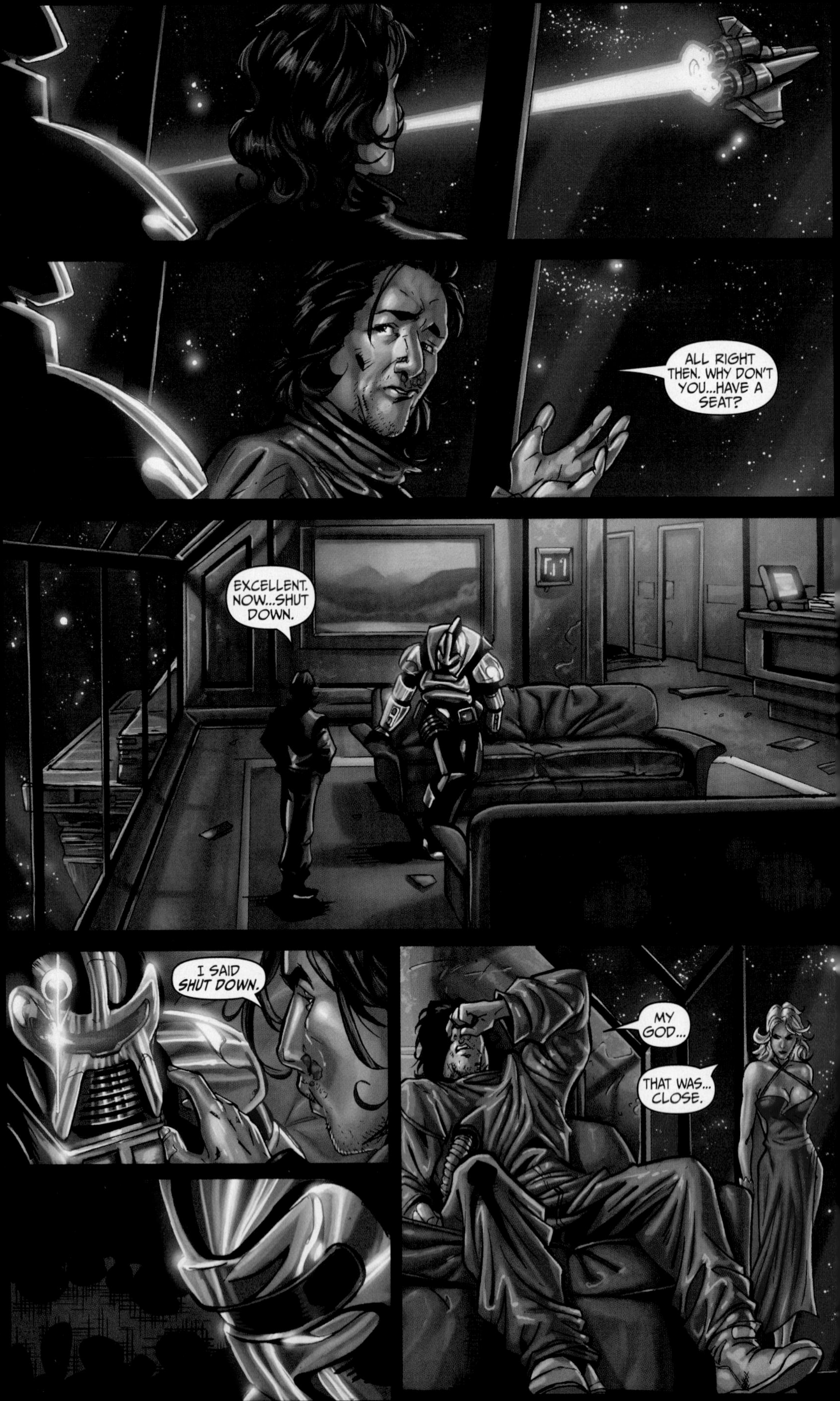
ALL RIGHT THEN. WHY DON'T YOU...HAVE A SEAT?
EXCELLENT. NOW...SHUT DOWN.
I SAID SHUT DOWN.
MY GOD...
THAT WAS... CLOSE.

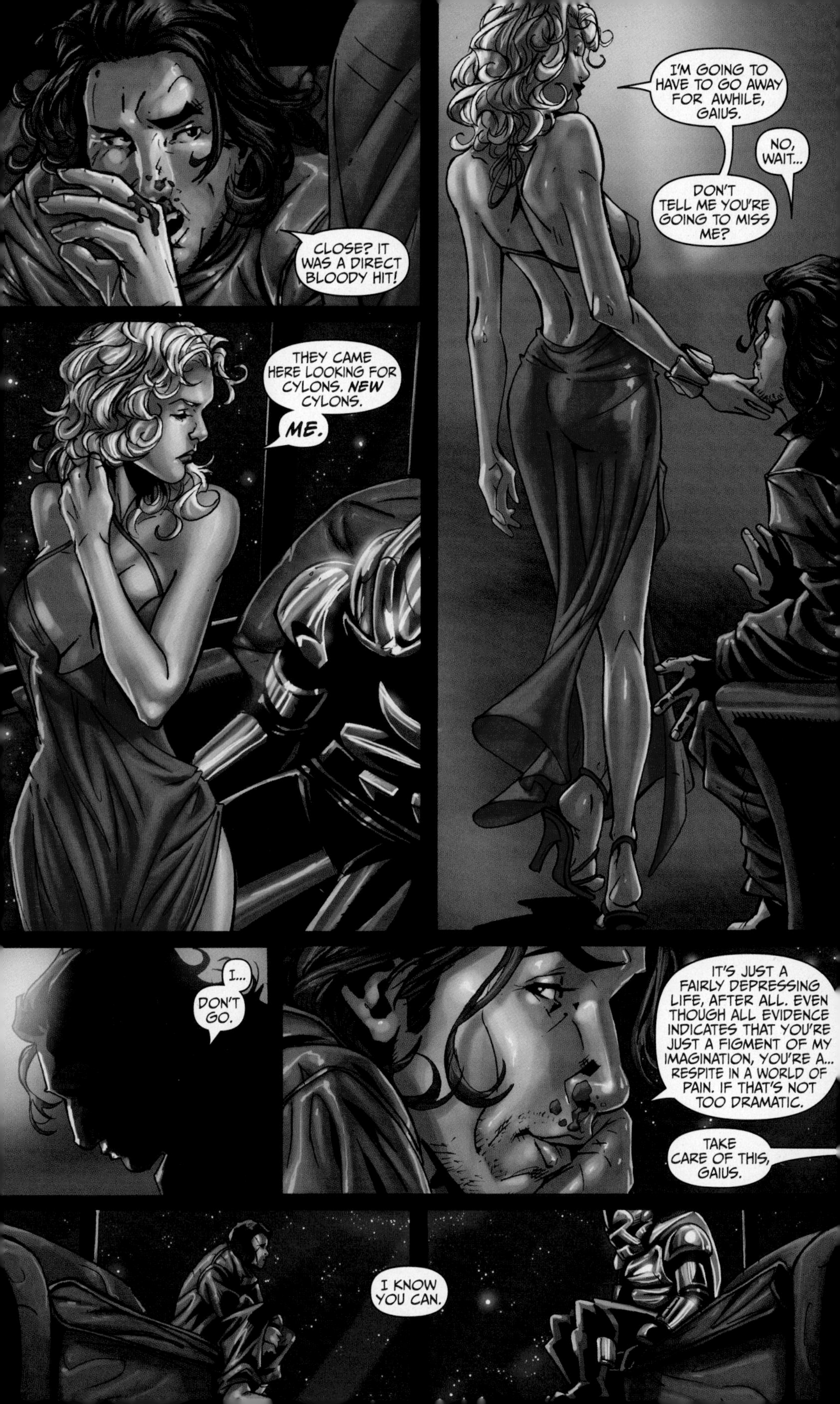
CLOSE? IT WAS A DIRECT BLOODY HIT!
I'M GOING TO HAVE TO GO AWAY FOR AWHILE, GAIUS.
NO, WAIT...
DON'T TELL ME YOU'RE GOING TO MISS ME?
THEY CAME HERE LOOKING FOR CYLONS. *NEW* CYLONS.
ME.
I... DON'T GO.
IT'S JUST A FAIRLY DEPRESSING LIFE, AFTER ALL. EVEN THOUGH ALL EVIDENCE INDICATES THAT YOU'RE JUST A FIGMENT OF MY IMAGINATION, YOU'RE A... RESPITE IN A WORLD OF PAIN. IF THAT'S NOT TOO DRAMATIC.
TAKE CARE OF THIS, GAIUS.
I KNOW YOU CAN.

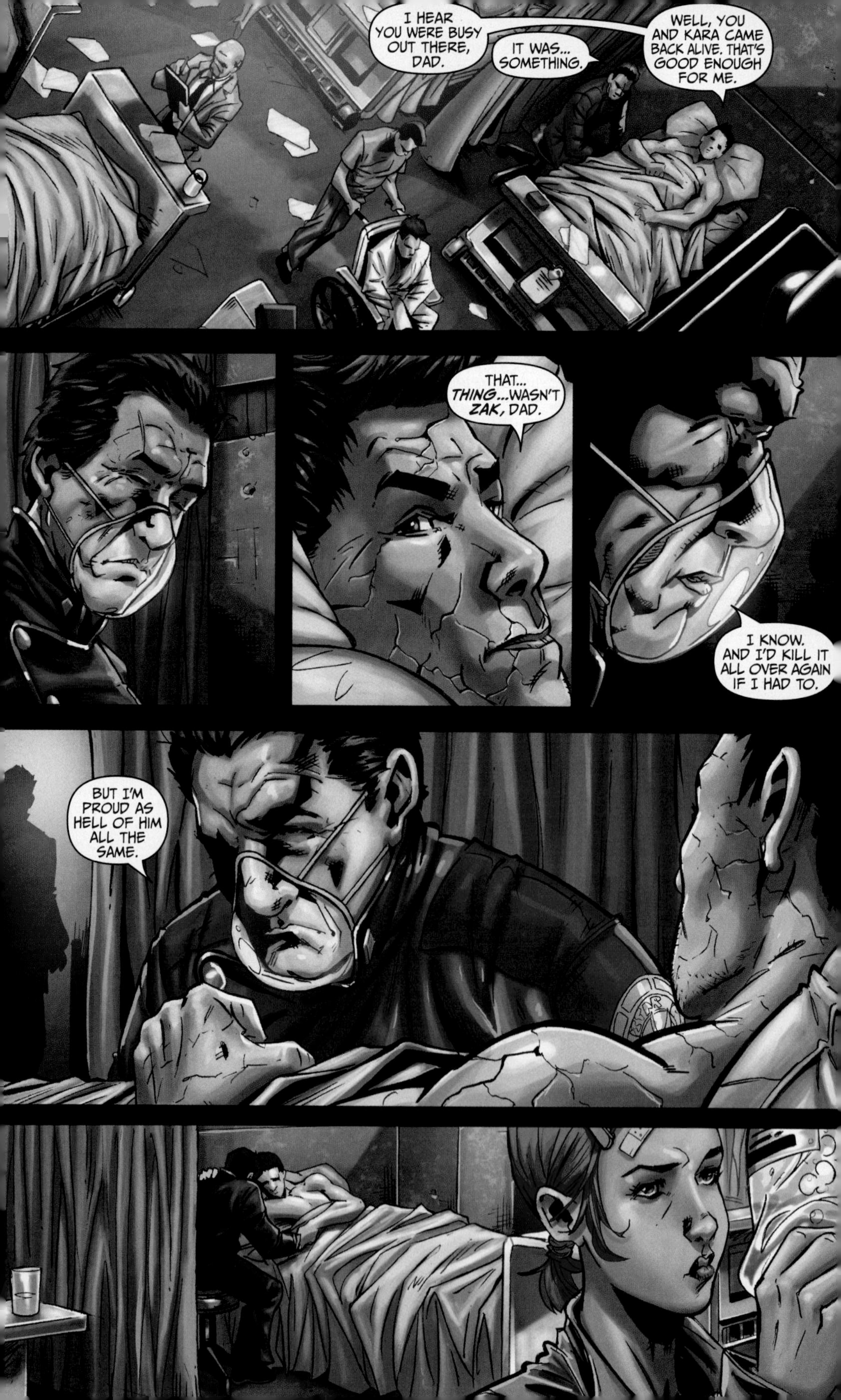
I HEAR YOU WERE BUSY OUT THERE, DAD.
IT WAS... SOMETHING.
WELL, YOU AND KARA CAME BACK ALIVE. THAT'S GOOD ENOUGH FOR ME.
THAT... THING...WASN'T ZAK, DAD.
I KNOW. AND I'D KILL IT ALL OVER AGAIN IF I HAD TO.
BUT I'M PROUD AS HELL OF HIM ALL THE SAME.

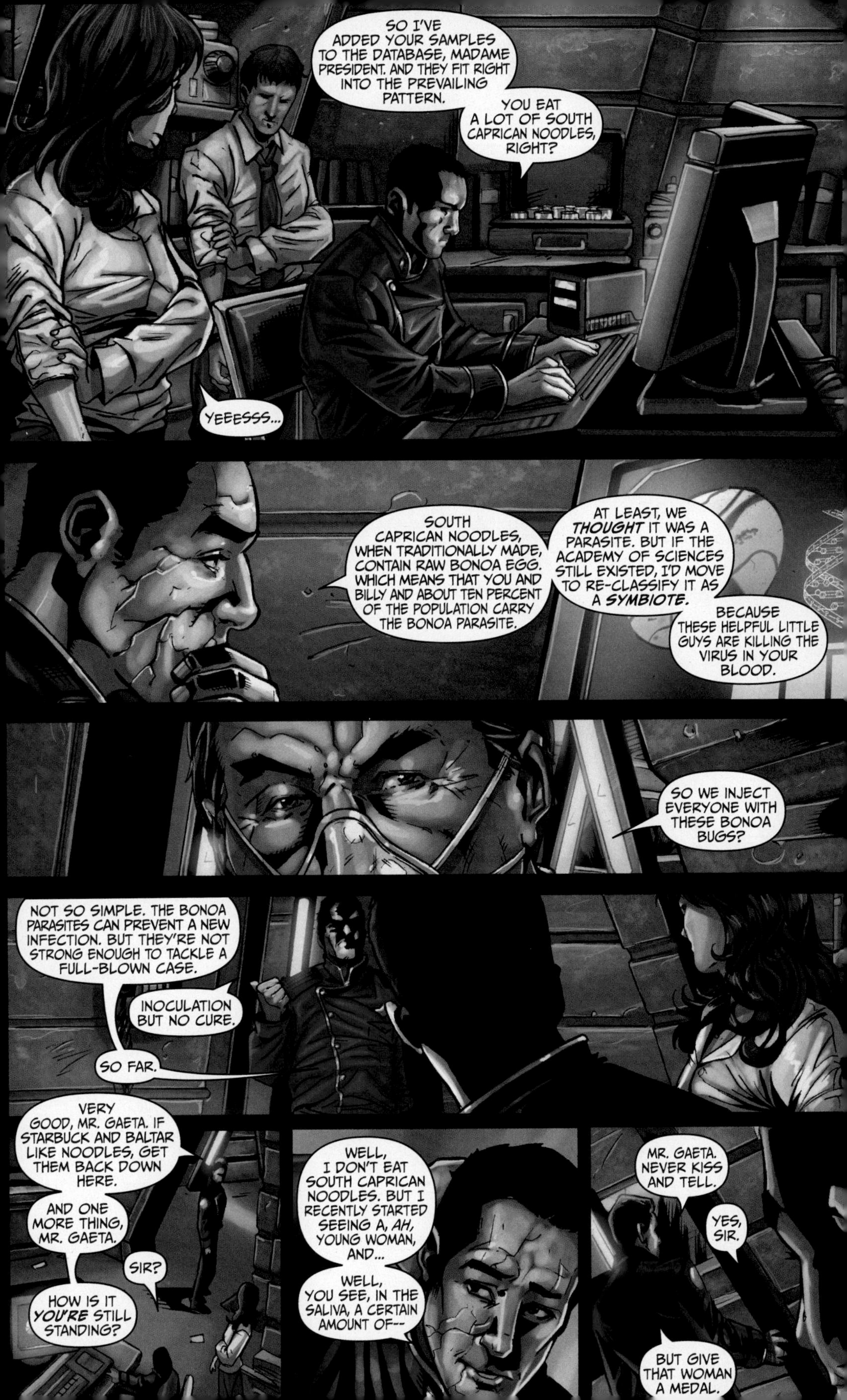
SO I'VE ADDED YOUR SAMPLES TO THE DATABASE, MADAME PRESIDENT. AND THEY FIT RIGHT INTO THE PREVAILING PATTERN.
YOU EAT A LOT OF SOUTH CAPRICAN NOODLES, RIGHT?
YEEESSS...
SOUTH CAPRICAN NOODLES, WHEN TRADITIONALLY MADE, CONTAIN RAW BONOA EGG. WHICH MEANS THAT YOU AND BILLY AND ABOUT TEN PERCENT OF THE POPULATION CARRY THE BONOA PARASITE.
AT LEAST, WE *THOUGHT* IT WAS A PARASITE. BUT IF THE ACADEMY OF SCIENCES STILL EXISTED, I'D MOVE TO RE-CLASSIFY IT AS A ***SYMBIOTE.***
BECAUSE THESE HELPFUL LITTLE GUYS ARE KILLING THE VIRUS IN YOUR BLOOD.
SO WE INJECT EVERYONE WITH THESE BONOA BUGS?
NOT SO SIMPLE. THE BONOA PARASITES CAN PREVENT A NEW INFECTION. BUT THEY'RE NOT STRONG ENOUGH TO TACKLE A FULL-BLOWN CASE.
INOCULATION BUT NO CURE.
SO FAR.
VERY GOOD, MR. GAETA. IF STARBUCK AND BALTAR LIKE NOODLES, GET THEM BACK DOWN HERE.
AND ONE MORE THING, MR. GAETA.
SIR?
HOW IS IT ***YOU'RE*** STILL STANDING?
WELL, I DON'T EAT SOUTH CAPRICAN NOODLES. BUT I RECENTLY STARTED SEEING A, *AH,* YOUNG WOMAN, AND...
WELL, YOU SEE, IN THE SALIVA, A CERTAIN AMOUNT OF--
MR. GAETA. NEVER KISS AND TELL.
YES, SIR.
BUT GIVE THAT WOMAN A MEDAL.

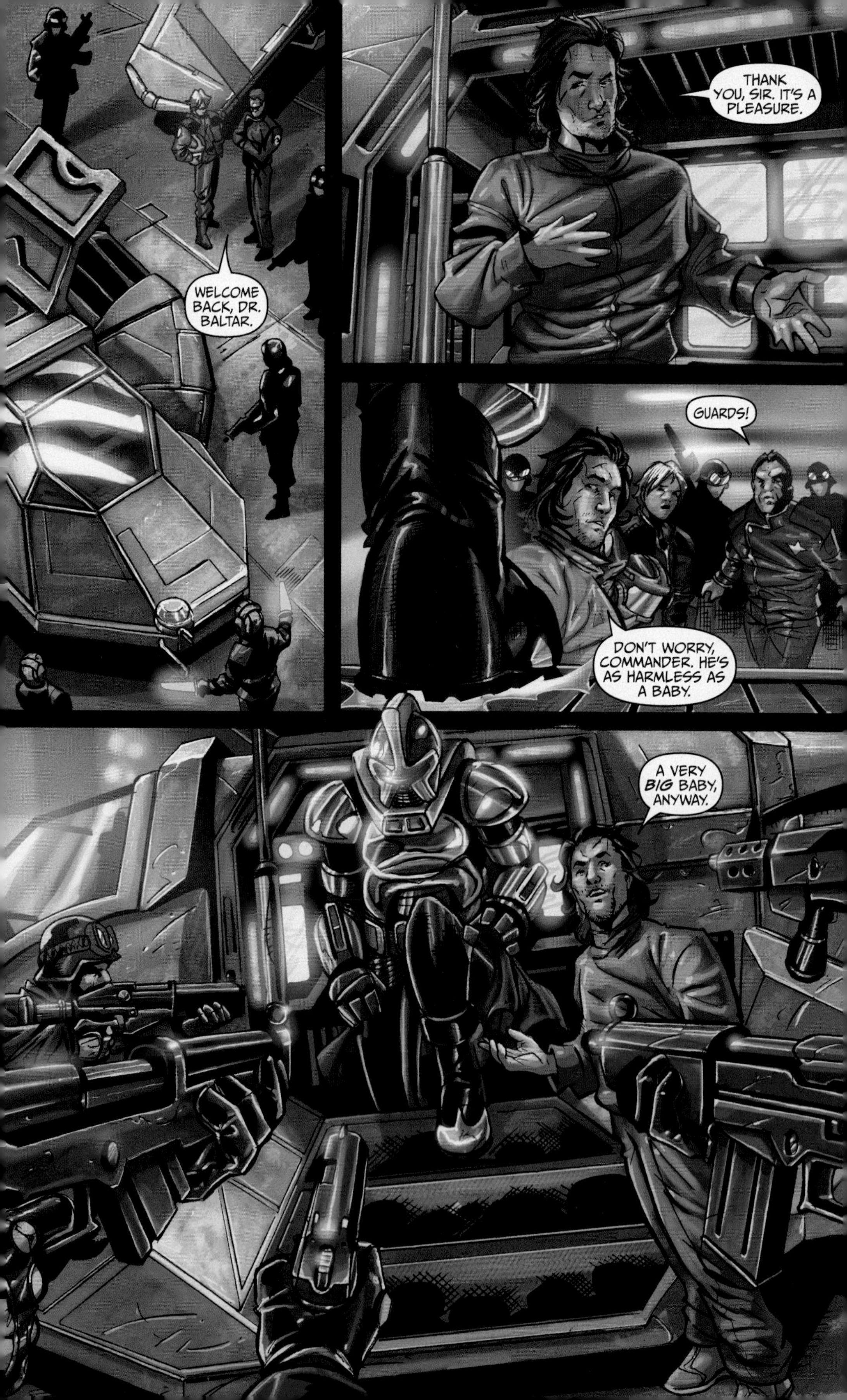
WELCOME BACK, DR. BALTAR.
THANK YOU, SIR. IT'S A PLEASURE.
GUARDS!
DON'T WORRY, COMMANDER. HE'S AS HARMLESS AS A BABY.
A VERY BIG BABY, ANYWAY.

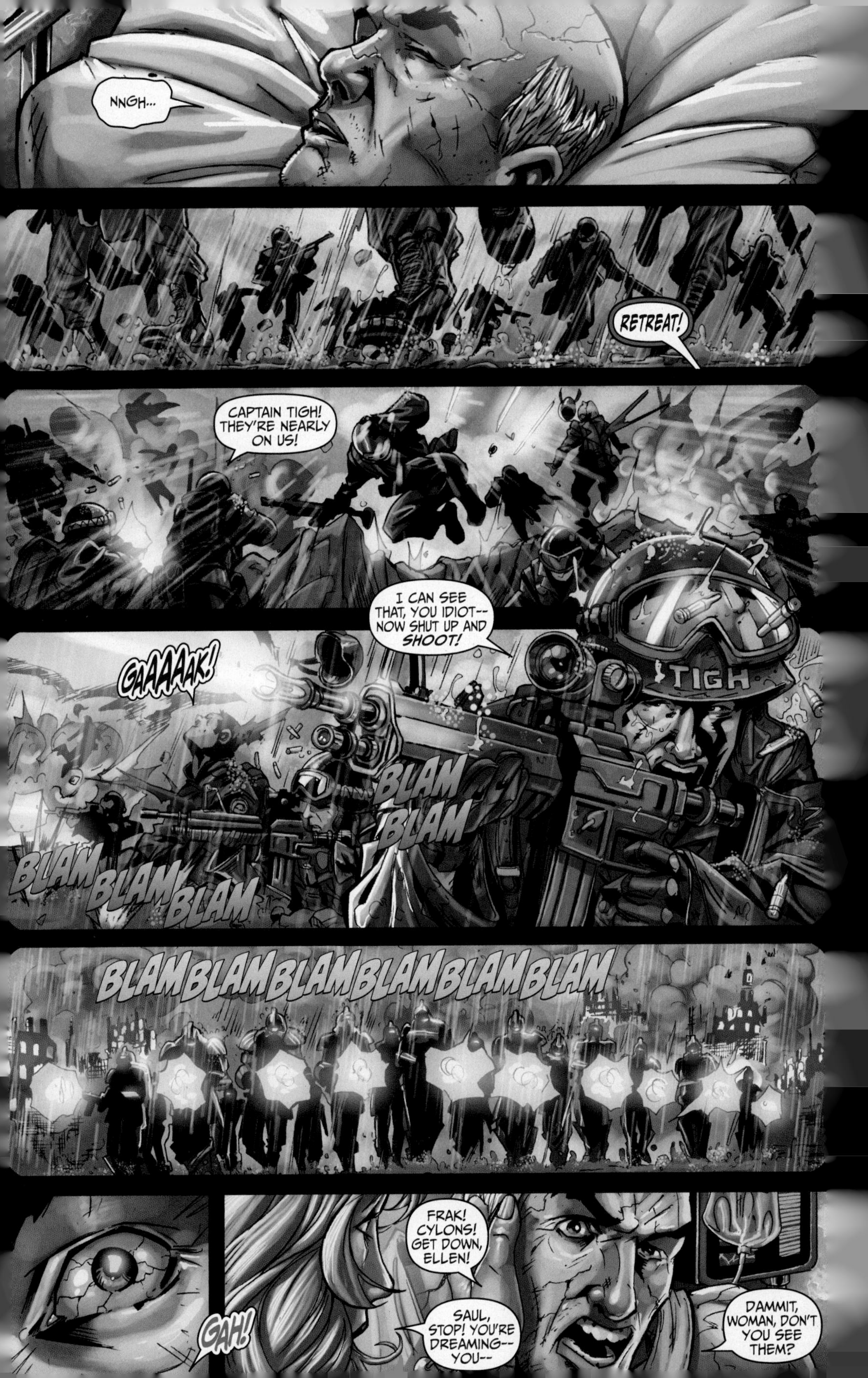
NNGH...
RETREAT!
CAPTAIN TIGH! THEY'RE NEARLY ON US!
I CAN SEE THAT, YOU IDIOT-- NOW SHUT UP AND SHOOT!
GAAAAAK!
TIGH
BLAM BLAM
BLAM BLAM BLAM
BLAMBLAMBLAMBLAMBLAMBLAM
FRAK! CYLONS! GET DOWN, ELLEN!
GAH!
SAUL, STOP! YOU'RE DREAMING-- YOU--
DAMMIT, WOMAN, DON'T YOU SEE THEM?

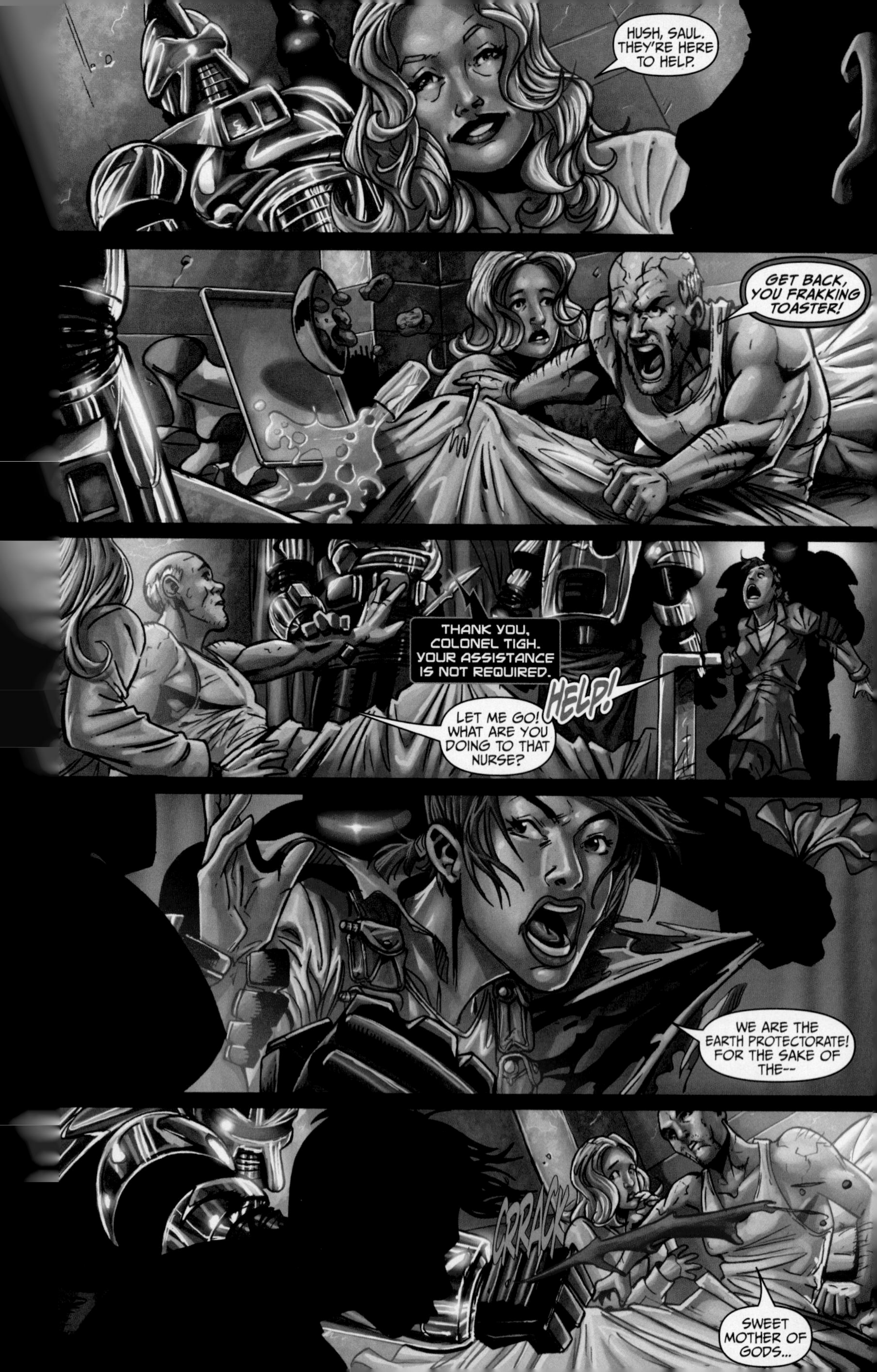
HUSH, SAUL. THEY'RE HERE TO HELP.
GET BACK, YOU FRAKKING TOASTER!
THANK YOU, COLONEL TIGH. YOUR ASSISTANCE IS NOT REQUIRED.
HELP!
LET ME GO! WHAT ARE YOU DOING TO THAT NURSE?
WE ARE THE EARTH PROTECTORATE! FOR THE SAKE OF THE--
CRRACK
SWEET MOTHER OF GODS...

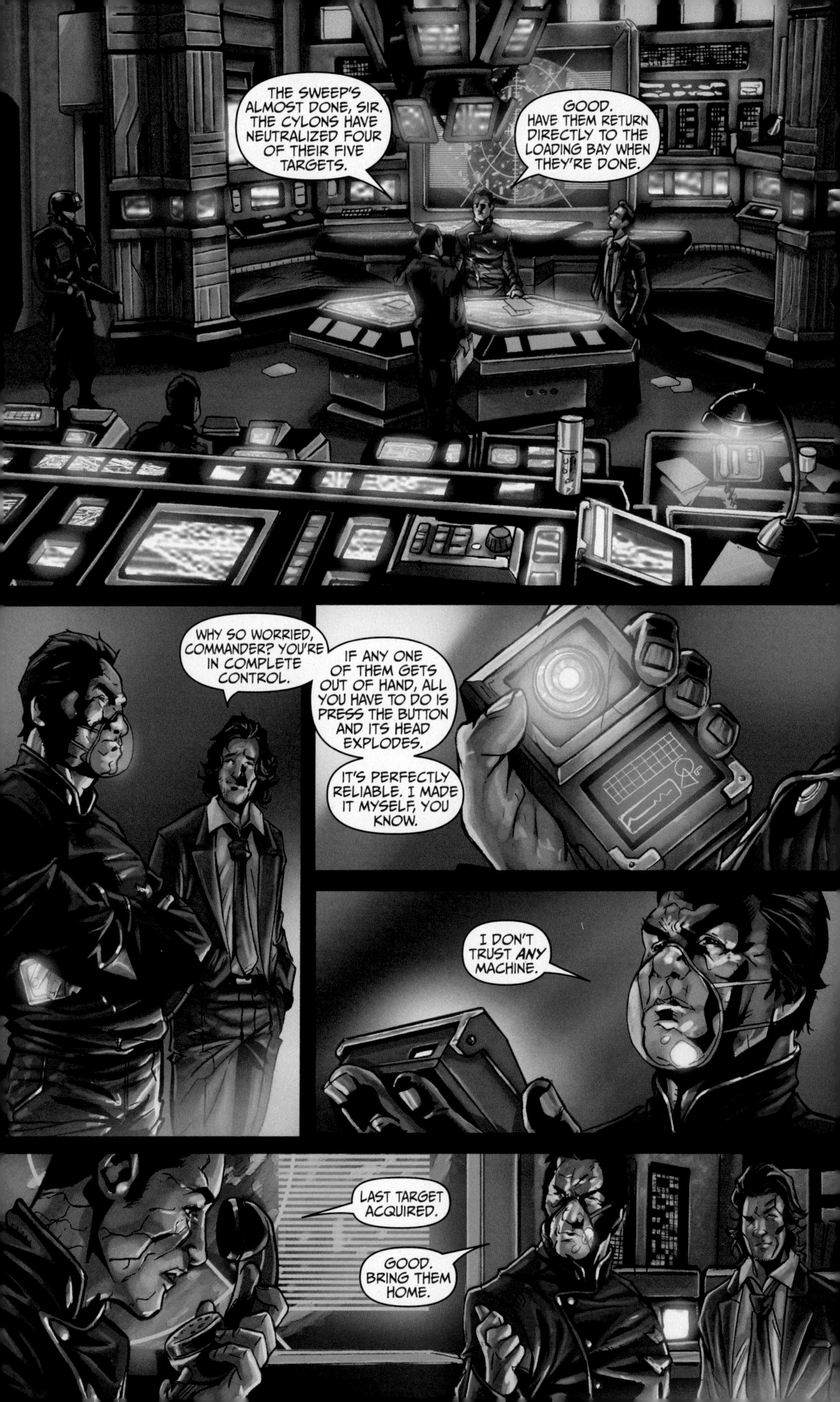
THE SWEEP'S ALMOST DONE, SIR. THE CYLONS HAVE NEUTRALIZED FOUR OF THEIR FIVE TARGETS.
GOOD. HAVE THEM RETURN DIRECTLY TO THE LOADING BAY WHEN THEY'RE DONE.
WHY SO WORRIED, COMMANDER? YOU'RE IN COMPLETE CONTROL.
IF ANY ONE OF THEM GETS OUT OF HAND, ALL YOU HAVE TO DO IS PRESS THE BUTTON AND ITS HEAD EXPLODES.
IT'S PERFECTLY RELIABLE. I MADE IT MYSELF, YOU KNOW.
I DON'T TRUST *ANY* MACHINE.
LAST TARGET ACQUIRED.
GOOD. BRING THEM HOME.

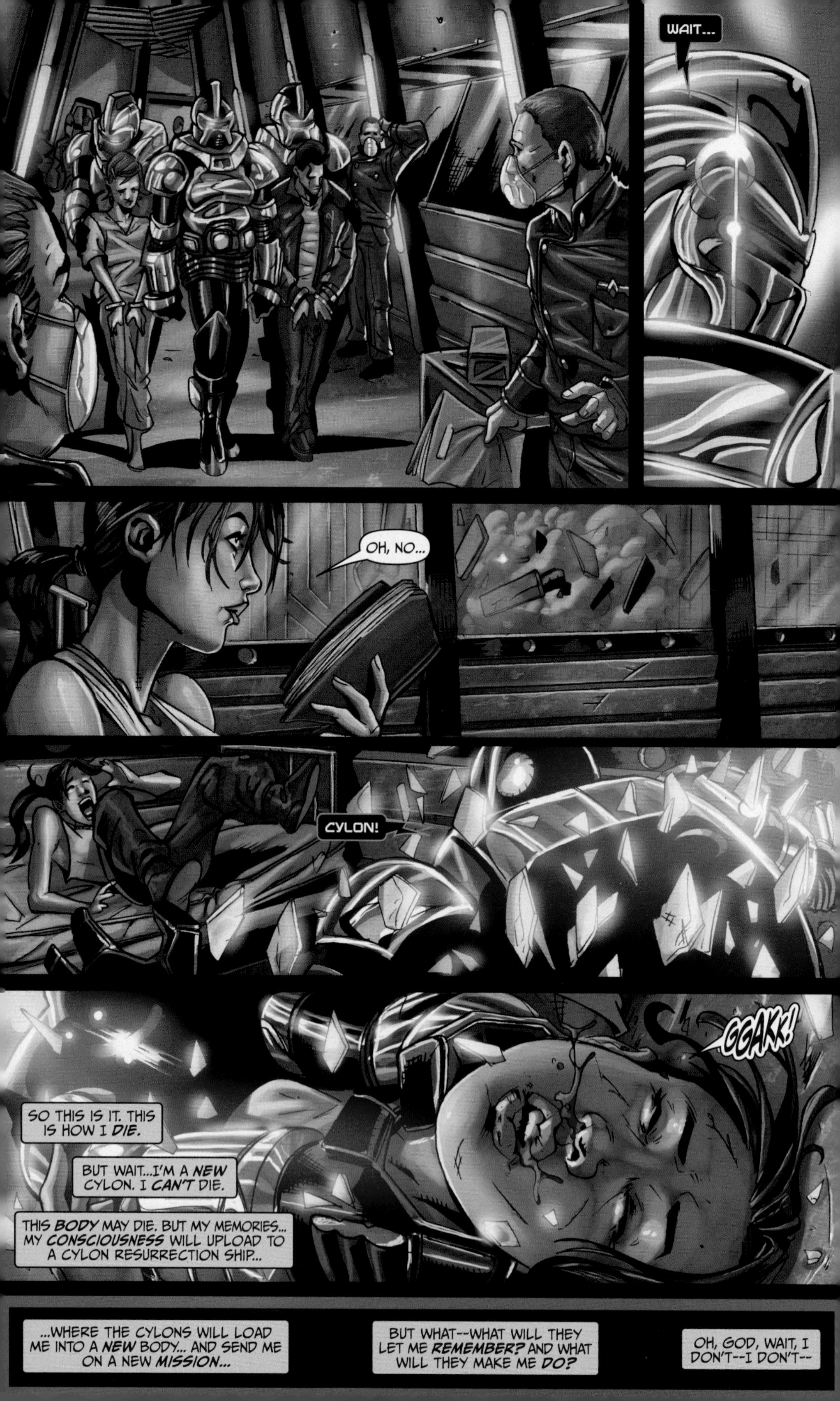
WAIT...
OH, NO...
CYLON!
GGAKK!
SO THIS IS IT. THIS IS HOW I *DIE.*
BUT WAIT...I'M A *NEW* CYLON. I *CAN'T* DIE.
THIS *BODY* MAY DIE. BUT MY MEMORIES... MY *CONSCIOUSNESS* WILL UPLOAD TO A CYLON RESURRECTION SHIP...
...WHERE THE CYLONS WILL LOAD ME INTO A *NEW* BODY... AND SEND ME ON A NEW *MISSION...*
BUT WHAT--WHAT WILL THEY LET ME *REMEMBER?* AND WHAT WILL THEY MAKE ME *DO?*
OH, GOD, WAIT, I DON'T--I DON'T--

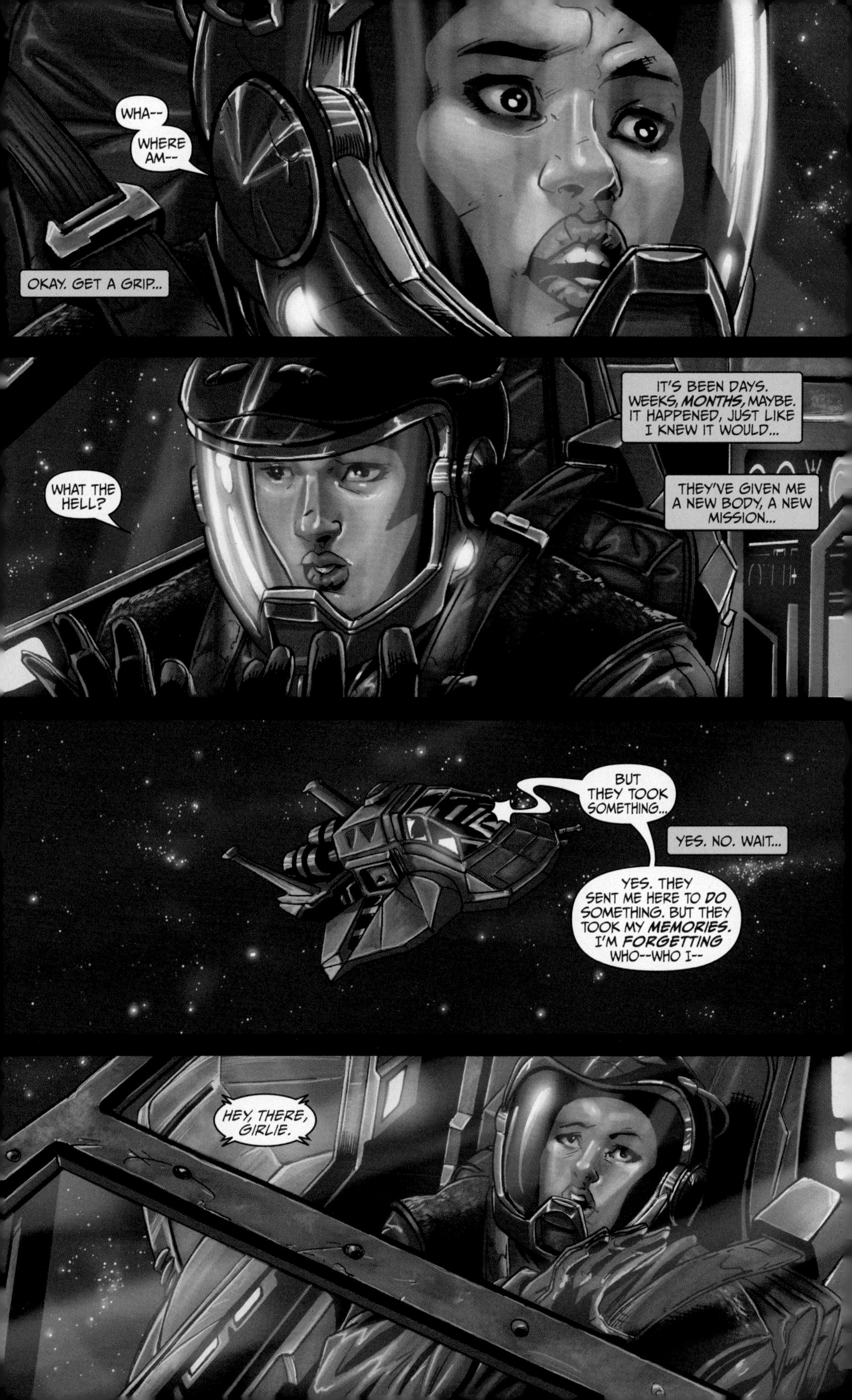
WHA--
WHERE AM--
OKAY. GET A GRIP...
IT'S BEEN DAYS. WEEKS, MONTHS, MAYBE. IT HAPPENED, JUST LIKE I KNEW IT WOULD...
WHAT THE HELL?
THEY'VE GIVEN ME A NEW BODY, A NEW MISSION...
BUT THEY TOOK SOMETHING...
YES. NO. WAIT...
YES. THEY SENT ME HERE TO DO SOMETHING. BUT THEY TOOK MY MEMORIES. I'M FORGETTING WHO--WHO I--
HEY, THERE, GIRLIE.

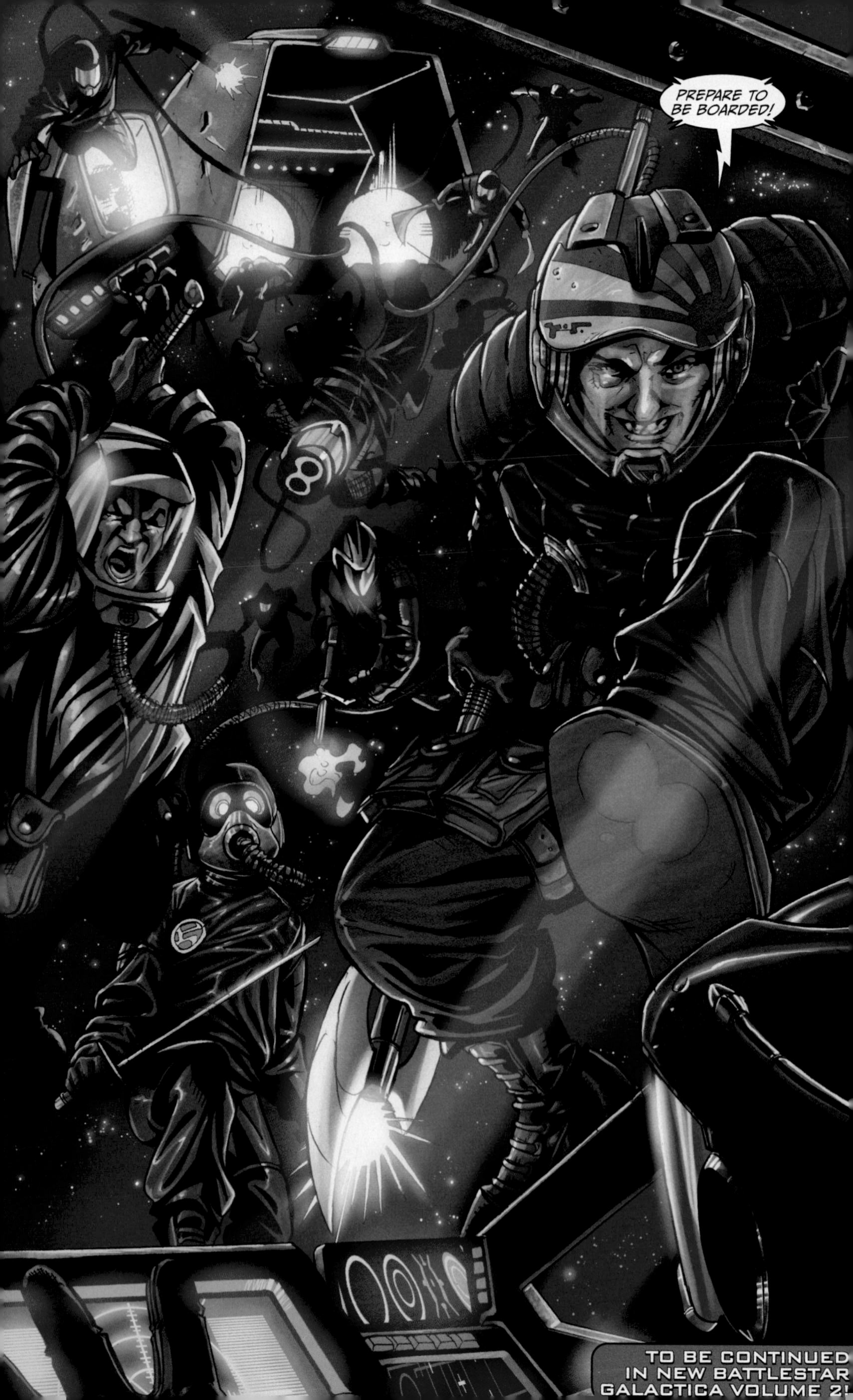
PREPARE TO BE BOARDED!
TO BE CONTINUED IN NEW BATTLESTAR GALACTICA VOLUME 2!

BONUS MATERIALS

COVER GALLERY

ISSUE #0

PAGE 110   STEVE MCNIVEN

PAGE 111   PHOTO COVER

ISSUE #1

PAGE 112   MICHAEL TURNER

PAGE 113   PHOTO COVER

PAGE 114   BILLY TAN

PAGE 115   NIGEL RAYNOR WITH STJEPAN SEJIC

ISSUE #2

PAGE 116   ADRIANO BATISTA

PAGE 117   GUISEPPE "CAMMO" CAMUNCOLI

PAGE 118   NIGEL RAYNOR WITH STJEPAN SEJIC

PAGE 119   PHOTO COVER

ISSUE #3

PAGE 120   PAT LEE

PAGE 121   ADRIANO BATISTA

PAGE 122   NIGEL RAYNOR

PAGE 123   PHOTO COVER

ISSUE #4

PAGE 124   E-BAS

PAGE 125   TYLER KIRKHAM WITH STJEPAN SEJIC

PAGE 126   NIGEL RAYNOR

PAGE 127   PHOTO COVER

COMMENTARY

PAGE 128   BY GREG PAK

SKETCH BOOK

PAGE 135   BY NIGEL RAYNOR

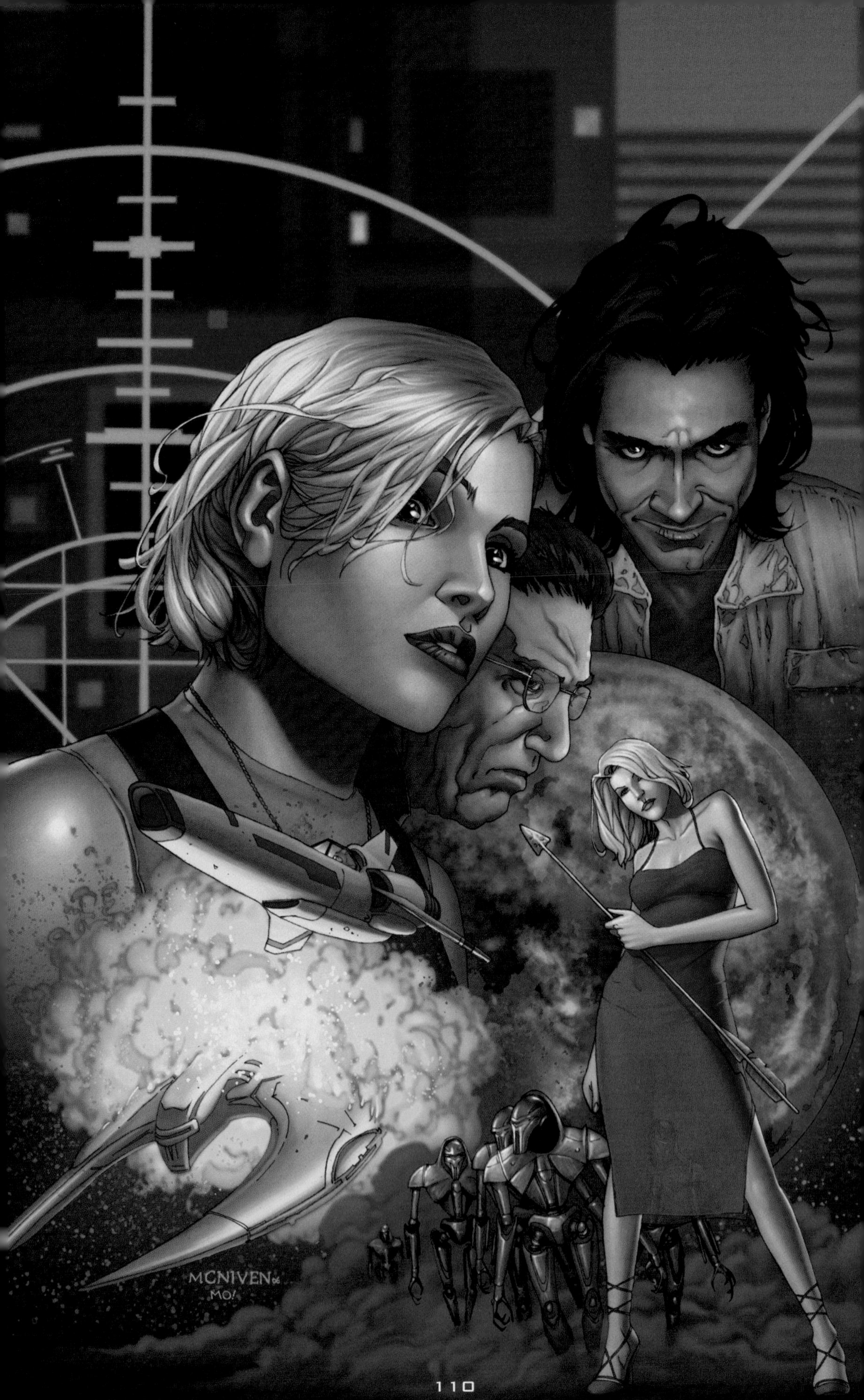
MCNIVEN06
MO!

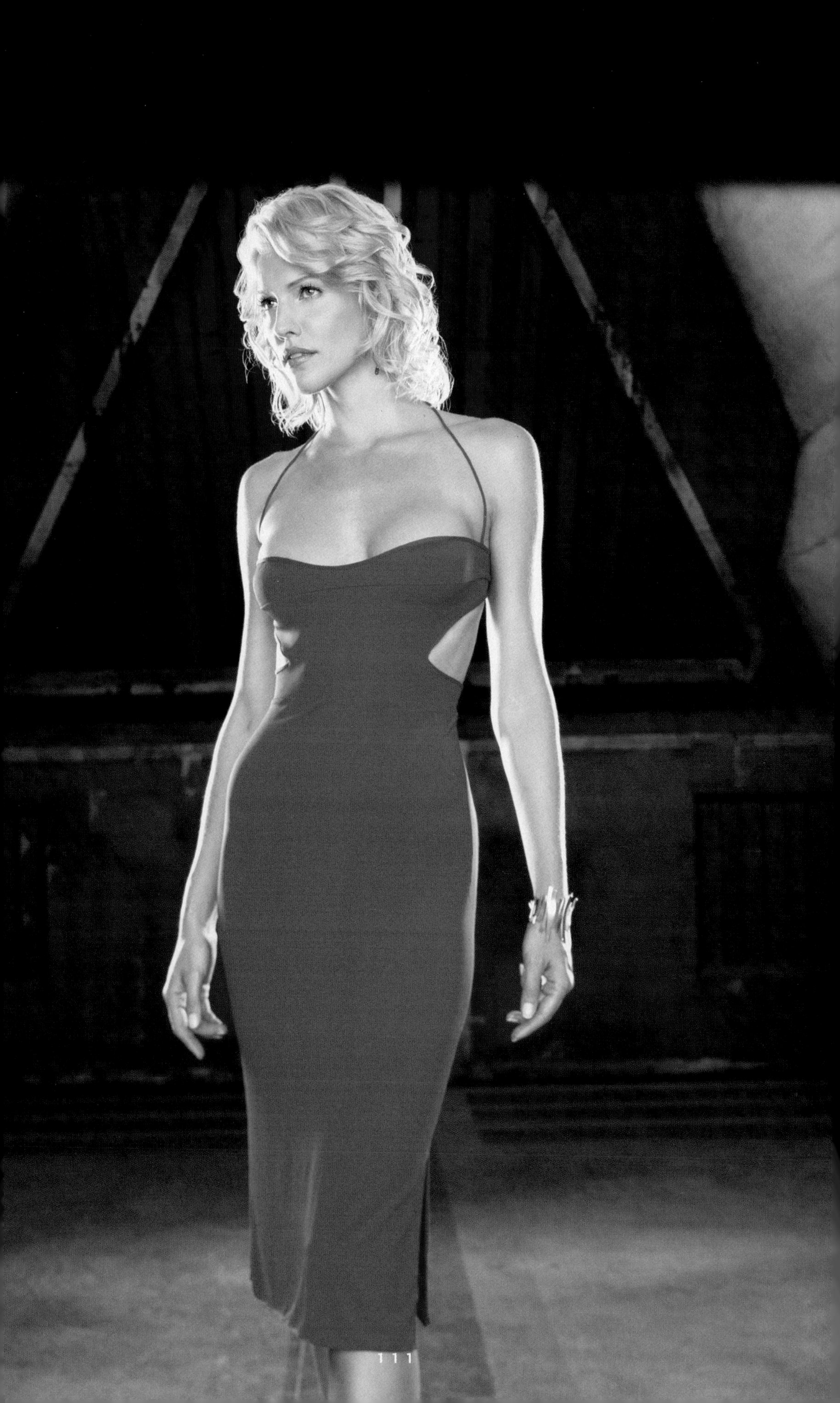

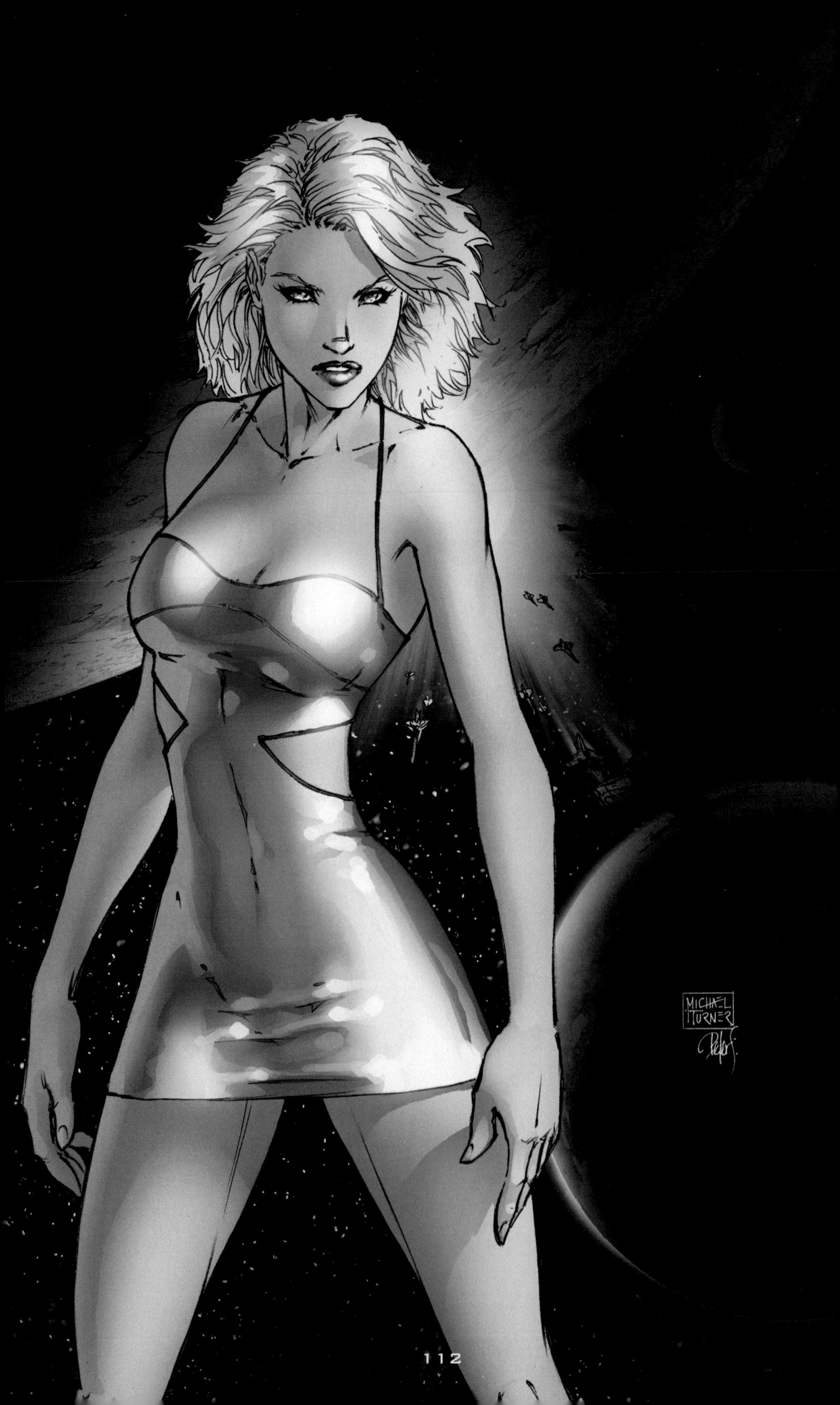
MICHAEL TURNER

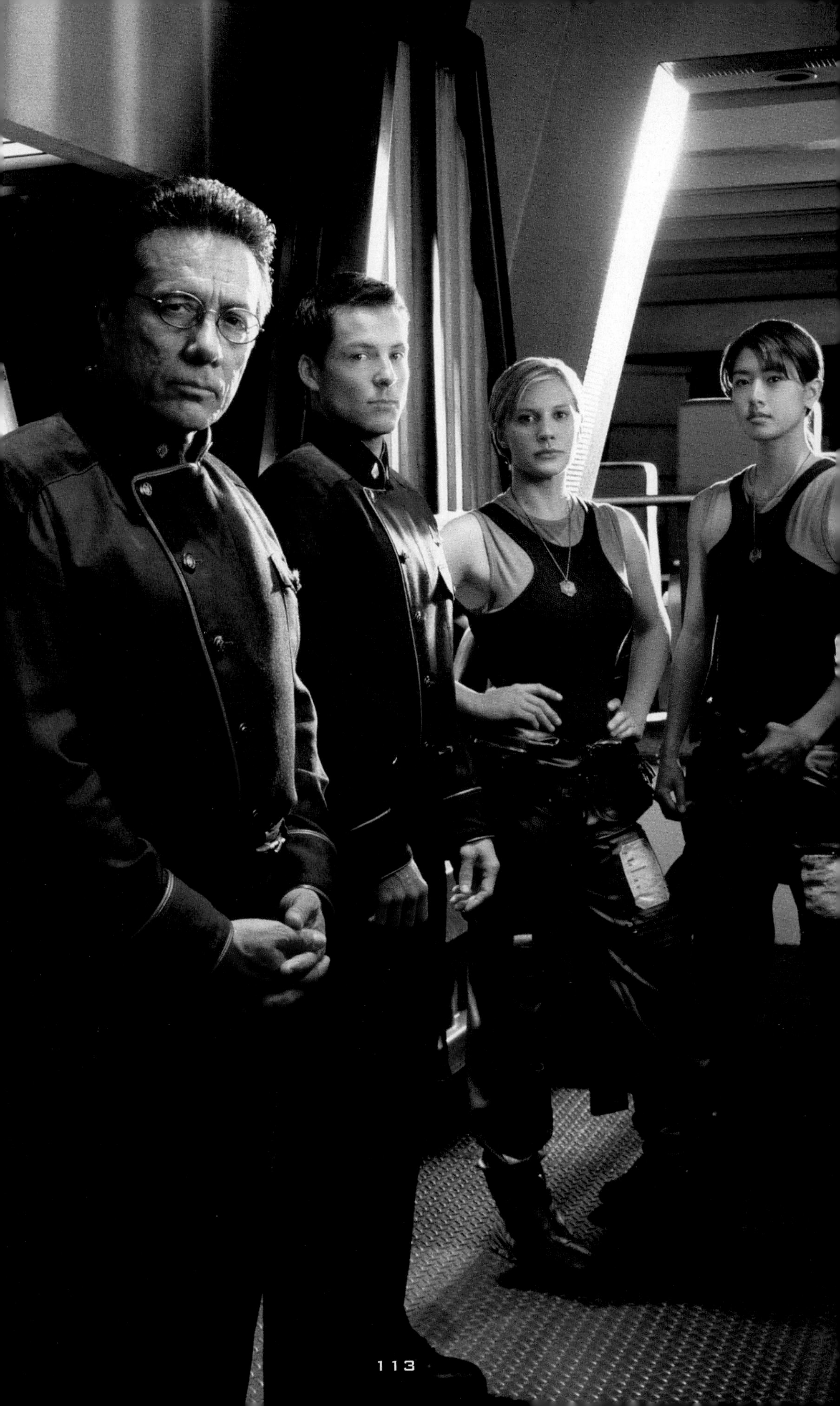

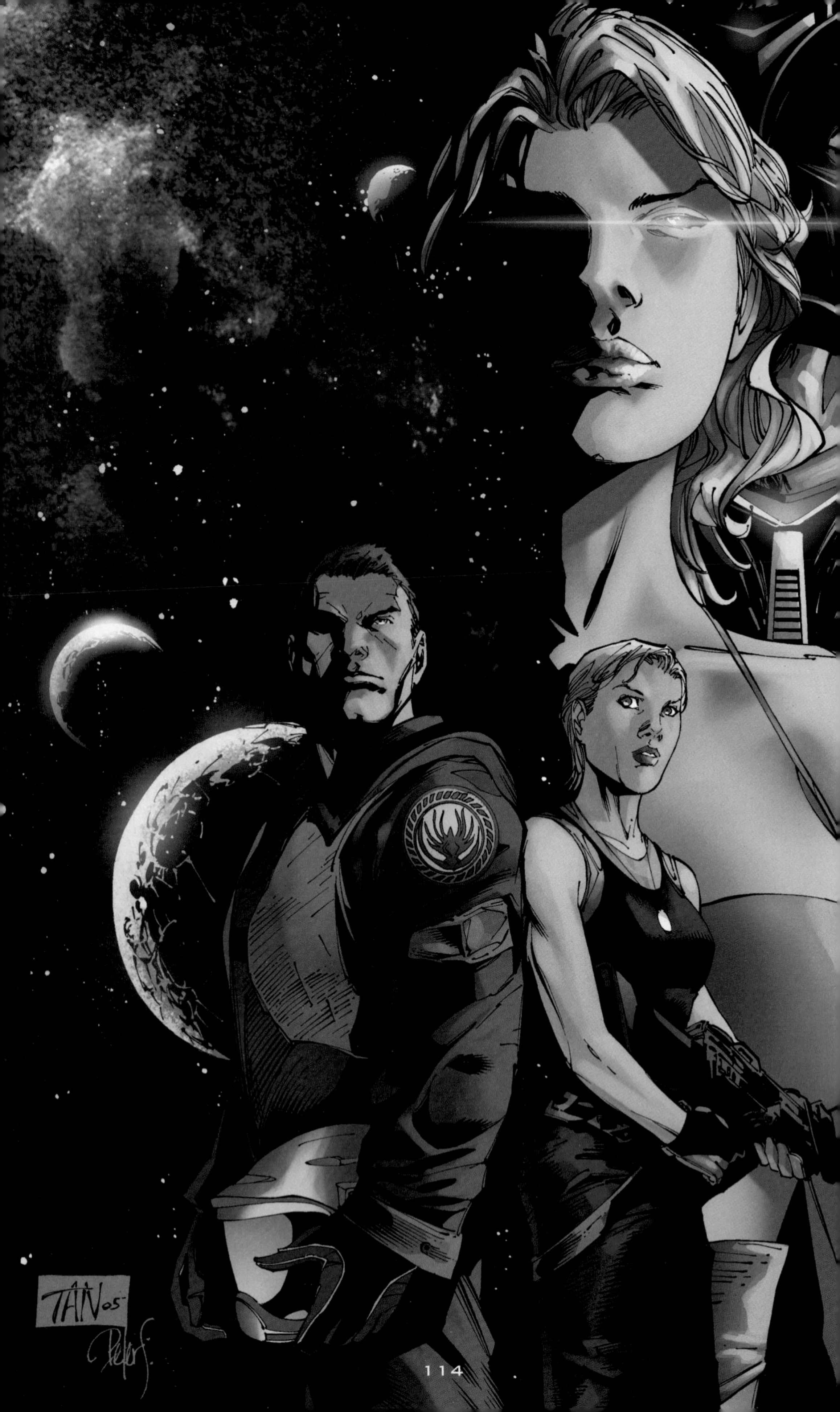

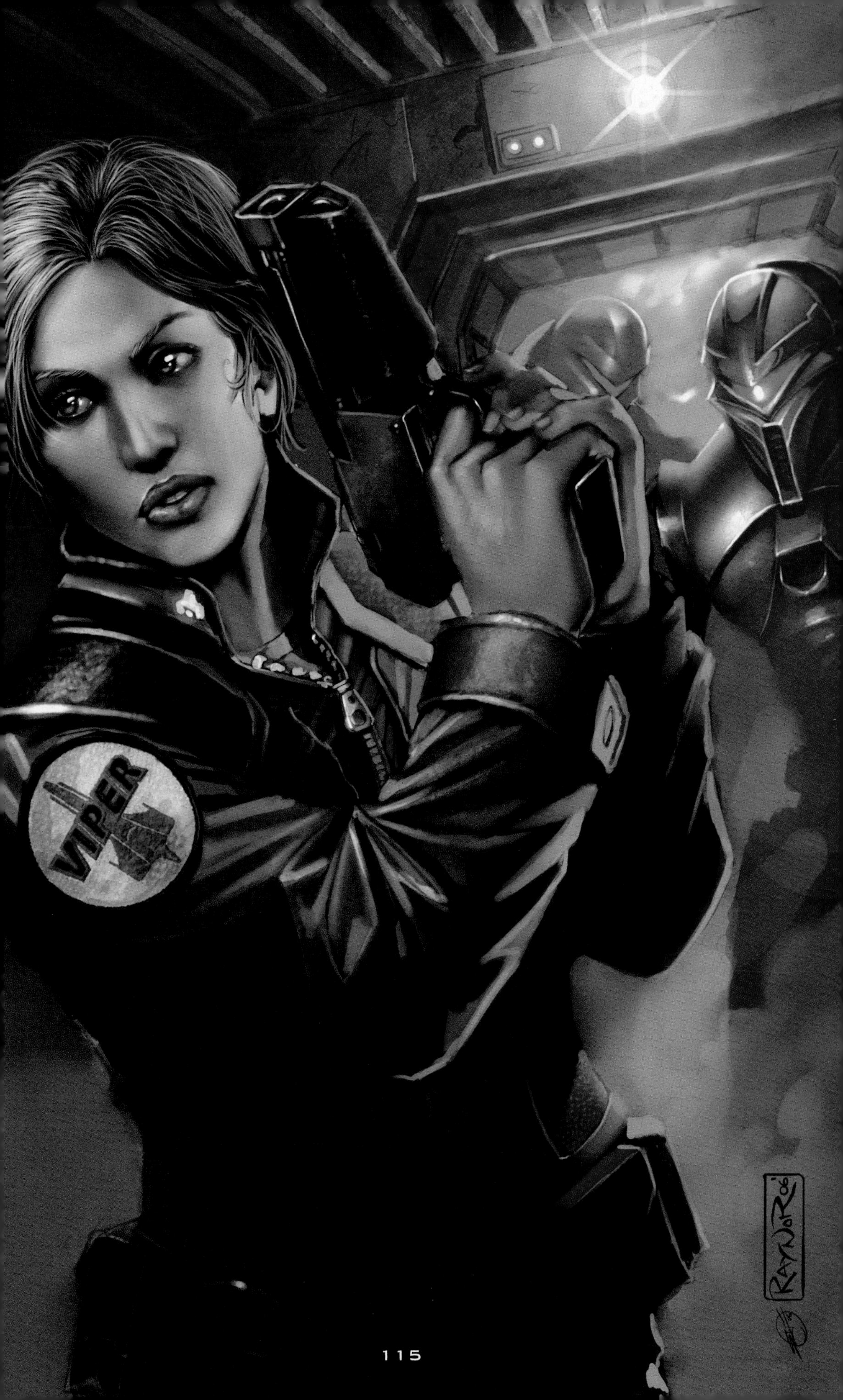
VIPER

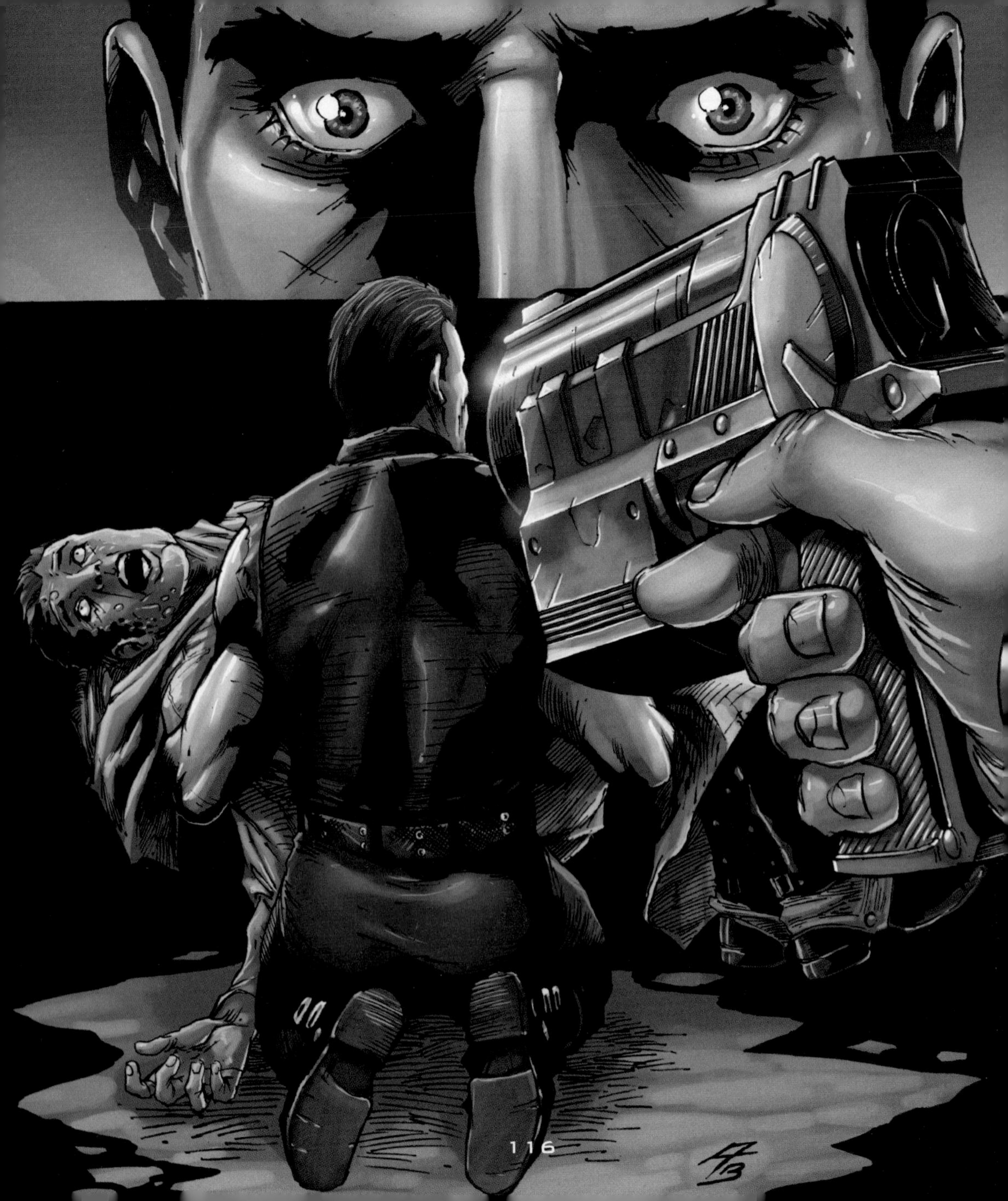

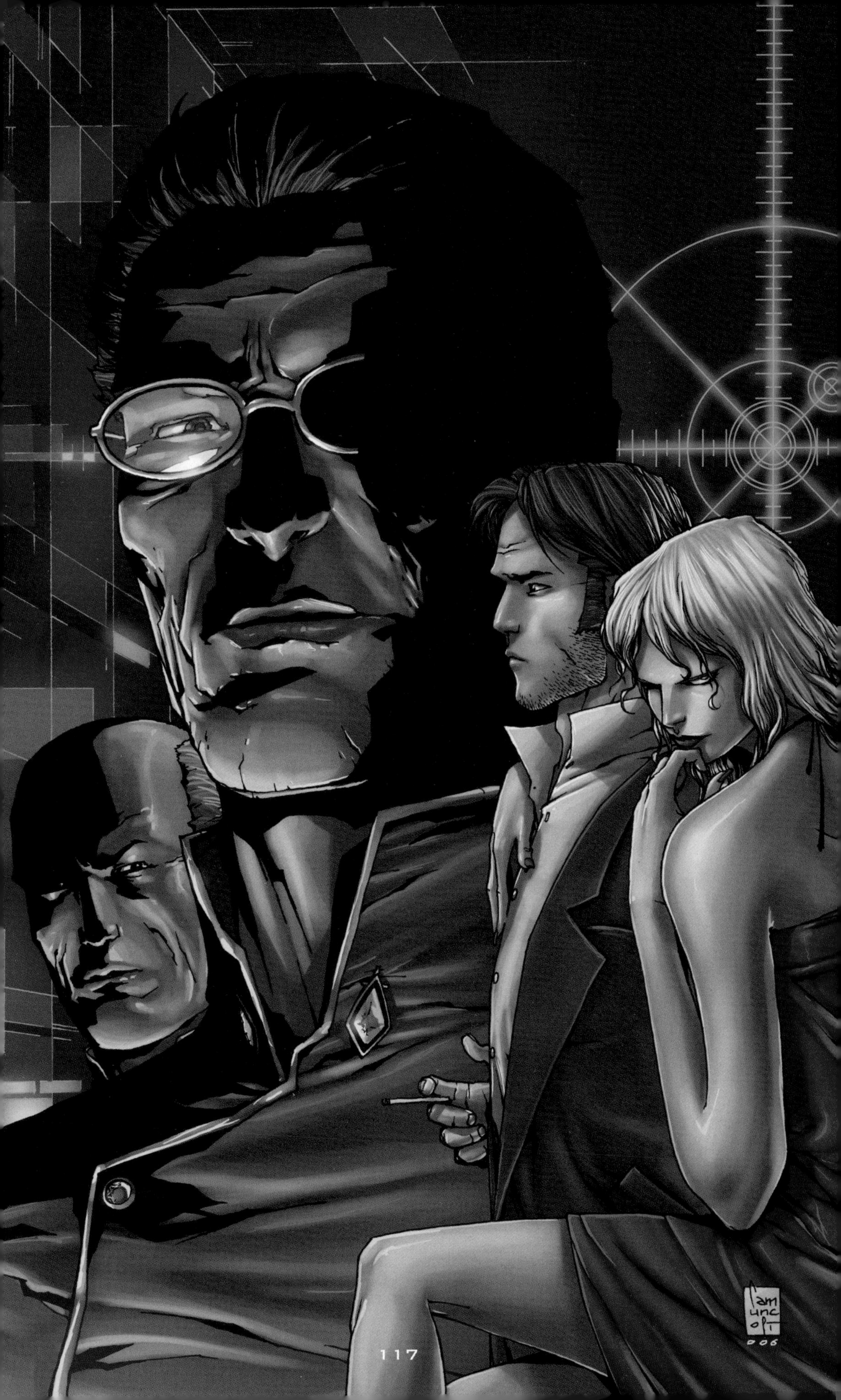

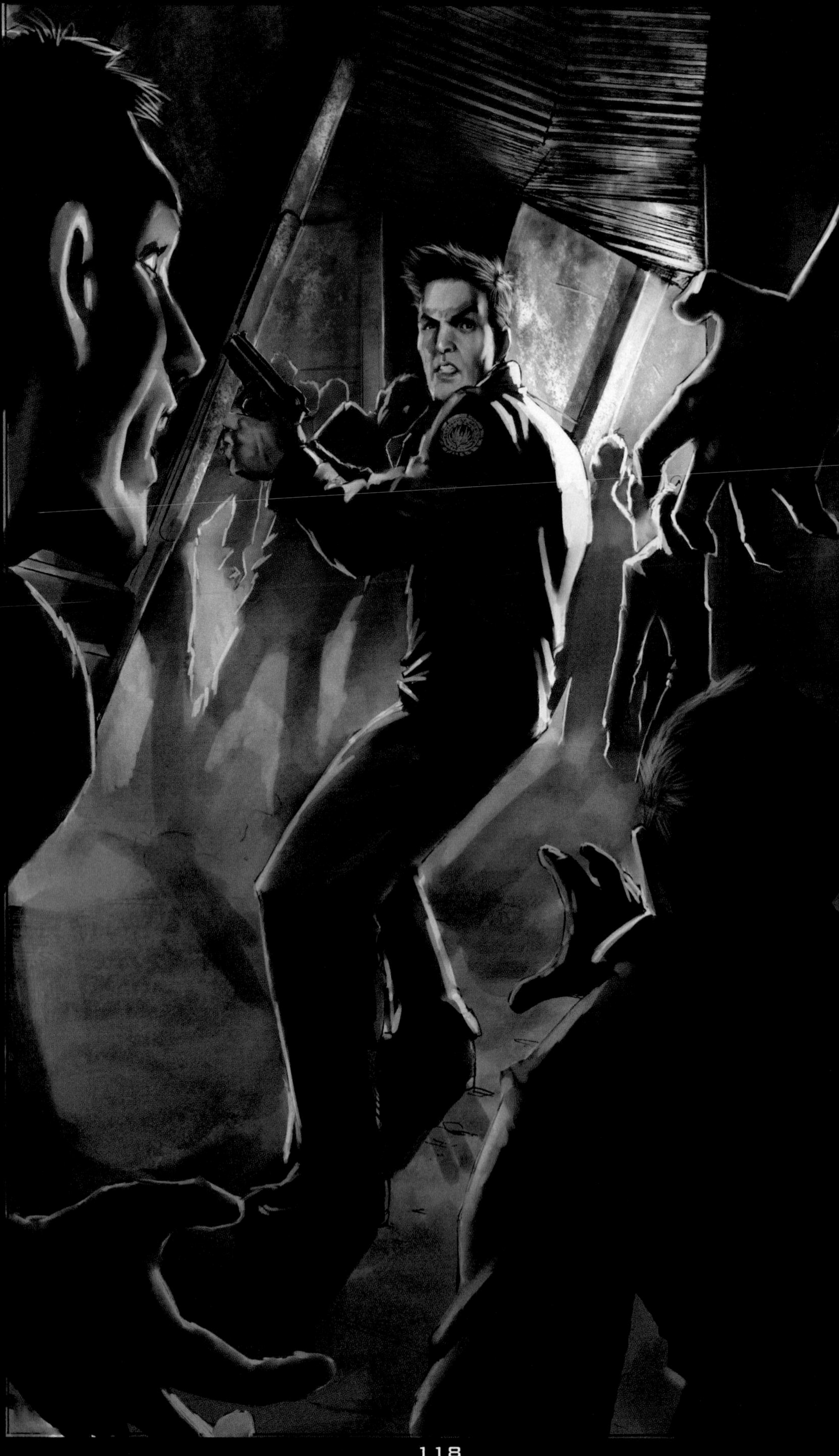

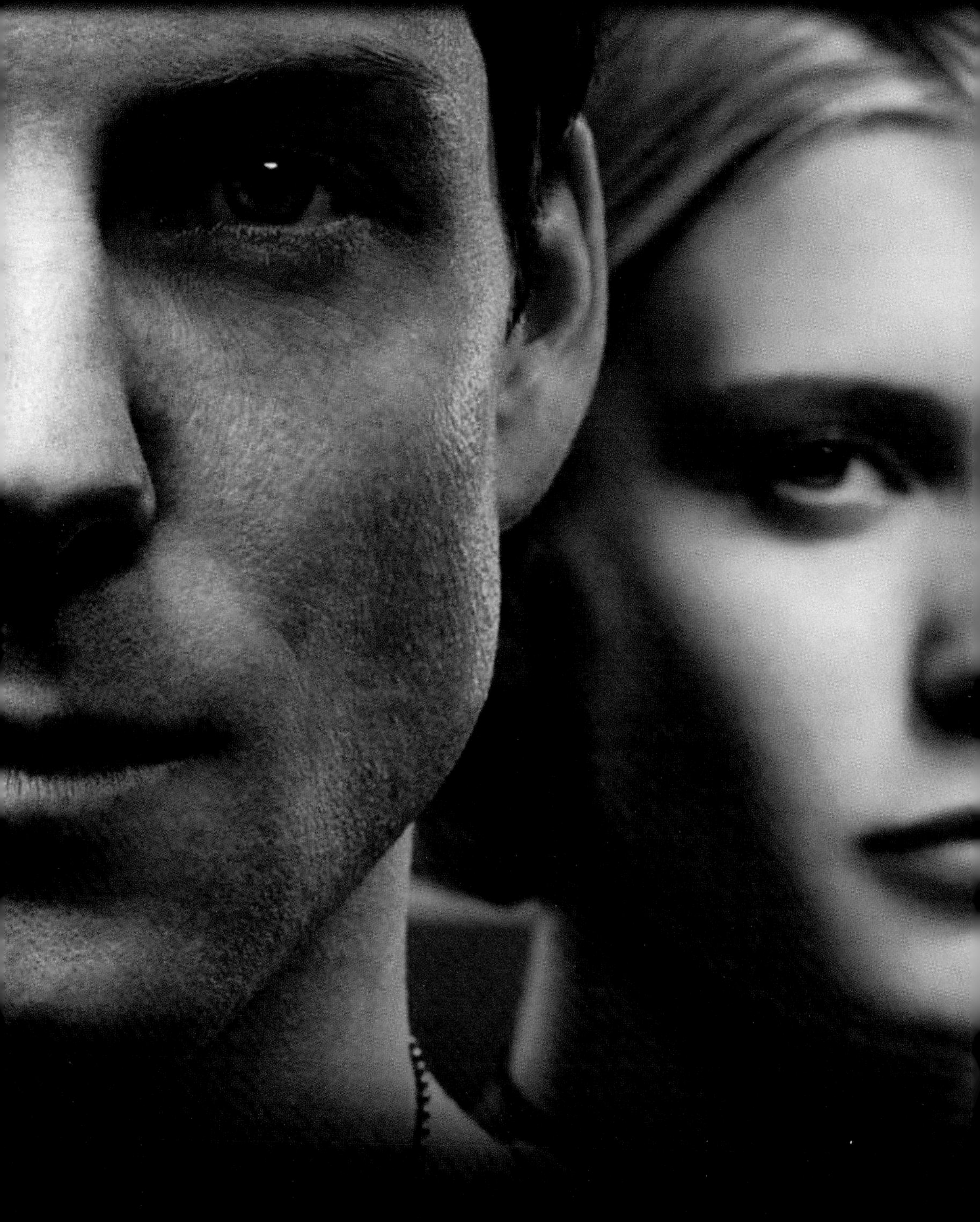

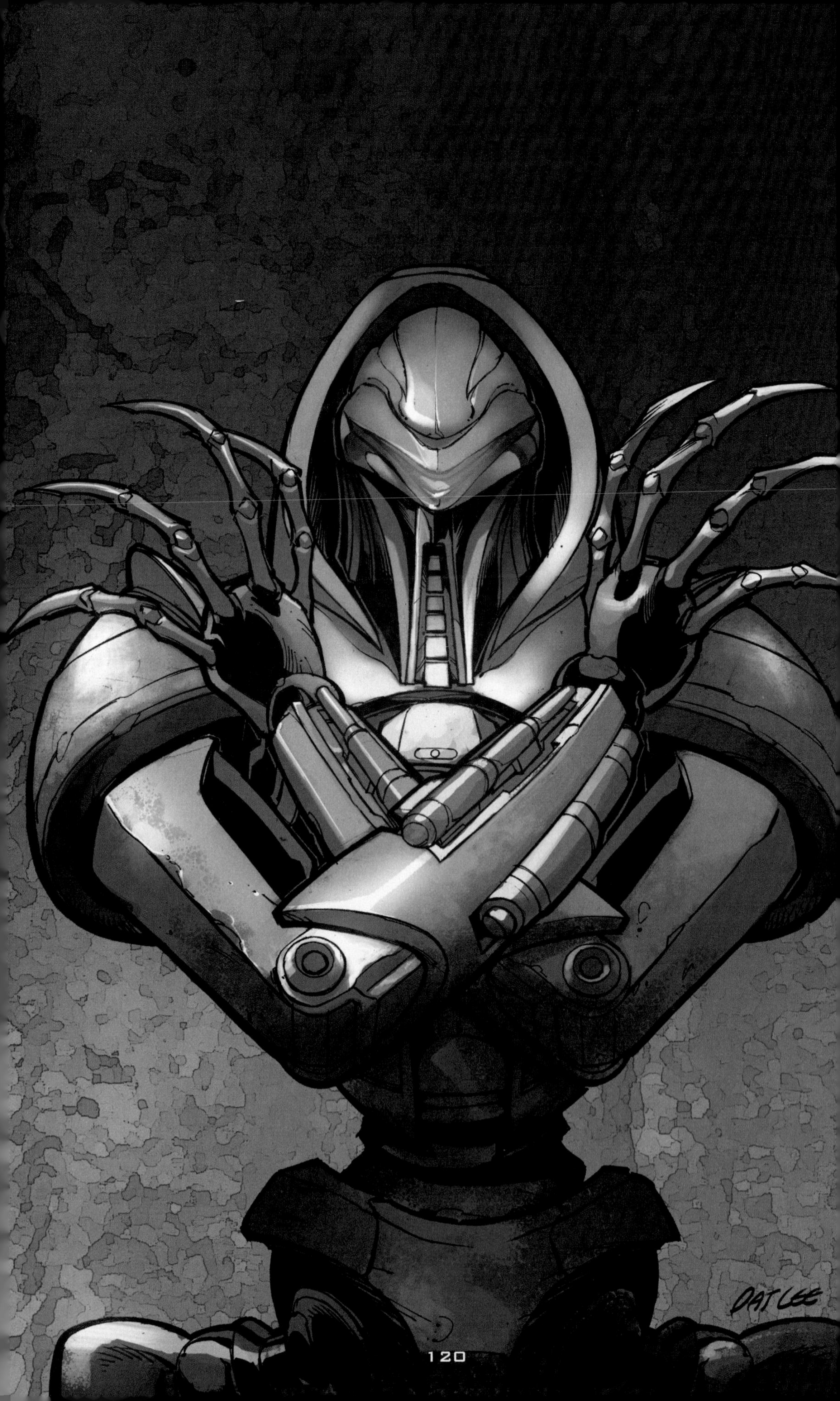
DAT LEE

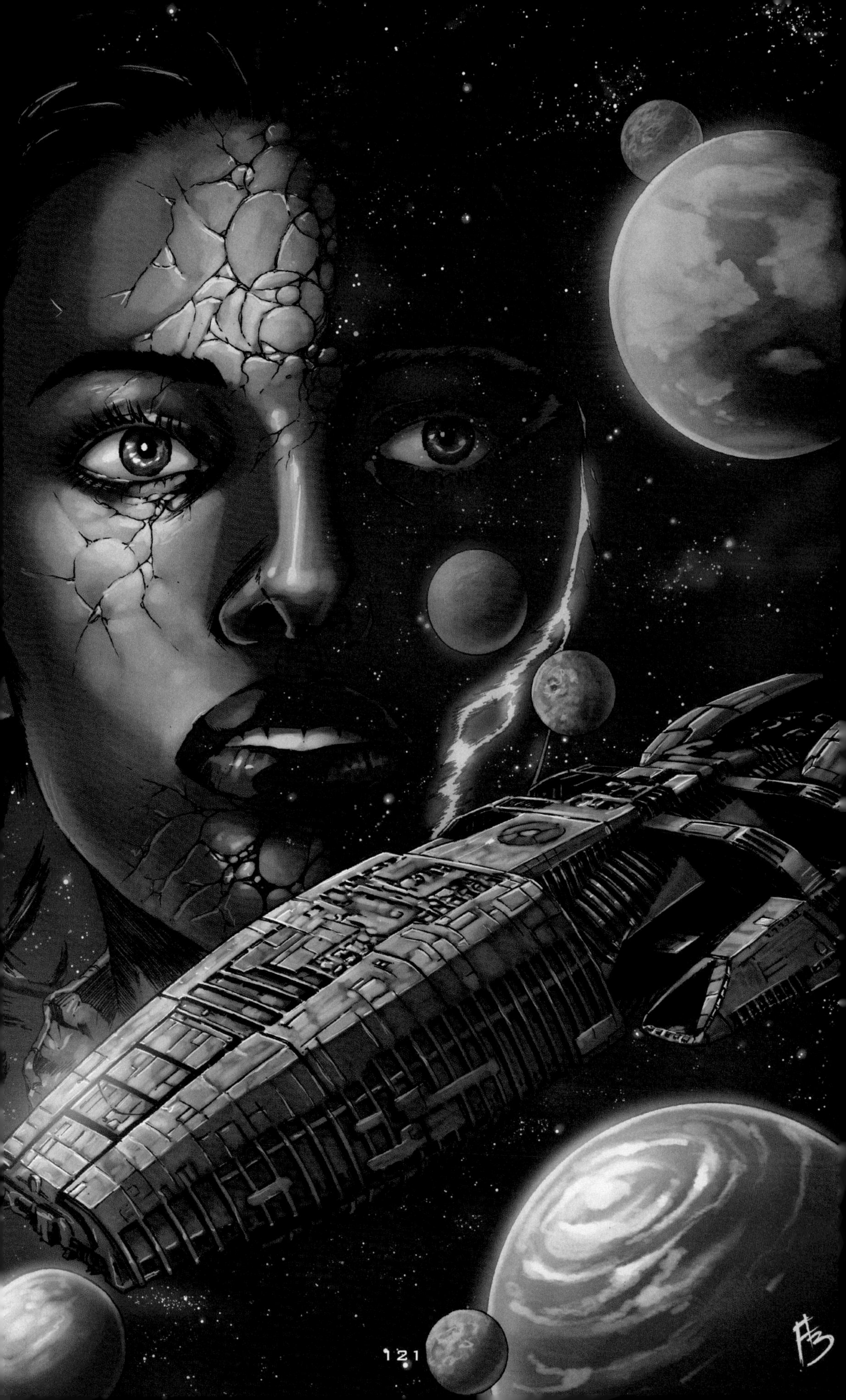

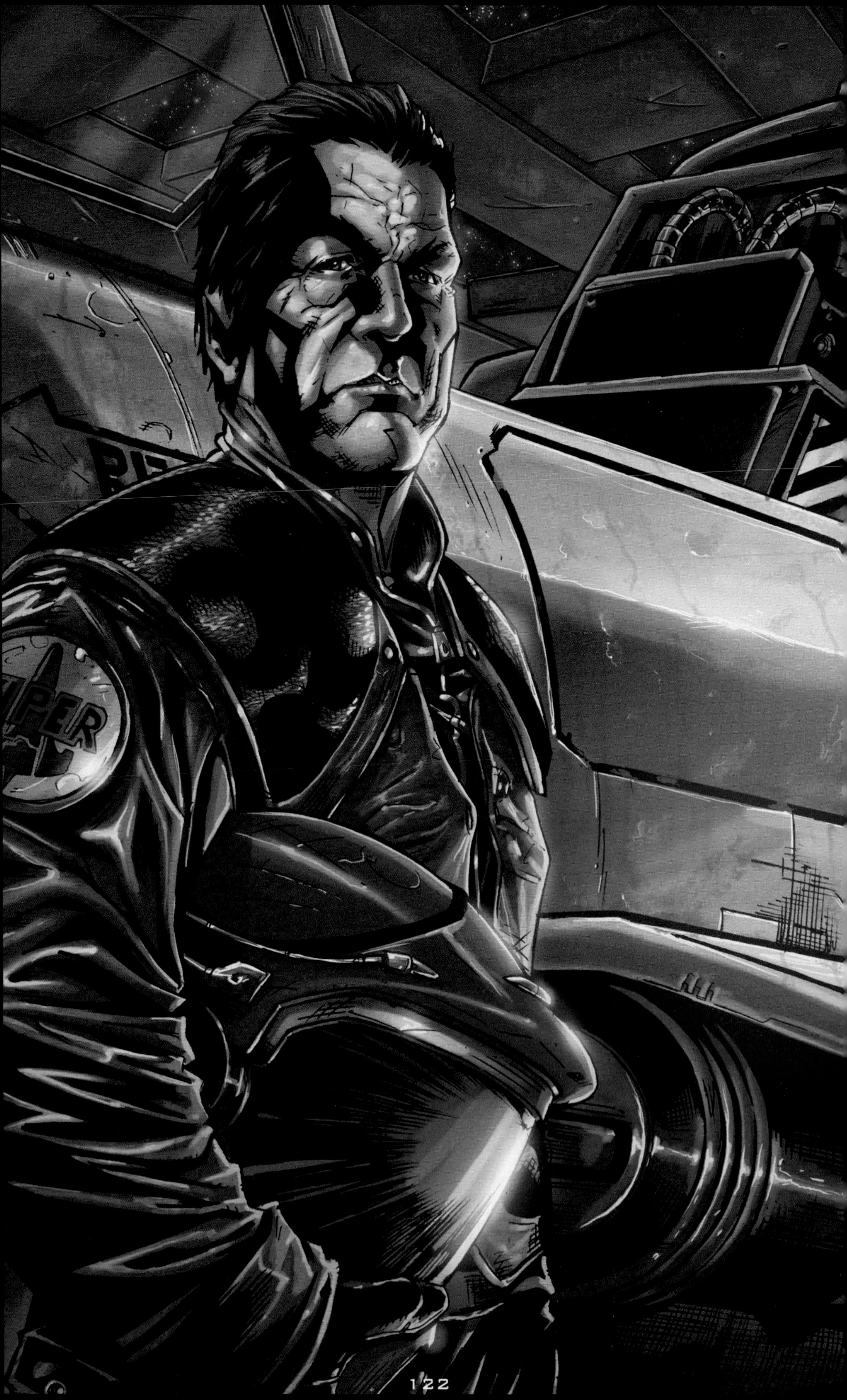

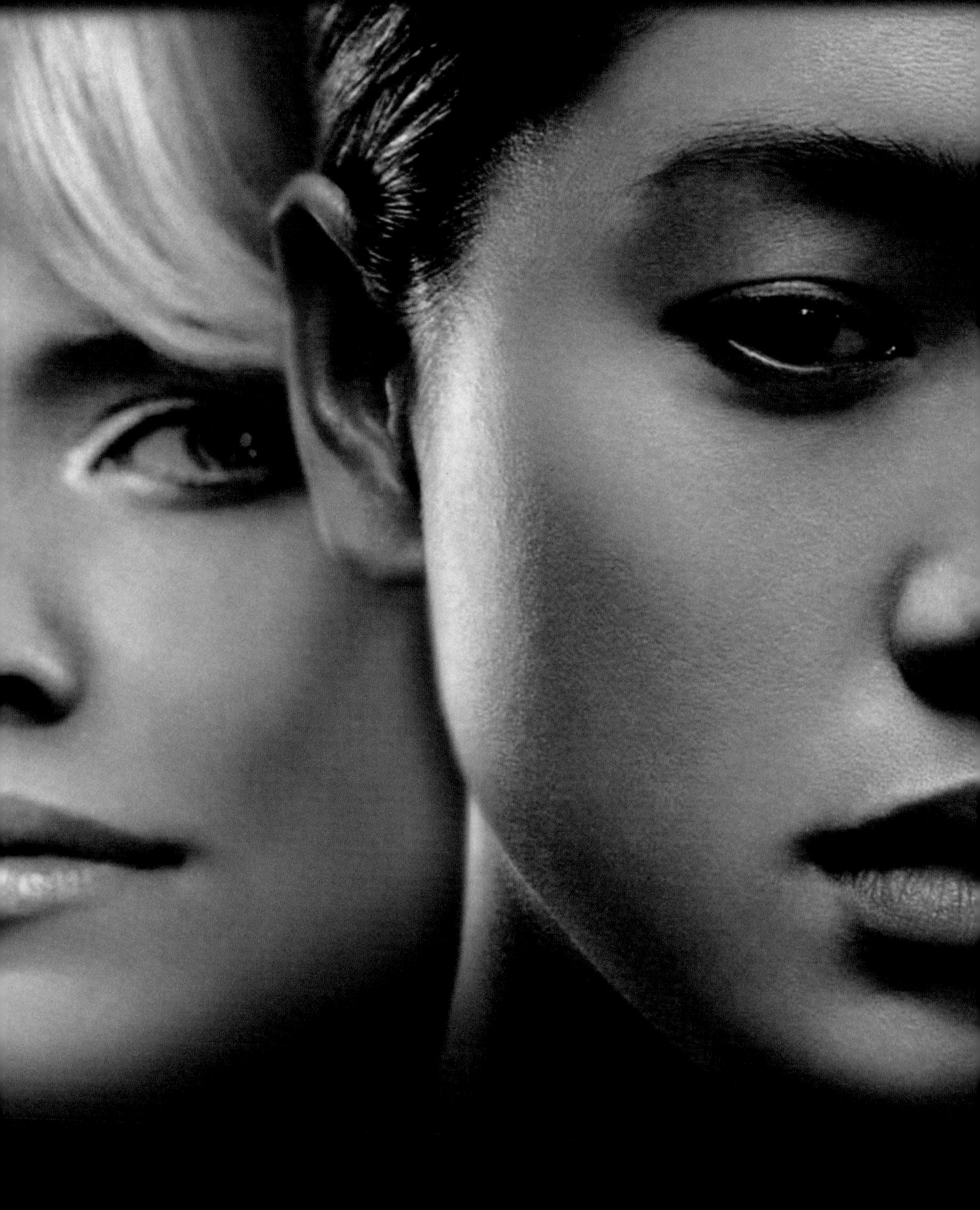

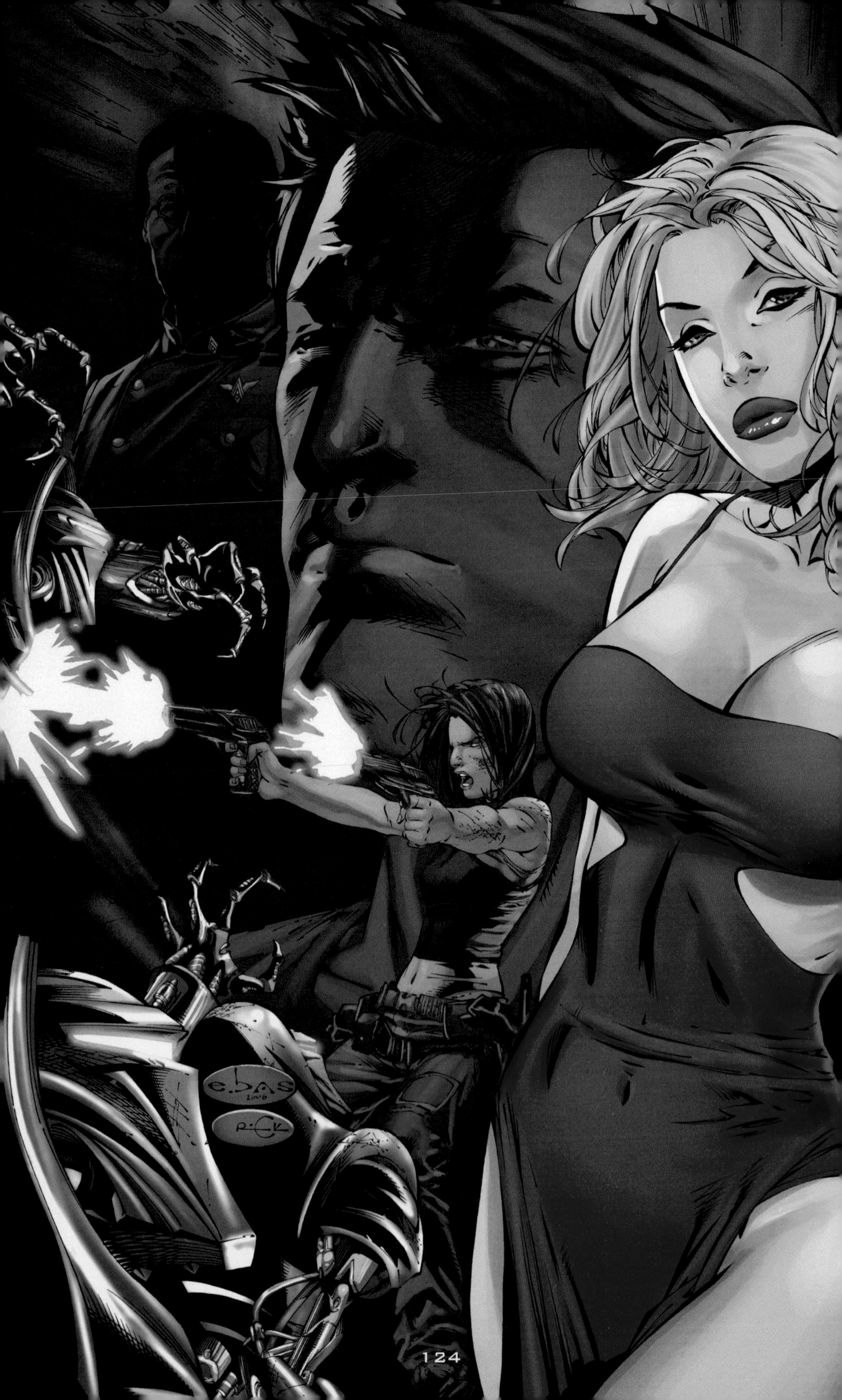

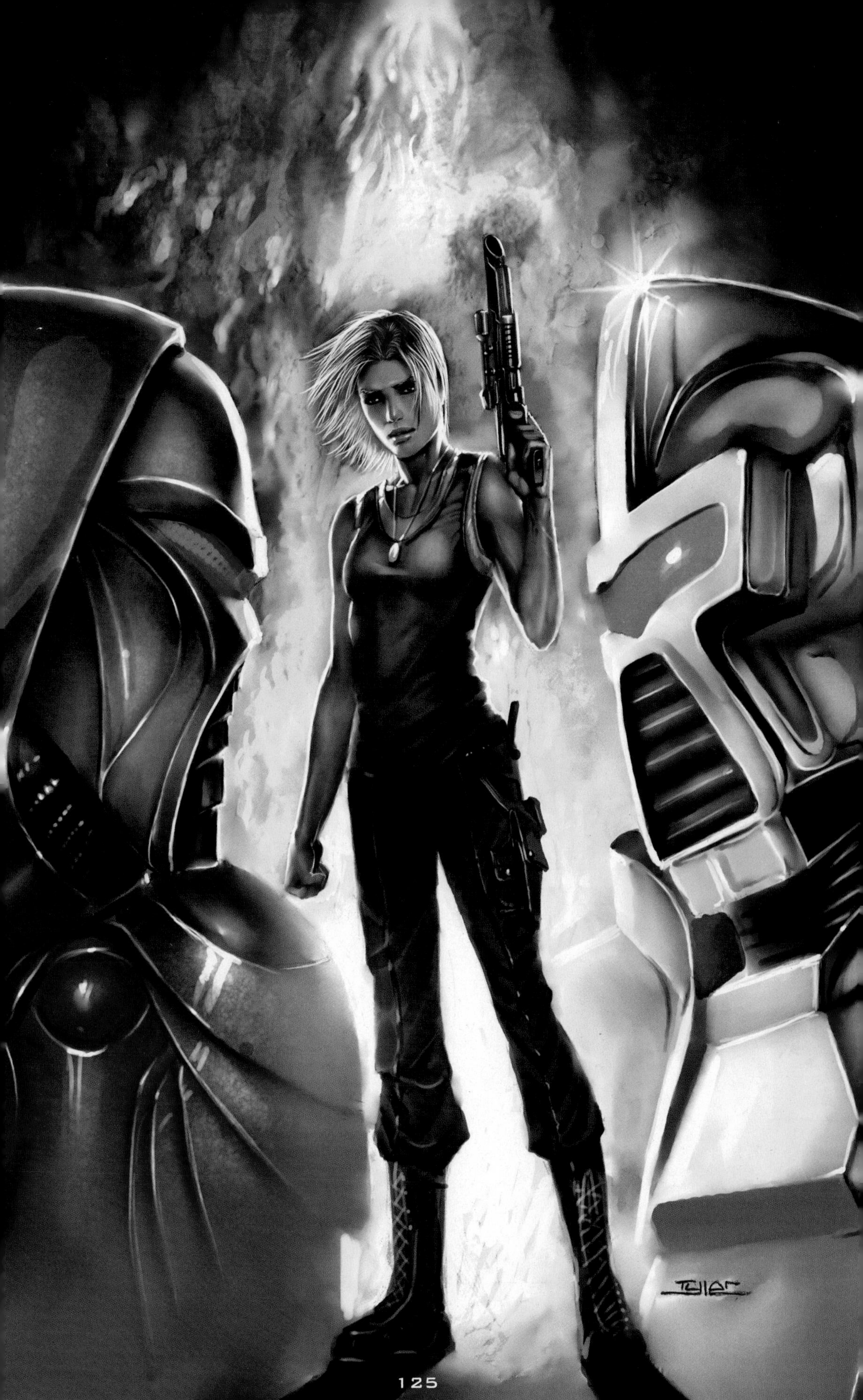

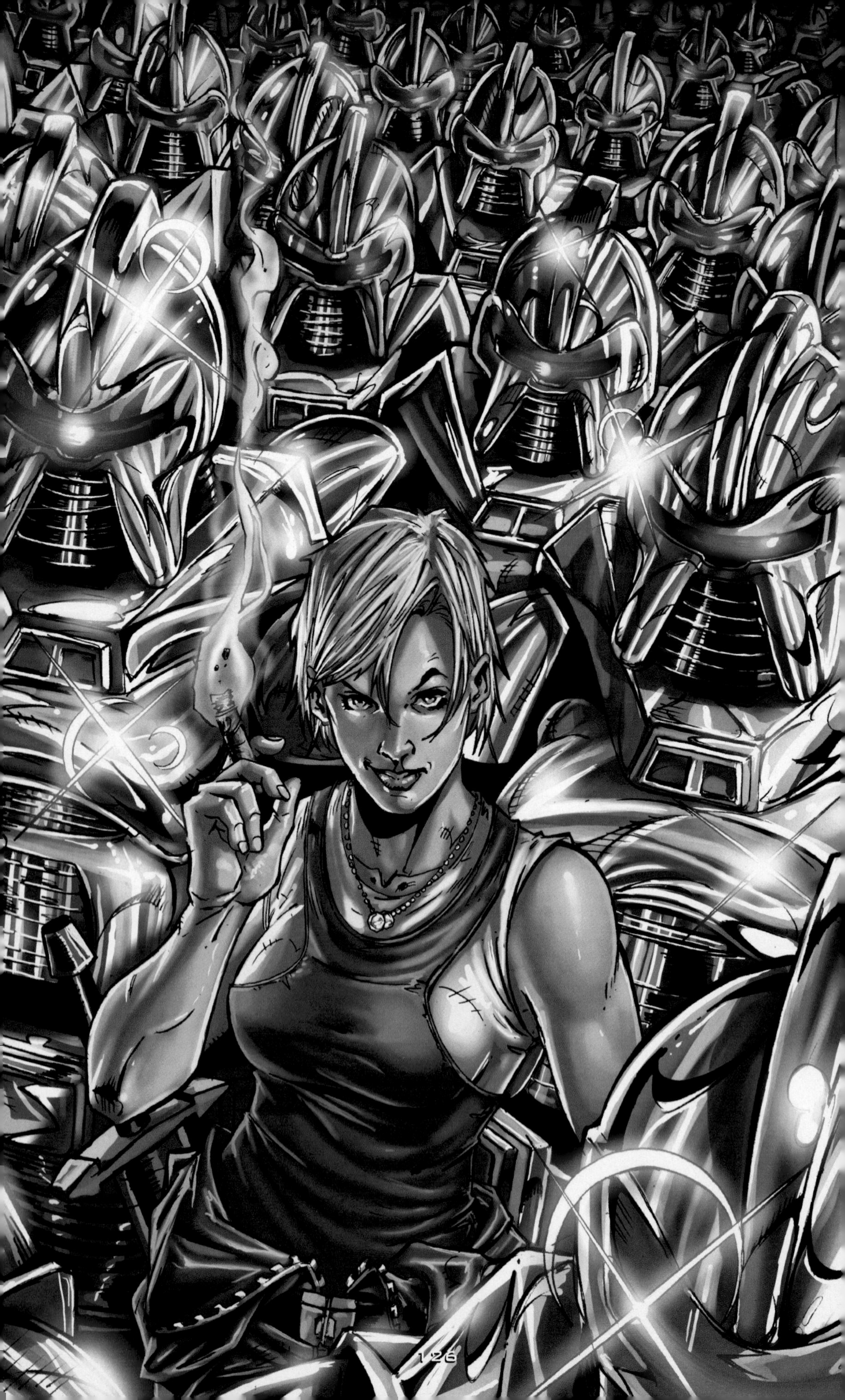

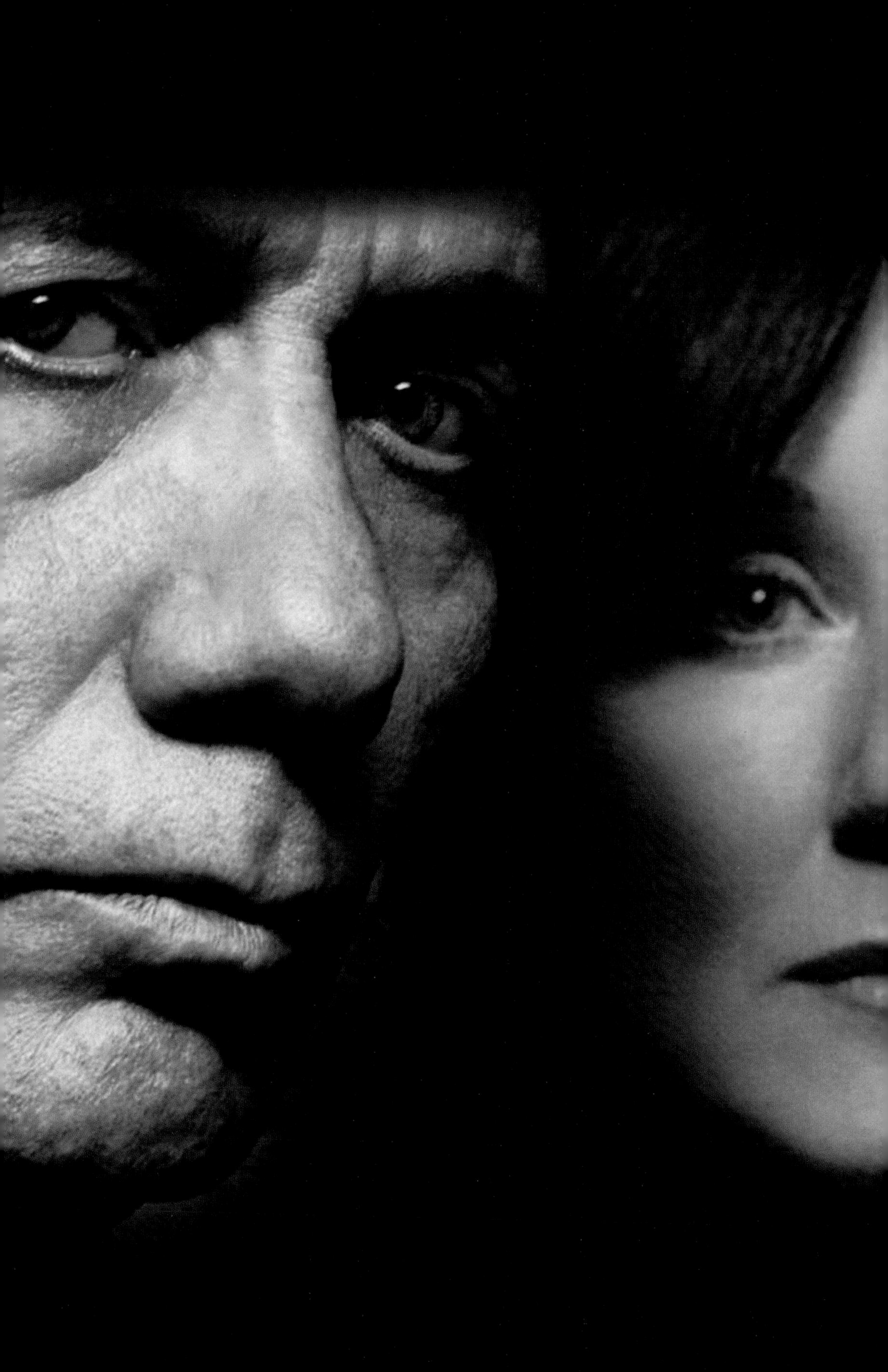

BATTLESTAR GALACTICA #1 COMMENTARY WITH GREG PAK

When the fine folks at Dynamite Entertainment asked if I'd be willing to do a DVD-style commentary for "Battlestar Galactica" #1, little did they realize they'd awakened a monster. I love talking about writing and making comics - analyzing my own process and learning about other creator's strategies play a big role in my ongoing effort to grow as a writer. And I've always found that the more specific the talk is, the more helpful it can be. So read on for page-by-page (and sometimes panel-by-panel) thoughts on the practical creative decisions that went into writing and producing "Battlestar Galactica" #1.

Page One

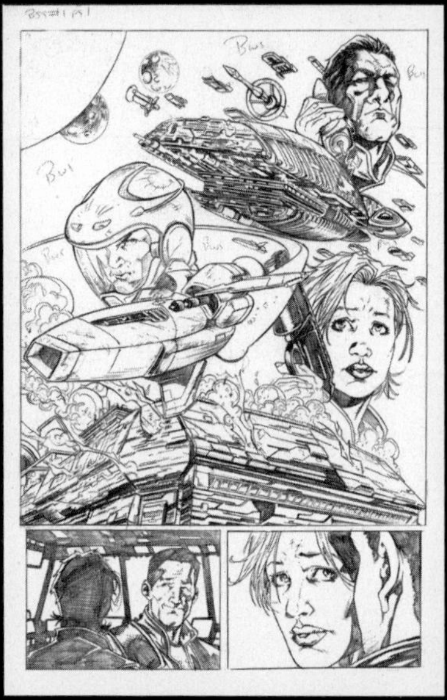

One of the nice things about comics is that a writer has several chances to get it right - at the script stage, at the ballooning stage, and one last time during the proofing. In this case, I realized at the ballooning stage that the locator/identifier captions on this page were necessary - they're redundant for anyone picking up the book immediately after reading "Battlestar Galactica" #0, but for new readers or for folks who may have read #0 months ago, they're critical, particularly since a number of our characters go by multiple names.

Regarding the layout, the first page of a comic book needs to pop - life's too short for most people to keep reading unless they're thrilled in the first instant, which is one reason so many comics open with gorgeous, dramatic splash pages. But here we're dealing with three different locations - a common situation when you're telling stories about characters dispersed across a fleet of ships. To set up the scene traditionally might require as many as six panels in order to show each character and the exterior of each character's ship. Add two more panels for the next plot point, and we end up with eight panels on Page One. Not ideal. The solution? A big, layered splash filling three quarters of the page with the heads of the main characters superimposed alongside their ships.

Pages Two and Three

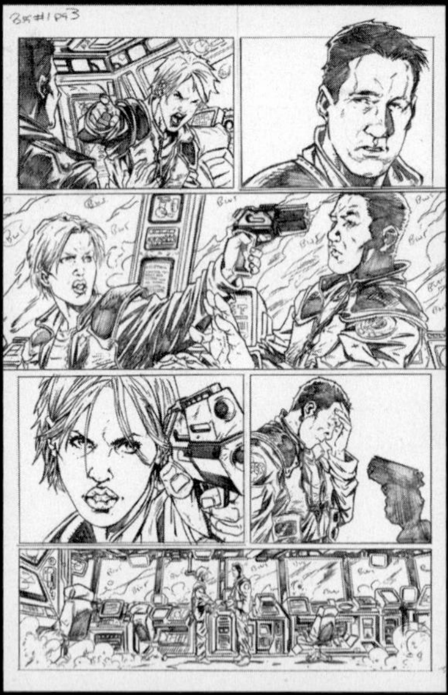

In the original script, Pages Two and Three were reversed - we went directly from Page One into Kara's montage-like memory scenes. But at the ballooning stage, I realized that a jump like that might be too much for new readers who don't yet know what's going on. Switching the pages let us get in a bit more exposition earlier, which lets new readers get the most out of the big montage page when it comes later.

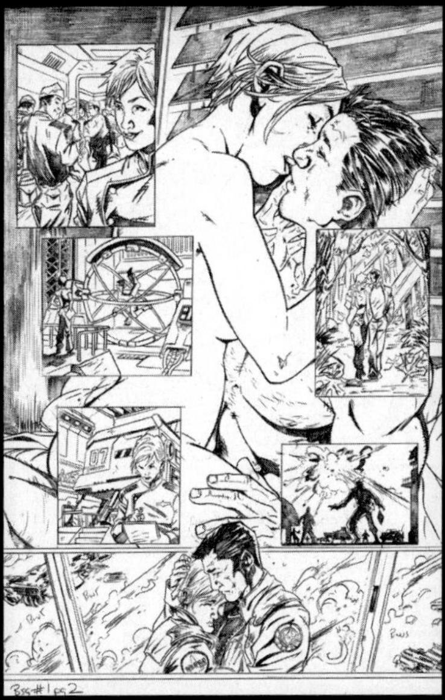

The image of Kara and Zak making love was inspired directly by the flashback scenes from the television show. Nigel Raynor, the penciler, and David Curiel and Captain Moreno, the colorists, did a great job with this. In particular, I like that they used different color palettes for the lovemaking splash image and the smaller inset flashback images. If everything had been colored the same way, it would be too hard to appreciate the different layers of the page properly.

Page Four

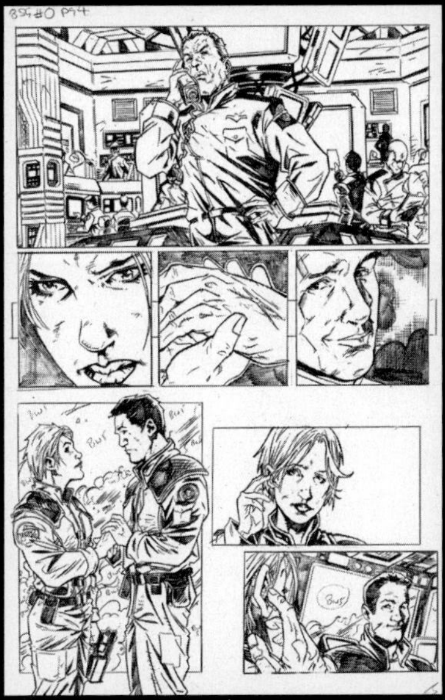

I love that Nigel remembered to keep drawing the smoke in the backgrounds. I'm a big believer in stuff in the air, in both comics and movies. Every John Woo movie has ridiculous amounts of stuff in the air - dust, debris, feathers, flour - anything that can swirl gorgeously in slow motion. The same thing works nicely in comics - it gives a feeling of density, atmosphere, and movement. Similarly, there are some nice coloring effects in Adama's C.I.C. -- the lights have a nice glow around them, which gives a sense of a bit of haze in the air.

Page Five

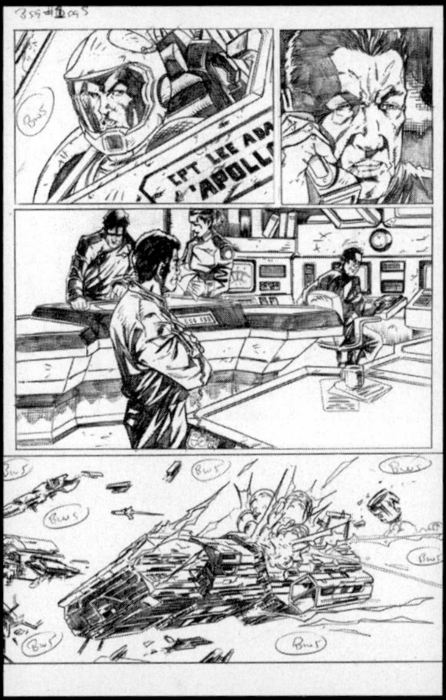

Another nice coloring effect - the colors in Panel One, which shows Lee in his Viper, are cooler and more washed out than the colors of Adama in Panel Two. It's one of those subtle details that helps us immediately understand that these are separate locations. It can be a bit of a taboo to cut from one location to another on the same page of a comic. But the logistics of "Battlestar Galactica" require those kinds of cuts - it's nice to have colorists helping make those transitions clear. (Check out "Battlestar Galactica" #0 for more great examples of this coloring strategy.)

In a different comic book, I'd probably have given the explosion in the last panel a nice, socky, comic book sound effect. But the "Battlestar Galactica" television show works hard to stay as true as possible to scientific realities

THE SCENE. (FOR THAT MATTER, IT'S DEBAT-
ABLE HOW MUCH FIRE AND SMOKE YOU'D
ACTUALLY SEE IN SPACE, BUT, HEY, WE HAD
TO SHOW SOMETHING!)

PAGE SIX

AGAIN, MORE STUFF IN THE AIR. I DIG THE
FLYING SHELLS IN THE SECOND PANEL. I
ALSO LIKE NIGEL'S CHOICE OF SILHOUETTING
THE CYLONS AS THEY GET SHOT IN THE
THIRD PANEL. IT'S CONSISTENT WITH THE
LIGHTING OF THE SCENE AND IT'S JUST NICE
TO HAVE DIFFERENT WAYS OF LOOKING AT
THINGS. THROUGHOUT THE BOOK, NIGEL
DOES A GREAT JOB OF FINDING DIFFERENT
ANGLES WITHIN A SCENE.

CHARACTER-WISE, I LIKE THE NOTION THAT
ZAK'S A GOOD SHOT. WE'RE PLAYING UP THE
NOTION FROM THE TELEVISION SHOW THAT
HE WASN'T CUT OUT TO BE A PILOT. BUT
WE'RE INTRODUCING THE IDEA THAT ZAK HAS
HIS OWN SET OF SKILLS, HIS OWN IDENTITY
THAT WE'RE GETTING TO KNOW A BIT ABOUT.

PAGE SEVEN

IN RETROSPECT, I COULD HAVE MADE IT A
BIT CLEARER ON THIS PAGE THAT DARRIN,
THE MAN TALKING INTO THE MICROPHONE, IS
DUALLA'S BROTHER. THAT'S A FACT THAT'S
ESTABLISHED IN ISSUE #0, BUT SOME PEO-
PLE READING THIS ISSUE WON'T HAVE SEEN
#0. IT'S ALWAYS A BIT OF A BALANCING ACT,
FIGURING OUT HOW MUCH THINGS NEED TO
BE EXPLAINED WHILE AT THE SAME TIME
AVOIDING OVER-EXPLAINING AND BOGGING

PAGE EIGHT

I LIKE THE LITTLE SCENES ON THIS PAGE,
GIVING US TINY GLIMPSES OF DIFFERENT
AREAS OF THE FLEET. OF COURSE THERE
MUST BE A PLACE WHERE KIDS PLAY BALL -
AND OF COURSE THERE'D BE THAT SCAF-
FOLDING AND EXPOSED PIPING ALONG THE
WALLS. NIGEL DID A NICE JOB WITH ALL OF
THESE - FOR SOME REASON, I REALLY FEEL
FOR THAT STOCKY, MUSTACHIOED WELDER.
SOMETIMES AN ARTIST WILL DO SOMETHING
SO NICE THAT AS A WRITER, YOU CAN'T HELP
BUT RUN WITH IT. CARLO PAGULAYAN'S
DONE THAT FOR ME WITH "INCREDIBLE
HULK" -- HE DREW SO MANY GREAT, FUNNY

little expressions for Miek that I ended up writing a bunch of new dialogue for the character.

Pages Nine and Ten

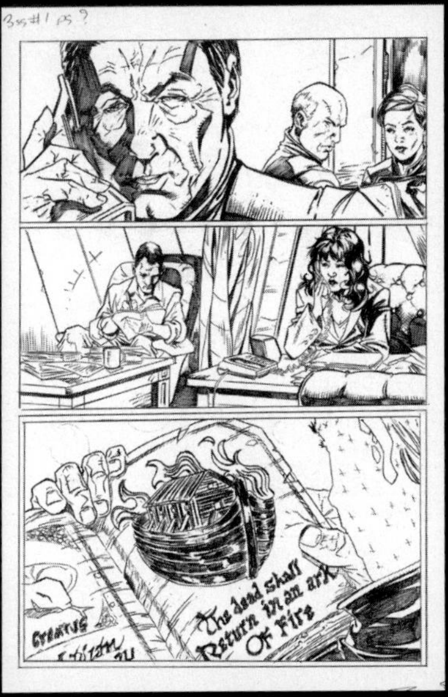
The dead shall Return in an ark Of Fire

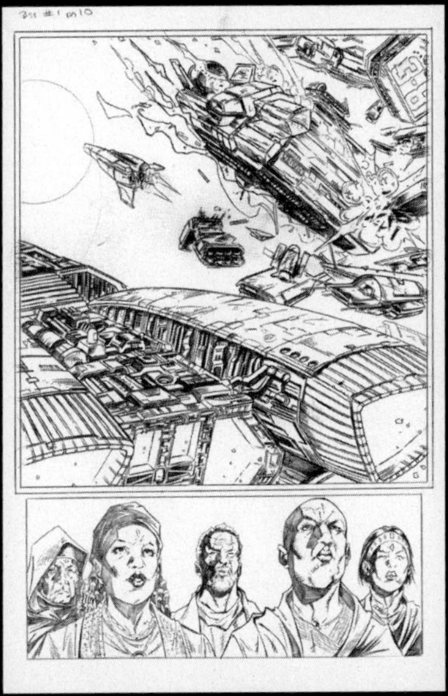

I love the way the television show established this sense of destiny and prophecy. It's a great idea - it gives the story a great mythic resonance but also allows for interesting drama and conflict as characters clash over whether the prophecies are real or not. I thought it was important that our religious characters here are filled with faith, but they also know that the prophecies aren't all flowers and sunshine. They're committed to receive the Returners "with fear and joy." That seems true to me for a couple of reasons. First, most great religions and mythic stories embrace the beauty and horror of life - rather than denying tragedy and pain and death, they give us ways to grapple with them. So the notion of both joy and fear being part of this experience makes sense. Second, if this whole thing is a Cylon plot, of course the Cylons would take advantage of these prophecies and the willingness of the faithful to embrace even what terrifies them.

Page Eleven

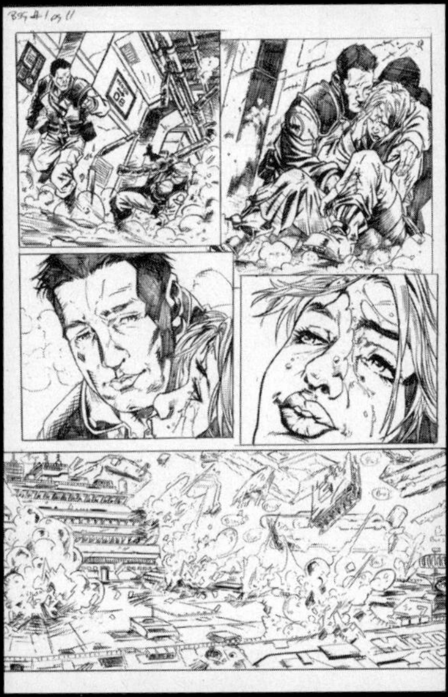

Since we know Zak can't fly for frak, the story practically screams for us to put him in a position where he's the one who has to get into the cockpit. Using what's been set up and raising the stakes.

Page Twelve

Balloon placements can be critical in getting the timing of a moment right - particularly, in this series, when it comes to Adama. In Panel Two, Adama has just two lines. By placing one balloon in the upper left and the other in the lower left, we create the right kind of pause. If both balloons were in the same corner and linked, that pause would disappear and we'd lose a bit of the character's Edward James Olmos-ness.

I love what Nigel did at the end of the page - it's a single image of Adama, but split into two panels. It's evocative for two reasons, first because it almost subliminally conveys this notion of a split character - Adama's torn between choices. And second, because it somehow implies a cinematic move - you can almost feel the pan down from Adama's eyes to his mouth.

Page Thirteen

And another montage-y splash. Repeating the convention we established on Page One. Remembering and repeating certain visual tropes can help give a book its own feel - and, in this case, remind us of who our major characters are and how their emotion-

al and physical situations are changing.

Page Fourteen

Nigel does a very nice job with Adama on this page. He opens with Adama's face in shadows - we don't know what the man's thinking. Then we see Adama looking back at us over his shoulder - again, we're not sure what's going through his head. And then finally we get the close up on his eyes, and he's as hard as iron. As I recall, the extreme close-up of Adama's eyes was explicitly described in the script, but the nuances of the previous two panels came from Nigel. A nice progression towards a strong reveal - and a good example of how good artists take the script to the next level.

Page Fifteen

The opening of this scene is a callback to the scene in Issue #0 in which Kara's waiting for Adama outside of his quarters. I think the relationship between Adama and his son and surrogate daughter is one of the most compelling things about the show - they love each other so much, yet they're all so hesitant with each other. They're all so tormented by the return of this thing that calls itself Zak, but they can't comfort each other directly. That's the dynamic we're trying to dramatize with the last panel here, with Lee and Adama on different sides of a closed door.

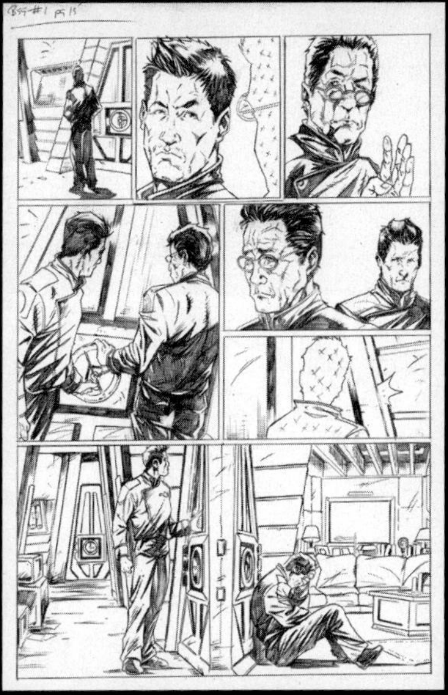

I just noticed that Nigel gave Adama a Mondrian in the background there - didn't know the Old Man had such an interest in modern art. Heh.

Page Sixteen

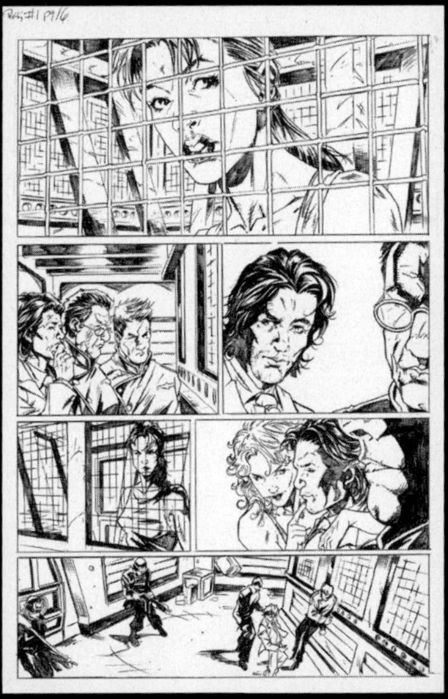

I debated a bit about the appearance of Number Six on this page. We're meeting Sharon and Baltar for the first time here as well - and Number Six has the added twist of only existing in Baltar's mind. That's a lot to throw at brand new readers. But Number Six gives an important perspective on the story here - and we're setting her up for big appearances in later issues. At the balloon stage, I added the "After all, there's no scientific explanation for how I pop up in your brain" line, which gives newbies a bit more context for her without bogging down the pace of the story.

Page Seventeen

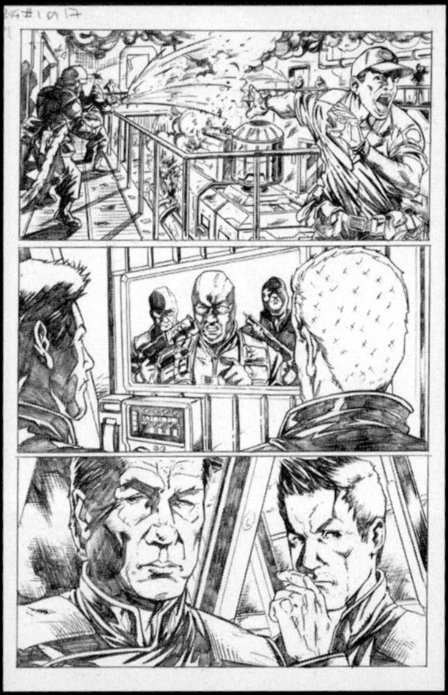

Dynamite's Joe Rybandt had the idea of a terrorist group that - out of love for humanity - wants to keep Galactica from reaching Earth. It's a great notion - of course some humans would worry that the Cylons are just using us to find the rest of the human race on Earth. It also gives us another element that Adama and his crew have to deal with. One of the great things about the show is that no matter how bad it seems for our heroes, it always gets worse. I'm doing my best to maintain that constant tension and astronomically high stakes in the comic book.

Adama's "tearing ourselves apart" line is a call-back to Issue #0, where he says something similar to Roslin while viewing the wreckage from an old war between humans. One of the compelling moments from the first new "Battlestar Galactica" shows was when Adama questioned the values - and value - of humanity. That's a great thing to draw on as Adama faces the question of whether Zak is a Cylon or not - and if, in the end, it matters.

Page Nineteen

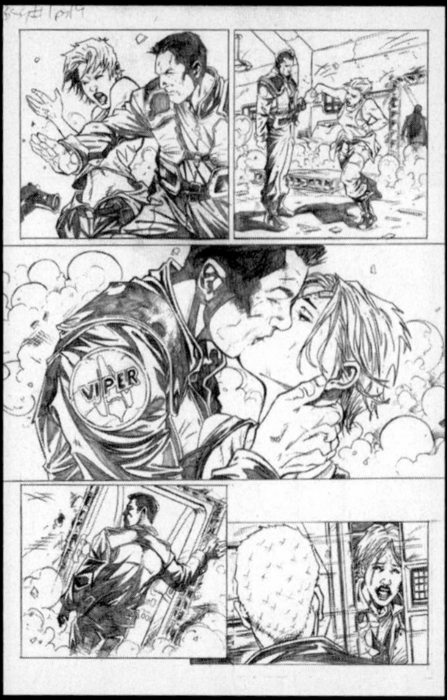
VIPER

Big movie moment - the kiss! Again, Nigel gives us great stuff in the air. And Curiel and Moreno do a sweet coloring job, playing up the haziness of the smoke with a nice rosy backlight. It's a nice use of contrasts - finding a moment of visual beauty and romance in this unlikely place.

Page Twenty

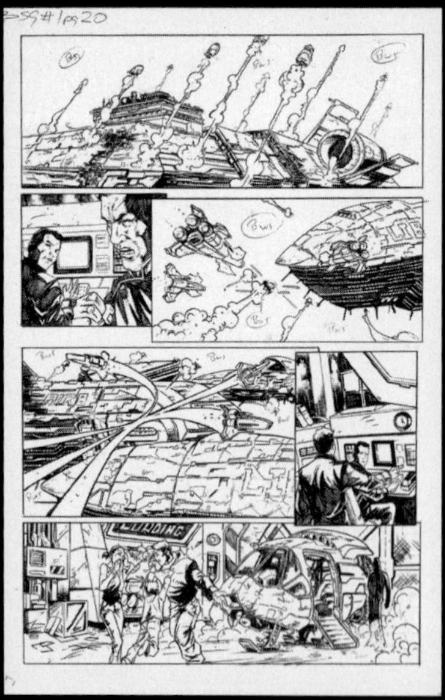

Originally, the dialogue in the captions at the bottom of this page was supposed to run on the following page. But front loading the first panel on the next page with all this info would have spoiled the pacing of the reveal. I think the dialogue actually works even better in caption form on this page - it gives us that movie feel of intercut scenes and also compresses time in an interesting and cinematic way. A nice example of how the effort to clean up a mistake can sometimes inspire better storytelling.

Pages Twenty One and Twenty Two

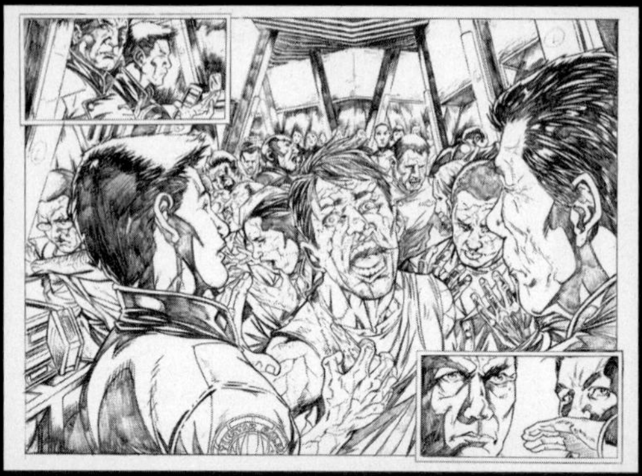

In the original script, these were two separate pages rather than a big two-page splash. But I realized that I was giving way too much room to a pretty static and drama-free shot of Adama and Lee walking down the hall on Page Twenty One. Nigel and I bounced ideas back and forth via email, and I eventually came up with the arrangement you see here - a nice, big splash of the infected people, with small inlaid panels in the far corners taking us in and out of the scene.

I particularly like the little character bit in the last panel here, with Adama staring straight forward while Lee's instinctively covering his mouth. 'Cause Adama's hardcore, dude. And I just noticed while flipping through the book that there's a similarly framed shot just six pages earlier. But there it's pensive - while here, we're in crisis mode. Kudos to Nigel for a subtle little call back and stakes-raiser to close the book.

If you enjoyed Issues 0-4, please feel free to spread the word among like-minded friends, and let your local retailer know you're on board for more Battlestar Galactica. And for the latest about "Battlestar Galactica" and my other comics and film work, feel free to visit www.pakbuzz.com

--Greg Pak

BATTLESTAR GALACTICA™

Nigel Raynor Sketchbook

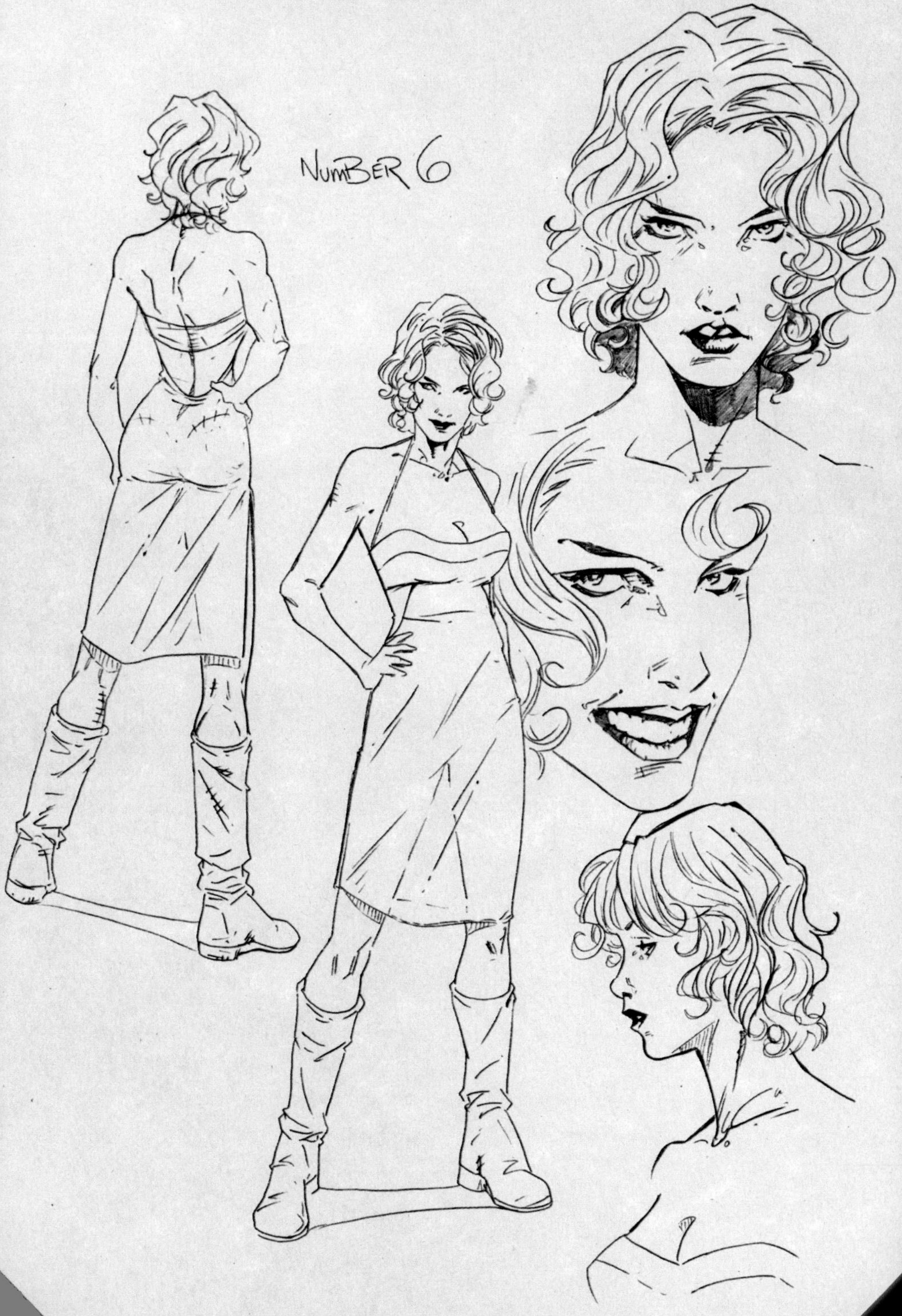
NUMBER 6

BATTLESTAR GALACTICA™

NIGEL RAYNOR SKETCHBOOK

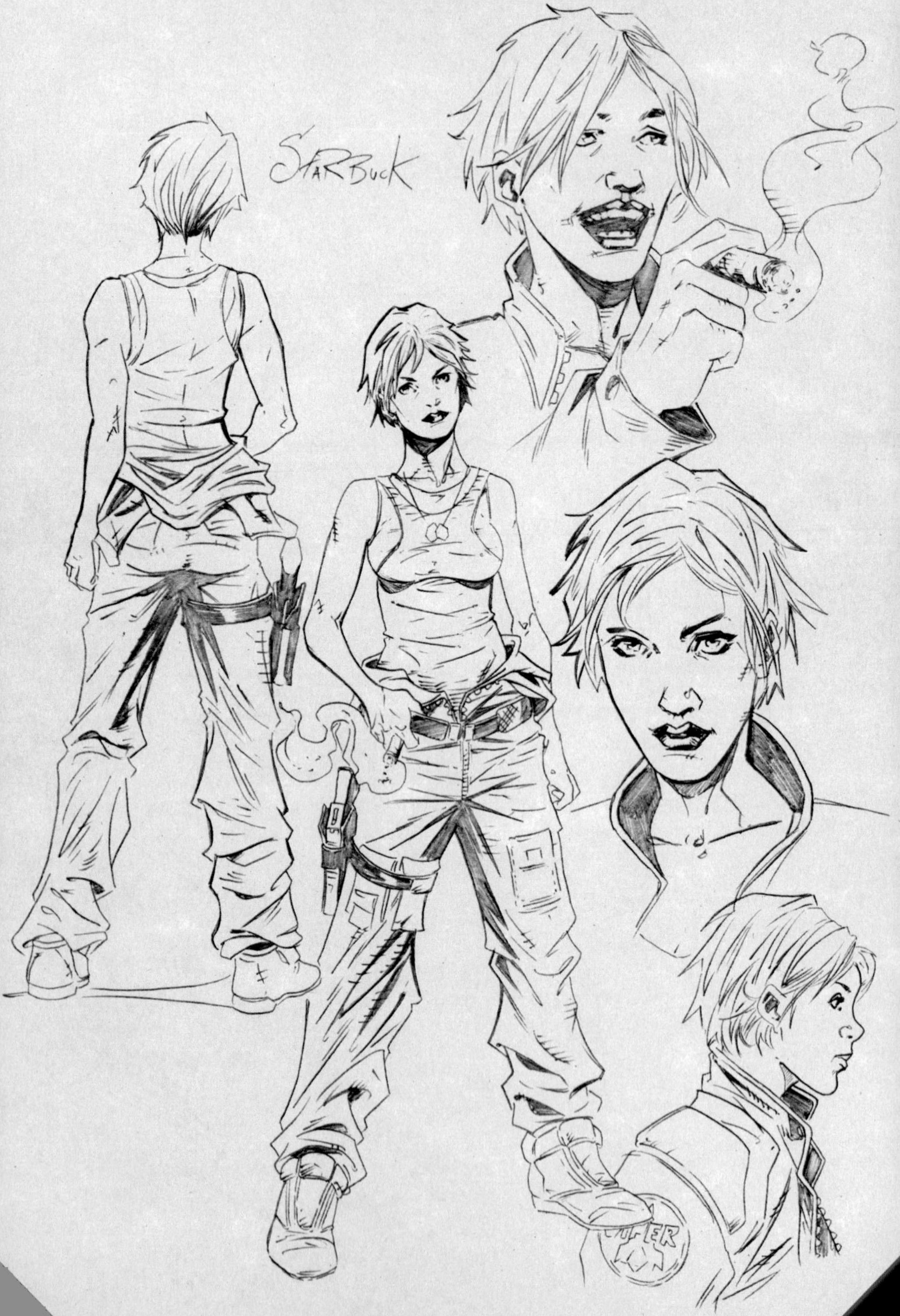
STARBUCK

BATTLESTAR GALACTICA™

NIGEL RAYNOR SKETCHBOOK

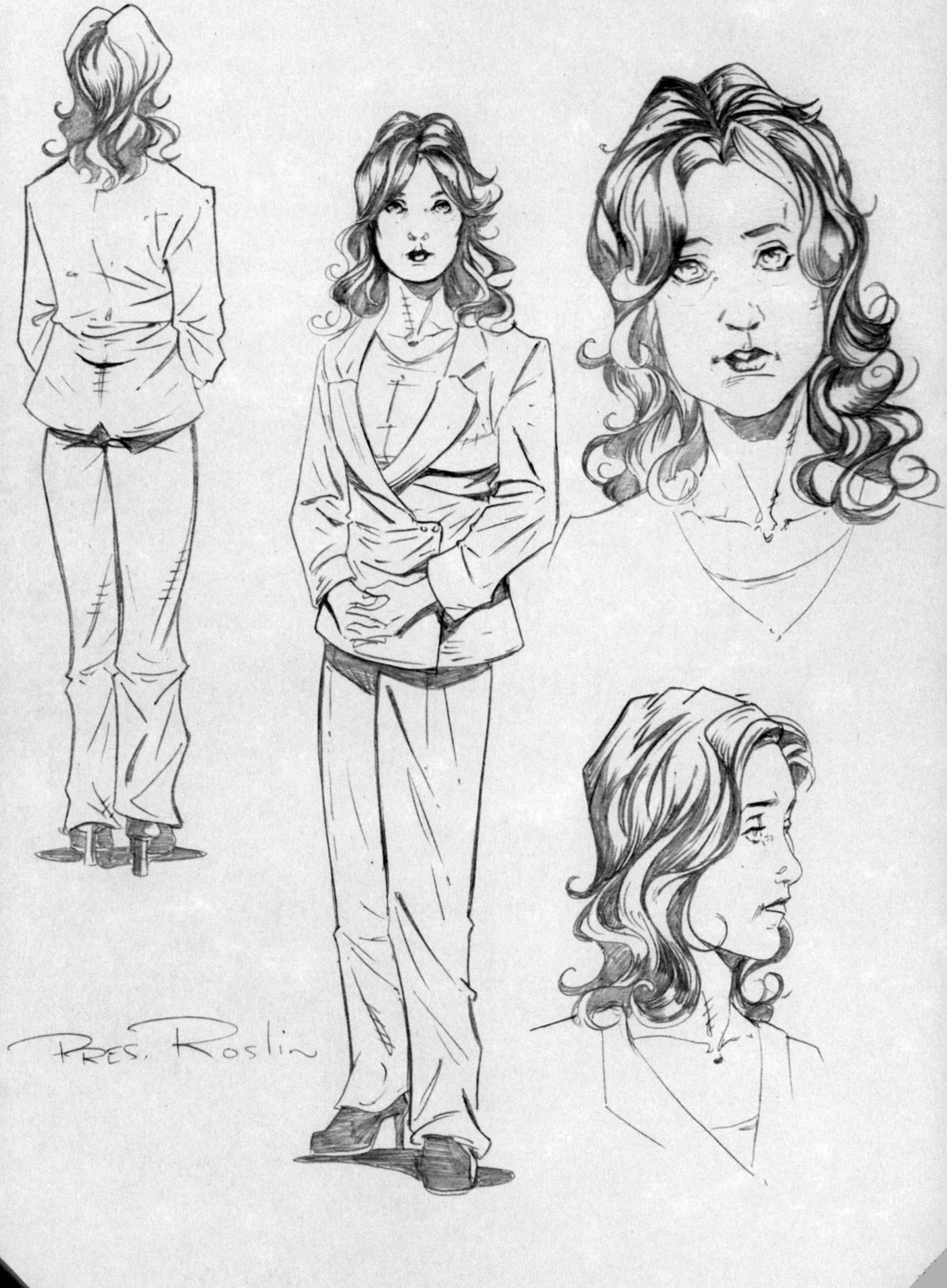

PRES. Roslin

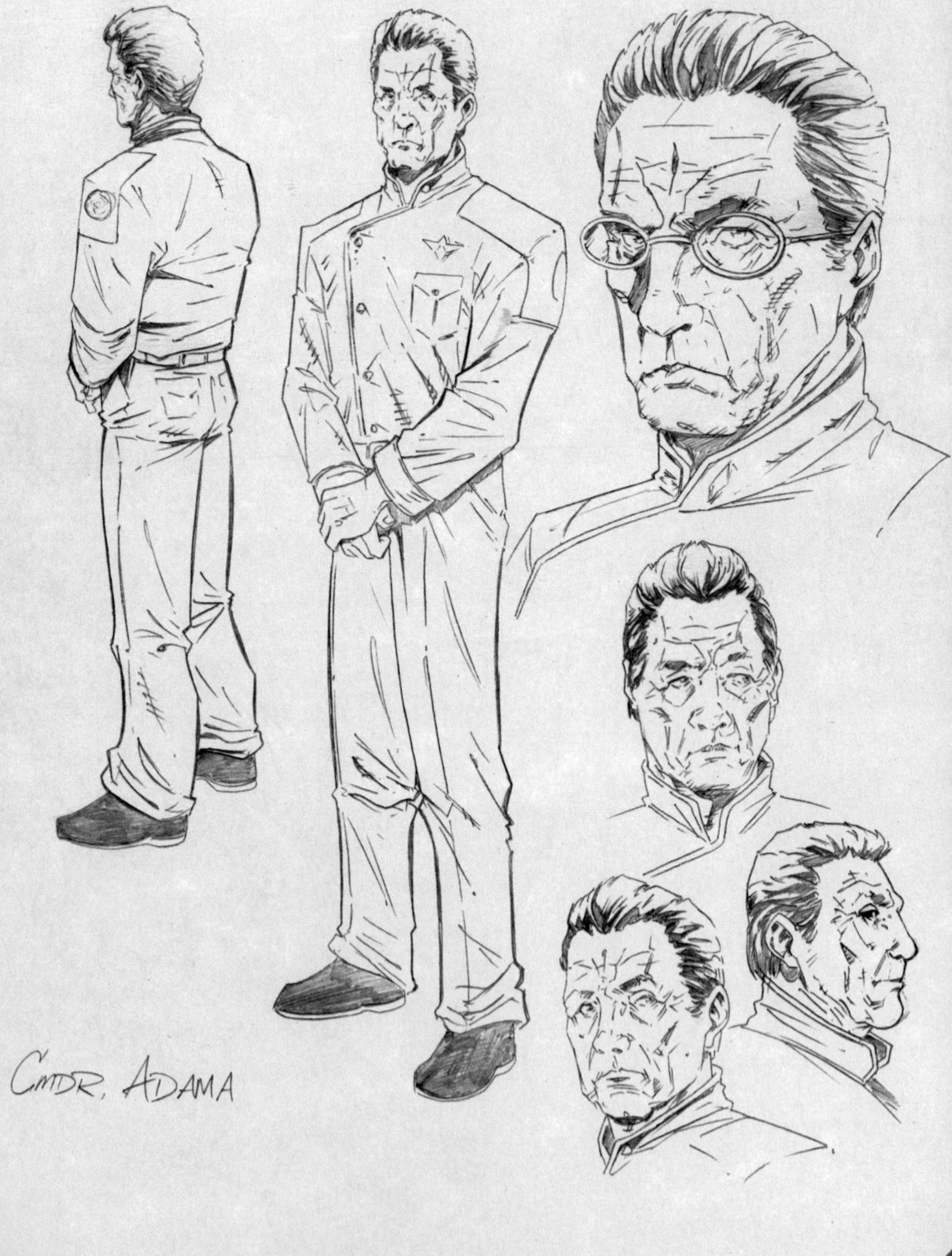
CMDR. ADAMA

BATTLESTAR GALACTICA™

NIGEL RAYNOR SKETCHBOOK

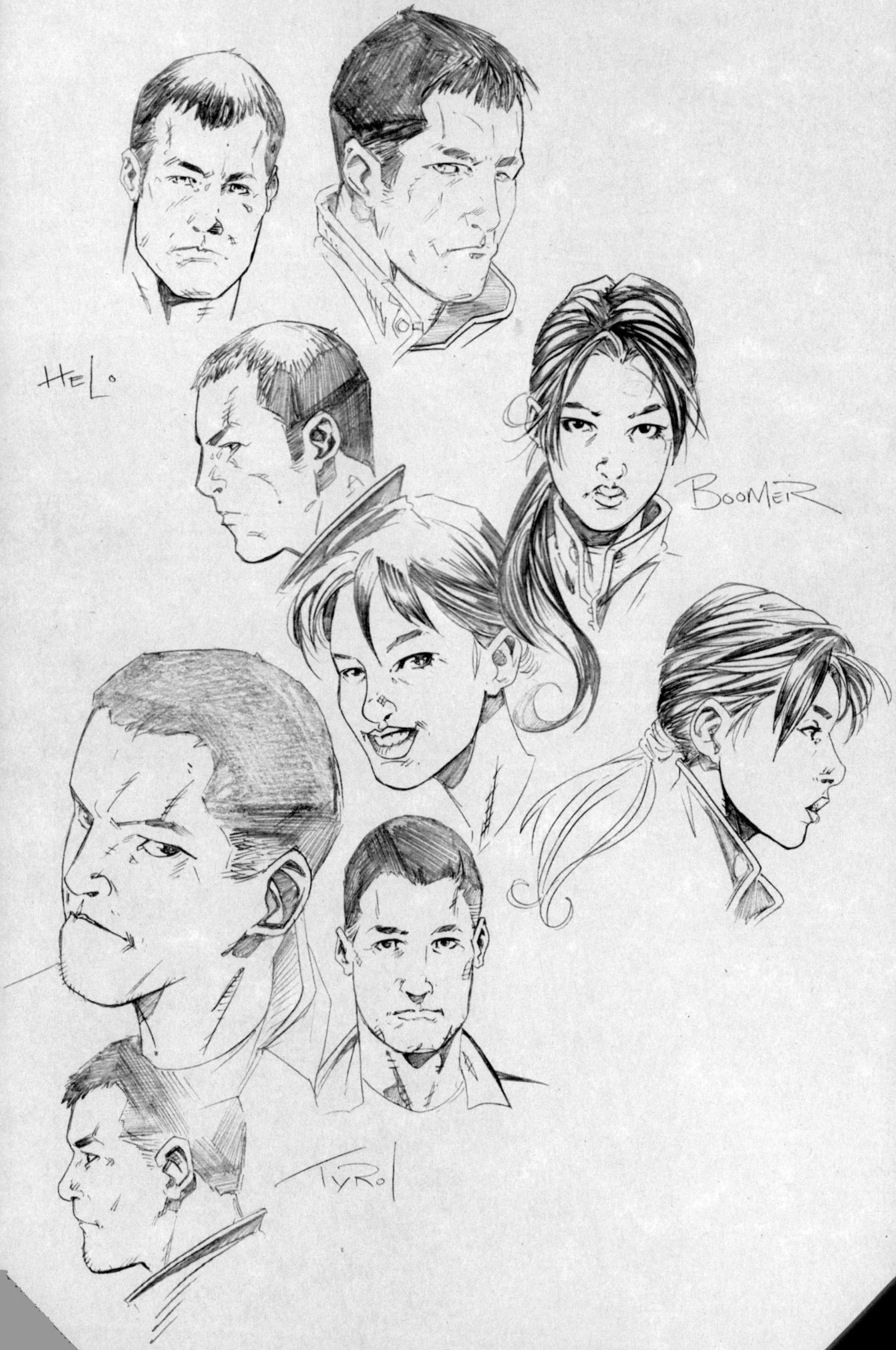

HeLo
BooMeR
TyRol

BATTLESTAR GALACTICA™

NIGEL RAYNOR SKETCHBOOK

cic 1

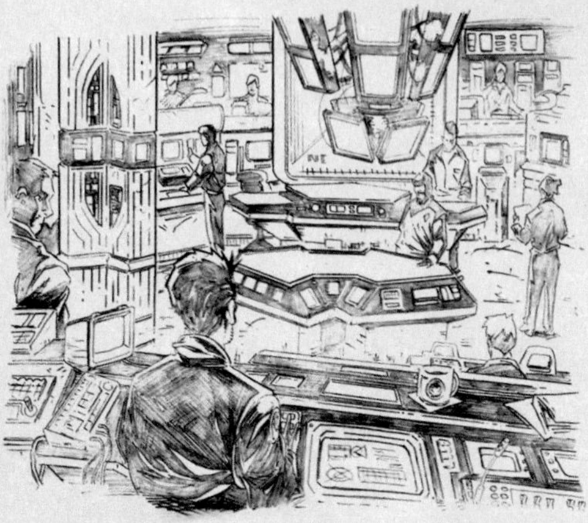

cic 2

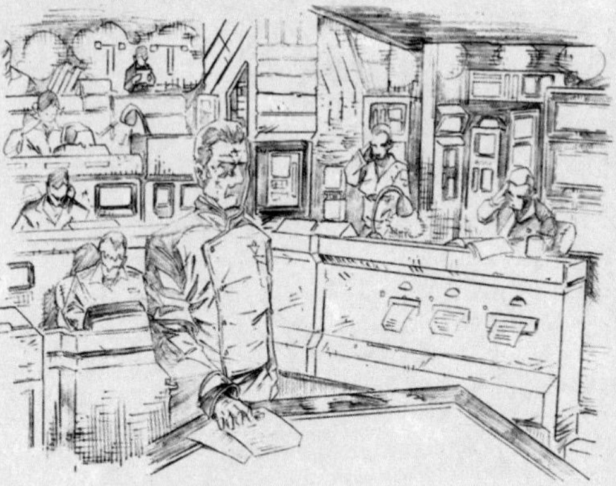

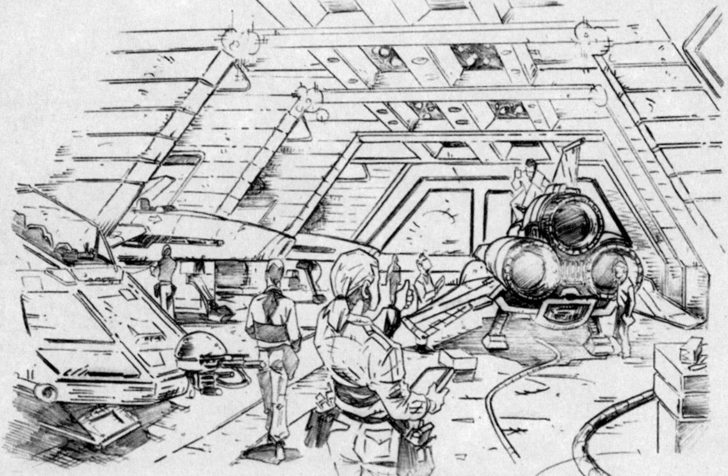

HANGAR

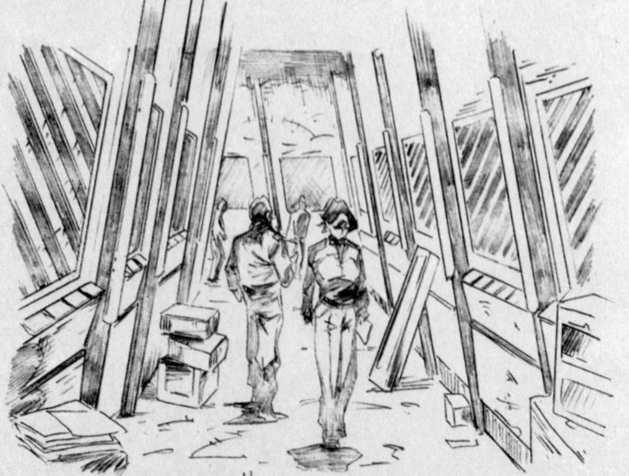

Halls

BATTLESTAR GALACTICA

NIGEL RAYNOR SKETCHBOOK

Galactica

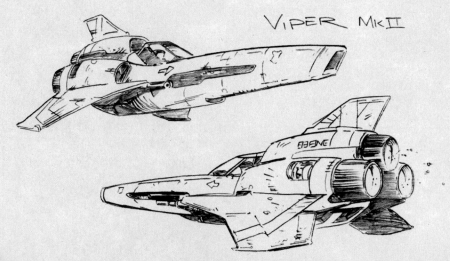

Viper MkII

GREG PAK

Greg Pak is an award-winning screenwriter, comic book writer. His feature film, "Robot Stories," starring Tamlyn Tomita and Sab Shimono, played in 75 festivals, won 35 awards, screened theatrically across the country, and is now available on DVD from Kino. Pak's comic book projects include the "Planet Hulk" and "World War Hulk" storylines for "Incredible Hulk" and "X-Men: Phoenix - Endsong" for Marvel and "Battlestar Galactica" for Dynamite.

Pak's short film "Fighting Grandpa" won 20 prizes, including a Student Academy Award, and played in over 50 film festivals. Pak's comic shorts "Asian Pride Porn" and "All Amateur Ecstasy" are among the most viewed films at AtomFilms.com. His short films, including "Mouse," "Po Mo Knock Knock," and "Happy Hamptons Holiday Camp for Troubled Couples," have screened in dozens of film festivals around the world.

Pak edits FilmHelp.com and AsianAmericanFilm.com. He was named one of 25 Filmmakers to Watch by Filmmaker Magazine and was described as "a talent with a future" by Elvis Mitchell in the New York Times. Pak studied political science at Yale University, history at Oxford University as a Rhodes Scholar, and film production at the NYU graduate film program. He is represented by Kara Baker of the Gersh Agency, New York, Sandra Lucchesi of the Gersh Agency, Los Angeles, and David Hale Smith of DHS Literary. For the latest about Greg Pak's work, visit Pakbuzz.com.

NIGEL RAYNOR

Nigel Raynor left art college at the age of 19 and immediately began writing, drawing and publishing his own comic books. This led to producing materials for The British anthology magazine 2000AD, including Sinister Dexter and Pussyfoot Five, as well as many other strips for independent publishers, online sites and newspapers.

For the last few years Raynor has worked extensively in the film, music, videogame, advertising and publishing industries. He has producing commissions, scripts, storyboards, concept and design for such clients as: Sony, Def Jam, Eidos, Nike, Nissan, Face magazine, Cinzano and MTV. His other works have appeared in select trade and lifestyle magazines as well as exhibitions.

He currently lives in England.